"A favor, you say, Sibyl? You have only to ask," Hunter assured her. "Tell me what I can do to help you."

"I have a secret," Sibyl said. Firelight dappled her neck and face, and turned her upswept fair hair to gold. Her throat moved sharply. "A secret longing." She swallowed. "I have come to you because...Hunter, I have come to you because you are the only man...Hunter, I need you."

This was amazing. Wonderful but amazing. This shy little woman—this woman who had seemed shy until now—coming to him to declare herself? He could not immediately meet her eyes and gazed instead at the wide green satin ribbon tied around the base of her high bodice. "You are usually quiet," he managed, "but not usually completely tongue-tied."

Now, she thought. "I'm going to have a child," she said. "I mean a baby." To her horror, her eyes filled.

"Hush," he said. "There's no need to cry. Please don't cry, Sibyl, I beg you." He paused, and then said briskly, "Sibyl, I must be blunt. You are my friend and if I have my way, you will always be my friend. But there is something very serious going on here. You are to answer me direct. There can be no deceit, no fabrication."

Nor would there be. "I shall explain myself with complete honesty."

"Sibyl, this is painful for both of us, but if I am to help you, I should know when you anticipate the arrival of the child."

Her eyes lost focus. A soft smile settled on her lips. She looked up into his face and he found her the loveliest creature he had ever seen.

Damn it all, he was only a man, a man who had fought his feelings for Sibyl for too long. And then he kissed her.

Also available from
STELLA CAMERON
and MIRA Books

ALL SMILES

Watch for Stella Cameron's newest historical romance

A USEFUL AFFAIR

March 2002

7B
STELLA
CAMERON

MIRA

ISBN 1-55166-795-9

7B

Visit us at www.mirabooks.com

Printed in U.S.A.

For our own sweet Serena.

Prologue

7 Mayfair Square, London, 1822

Ghost in a post.

I ask you, is that any way to address a man of my distinction, a man who would welcome death—again—rather than face the latest developments in the house I built for my family? That is, my family throughout the generations to follow me, not, I repeat, not for lodgers!

And to turn the knife in the wound of my misery, that knave, Shakespeare, has dubbed me "Ghost in a Post" on account of my dwelling place in an exquisitely carved newel post at the foot of the staircase at Number 7. He is not enjoying quite the popularity he achieved in his former state, and mortification—I am also known for my dazzling wordplay—makes his tongue vicious.

But I am remiss. The late Sir Septimus Spivey at

your service. Knighted in 1712 for my architectural achievements; unparalleled in my vision, skill, innovation, and all-around brilliance. Number 7 was and is my most prized accomplishment, and the present owner, that wretched great-granddaughter of mine, Lady Hester Bingham, takes in paying guests! Protégés, she calls them. Poppycock, I say to that.

A less compassionate fellow would have tossed aside all regard for the feelings of these wretched interlopers. Not so Sir Septimus. Oh, no, no. From the instant my ghostly skills allowed it, I set about removing the strangers in a most kindly manner. There wasn't a single married tenant, so I decided to marry them off. Guide them—with a trace of inelegant but necessary haste—into connubial bliss. Elsewhere. There, I am a benevolent spirit if ever there was one.

But am I given credit for my efforts, for my accomplishments? Never. Two former residents, the former Miss Finch More and the former Miss Meg Smiles, are well-wed, well-fixed, and annoyingly—no, I mean gratifyingly happy. All I asked was that Latimer More depart with his sister, who has become Viscountess Kilrood, and that Sibyl Smiles become a member of her sister Meg's, now Countess Etranger's, household.

Each of those nincompoops, Latimer More and Sibyl Smiles, chose to continue living in their re-

spective rooms, meaning of course, that I have not succeeded in emptying a single flat!

That state of affairs is about to change. After the last debacle I needed a good rest. Now I am refreshed and I have selected Miss Sibyl Smiles as my next victim—I mean as the next beneficiary of my valuable attention, of course. I have already been hard at work for some time and had thought that at last I had a simple task ahead.

Females. I should have known that even so placid an example as Sibyl Smiles could become difficult. Her sister, Meg, is a headstrong creature, a daring and unpredictable specimen if ever I saw one. Sibyl is the pale shadow, or I should say that she used to be the pale shadow. I cannot imagine what has come over her, unless it is jealousy of her sister, and a determination to prove that she, Sibyl, is capable of equally flamboyant and unsuitable behavior. Oh, I am almost certain she trembles within. I have seen how she gathers courage to embark on each outrageous step she plans, but embark, she does. And what if she accomplishes her aim to achieve independence of the most extraordinary kind? Well, then, I shall not only be foiled again, but doubly foiled again.

You see, my plan is that at last that cold fish, Hunter Lloyd, Hester's nephew and another unwanted occupant at Number 7, will decide that a man in his position—barrister, y'know, and about to be knighted, although I cannot imagine why—must have a wife and a residence of his own. So, Hunter marries Sibyl. Sibyl marries Hunter. The result is obvious, or so I had hoped.

Drat, I see Henry VIII coming this way. Seems to be forever trying to gather all those wives together. Says he wants to make amends. Can't imagine why he doesn't accept that there are things even a king can't put back together.

Fellow talks too much. Rude, too. I must make myself scarce.

But as to Sibyl and Hunter? I mustn't dash off without telling you the serious problem I must overcome there.

I believe Hunter may have noticed Miss Sibyl. His gaze lingers, y'know. But Miss Sibyl's mind is elsewhere. She is rehearsing; making ridiculous faces in front of the mirror. Practices walking with a devil-may-care swagger. A strut. The silly chit is determined to put on a self-assured air, a worldly air, even. With her newfound friends, a group of drab, bluestocking creatures destined for the shelf, she is devising a plan to obtain what she wants most in life.

Miss Sibyl Smiles wants a child.

She does not want a husband.

I shall overcome.

1

How, Sibyl Smiles wondered, did one tell the dearest of sisters that one had decided to have a child, but that one had no plans to marry?

These rooms at number 7 Mayfair Square were home to Sibyl, just as they had once been home to her sister Meg, Countess Etranger. Here Sibyl felt safe and among good friends who would accept and protect her no matter what she did. Well, at least, she hoped that would remain true.

"That's it," Meg announced, getting to her feet. "I have watched you dither and posture—in a most un-Sibyllike manner, I may add—for quite long enough, sister. This was to be our time together to share our hearts as we always have. You know Jean-Marc and I can only be in London for a few days. And my sister-in-law is all but stamping her feet while she awaits her turn to come to 7B. She is longing, she says, for her own private moments with you—whatever that may mean."

Sibyl said, "I'm sorry if I disappoint you and

Princess Desirée," but kept her chin high. Under no circumstances must she reveal the price she paid for so much contradictory behavior.

"*Disappoint* me?" Meg, regal and irresistible in her favorite yellow, raised her own chin. "Can this be my darling Sibyl talking to me so? Shed all this false behavior. Now, Sibyl, if you please. First, kindly explain what has brought you to such a pass where you have decided to become an actress before even me?" Delicate lily-of-the-valley sprigs peeped from beneath the brim of Meg's bonnet. She wore a triple white ruff. The edges of her promenade pelisse were embroidered with the tiny bell-shaped lilies and more sprigs were to be seen on her yellow satin half boots.

"Sibyl," Meg said, frowning. "Please explain."

"Hm," Sibyl murmured, clearing her throat. "I thought you would bring Baby Serena with you."

"Serena is sleeping. As you will find out when you marry and become a mother yourself—and if you insist upon caring for your child with the minimum of help from a nanny—well, then you'll decide the less one disturbs a sleeping baby, the better."

Sibyl was all but moved to cry. At least Meg said, "when" Sibyl became a mother, not "if". But she did insist on mentioning the expectation of a husband in the picture.

"*Sibyl,* please."

"I am not different at all," Sibyl responded, well aware that her voice was high, thin and forced. "I go about my daily business exactly as usual. I have fewer pianoforte students at the moment, but that isn't unusual when the weather is so bad. It must be a matter of your not being with me very often, so you forget how I really am."

"Bosh!" Meg moved close to Sibyl and studied her face closely. "Your complexion is lovely. But then, it always was. Your eyes are bright. They always were bright, the brightest blue and very appealing to many men, I might add." She shook her head to warn Sibyl away from protests. "Indeed, sister, you do look wonderful. That hair. What I wouldn't give for your pale, shining hair—also of great interest to the gentlemen, I may add—rather than my own ordinary brown mop."

"Your *mop* is chestnut and thick and Jean-Marc considers you the most beautiful woman ever—which you are. So enough of that and enough study of my person, if you don't mind. I can hardly wait to visit darling Serena."

"Oh, no, no, no, I am not so easily diverted. When I arrived, three very dour ladies were leaving you. Two of them looked upon me with disdain. I cannot explain their reactions otherwise. The third appeared to have the makings of a pleasant enough person, or she might have had she actually looked at me. What, Sibyl, is going on?"

"When is Desirée coming?"

"That is the end of this nonsense. You are hiding something and it must be serious or you wouldn't be so evasive. Foolishly evasive, and that is not like you. Incidentally, I am particularly fond of you in that soft blue. You are ethereal, Sibyl, a vision of gentle beauty, when you aren't trying, and failing, to appear haughty. Or is that demeanor supposed to suggest a devil-may-care attitude? Did I actually see you walking with a sort of...*strut?*"

Sibyl could not stem the rush of blood to her neck and face. "No such thing. I feel you are examining me and looking for flaws, so I am awkward, nothing more. And the only thing different about me is that I, too, wish to have a baby. Why not? Why should you be the only one to hold and adore a creature of your own blood and bone? Why is it that you assume I will be forever content to teach children to play the piano, to watch you with Serena and the other children you will undoubtedly bear, and to occasionally hold them, but never to have my own sweet ones to lavish with my love?"

Astounded, Meg saw when Sibyl ran out of breath. She slumped onto the chaise that had finally had its ancient rose-colored upholstery replaced with blue-and-gold tapestry.

Meg didn't know what to say—a quite extraordinary turn of affairs for one who was gifted with quick wits.

At last she recovered a little and said softly, "You are eight and twenty. Hardly ancient. You will have your own children, dearest. Why should you think I expect otherwise?"

"I'm tired of waiting. There is no eager husband panting to sweep me away. I do not grow younger. The time for me to bear children is now, and that's what I've decided to do."

Silence fell in the sitting room at 7B Mayfair Square. The tea Sibyl had poured for both of them grew cold and fragrant slices of caraway cake no longer seemed appealing. Meg studied Sibyl's bowed, blond head and had to turn away. She went to the windows and drew a white lace curtain aside. Across the square at Number 17—formerly 16 and 17 but converted into one quite magnificent home by the Count's father—Jean-Marc would be attending to the business that had brought them to Town. Desirée was no doubt pacing impatiently until she should be allowed to come to Sibyl, and darling Serena would soon be waking and demanding her mother's breast. The latter was considered not at all the thing in her circles, but no expectation of society would dictate the manner in which she cared for her children, and Jean-Marc was delighted with the decision.

Unwillingly, Meg made herself consider what Sibyl had actually told her. "I will not question your sincerity in this matter," Meg said at last. Perhaps she had misunderstood Sibyl. "You have met someone who has asked for your hand. You do not love him, but you have accepted him because you want a child at once. That is what you mean?"

"No." There was only determination in Sibyl's tone. "There isn't a man in my life."

Meg flinched. She faced her sister again. "Then I implore you, most desperately implore you, to—to—to, well, *not to.*"

"Not to have a baby?" The facade began to slip and Sibyl sounded as if tears could not be far away.

"Not to—to embark upon a course that could bring shame upon both you and an innocent child."

Sibyl's frown was quite magnificent. Her fine brows met. "How could I do that? Whatever I have to do will be in order to have a child, nothing more. I am not a green girl in search of pointless adventure."

Oh, my. "We need to talk much more. Clearly I had assumed you were more a woman of the world than you are. In fact you are not a woman of the world at all. You are, most certainly, a green girl." Meg was unaccustomed to being flustered. She tugged on her gloves. Took them off again. Put them on again. "I must go to Serena. May we meet late in the afternoon the day after tomorrow? We could talk here—and I will be prepared to be blunt and informative—and then would you come home with me to Number 17 for dinner? Jean-Marc is already agitating because there are no firm arrangements for a visit. He wanted you to come this evening."

"You only arrived last night. And I wish I could come but I have late students both today and tomorrow."

"Quite so. But you know how Jean-Marc is. Very definite about what he wants." *Very definite,* Meg thought and felt pleasantly warm. "So, will that work?"

"Yes, that would be nice."

"Desirée will not be able to contain herself until then. Could you bear it if I let her come to you today?"

Sibyl adored Princess Desirée of Mont Nuages, Jean-Marc's half sister, who was destined to rule the principality on the French-Italian border after her father's death. "I shall be the one to pout if she doesn't come," Sibyl told Meg. "Will she forgive me for asking her to wait two hours? I am a little tired from my morning's exertions."

"With that boring group of females?"

"What a nasty thing to say," Sibyl said, more sharply than she had intended. "The ladies are my friends. They have been kind and supportive. I hope to have the opportunity to introduce you. You will find each of them interesting. They are free thinkers and intellectuals. They do not subscribe to the appointed boundaries for women, the boundaries appointed by men."

Meg smelled true danger here. "I shall look forward to meeting them. And Desirée will come to you in two hours."

Sibyl said her goodbyes, saw Meg out and watched her cross Mayfair Square to Number 17. Then she shut the front door and leaned against it. She closed her eyes and let out a long, long breath. "Now I must hope he is at home," she said quietly, looking upward toward the third-floor gallery. "Please be at home, or I'm going to lose my nerve, Hunter. You need never concern yourself with the incident once it's done. After all, how difficult can it be to perform whatever is necessary?"

I shudder. Do you see why my home in this newel post is so perfect? I can observe all comings and goings. But saints preserve me. Unless I am less astute than I know myself to be, the dratted woman is going to...no, I cannot allow myself to visualize the act she had in mind. She's going to ask Hunter to help her have a baby, isn't she? And she doesn't want anything else from him. If she succeeds, she'll be even more entrenched in my house—with a squalling brat! But if she thinks I'll stand idly by while she entices Hester's nephew to—to—well, you know what she wants him to do—she's absolutely wrong. Hunter is far too principled a man to agree to tumble into bed for nothing more than an interlude of potentially wild sexual gratification.

"Gadzooks. What am I saying? I must act at once."

"Her Royal Highness, the Princess Desirée of Mont Nuages," Old Coot, Lady Hester Bingham's ancient butler, announced with relish. He pushed open the door to Sibyl's sitting room and hobbled far enough inside to allow eighteen-year-old Desirée's entrance. "Will you be requiring refreshments?" Old Coot asked, his bulbous eyes darting about the room with the customary disapproval at Sibyl's changes.

"That would be nice," Sibyl told him, thinking at the same time that the housekeeper, Mrs. Barstow, who was also Lady Hester's companion, would be furious at the extra work.

At last the door closed and Desirée shed her royal demeanor to fly in a rustle of fine, pale-mauve satin to throw her arms around Sibyl. "It has been forever, dear Sibyl. And I have missed you. Why must you be so difficult and refuse to live with us?''

''Let us enjoy our time together, Your Royal Highness,'' Sibyl said, too emotionally drained for yet another battle. ''I am to dine with you the day after tomorrow and I know Jean-Marc will pose the same question again. May we be friends together for now and let the rest go?''

Desirée removed a saucy, purple velvet concoction from atop her prettily dressed light-brown hair and tossed it aside together with an oversize bag she'd brought with her. She planted her hands on her hips. ''We *are* friends. The greatest of friends.'' She pointed at Sibyl. ''But we may become enemies if you ever call me *Your Royal Highness* again. Such silliness. Promise you won't.''

Sibyl considered, then agreed. This had been such a difficult day. At her knock, Hunter had opened his door and smiled, and seemed glad to see her, but within seconds a note ''of the highest importance'' had been thrust into his hand by one of the maids and he'd had to leave. With visible reluctance, it was true. But now Sibyl must gather her courage all over again and at the moment she simply didn't have enough strength.

''This room is lovely,'' Desirée said. ''So elegant, yet so cozy. It exactly suits you, Sibyl. A charming room for a charming woman. There.''

Sibyl laughed and waved Desirée into a delicate gilt chair for which Sibyl had made the needlepoint covering herself. "You are a terrible little flatterer," she said. "And I am suspicious that you may be about to reveal some wicked plot with which you want my help. Am I right?"

"Per'aps." Occasionally Desirée's native French made her already charmingly-accented English even more charming. "You have not asked about my beloved Halibut. I think you do not love him anymore."

Halibut was Desirée's enormous gray tabby cat, who ruled all he saw. Even Jean-Marc doted on the creature.

"I already know Halibut is enjoying his visit to Number 17 and that he is as impossible as ever. Now, miss, kindly tell me what it is that makes your eyes glow with mischief."

Desirée made a rush to pick up her rather ugly brown bag and took it back to the gilt chair, where she set the bag on her lap. "You are going to like what I have in my mind," she said. "Your Meggie enjoys her married state, but she is become altogether too secretive. Before she and my tyrannical brother married, she was willing enough to consider examining a certain matter with me. Now she merely looks smug and tells me I will learn all when the time is appropriate. La-la to that. I am finished with patience and will unravel the mystery now. With your help, because you are so much more free to move about than I am."

Sibyl shifted to the end of the chaise and raised her feet to the seat. "I'm almost certain this is not going to be an appropriate topic for us to discuss," she said. "But I'm prepared to consider it." In truth, her curiosity was popping.

With great care, Desirée removed a large, heavy, leatherbound book that showed signs of great use. Badly worn gold tooling decorated the spine. Desirée paused, her large gray eyes busy in a close examination of Sibyl. "What is different about you?" she asked abruptly. "And you are different. You walk differently and talk differently. You seem no longer shy. How can that be? It's wonderful, of course. For a few moments I was aware of the change, but too busy with my own mission to take careful notice. I am a selfish creature."

"I am not changed," Sibyl said, regretting the lie but by no means ready to discuss such things with yet another sharply observant female. "And you are not selfish. Now, what is the book?"

Desirée's eyes narrowed. She said, "Yes, the book," quite slowly. There would be further observations on Sibyl's demeanor.

"Sibyl," Desirée said, intensely earnest. "Like me, you are a woman with little knowledge of the male. This has irked me for far too long and I am determined to change that state of affairs. I urge you to join me in my quest."

Sibyl made a noncommittal sound but thought that Desirée would find the gatherings Sibyl had with her newfound friends most enlightening. They had certainly broadened Sibyl's knowledge of the workings of the male mind. What she had learned made her sad, but it also made what she intended to accomplish easier. Men didn't fall in love, not really. And children didn't mean to a father what they meant to a mother. Men were…missing areas of the mind taken for granted by women. Very sad.

"This book is an example of the nonsense we women have tolerated," Desirée announced earnestly. "The wool has been pulled over our eyes. We have been fobbed off with mythical depictions, vague allusions to grand—um—grand but hidden delights of incredible beauty and fabulous proportions. These stupendous *parts* we are led to believe, are the very cornerstone of the human race, the pinnacles of pleasure and fulfillment upon which all women should clamor to worship, to, in fact, surrender their very selves. But—" Desirée pointed darkly to the book "—without ever looking upon the pinnacle or ever experiencing the slightest pleasure, though this, I am assured, is most unlikely. And should it happen, she must never let it show."

Sibyl quaked at her companion's fiery ardor. Despite insights into the minds of men, she knew little about their bodies. "There has indeed always been the most outrageous inequity in these matters," she said.

"Just so." Desirée sprang to her feet and crossed to sit beside Sibyl on the chaise. "I knew we were meant to work together. Think of it, Sibyl. From my studies to date I have discovered that... Oh, look at the book first. This is intended for study by artists, sculptors in particular, which explains a good deal." The great book was opened, and extremely well-thumbed pages turned until Desirée found what she was looking for. "There are many pictures. Far too much statuary, but at least I now understand the vagaries of that. I think we can dismiss statues of the male as representational efforts designed to glorify—*and to misrepresent.* If they weren't, there would be no need for what you will note here—a decision to use, or not to use *black squares.* The paintings and sketches from life are of the greatest interest. See." She turned the book and balanced it on Sibyl's limbs.

Confronted with a detailed drawing of a handsome, muscular person of the masculine variety, Sibyl gasped.

"Yes." Desirée bounced with enthusiasm. "He's my absolute favorite. Look at his face, his mouth.

Oh, Sibyl, do look closely at that mouth. And his hair, so dark, and the way it flows over his shoulders. And his shoulders and arms! He appears—*feral.* A creature of the wild, and so exciting he makes me tremble in the oddest places."

Sibyl couldn't think what might be the appropriate comment, although she believed she had felt similar tremblings—and enjoyed them.

"Do you not think him beautiful?"

"Oh, I do, I do indeed," Sibyl said, unable to take her eyes from the drawing.

"But," Desirée said with palpable satisfaction, "this is the best of all. They missed! Their black square—you'll notice there's one on every picture, except those of statuary—but their black square went a little awry here. Look."

Sibyl did look. She peered closely at the black square to which Desirée referred.

"Just there," Desirée said, placing the tip of a fingernail on the page. "See? There is hair there, isn't there?"

"Oh, dear." Sibyl fumbled for her fan and flipped it open. She was so hot. "I do believe there is, but we really shouldn't be looking."

"Of course we should. This is a book. Books are for looking at. By the by, this is a perfect example of what I mean about statuary. There are no black squares on the statuary, which means there is nothing real enough to enlighten one, otherwise the salient parts would be covered like they are in the drawings. Of course—'' Desirée paused, chewed her bottom lip thoughtfully ''—yes, it could be that the intention is to make sure women are not frightened by the truth. Hmm.''

Sibyl fanned herself more vigorously.

''I must concentrate,'' Desirée said. ''There, you see? Right there, the edge of something round. I assure you that I have been very diligent in my study. There is something round, then consider this.'' She ran her fingernail from the ''something round'' down the hint of something else not completely obscured by the black square. ''Do you know what I think that is?''

Sibyl shook her head. She bent over the book and said, ''There's a little hole in the page here.'' She tapped a corner of Desirée's black square.

Desirée waggled her head and failed to hide a smirk. ''La-la, I was just trying to see if—''

''If you could see underneath?'' Sibyl finished for her. ''You naughty girl.''

''I think—'' Desirée's hesitation and her triumphant expression were almost an implied drumroll ''—I think *that* is the pinnacle. The real thing rather than the flowery embellishments flaunted on park statues. *Alors,* sometimes they even put on the small leaves! Ivy, or other unlikely decorations. One assumes that men do not tuck leafy vines inside their trousers. But then, we cannot be sure about—''

''But the pinnacle is purely euphemistic,'' Sibyl rushed to point out. ''And how can a pinnacle point downward?''

''Aha,'' Desirée exclaimed, clearly incredibly pleased with herself. ''That's what we have to find out. Does it always point downward? Is what appears to be the beginning actually the end, in which case it would be pointing upward? Or—'' there was another dramatic pause ''—does something happen to it for some reason, something that makes it change direction, perhaps even shape or size? And does that happening have something to do with all this secrecy? Perhaps it becomes incredibly ugly or becomes beyond the control of its owner. After all, we do know that somehow the male has the power to make a woman increase. If not with this, then what? My nurse, who got very cross with me for my curiosity, told me kisses were a woman's downfall. I was never to allow a man other than my husband to kiss me, and only then when I wanted to have a child. How ridiculous. Jean-Marc kisses Meg all the time yet she has only Serena.

''If only Meg would tell us the secrets. Think of the time it would save.'' She leaned to whisper in Sibyl's ear, ''She and Jean-Marc pretend to pass the night in separate bedrooms. It's a lie. I happen to know he goes through the dressing room to join her *every night,* and remains there. Then when they appear at breakfast, they touch each other and smile, and look most pleased with themselves. Would that happen if they hadn't been having an exciting time before they arrived?"

"This is unsuitable," Sibyl said weakly. And she didn't want to accept that Meg now kept things from her when they had once shared everything.

"That's another thing," Desirée said as if she hadn't heard Sibyl's caution. "Meg shows pleasure about something, doesn't she? She shows she's enjoying herself. So much for the instructions we unmarried females are supposed to follow."

"I repeat," Sibyl said. "We should not discuss such matters."

"Perhaps, but we will pursue the subject for the highest possible cause. To enlighten our sisters—and ourselves. At least if we go to our marriage beds prepared to be completely horrified, we may bear that horror in hopes of eventually discovering the secret that makes Meg so happy. I rather think it could take many experiments first—but perhaps one learns to make the best of them, especially if there is something about diligent practice that may cause a woman to bear a beautiful child like Serena."

Sibyl's eyes went to the drawing once more. Many experiments first? Surely not. Oh, my. In future it was going to be difficult to look Hunter in the face.

2

Success had made little difference to Latimer More's appearance, Hunter mused, for no reason other than to engage his mind while Latimer remained deeply sunk in thought. The man had a good tailor these days, but his manner remained vague on occasion and hard work hadn't put a day on his face.

As soon as Latimer returned to his own rooms downstairs at 7A, Hunter intended to go in search of Sibyl. The so-called urgent message that had interrupted her unexpected visit had proved to be a puzzling and annoying hoax. When he'd arrived in chambers, not a soul awaited him there. Eventually he'd given up on meeting the Mrs. Ivy Willow who had written of her ''desperate plight,'' signed her name, and arranged for a man to deliver her summons to Number 7. Then Hunter had returned home to find Latimer waiting for him. During the years Latimer had lived in Mayfair Square, they had formed a firm friendship and regularly raised a glass together.

"Could this be anything to do with the other, d'you think?" Latimer asked, looking up from Ivy Willow's note. "Perhaps there was a plan to lure you out and, you know, finish you off?"

Hunter studied his friend's serious, very dark eyes and found no hint of humor there. "The thought had crossed my mind." He'd received threats. If he didn't refuse the knighthood about to be bestowed on him by King George IV, someone would make sure he didn't live to be called Sir Hunter anyway. "But I think this is too soon. They want to torment me, whoever they are. I don't put much stock in their warnings. Probably nothing more than a practical joke. Sooner or later the culprit will leap out, no doubt thrilled with his nonsense."

"That's not what you think," Latimer said, leaning forward from Hunter's favorite leather chair. The late January afternoon had grown cold and he held his palms toward the heat of the fire. "You're not a man to mention something like this if you're not concerned. I'm concerned, too. Think what it could mean to me. Looked forward to saying, 'my good friend, Sir Hunter,' I have. Might even have tossed around a few hints already. I assure you that 'My late friend, Hunter Lloyd, was a good barrister,' doesn't cut the mustard at all. Sounds embarrassingly boring, in fact.''

''Sorry about that,'' Hunter said, grinning. ''I do appreciate your concern and I'll try not to humiliate you by dying.''

Latimer smiled slightly himself. ''Glad you've decided to take matters seriously. Chillworth gets back from the Continent shortly. He'll lend a hand, keep a lookout with me. In the meantime I'm in a position to offer you my services.''

Adam Chillworth was the painter who lived in the attic, 7C. Presently he was touring France, Italy, and wherever else a painter felt he should pay homage. There had been talk of Austria and even Greece.

''Good of you to offer,'' Hunter told Latimer. ''Not necessary just now, though. Don't worry, I'll shout if things change. Listen to that rain. That was sudden.''

Latimer was not to be diverted. ''You're not yourself.'' He crossed his ankles atop Hunter's comfortably worn footstool and wiggled an expensively shod foot.

Hunter shook his head a little. ''Can't imagine what you're talking about. But I am glad your business is going so well. Everybody wanting exotic imports, are they?''

''Something like that. You're grim, Hunter.

Down in the mouth, if you'll forgive me for saying so. You need something to cheer you. A wife, perhaps."

Now there was a subject Hunter had no intention of addressing. "Your glass is empty," he said, and caught up the decanter of whiskey. "I'll join you in a spot more."

Latimer didn't argue, and he didn't protest when Hunter jerked the footstool from beneath his shining boots and sat on it.

They sipped in companionable silence before Latimer said, "You're avoiding things, old man. That's not like you at all. Doesn't have to be a grand passion, y'know."

Hunter took a moment to catch Latimer's meaning. When he did, he took too large a mouthful of liquor, and coughed when it hit his throat.

"We both know there's plenty of that to be had elsewhere than in the marriage bed," Latimer said, drawing himself up straight. "A nice, reliable homebody of a piece is what you need. Choose a girl who'll run your home well, and—"

"Latimer," Hunter interrupted, "what has made you an expert in this matter? Have you been keeping things from me? Got a wife somewhere, have you? Of course you have. I should have known as much. She's what drove you to establish your reputation elsewhere, no doubt." He leaned closer. "I know we made a pact never to discuss our, er, *hidden* lives, but perhaps we've matured and we're ready to be open, at least with each other. After all—we're well-known in certain quarters, but have we changed?"

"Most daring lover in all England?" Latimer said without even a ghost of a smile now. "That's been a useful fiction on occasion, although I've had my moments. You may be right. I certainly don't have the same interest in leading a double life. Not, of course, that I could ever compete with a man like yourself."

Actually, although they'd spent many a night on the Town together some time ago, they'd never been moved to discuss the topic before. "What's it like?" Latimer said, almost offhandedly. "The fastest recovery thing? More climaxes than any man alive? Not that I've seen you about much recently. Lost the urge, have you?"

"I say." Hunter coughed and found a handkerchief to wipe his mouth. "Are we too frank with this, d'you think? Another piece of fiction, that. And why isn't it possible I've found myself a mistress, tucked her away, and we have a perfectly satisfactory, or should I say, compatible arrangement?"

"Because you don't, that's why. I think you've grown tired of aggressive women, as have I. These days you're either in court, or here in these rooms.

Most of the time, anyway. You ride obsessively, but always alone. You are never still. It has been suggested that your need for excessive physical activities is a sign of certain other frustrations. According to...well, as far as I know, your name has never been linked to any particular woman's."

"According to whom?" Hunter turned sideways on the footstool and looked directly at Latimer. "Who have you been talking to about me?"

"A man of honor never breaks a confidence," Latimer said. "It's time you had a home of your own. I can't imagine why you continue living here."

"I can't imagine why *you* continue living here. You also need a home of your own. And a wife."

"We are not discussing me. You are more than well-fixed."

"So are you," Hunter pointed out.

"You haven't done a thing to these rooms as long as I've known you. Good carpet. Ottoman. I've always admired it. The plasterwork is splendid." Swiveling from the chair, he narrowed his eyes to study the room. "One could never fault Chippendale. Burled walnut's always been a favorite of mine. Your desk is a corker. No, it's the walls. All that red. Contemporary brothel, I'd call it."

The damned impertinence of the man. "I'll let the brothel comment pass. Unless I'm mistaken, you've done very little to your rooms. And I'm fond of the familiar. I like my surroundings, thank you.''

''No sense of adventure,'' Latimer muttered. He went to one knee before the fire, added coals from a brass scuttle, and used the bellows to encourage the flames.

''What did you say?'' Hunter asked. ''No matter, I heard what you said. *I* have no sense of adventure? What exciting escapades have you embarked upon of late?''

Latimer brushed his hands together and rose to his feet. A tall man, he appeared even more so when looking down at Hunter on his stool. ''Don't change the subject. First we must deal with any threat to you, but then it will be time for you, and perhaps for me, to consider our needs.'' He picked up a glass flask he'd sold to Hunter only months before. ''I still admire this. The Venetians have always had a certain flamboyant flair. Practice makes perfect, or so they say.''

''About Venetian glass?''

Latimer laughed and set the flask down on the mantel again. ''I was thinking about women. It's a man's job to teach his wife what pleases him, and to learn to please her.''

Now here was an interesting turn of events, Hunter thought. He got up and strolled to the massive burled-walnut-and-leather desk that had been his father's after it had been *his* father's, and after it had belonged to Sir Septimus Spivey. "I do believe it is you who are considering the intricacies of marriage after all. And you are a forward-thinking man, I see, or perhaps an individual in your thoughts. Tell me how you come to the conclusion that a man must learn to please his wife."

"I shall." Latimer ran his fingers through thick brown hair and commenced to pace. "What could be better than to have a wife who cannot wait to have you join her beneath the sheets? Or wherever. Who could have designed the notion that a man's pleasure will only be complete if he takes his wife, and spends himself on an inanimate body taught to remain still and unresponsive?"

Hunter sat behind the desk and leaned back in his chair. He swung his feet on top of the desk and stared at the ceiling with its carvings of scrolls and pens, books of various sizes, the whole wound about by fanciful ribbons. "This is amazing," he said at last. The subject began to arouse him. "I have long had much the same thoughts. To tell you the truth, the idea of a woman fearing me, physically, is abhorrent. Oh, certainly, there should be no straying from the fact that the man is the provider, the master of his own house and family, but why not marry for...marry because one *likes* the girl as well as desires her, and because she's mad about you? Imagine what that could lead to."

"Oh, yes," Latimer said on a long sigh. "Yes, yes. *Passion.* None of this nonsense about the woman keeping herself as covered as possible. Gad, where's the passion in that, I ask you?"

"No passion at all," Hunter agreed, drinking deeply of his whiskey.

"No," Latimer said. "See, if you will, a willing woman waiting for you every night—"

"Laughing," Hunter cut in. "Abandoned. Already naked and with outstretched arms."

"Ready to tear off your clothes," Latimer added, a faraway look in his glittering, almost black eyes. "Pulling you to her."

"Kissing you and begging for—"

"Passion." Latimer nodded emphatically. "In all its limitless varieties, hmm?"

Hunter bared his teeth and enjoyed feeling his manhood rise to the occasion. "Passion, indeed. No pretense. No long-suffering tolerance and silent acceptance of the inevitable. Dammit, what kind of a man is fulfilled in the arms of a female who doesn't want him?"

"Not I," Latimer announced in ringing tones.

"A woman with soft but strong hands to soothe or to take you to—"

"Passion." Latimer sighed. "Ah yes. A woman with no need to feign ecstasy."

"Ah, what nights those would be." Clasping his hands behind his neck, Hunter saw a clear image of a woman smiling down at him. "And mornings."

"And afternoons." Latimer set down his glass and crossed his arms. "Yes, very well. You know what you want. Now you should set about finding it—or her."

"Me? What about you? You obviously want those things for yourself."

For once Latimer didn't retreat into either silence or his dour wit. "I suppose I do," he said. "And I shall consider the matter. But I am not so cast down and lonely as you are. No, don't argue, you *are* a lonely man. I've seen it in you."

Lonely? The idea hadn't exactly occurred to Hunter.

"Do you want children?" Latimer asked, and when Hunter wasn't quick enough with a response, added, "You aren't getting any younger. Get on with it, man. Passion, lots of practice, then a child, then more passion. And more children if that's what you want."

Hunter laughed; he couldn't help himself. "You bounder, More. A man in his thirties is in the prime of life—and we are of an age, you and I."

"Then we'd both better be thinking about it,

hmm? A charming, warm, welcoming, ardent wife. And in good time—that is soon—an infant at her breast.''

A tightening within him bemused Hunter. ''Well, if you say so. But first things first. Wedding and bedding before babies, I think.''

Soft tapping at the door wiped away the pleasant visions. ''Come in,'' he said sharply.

The door opened a few inches and Sibyl poked her head into the room. She said, ''Forgive me for pursuing you, Hunter, but I do need to be alone with you,'' before she noticed Latimer, who was once more before the fireplace.

Instantly, Sibyl blushed fiercely and neither came into the room nor withdrew.

Smiling, Hunter got to his feet, but before he could welcome her Latimer said, ''Good to see you as always,'' and Hunter didn't miss either the man's stilted tones, or the way he glanced from Sibyl to Hunter. ''I'll be on my way then. Consider what we've talked about, Hunter. But have a care.''

There was an implied warning in those words, and it wasn't regarding Hunter's personal difficulties with threatening letters. Latimer was letting him know that he assumed he might be trifling with Sibyl's affections—perhaps compromising her even. Hunter understood the protective feelings Latimer had for Sibyl. Hunter shared those feelings. But he resented the implication, dammit.

Latimer opened the door wider and stood back while Sibyl entered. He looked into her upturned face and his expression softened. "You look well," he told her. "But then, you always do, and green becomes you."

With that he was gone, leaving Hunter and Sibyl alone, and Hunter with a muddle of disquieting thoughts and questions.

"Is this still a bad time?" Sibyl asked as soon as the door closed again. "I apologize if it is, but I have something to ask you and I want to do so before my courage deserts me."

3

Sibyl had changed her frock since their earlier encounter. She crossed the well-worn red carpet, the skirts of her green chintz dress rustling softly.

Damn Latimer anyway, Hunter thought, he'd said exactly what Hunter would like to have said to Sibyl.

"I was only joking, of course." She smiled, and played casually with the double ruff at her neck. "Courage isn't likely to desert me, not when I ask a favor of a dear old friend."

"Glad to hear that," he said, but felt unaccountably disquieted by the impression that she had either become more bold, or pretending to be so.

"Come," Sibyl said. Her already straight back became straighter and her chin rose. "Sit by the fire with me. I have a proposition for you."

Green did become her, but then, for longer than he wanted to consider, everything about Sibyl had enchanted him.

"Hunter? What's the matter with you? Surely you are not grown hard-of-hearing already."

He hadn't been mistaken. Something was definitely amiss with Sibyl. She had a quiet, gentle nature and was not given to forwardness. Already on his feet, Hunter smiled at her. "You think I am so old I can't hear anymore, hmm? Then I had better accept your invitation to come closer and sit in front of my own fire."

"Do that." If she'd noticed the mild rebuke, she gave no sign.

Beyond the windows, the afternoon grew dimmer. The rain beat the windowpanes even harder. Hunter took a moment to close heavy, deep-red velvet curtains.

Sibyl loved Hunter.

He treated her as a friend, perhaps almost as a sister. Before long he would become Sir Hunter, and must surely move to a more extravagant home and think about marrying a suitable woman. Even if he had ever noticed her as a woman, her simple beginnings as the daughter of the late Reverend and Mrs. Smiles of the tiny village of Puckly Hinton held no promise of increasing his social standing.

If he knew what she was thinking, he'd be embarrassed for her.

The hopelessness of it all struck her hard. Yet

this was the time to be composed, and as casual as one could be under the circumstances.

He wore black, as he usually did when he went to his chambers each day. She knew these things because his habits marked her days like clock chimes. She listened for his feet on the stairs both morning and evening, felt disappointed if she did not hear them. When he stepped onto the tiles in the hall, she stood in secret behind a curtain, where she could watch him leave the house. She didn't have to see him in the flesh to imagine the angle of his head when he tilted it on entering or leaving his carriage, or the glint of sun on light-brown hair—in green eyes. And she'd seen him on horseback. What a figure he cut. Yes, she knew what he wore, the way his coat fitted his shoulders and straight, solid back. The struggle not to study his capable hands was hard. And his legs... He turned toward her and she looked at the fire.

"A favor, you say, Sibyl? You have only to ask. Anything, dear girl, you know that."

Anything? Oh, she did hope so. "Please sit with me." She smiled and did what she had never done before, held a hand out to him. Unless she could convince him she'd become a confident woman of the world and capable of surviving difficulties on her own, he would never agree to help her.

Hunter looked into her eyes, then at her hand.

She felt his struggle, his surprise. And she saw when he made up his mind between ignoring her gesture and accepting it carelessly.

His fingers were as warm and firm as she'd imagined they would be, and she felt the toughened places where he so often held the reins. Her own frivolous laugh, practiced many times, felt painfully false.

Sibyl could not stop herself from glancing at his hand enfolding hers. For one mad instant she would have raised his fingers to her lips and kissed them.

"Sit in your chair," she told him in a breathless voice that annoyed her. "You look tired. I know I am. A new student just left. A little girl who does not like to sit still in one place for one minute. She would rather dance while *I* play." She smiled at him.

When he did nothing but remain standing, staring at her, Sibyl sat on a footstool and tugged on his arm until he sank into the chair beside her.

Hunter kept a smile on his mouth and made sure no hint of concern showed. Sibyl didn't take her hand from his and he couldn't make himself let her go.

The color in her cheeks was too high, the glitter in her eyes too bright, and she might take courage from the coquettish incline of her head, the pretty moue, but he heard her rapid breathing and saw the sharp rise and fall of her breast. And her hand was far too cold.

"You are chilled," he said, holding that hand between both of his and chafing the skin. "I shall ask Barstow to get you some tea."

"No, thank you."

Much too quick a reply, Hunter thought. "Take a chair instead of the stool and get closer to the fire, then."

She shook her head.

"Then tell me what I can do to help you."

In another subdued rustle, Sibyl stood up, stood at his very knee and clasped her hands at her waist. She said, "Please don't get up," when he made to rise. "There's a wind now, too. I believe we shall have a violent storm."

The very old lantern clock that had belonged to Hunter's grandfather chose that instant to chime, and Sibyl jumped, then laughed self-consciously. For all her newfound forwardness, she was beyond anxious and the laugh, the smile, the sway of her body, didn't hide the fact from Hunter, not for a moment.

His present angle on her was new. He had never been seated while she stood, and stood so close. Did she feel any trace of what he himself felt, the inner tension, the heightened awareness that traveled just beneath his skin?

Of course she didn't.

Gently born women couldn't be expected to know such sensations, although, as he and Latimer had discussed, there ought to be a way to teach them....

"I have a secret," she said. Firelight dappled her neck and face, and turned her upswept fair hair to gold. Her throat moved sharply. "A secret longing."

Hunter swallowed, too. How did a man respond to such a statement?

"I have come to you because... Hunter I have come to you because you are the only man... Hunter, I need you."

This was amazing. Wonderful but amazing. This shy little woman—this woman who had seemed shy until now—coming to him to declare herself? He could not immediately meet her eyes and gazed instead at the wide, green satin ribbon tied around the base of her high bodice. Certainly Sibyl was, as he'd always thought her, small, but so much in proportion. Her hips were far from boyish and her breasts would be just right in his hands, beneath his lips....

How fortunate he was sitting, and that Sibyl was unlikely to examine any part of his person too closely.

She must not, Sibyl knew, lose her determination

now. Whatever it cost her, the request must be made, for she would never again find the nerve to ask him.

His lips parted as if he intended to speak, but he closed them again and tapped his steepled fingers together. Long fingers. There were fine but definite hairs across the backs of his hands and the palms were broad.

"Sibyl?" he said quietly.

Now. She must say it now, ask him to do whatever had to be done—exactly. Her glance swept quickly downward from his hands. Just as quickly she averted her face. If she dared to conduct a longer study she could compare what she saw with the book Desirée had left with her. As it was, she'd seen a definite suggestion of the sort of shapes they'd decided were beneath the black squares. *More than a definite suggestion.*

Peeking pointedly at unmentionable things! She was a loathsome disgrace and should leave at once.

"You are usually quiet, but not usually completely tongue-tied," Hunter said.

Now. "I'm going to have a child," she said. "I mean, a baby."

Hunter's expression became fixed. Slowly, he dropped his hands to the arms of his chair. He didn't understand what she'd said, that much was obvious.

"Since you are, or have been, by way of a close

friend—or should I say, a generous neighbor—I thought I might speak to you about this."

"Good God." Damn it all, he'd better misunderstand her or someone was going to pay. No. No single woman would admit to such a thing if it weren't true. Hunter sprang to his feet so abruptly, he bumped Sibyl and she lost her balance. He caught her as she would have stumbled onto the hearth. Holding her in his arms, his instinct was to gather her to him, to kiss and comfort her.

He must cool the heat within him. He must do or say nothing that he would regret all too soon. His reactions confused him. She confounded him with horrendous news and his desire for her overtook him completely.

"Oh, Hunter," she whispered and her eyes shimmered too brightly.

"Hush," he said. "There's no need to cry. Please don't cry, Sibyl, I beg you." If she did he would have no idea what to do about it. With great care, he turned her around and pushed her gently into his chair. "Do not move from there. I'll get you something to drink. Here, put your feet on the stool and rest." When women were increasing they needed lots of rest. Yes, he did know that. They certainly did *not* need *passion.*

He lifted her feet and placed them on the stool, put more coals on the fire, used the bellows and cast about for a lap pad to warm her. Of course there wasn't one. He'd never use such a thing. "Sit there, now, Sibyl. I insist, so don't argue. I'll be back almost before you know I'm gone." He rushed to the door that led to his bedchamber and said, "Don't move a muscle," raising a forefinger and assuming a fierce expression.

Sibyl saw him go into the next room and finally remembered to take a breath. He was behaving so strangely. Did he think she was ill? She certainly didn't dare to disobey his instructions. The trembling in her limbs crept throughout her body. Forceful behavior undid her, and usually reduced her to tears. But he had begged her not to cry. However, he had been forceful, too. Tears wouldn't help. He had sensed her discomfort, that was all, and in typical Hunter manner was attempting to comfort her.

He reappeared carrying a patchwork quilt in his arms. Very large and made of dark shades of velvet, the pattern was of linking ovals, the individual pieces embroidered with depictions of animals and birds—and women, unclothed women.

Hunter became too busy tucking the warm quilt around her to note how she looked repeatedly from the voluptuous little females to his face. At last she kept her eyes lowered and hoped he would never notice. One of the last things she would have expected of him would be that he liked such vulgar things, and on his bed, of all places.

Rubbing his hands together, he bent over her and looked closely at her face. "You're very pale. I should have noticed that before. You need something more to warm you. Would it be inappropriate for you to have a little sherry?"

She had tasted it on several occasions and liked the flavor, and the warmly secure sensation it caused. "Quite appropriate. Thank you, Hunter." A secure sensation would be most useful.

He went to a tall, red lacquer Chinese cabinet and opened double doors at the top. From inside he produced a dark-colored bottle and a small, blue crystal glass, which he only half filled with sherry. His frown tightened her chest. The dramatic arch of his brows sent a little shiver through her. Then he looked up at her with his dark-lashed eyes that could be any shade of green. They were deep, shadowy green now.

"Here you are," he said, and she thought she heard anger in his voice. "Don't drink quickly. You aren't used to such things."

Sibyl accepted the glass and dutifully took a tiny sip. It was enough to burn deliciously in her throat, and tread a warm path through her veins. Quickly, she sipped again and closed her eyes, holding the glass in both hands.

Hunter remained standing. He stood over her with his feet braced apart, his hands clasped behind him, and a harsh, tense set to his lean features. His black waistcoat fitted his broad chest without a wrinkle, fitted and narrowed at his waist. He was flat there. With his feet apart, his trousers clung to large, hard muscles in his legs. She'd noticed them on a number of occasions, particularly when he was on horseback. Sibyl sighed. The sherry was a most useful focus that allowed her to study him covertly. If an artist were to draw him without clothes, and put the picture in a book, it would need rather a large black square.

"You're blushing, Sibyl. Why? Or are you hot?"

She knew she grew even redder and tried another swallow of sherry.

"Don't drink so quickly. How obtuse of me. It's the sherry that overheats you. Sibyl, I must be blunt. You are my friend and if I have my way, you will always be my friend. But there is something very serious going on here. You are to answer me direct. There can be no deceit, no fabrication."

Nor would there be. "I shall explain myself with complete honesty."

"Very well then. Are you comfortable?"

"Yes."

"You don't feel ill?"

She hesitated before saying, "No." In fact she felt light-headed.

"You do feel ill." He took her glass and before she could protest, swept her up into his arms and marched with her into his bedchamber. "You have nothing to fear. Your honor is safe with me. I shall lock the door to the passageway and make sure we are not interrupted. You may take as long as you need to tell me everything." He set her on the bed and pulled pillows up behind her back. Then he settled the quilt about her once more.

He left the room, presumably to lock the door to the corridor and was back almost at once. "Drat the fire in here," he said. "Almost out. We shall have to hire some younger help. Old Coot will just have to understand. It's time I became more insistent with Aunt Hester."

A little of Hunter's adept ministrations and the fire soon crackled against the blackened chimney breast.

Sibyl Smiles, spinster of very little experience, was ensconced in the bed of Hunter Lloyd, Barrister at Law and soon to be Sir Hunter Lloyd. Alone. With him in the room. With him wiping his hands on a towel and frowning at her, observing her with eyes grown dark with an emotion she was sure she wouldn't like to have completely revealed.

"You're going to have..." He approached the

bed and sat down beside her. "You're going to have a baby. Isn't that what you said, what you meant?"

"Yes." She pushed her shoulders back. "That is exactly what I said."

He covered one of her hands and held it. He held it too tightly and it hurt, but she couldn't allow herself to cry out. "Sibyl—" He spoke through clenched teeth and muscles flickered in his cheeks. "I—Sibyl, who—I mean, shouldn't you be speaking to another man about this?"

"Impossible," she told him. "Absolutely not."

"You are afraid of the reaction?"

"Very afraid. But I am not afraid to talk with you, not really. I trust you completely, Hunter." Even saying the words brought a rush of sad, sweet longing. "I would do anything for you and I know you will stand by me." What ill fate that she could never expect him to return her feelings.

Quite unexpectedly, he propped an elbow on his knee and rested his forehead on a fist.

"Hunter?" Sibyl asked tentatively. "I have concerned you. Please, that is the last thing I should wish to do." She was selfish in taking this path, but to turn back now would mean to close the door on her dream. And she would be a good mother, too. The world needed lots of good mothers.

"Extraordinary," he muttered. "Unthinkable.

Can you go to Count Etranger? Surely he would do what's necessary.''

Horrified, Sibyl caught at Hunter's hand and pulled on it until he raised his head. ''Out of the question,'' she said, sitting up and putting her face close to his. ''Awful even to consider. Please promise you won't breathe a word of this to him—or to anyone unless I tell you it's all right.''

He was handsome, with a clear-cut mouth she felt she knew well without ever having touched it. Firm and full, and when he smiled, the upper lip arched away from his eyeteeth and dimples appeared beneath his cheekbones. Those were the times when he appeared very young.

''I won't say anything to anyone without your permission,'' he said.

His breath passed softly over her lips. She was close enough to see how thc light changed in his eyes, and to make out the chips of black and gold there.

He didn't move away. Neither did she. He looked at her with deep concern, the concern of a man who cared. Only inches and her lips would touch his.

Hunter was looking at her mouth.

She pulled her bottom lip between her teeth.

He drew in a great breath and let it out slowly. ''Sibyl, dear, about the man you should be talking to about this…''

"There is no other man whom I believe in as much as you." Her expression was sweet and trusting. Hunter entertained wild notions. He could take her somewhere safe and hide her there until this was all over. He could find out the wretched man's name and prosecute him for trifling with an innocent woman.

What would she say if he told her about his somewhat lurid reputation in parts where, even now, his name wasn't known, or that in his own world he could not attend any function without being pursued by eligible, marriage-hunting misses and their anxious mamas? How would she react if he opened his heart and said she was the only woman he wanted as a wife, but that up to now her shy nature held him back for fear any sign of his ardor would repulse her.

What could have brought her to such a pass? With child, but not, apparently, with so much as the possibility of a husband. "Sibyl, this is painful for both of us, but if I am to help you, I should know when you anticipate the arrival of the child."

Her eyes lost focus. A soft smile settled on her lips. She looked up into his face and he found her the loveliest creature he had ever seen. He could not imagine what impulse made her do so, but she took up his hands and held them to her cheeks. Her eyes closed.

Peace spread across her features.

Slowly, she brought her temple to rest against his jaw. He felt the rise and fall of her breasts against his forearms.

Damn it all, he was only a man, a man who had fought his feelings for Sibyl for too long.

Hunter took a deep breath. He took his hands from beneath hers and framed her face and ears. Very gently, he blew wisps of stray hair away from her forehead.

And then he kissed her. He kissed her lips with tenderness, feeling the shape of them, the texture of them, the slightest brush of her teeth against his bottom lip. He opened his eyes, but hers were closed and the needy intensity in her features turned his heart. A lost one in need of a strong man's comfort and protection. And protect her, he would.

They embraced, and they kissed again and again, the light kisses of the very young, or the very inexperienced, because he allowed her to set the pace. Sibyl didn't part her lips—not until he parted them for her. She grew quite still then, but rather than appear shocked or disgusted, her puckered brow showed how hard she was concentrating. Oh, she concentrated, and she learned quickly. Hunter pushed her back onto the bed and came down on top of her. He couldn't stop, couldn't slow down. And Sibyl wasn't doing anything to help him. She stroked his face and his hair, shakily rubbed his shoulders, then slipped her hands inside his waistcoat to his smooth linen shirt.

Blood beat in his veins, beat in his ears. His heart thundered, and he felt the answering rapid beat of Sibyl's.

She unbuttoned his waistcoat and touched his chest and stomach lightly, smoothing over his shirt and panting softly.

A darkness formed inside his head. His focus had centered on her and he no longer controlled that part of him that was driven by passion…or lust.

The ruff was easy enough to dispense with, and her frock was quickly undone down the back. Hunter kissed her hard, opened her mouth wide and sucked her lower lip between his. And he pulled the frock from her shoulders, taking her chemise with it.

Then her breasts were bared and he'd been right. On so small a woman, they were voluptuous, very round and with such pink nipples.

He was lost.

Once more he kissed her lips, then he cupped her breasts and pushed them upward, no longer caring how obvious his erection must be. How she must feel it.

"You are beautiful," he told her. "Your breasts are the most desirable ever. Perfect." And he trailed his tongue in circles around one, each circle a little smaller than the one before until he reached the edge of puckered pink flesh. He stopped and took the nipple between finger and thumb, squeezed and pulled lightly.

She made the first sound in minutes, a thin moan while she arched her back. Hunter used his tongue on her other breast and this time when he reached the center he took her flesh between his teeth and suckled.

Her head was angled backward. She groped to touch him wherever she could reach. Hunter swept up her skirts and pressed his hands through the gap in her drawers and into the warm moist place where the tops of her thighs came together. Sibyl writhed, and he sought out her most private places. With one knee, he kept her legs apart.

Sibyl forced a hand downward between them and he all but yelled when she took hold of him and squeezed. He felt her shudder and at first thought she was frightened, or repulsed, but her other hand joined the first and she cradled him, used her fingers to trace the shape of him.

It was mad. A heated grappling madness between a lonely man and a woman who had come to him only for help.

"Damn it."

Sibyl had stopped moving, too. Any fool could

see she was stricken by their behavior. He withdrew her hands and pulled down her skirts. For far too long he held her wrists together above her head and stared at her breasts. He released one of his hands and passed his palm back and forth over her erect nipples, half crazed and half borne away by the thrill of her helpless attempts to thrust herself upward at him.

At last he eased the chemise and frock back into place, pulled her to sit up and lean against him while he fastened the back of her dress. The ruff could wait.

"I'm sorry," he said. "What a weak thing to say. I don't understand myself. I should never have treated you like that."

"The way I wanted to be treated, you mean? I didn't try to stop you."

"Because you are needy, and because you trust me to do nothing that would hurt you." *How could he hurt her more than he already had?* "I was wrong, *wrong,* and after all you've been through. Unforgivable. Please don't argue. I must deal with my own feelings." His feelings were that he'd taken advantage of her when she was in no condition to stand up for herself.

Sibyl hardly dared look at him. He had...well, he *had,* and she'd adored every second. Until now. Now she felt foolish and forward, and he was angry, no doubt because he had given in to this animal reaction she and the ladies had discussed. It was behavior that meant nothing other than some physical satisfaction to a man, whereas a woman was especially at risk during such times because her heart and mind—and body—responded and, if she really cared about the man, she could make the mistake of thinking he returned her feelings.

But at least she had brought him that physical pleasure she knew men not just enjoyed, but needed. She would do anything for him.

He moved to the very edge of the bed and sat with his head bowed. "There is no other man you will let me speak to on your behalf."

The thought horrified her. "No. Please, no, Hunter."

"When do you plan to have your baby?"

"That remains to be seen. And please, don't give another man a thought. You know I have meetings here, each week? Sometimes twice a week?"

He had seen the small parade of haughty females who closed themselves inside 7B with Sibyl. On occasion he had encountered their type at The Inns of Court. Women with causes, God help him. Women who sought defense because they had brought themselves to pretty passes through their determination to prove they were either superior to men, or that they didn't need men at all. "I'm aware of your visitors,'' he said. ''What do you discuss that keeps you closeted for so long?''

''Matters of the highest importance to women. The problem of causing—I hope you will forgive me if I sound bold—but the problem of causing men to recognize the strength of our minds, our ability to make our own decisions, our understanding of matters men have formerly thought to keep from us. Such as politics, matters of national interest, reform. And the more complex and private workings of our bodies—and theirs. And—'' Sibyl rushed her words and showed how flustered she was ''—and the idea that not all women truly *need* men to protect them.''

I'll be dashed. This was exactly the type of thing he'd feared and it explained why Sibyl was foolish enough to think producing a child out of wedlock was other than a personal disaster. ''Is that so?'' he said, stalling, taking his time while he considered how to enlighten his friend. His friend, hah! He had stepped over the line of mere friendship and taken her with him.

''Yes,'' she told him. ''And we learn more with every meeting. Are you aware of the work of Prévost and Dumas?''

''I can't say I am.''

''Fascinating,'' Sibyl said. If only she could quell the league of nerves that jumped in her stomach.

"They have proved that the sp-sperm—only formed by the male, by the way—is essential to fer-fertilization. For babies, you know. Making it possible for them to, well, *be.*"

Good grief. "Ah, is that so? I do believe I had read something of the sort."

"Yes," Sibyl said, "which means, of course, that even women who would prefer to avoid contact with men must sacrifice themselves to gain a certain end. However, what I come to you about now is my own private concern."

"It would be."

He regarded her inscrutably, which served to make Sibyl increasingly unhappy, if that were really possible. "Will you help me, Hunter?" Never had so few words cost her so much.

"Help you do what, exactly, Sibyl?"

She was ever more enchanting, Hunter thought. He would never again be able to pretend that his interest in her hadn't passed beyond polite admiration and liking. He desired her. How many nights had he already spent tossing and turning and visualizing her sleeping a floor below—in a bed almost exactly beneath his own, in fact. After the events of the past hour, he was doomed to do more than visualize. He would see her exactly as she was and would need even longer early morning rides—or a return to his old ways for an interval.

He didn't just desire her, he lusted after her, God help him. But some other blighter had taken advantage of her and he was faced with the biggest dilemma of his life. If he married her quickly, there would still be gossip about an "early" birth, but that would gradually fade.

Surely, Sibyl thought, he would agree to at least consider what she had in mind. Surely he would after she explained her odious alternatives. "I've entertained a number of options," she told him. "I could go into the country, to a farm perhaps, where I understand there is usually an abundance of healthy men but often a shortage of unmarried females. I could find a position. And such a situation might provide me with the result I need."

Hunter struggled to interpret her meaning. Could it be that she thought to marry a farmer? For what purpose?

"Or," she continued, pulling the dark velvet quilt around her, "in a great house. I could enter service for as long as necessary. One hears tales of liberties taken by some who are privileged but unscrupulous. Very unpleasant to consider of course, but the end could justify the means, don't you think?"

This was not going well, Sibyl decided. Hunter was supposed to want to save her from such courses, but he didn't show any sign of offering to help.

"Could it?" he asked after what seemed a very

long time. He got up and lighted the lamps. The flames rose and fell, shifting shadows over his face, his eyes. He studied her, unblinking. This room, furnished in beautiful but heavy old furniture of mostly oriental origin, fitted him. Here he was not the Hunter she knew, but a darker, more unfathomable man.

She breathed in loudly and cast about for an inspired explanation. "One of my ladies knows all about these things. But she chose yet another solution and I'm not sure I could manage it at all. There are places called *nunneries.* They are not what you think at all, although the person who oversees them is called an abbess."

It was with difficulty that Hunter stopped his mouth from falling open.

"I think you have some idea what I'm talking about," she said, her voice growing smaller. "These places are sometimes called houses of ill repute. Miss Phyllis has a wealth of information on them. I can't say I'm completely clear, but Miss Phyllis insists one need probably be there only a short time to accomplish whatever, but I'm just not sure. She did not actually take that course."

"Sibyl," Hunter said when the shock began to subside a little, "are you speaking of... Well, no, of course you aren't. I misunderstand you."

"I don't think you do. The lady I mention found a way to accomplish her needs and went to the Continent for the final event. Then returned with the child afterward. It's being done all the time, by all manner of women who have no man in their lives. I'm prepared to do the same. All I need is someone willing. It was suggested that the simplest thing is to find a way to get the gentleman in his cups. Awful, I know and useless to me under the circumstances, since I should require his guidance. Also, I would not consider taking advantage of another person. But however this is done, I will never expect the man to take any responsibility afterward."

Hunter was too warm, sweating even. So she wasn't with child, only intending to become so. What in the name of heaven could possibly cause Sibyl to think of such appalling measures, much less try to act on them?

"Hunter?"

He held up a silencing hand and willed his mind to be quiet. Her proximity on his bed didn't help. "I think I understand you now. I have no right to do so, but I absolutely forbid you to resort to any of these revolting and extremely dangerous notions. For you to mention them shows how little you know of the world."

"I know a great deal," she said, but she quaked before his anger. "I am a spinster of a certain age and have no particular interest in marriage. Soon it will be too late for me to realize my fondest hope and that would be a shame because I know I should be very good at it—at being a parent, that is."

"Absolute tripe," Hunter thundered. If nothing else, he would intimidate her out of this. "You are far from the time when you need worry about this. And think, Sibyl, how would you explain such a thing to others? Your returning from wherever with an infant?"

She felt herself blush. "I will have rescued a foundling while I am on the Continent, of course. You have no need to concern yourself with details. I have no desire to take any of those other steps I mentioned, but what I require cannot be accomplished without a man." The next breath she took was so hard. She would tell him what she would like, tell him straight. "What could be better than to know the father of one's child is an honorable man, a man one likes so much."

This was an encounter he would never forget. "Certainly sounds like an absolute requirement to me." She had no interest in a husband, but he would save her from herself, no matter how difficult that proved.

Sibyl could scarcely hear for the pounding of her heart. "Then we are agreed. Surely you know the man I would choose, don't you? There is only you who could be the perfect one. Will you do this for me, Hunter?"

4

Sivey here.

Whatever I might have anticipated, this would not have been close.

I am bewildered. Saddened, even.

Forget I said that. Of course I am not saddened. The enemy is always the enemy.

But Sibyl is such an innocent. And Hunter actually made me pity him. After all, blood is thicker than water and the boy is... No. I must do what must be done and return to my post, newel post, to rest. My mind is tired and I become maudlin.

Now, how to accomplish the imperative?

As in past difficulties, the answer—even if not particularly comforting—would be to employ a suitable candidate as my emissary. My earthly emissary, one with an earthly body I could use to help my cause. How unfortunate I spent so much effort finding Ivy Willow, only to have her become wilful and withdraw before Hunter arrived in Chambers. In the end I couldn't keep control of her. Her nat-

ural fear simply shut her mind to my instructions and she ran away, leaving me with a long flight home, I might add. And flying is still not my strongest talent in my new state.

Wait, this may not be at all unfortunate. Hunter hasn't seen the woman, so? Yes, she will still be perfect. Young enough for the job, and not unattractive. That may be important.

I will go to her and reestablish an attachment at once. Sad, lonely creature that she is. The man she hoped to marry married another and she's lived alone ever since. I shall relieve her of that unhappiness for at least a while. Yes, I am certain she will thoroughly enjoy the part I have for her to play.

Sibyl's latest faithful friend. A new member of that nasty club or whatever they consider themselves when they meet at 7B.

Her name must be changed, of course. But this is a splendid—and selfless—idea. I will be helping Sibyl by stopping her from disgracing herself, and helping Hunter by removing the shocking burden that she has placed upon him.

Now, I have not fully explained what is going on. There are elements about which you can have no knowledge and they are the underhanded ideas of my addlebrained great-granddaughter, Lady Hester. You see, Her Ladyship is the most selfish crea-

ture I have ever encountered. She has not one whit of concern for anyone but herself.

If you can believe this, and I do not know why, she cannot bear to consider having Sibyl leave Number 7. She does not know anything of Sibyl's amazing scheme, but she has seen the way Hunter and Sibyl look at each other, and pretend not to look at each other, and she's afraid Hunter will get around to asking the girl to marry him. After all, or so she thinks, he is to be knighted and will move to a house of his own. Since he at least attempts to restrain some of her impetuousness, she wants him to leave. She does not want Sibyl to leave—not ever. So—rather than put the happiness of two young people before her own, Hester intends to come between them.

Fool!

Of course there can be no bastard child. But there can be a wedding and a bedding—far away from here. The result being the reclaiming of two apartments—at last.

And these people would be blissful together, I can just see how happy they would be.

Not that I care. Why should I?

I am the slightest bit befuddled. The Reverend Smiles, Meg and Sibyl's departed papa, who speaks with me often, only grows more elevated and well thought of among the Important Ones up there. He shows signs of gaining his heavenly wings at any time. Being still in a suspended state and awaiting some decision about my future, this is not an eminent creature I can afford to annoy. After all, he was quite kind and friendly when he asked me to keep an eye on his daughters. I like to think Meg's marriage to Etranger resulted in a recommendation up there—in the higher place where I would very much like to strut. Strum, I mean, on a harp. But he awaits news of Sibyl daily and he has already shown signs of disappointment in me. You see, in his position, when he is studying strenuously for the Bar—for want of a better description, people like Smiles are by way of being politicians who decide the big stuff, and, therefore, must be lawyers—while he is studying for the Bar, and for some time afterward, he is not allowed to have anything to do with those still in the rudimentary stages on earth. So I have been appointed to do what I can in his stead. Fine line that, helping him while I help myself.

Back to the frightful Hester. She intends to bring the daughter of a friend to stay in Mayfair Square. Her mother is an ambitious female intent on clawing a way into society. For now, my beleaguered descendant, Hunter, seems a desirable escort for the girl, perhaps even a desirable match. Then Hester would get her wish and Sibyl would remain while Hester's socially appropriate friend—Hester does have a large portion of the snob in her—would expect Hunter to set up home much more grandly elsewhere.

Now I ask you, would that be fair to either dear little Sibyl, or to Hunter, who is indeed an honorable man I'm glad to count a member of my family?

You are so right. It is not.

I shall protect them from themselves. Help them along a bit—with Ivy Willow's assistance. Hunter and Sibyl should marry and leave this house together.

Oh, oh, I believe I'm having a spell. I don't feel at all like myself. I shall glide to the place where my new helper lives her empty life and be more firm about putting the final touches to her preparation.

Spell? What am I babbling about. No spell at all. I'm not becoming overgenerous, just protecting my home. No whimpering, whining infant shall disturb my peace. Oh, the thought makes me beside myself. I'm on my way at once.

Drat, here comes another friendless nuisance. I shall dispatch him at once.

"Out of my way, Mr. Fawkes. No, I shall not lend you an ear, you traitor!"

5

"Even if Sibyl were forced to be late for some reason, Lloyd is a prompt fellow," Jean-Marc, Count Etranger, told his wife. "Then there is Latimer More and Lady Hester. How extraordinary that they are *all* late."

They waited in the green salon, Meg's favorite room whenever they deserted Riverside, their estate in Eton, for London. Princess Desirée hovered in a corner, swaying her two-toned pink-striped skirts.

"Sit down, there's a good girl, Desirée," Jean-Marc said, well aware that his young half sister was sulking, and why.

"I am too distraught to sit," she said, making a fine profile that showed off a beguiling knot atop her head, through which strands of pink jade beads had been threaded. "How can it be that Adam Chillworth is still on the Continent? He left an absolute age ago. Sibyl wrote to us at Riverside about it. Is it not so, Meg?" She pouted.

"You should not be concerned with Chillworth's

whereabouts,'' Jean-Marc said firmly. ''He is a fine artist and I can understand your interest in his work. And of course you must be anxious for him to continue your portrait. But he is very much a man of the world, with a man of the world's needs—''

''Jean-Marc,'' Meg exclaimed.

An impressively large and elegant man with the regal bearing of one who carried considerable burdens for his father's country, he grinned and strode to catch his voluptuous wife about the waist and sweep her from her feet. ''Do not censure me, my lady. Remember I am your lord and master.''

''Hmph.'' She prodded the middle of his chest. ''You'd like to believe that, wouldn't you? Now put me down.''

''We need a few moments of privacy to discuss what I should do—as head of the household, *chérie.* This may be our only opportunity.''

Meg planted her hands on his shoulders and tried, but failed, to glare at him. ''Don't be outrageous. What can you be talking about?''

''My sister-in-law, Sibyl, of course.'' A French accent made his perfect English irresistible. He put his mouth to her ear. ''I must take care of all my girls.''

A moment of panic was quickly quelled by Meg. ''You are a bounder, sir. Sibyl has chosen to be her own mistress and would not appreciate your interference. You promised to say nothing. I spoke to you in confidence."

"In confidence," he mimicked, inclining his head. "As if I didn't know you only confided in me because you needed my superior problem-solving powers. But don't worry, I will do nothing to arouse suspicion."

"Jean-Marc," Meg wailed, disregarding Desirée's presence. She was bound to learn of the Great Dilemma before long. "I shall never forgive you if you embarrass poor Sibyl. Now put me down at once."

He did so, but trapped her against him. He glanced at her décolletage and whispered in her ear again. "Nursing my angelic Serena does beautiful things for your already spectacular charms."

She frowned, unconvincingly, and said, "Unhand me, sir. How would it look if our guests arrived for dinner to find us in such a position?"

"They'd be jealous, wouldn't they, Desirée?"

"You are mean. You deliberately flaunt your happiness before me. And you should be more capable of composure at your age." Desirée's accent was much heavier than her half brother's, and her English was not as good. "You are also so satisfied with yourself that my pain goes unnoticed."

"Never, Desirée. I understand the pangs of young love."

"Who said anything about love?" Desirée wanted to know, and in rude, ringing tones. "It is merely that the company at dinner promises to be a great bore and Adam invariably makes an attempt to entertain me."

Jean-Marc could grow very tired of this young woman on occasion. "A boring meal causes you pain, Desirée? You are an even more spoiled creature than I thought."

An abrupt rap on the door preceded Rench, Jean-Marc's butler of some years. A tall, thin man, he inclined a head of thin silver hair and said, "Mr. Latimer More has arrived with Miss Sibyl Smiles. And Lady Hester Bingham escorted by Mr. Hunter Lloyd. I have taken the liberty of showing them directly into the dining room. Cook is annoyed that her soup grows cold."

"Is that a fact?" Meg said. "Kindly come to us before you make such decisions in future. We shall appear rude and I'm afraid that must come before cook's spectacular temper. Let us hurry to join our guests, Jean-Marc."

"Our guests are also old friends, and a relative," he pointed out. "They are most comfortable with each other and will not even miss us. Desirée, turn up the corners of that pretty mouth. It's time you got to know Latimer More better. He is a cultured man with a great deal of knowledge about rare artifacts, and could engage you in interesting conversation."

"About old stuff? He rarely says a word."

"If you so desire, I am sure you can have him chattering in no time. What man could be immune to your charms?"

The princess made a growling sound and marched ahead of her half brother and sister-in-law.

Meg clung to her husband's arm and hung back. "Promise me you will not say a word of what I told you," she pleaded.

"You've got to admit Sibyl has surprised us," he responded, walking slowly across the stone-floored foyer with its scatter of excellent silk Persian rugs. "You think she wants Hunter as a father for her child, don't you?"

Meg groaned. "I don't know what she wants. It is all outrageous. She thinks she's growing too old to have children at all, so she's convinced herself no man would want her and that she must find one who is—"

"Willing to take on the odious job of making her with child. Poor, poor, fellow."

At that, she smiled. "Where does Sibyl get her ideas? I will deal with it, Jean-Marc. She may seem gentle and quiet—although she's pretending otherwise at the moment—but she is also very independent."

"Fear not, I shall do nothing to embarrass anyone."

The doors to the dining room were thrown open by two flunkies in white wigs and the royal livery of Mont Nuages. The black-and-gold quartering blazed with the Crown Prince's red, white and purple coat of arms, the coat of arms bestowed upon Jean-Marc by his grateful father in recognition of a faithful bastard son's service.

Strains of violin music sounded from the small gallery at one end of the long room. Servants were at their stations, hands at sides, staring straight ahead, and the table was a shimmering masterpiece of crystal, china and silver. Cascading fruit and flowers, heaps of sweetmeats, nuts, and exotic delicacies, were tucked into the bowls of a many-tiered, silver epergne, to form a spectacular centerpiece.

And there was Lady Hester Bingham, resplendent in her favorite mauve with a mauve turban to match. A very fine figure she cut. In her fifties, with smooth skin and bright-blue eyes—and fine blond hair when it wasn't covered—she could have replaced the late Lord Bingham in her affections many times over. Lady Hester was completely composed and obviously looking forward to the evening immensely. Upon sighting Jean-Marc, she wiggled her fingers at him and executed a graceful curtsey.

Jean-Marc bowed as he and Meg drew closer. Cook's soup certainly smelled delicious and from the array of covers already passed through to sideboards that stretched the length of one wall, this would be quite the feast.

"Good evening, my lord," Latimer More said. "Forgive us for arriving early."

Meg went to him at once and spoke quietly with him. No doubt thanking him for trying to take the blame for their hosts' graceless welcome. Jean-Marc grinned at Latimer and said, "I'm still hoping you'll surprise me with particularly obscure netsuke toggles. Ivory. I want to surprise Meg with them. She would have fun wearing tiny carvings at her waist."

"Indeed, I haven't forgotten. I have heard of a rare, early eighteenth century set and I may be coming to you soon, but I will not say another word about the pieces yet."

Latimer More, Jean-Marc noticed as always, made a striking figure and must be ripe for the picking.

And then there was Sibyl. A simple green taffeta gown suited her fair coloring, and her alluring figure. She might not please a man who preferred a good deal of flesh, but she was beautifully made and moved with natural grace—and was dashed pretty.

She also showed disturbing signs of being both dejected and awkward. He went to her side and linked their arms. "Dear Sibyl," he said, and was instantly in no doubt that he was much too hearty. "Do you know how much it means to marry the woman of your dreams and to discover that with her you have inherited a new sister who is as intelligent as she is beautiful? Even if it does take days to get her to come across the square for dinner."

That prodded a smile onto her lips. She tilted her face in a manner that reminded him of Meg, and gave him a wicked look. "I have my students. If I were Meg I should keep a close eye on you, My Lord. You are entirely too glib."

"Glib?" Slapping a hand on his chest, he fell back several steps. "Me, glib? An honest man who only speaks his mind? And in this case I definitely do, miss, so tame that cutting tongue of yours. I see Hunter is also quiet. My, my, there must be something dour in the air at Number 7. How are you, old friend?"

Hunter was, as ever, impeccably turned out, his evening clothes enviably flattering to an already fine form. Little wonder Sibyl fancied the man—if only as father to her child. Absurd subterfuge, of course. She must be in love with Hunter and if Jean-Marc had his way, that situation would be sorted out in short order, and his beloved wife's peace of mind restored. And Hunter and Sibyl would make a first-class match, of course. Jean-Marc was already considering a suitable inducement for Hunter, should any be necessary. Meg seemed to think Jean-Marc should leave well enough alone, but he would not stand still for any serious threat to Sibyl's reputation.

"Please let us be seated," Meg said, all dimpled smiles. "Cook is a wizard and not a dish is to be left untasted. What soup did I decide on, Rench?"

"It's gone back to be reheated," he droned, frowning.

"Good," she told him, determined not to give in to his unfailingly negative behavior. "Then it will be good and hot. But what is it?"

"Lobster and shrimp in a minted cream sauce with ginger shavings is always good. If it's not ruined by being ignored."

Latimer closed his eyes and breathed deeply. "Wonderful," he said.

"How do you know it will be wonderful when you have never tasted it?" Desirée asked him, the epitome of petulance.

Latimer smiled at her and tapped his nose. "Superior smeller, my dear. Sniffs out good stuff at great distances. Reaches around corners and under doors in its never-ending quest to find the most beguiling scents. Not that I need to do more than stand beside you to be enchanted by your perfume. Lily of the valley, am I right? Soft, fragrant, and irresistible—like the wearer.''

Desirée dimpled and flipped open a beautiful painted paper fan with soft, white feathers at the tip of each spine. Jean-Marc noted that she colored prettily behind that fan and smiled to himself.

''Evening, Lloyd,'' he said, but with some apprehension. The man stood at a distance and didn't take his eyes from Sibyl. Jean-Marc feared that foolish woman might already have done what he'd hoped to stop, and approached the barrister with her outrageous scheme.

Hunter came a step or two closer and said, ''Good evening to you, my lord. You and Meg—the Countess—have quite perfected this house.''

''Meg, if you don't mind, Hunter,'' Meg said at once.

''Jean-Marc.'' He followed suit quickly. ''You're a handsome devil in evening dress, y'know. Difficult to compete with. But then, you always have had a distinguished presence.''

Meg contrived to step on his foot and Jean-Marc breathed in on a hiss. She exhibited no sign of remorse.

Very well, yet another lesson to be learned: he should consult his wife before speaking a word.

''Let's seat our guests.'' The announcement

brought forth the expected phalanx of flunkies to hold chairs. Meg had decided on the order for seating. Since they were only seven, she had placed herself at Jean-Marc's right hand, and Lady Hester at his left. Next to her was Latimer, then Sibyl. To Meg's right were Hunter, then Princess Desirée.

Everyone was seated and napkins placed on their laps when Jean-Marc announced, "No, this will not do at all. I know Desirée particularly enjoys Latimer's company." This earned him a prizewinning scowl from his charge. "Change places, Hunter, there's a good fellow."

The haste with which the two men changed places was humorous, if not lacking in decorum.

Meg watched Jean-Marc with suspicion, although she tried not to be obvious. The devil was up to something. How he would suffer if he created a disaster.

"Carry on, Rench," Jean-Marc directed and they were soon surrounded by the subtle clink of silver on china.

"What soup," Latimer said, emptying his bowl rapidly, but refusing more. "One of the things one misses when living alone is good food."

"Must mean you need a wife," Jean-Marc said. "Well, of course you do. It's time. I'm surprised Finch and Ross haven't borne down upon you with an array of eligible females."

Latimer groaned. "What makes you think they haven't? My sister and her husband will not be satisfied until they find a way to curtail my freedom. I'm not interested in empty-headed creatures who live for visits to the modiste, and for gossiping half the day. And I'll find my own bride, thank you all very much."

Meg stared at her soup, felt utterly helpless, and waited for Jean-Marc's next *subtle* attack.

"And how about you, Hunter?"

Oh, Jean-Marc, I knew you'd do it.

"My practice thrives, thank you," Hunter told his host. "There is never any shortage of wrong-doers, or people who want to prosecute them. It all keeps me very busy."

"I say," Latimer said. "The Greatrix Villiers case was a corker. Trying to snuff the king's good friend, no less. Then using stories of heroism on behalf of some poor innocent girl as his defense. A mystery girl who never came forward."

Hunter raised his brows and drank wine. He didn't comment. That Latimer should be the one to mention the case surprised him.

Latimer wrinkled his nose. "Look. This is us, not a bunch of strangers. Isn't it true that when you defend someone, you pretend to believe the client even if you really don't? Greatrix Villiers probably embellished a bit, but you couldn't have believed

DeBeaufort's story entirely. Most likely Villiers did interrupt him when he was forcing himself on this female, but you're an inspired barrister and you made sure the court found for him."

"We did prove that was the appropriate finding," Hunter said.

"But is this Neville DeBeaufort a bounder?" Latimer was not to be diverted. "I met your colleague, Greevy-Sims. He said he didn't envy you the job of dealing with DeBeaufort at all—or with his connection to the king."

This statement troubled Hunter. It wasn't like Charles Greevy-Sims to speak out of turn. Charles and Hunter had been partners for a number of years and Hunter admired the other man's expertise.

"Charles is a good friend and an excellent barrister," Hunter said. "He obviously thinks of you as a familiar. Best not to repeat anything he says in confidence."

"What bores these tight-mouths are," Lady Hester said. She'd finished her soup and the plate had been removed, to be replaced by a tiny pear-and-glacé citron salad that was a work of art. "What harm can it do to discuss these matters in circles such as this? After all, we're the kind of people who can be trusted."

"Of course we are," Jean-Marc said, observing

the rows of jet and diamond that filled the low neck of her gown. "Beautiful jewelry, Lady Hester."

Her hand went to her throat. "My husband adored me," she said.

And apparently didn't leave her as destitute as she would have everyone believe, Jean-Marc thought. Conversations were breaking out independent of the hosts. Hunter leaned toward Sibyl and spoke with inaudible urgency while she kept her eyes lowered and her hands clasped in her lap.

Jean-Marc cupped his chin and stared at Meg, who instantly gave him her attention. "Sibyl and Hunter are very serious about whatever they're discussing," he said in low tones. "I do believe Sibyl's mad scheme has already been aired."

"I will not believe it," Meg said. "And your naughty sister is flirting with Latimer, in whom she has no interest."

"She is her mother's daughter," Jean-Marc said stiffly. "We have nothing to fear there, but I begin to hope Adam Chillworth remains on the Continent indefinitely."

"Dream on, husband dear. I believe he is due home in a matter of days."

"Dash it all."

"Do you remember the nightgown I got from Paris, Jean-Marc?"

He looked at her with glittering eyes. "Refresh my memory."

"It is the color of ripening pomegranates and has the naughtiest design. Imagine cutting such cunning openings and surrounding them with lace and embroidery. Oh, never mind, I see you have forgotten."

Beneath the table, he carefully raised her skirt until he could find the way to her naked belly. He smoothed her there, and rubbed his thumb somewhat lower. Meg felt heat rush up her neck.

"Still think I've forgotten? Cunning peepholes to reveal all sorts of beguiling things?" He kissed her ear and whispered, "You *will* wear that gown tonight, madam, so that I may torture you to ecstasy through those holes. If not, and this is all a technique to tease, then be prepared for my own form of torture." He smoothed down her skirts, but rested his hand in her lap.

She smiled and toyed with the pear salad. "I had intended to wear it, but you make the alternatives sound very, very stimulating."

"Did you say something to me, Meg?" Lady Hester asked. Her salad was already gone. "I do hope I shall get to see Serena before the evening is over."

"You shall," Meg told her. "I shall take you to her myself."

Confronted by a crystal bowl filled with flavored ices, Lady Hester gave a blissful smile.

Meg was aware of intense emotion to her right, where Hunter and Sibyl sat. She strained to catch a word or two of their conversation, but it was hopeless.

"Trouble there," Jean-Marc murmured. "If I must interfere, I must."

"No!" Meg said at once, then dropped her voice. "Promise me you will do nothing, husband."

"Remember that I am an ambassador, Mont Nuages's ambassador to England. A diplomat, my love. Negotiation is my business."

"Not negotiation that deals with matters of the heart—the hearts of others. Promise me."

"I promise you I will only do what I consider best."

Meg sighed, uncomfortably conscious of a fervent discussion between Hunter and Sibyl.

"Listen to me and don't argue," Hunter murmured to Sibyl, pretending to play with a wineglass. "Regardless of what you say, you and I are in this together now—at least for as long as it takes you to promise me you will abandon your unthinkable quest."

"Unthinkable?" She smacked down her spoon. "Because you are not interested in fathering children? I have told you I understand your refusal. I

have no right to plead with you to change your mind and I shan't do so. Forget I ever spoke to you, please. I shall do the same."

"No, you won't. Never. My behavior—and I'm not talking about my efforts to dissuade you from a disastrous path—my behavior was beyond despicable and I must find a way to make it up to you. And kindly refrain from stating that I am not interested in having my own children. That is not the point, and it's not true."

She was silent so long, he met her eyes and instantly shook his head. "No, absolutely not. As I have already told you, I will have no part in behaving like a stallion just to produce an offspring and all the ghastly complications that would come with her or him. My recompense must take a different form. I cannot believe that you thought I would be willing to father a child for you—because you think I'm honorable—and then behave as if nothing different had occurred. The child would always be there and I should be perfectly aware that he was mine. Your request was a cruel outrage."

"You don't sound as if you're trying to make anything up to me. You sound as if your only interest is in berating me and making me feel debased. Well, I do, so I hope you, in turn, feel vindicated. And you need not worry because there are others I shall approach."

He took hold of her wrist beneath the table and actually leaned on her shoulder. "Men in high places who think nothing of compromising innocent young girls?"

"If young girls are all they want, then that will not work."

"For... You are young, Sibyl. You are not a child, but you are young, and very lovely. You are..." He closed his mouth before he said something he would truly regret. "I wasn't entirely certain what you planned to do on a farm, unless it was to romp in the hay like a milkmaid."

"Do milkmaids have a lot of children?" She sounded highly interested.

"You are incorrigible. I have no idea what they do. And you are never, ever, to as much as allow a brothel to enter your mind. Is that clear?"

"That's a house of ill repute, isn't it?"

He closed his eyes. "You know nothing. Yes, that's what it is. And women disappear in those places, then turn up in the Thames, abused and beaten to death. Or they are stolen for the white slave markets. I want to hear you say that you will abandon this mad scheme of yours altogether."

"I see." She peered at her lap, where his hand rested over hers. "I will not talk about this anymore."

"Yes, you will. I compromised you and I'm a

cad. I told you your honor was safe with me, then look what I did."

Her faint, knowing smile had an unwelcome affect on certain parts of him.

"You decided my honor was beyond help. That was my fault, so you have nothing to apologize for. I behaved like a hussy."

"You most certainly did not. You could never do any such thing. It's your naiveté that makes you especially vulnerable. You're a danger to yourself."

"Because I let you half strip me and fondle my breasts?"

"For God's sake, Sibyl, have a care what you say." He glanced around and wasn't fooled by a sudden burst of conversation. They had all been watching and trying to catch what was said. He accepted a plate of smoked salmon garnished with peppered butter sauce and gave his attention to the fish.

The pressure of Sibyl's hand, this time on his thigh beneath the table, came close to choking him. She ate slowly, as if concentrating on her food, but at the same time, kneaded the large muscle in his thigh, gradually taking her ministrations higher until he felt the edge of her hand in his groin.

The minx.

He was tempted to grab her and run with her to

a place where they could be alone. With difficulty, he continued eating.

"Do you still think I am not a hussy?" she said as she raised a forkful of fish to her mouth. "Wait until I have an opportunity to consult more books. I may truly shock you."

"You will do no such thing." He stared at her and they both stopped eating. "How long have you rehearsed this new, changed Sibyl I wonder? And at what cost? This is not you, not the woman I have known."

"It is the woman I have become," she said. "I discovered that shy, perpetually circumspect young women had no fun. And neither did they have their share of attention from men. Where is the appeal there?"

Helpless to lessen either the urgent exchange between her sister and Hunter Lloyd, or the obvious fascination they caused among the rest of the guests, Meg looked to her husband in mute appeal.

Jean-Marc shrugged and said to Desirée, "Ask Latimer when your friend, Adam, may return," and could not believe he had suggested such a thing.

"Adam's besotted with the romance of so much art and history," Latimer said, in a voice that had taken on a certain edge. "Isn't that right, Lady H.? He's been everywhere he intended to go and now he's going to all the places he insisted he *didn't* intend to go. No doubt he's also besotted by all those exotic females one encounters on the Continent, too.''

Jean-Marc heard Meg's soft groan.

''A young man must eat 'is oats, is that not so?'' Desirée said, visibly perturbed.

''Sow his oats,'' Lady Hester said obligingly. ''I certainly hope Adam Chillworth isn't sowing his oats all over Europe. I have never approved of men leaving a trail of fatherless children behind.''

Jean-Marc groaned this time. Hunter and Sibyl were finally silent and listening to the conversation around the table. Sibyl frowned as if concentrating on every word and finding the subject interesting. Hunter fell back in his seat and looked at the ceiling.

After a moment, Jean-Marc observed the oddest, and perhaps the most disturbing development of the evening. Latimer More was staring fixedly at Hunter, apparently willing the other man to notice his attention.

Not an unobservant man, not even of atmosphere, Hunter lowered his eyes until they met Latimer's and the two men gazed at each other. Latimer's narrowed gaze issued…a threat? *Mon Dieu.* Jean-Marc decided there was much more intrigue here than even he had considered. When Latimer shifted his regard to Sibyl, his expression softened and saddened in equal portion.

There could be no open hostility at this dinner table. "The king wants Greatrix Villiers executed, then, Hunter?" Jean-Marc said, perfectly aware of how clumsily he'd tried to change the subject again. "Do you think that'll come off?"

"We'll know when he's sentenced."

At least he'd created a diversion. "I was never clear about Villiers's motive. He was supposedly foxed the night before and hung about on Hampstead Heath trying to sober up before going home to his sister. Neville DeBeaufort thought he was invincible enough to take a woman there at dawn, daylight mind you, and assault her. Then, so the story goes, Villiers shot the fellow and the woman ran off. DeBeaufort didn't die and he said Villiers was a would-be murderer, and a thief. But there were no other witnesses to the actual crime and Villiers protested his innocence throughout. Then witnesses who seemed to know the king rather well babbled on about robbery being the motive, but DeBeaufort's famed missing ring and watch were never found and word has it that Villiers was an upright fellow of modest but adequate means. What do you say to all that?"

This was a perfectly unpleasant end to Hunter's perfectly bewildering day. "I was retained by Neville DeBeaufort. Everything you say is correct. Aware of every detail and of the witnesses at my disposal, I acted on Neville DeBeaufort's behalf and his assertions were found reasonable beyond doubt."

"Because you are an extraordinary counsel," Latimer said, much too tightly. "You are persuasive and accustomed to getting your way. You consider it your right to take advantage of anything appealing that comes your way and to turn it to your own ends."

"Latimer!" Pitiable concern seemed about to reduce Sibyl to tears. "What can you mean? Hunter takes advantage of appealing things in his work? Why, that makes no sense at all."

"What I say makes sense to Hunter," Latimer told her. "Doesn't it, sir? You are an unscrupulous opportunist."

Hunter was on his feet, but Jean-Marc was only a second behind him. He left his place and strode to place a hand on the younger man's shoulder. "This is my fault," he said. "I should know better than to introduce controversial matters of politics, theology—or law—at such a time. Please gentlemen, for the sake of our lovely ladies, let us discuss this over a glass of good hock. *After* the fairer sex has withdrawn."

The rigid set of Hunter's back didn't relax. Latimer, also on his feet, continued to glare at his neighbor. Jean-Marc laughed and said, "Thank you, my friends. I shall try to hold my careless tongue in future." He applied pressure to Hunter's shoulder and the man gradually sank back into his chair.

Latimer seemed disposed to remain on his feet until Desirée, whom Jean-Marc made a note to reward handsomely, sniffed most affectingly and said, "Does anyone have an 'ankerchief?" At which Latimer quickly produced one and sat beside her, then bent over her looking remorseful and said, "There, there. There, there."

The storm had passed. For now. But there was absolutely no doubt that Sibyl and Hunter were deeply involved with each other and not, unfortunately, in a happy manner. Latimer More was another complication. Jean-Marc would almost swear he was jealous of Hunter's closeness to Sibyl.

Another remove was made and, with a flourish, covers were swept from plates bearing roasted larks surrounded with browned bread crumbs and lemon sauce.

Jean-Marc was silently congratulating his wife's fine management of the household when he noted his half sister acting in a covert manner. The forefinger and thumb of her right hand crept onto the edge of her plate, where she had previously placed the most succulent pieces of lark. These pieces disappeared one by one and Jean-Marc deliberately knocked a spoon to the floor, waved a servant away, and bent to retrieve the silver piece.

Beneath the starched, white linen tablecloth, he saw Desirée's monstrous large cat, Halibut, slapping his lips around a proffered delicacy. To his amazement, he also saw that Hunter held Sibyl's hand firmly as she seemed determined to touch him inappropriately. Shaken, Jean-Marc returned his attention to Halibut, who had noticed him and decided to shamble on oversize feet to visit his favorite member of the family, second to Desirée, of course. The great, gray-striped animal wound his way around Jean-Marc's ankles and he selected a suitably tender morsel to pass down—and met Desirée's sparkling, and knowing eyes. He gave her a conspiratorial smile.

A footman entered the dining room and went directly to Rench with a folded piece of paper. Frowning, Rench read what it said and spoke with the footman in lowered tones. Then Rench approached Hunter and bowed respectfully at his shoulder.

"Sir," Rench said to Hunter. "There's a Mr. Charles Greevy-Sims waiting for you in the Rose Parlor. That's to the right of the Green Sitting Room, where I believe you've been entertained before. Mr. Greevy-Sims regrets interrupting you at dinner but has a matter of gravest importance to discuss with you."

"Thank you," Hunter said, and told his hosts, "Please excuse me for a few moments. My partner is here to see me on an urgent matter. I'll return as soon as I can."

With interest, Jean-Marc watched him leave the room. A stillness caused him to observe that Sibyl watched him not so much with interest as with anxious longing. Sibyl had helped Jean-Marc when his relationship with Meg was in the difficult budding stages. She had also been unfailingly kind to Desirée. Now the time had come to do whatever was necessary to secure her happiness.

6

Hunter was shown into the feminine Rose Parlor. Instantly he visualized Sibyl here and thought how perfect a room it would be for her to relax in, or to entertain friends—or play with her children. That kind of thinking must be stopped.

Charles Greevy-Sims looked frightful.

Evidently he'd chosen to wear his long, gray coat with a velvet lining of almost the same color while tramping through mud that was drying on gray-striped trousers fastened under the instep of his filthy boots. His cloth of silver waistcoat—hung, unbuttoned and askew, and his neckcloth, usually tied in some fussy manner, trailed from its knot. His blond hair stood out from his head in unruly clumps and he held his mud-flecked beaver by the brim and before him, as if warding off attack.

The man was mute and staring.

Hunter shut the door beside him and went straight to pour a glass of Madeira, which he pressed into

Charles's right hand. "What has happened to you? For God's sake man, don't hold me in suspense."

Madeira swung from side to side in the glass Charles raised in his well-made but shaking hands. He swallowed loudly, emptied the glass, and indicated he wanted more. "My carriage threw a wheel miles away. I walked, hoping for a cab. No luck."

Hunter obliged with more Madeira. "Sorry to hear it," he said.

"I went to your place," Charles said, his voice low and far from steady. He was a solidly built fellow who gave an impression of strength, but tonight he seemed shrunken inside his clothes. "Butler—Coot, I think—directed me here. I'm sorry to interrupt, but this could turn into a bloody nightmare. A woman came to see me. She had a lot to say about you, and she made threats. Then pretended she hadn't made threats, just come to inform you of things you might find useful."

The sensation in Hunter's stomach was unfamiliar and purely unpleasant. Then he remembered his earlier trip to Chambers. "Of course, the interesting Mrs. Ivy Willow. She sent for me and I went to meet her but she'd already left. She must have returned later."

Charles frowned and drank some more. His brow overhung deep-set blue eyes. "I don't know what you're talking about. This woman wouldn't give her name. Just said she's Villiers's widowed sister. Medium height. Nicely built. Dark hair and eyes and very white skin. A beauty if she weren't trying not to show how angry she was, or so I should think."

Hunter experienced another falling sensation in his stomach. "What did she want?"

"You. She wanted you. And revenge. Everything she said was in a calm, quiet voice, but her eyes were wild, Hunter. She intends to cause the firm a lot of trouble. We both know her type. Rigid. Mind on one thing and not about to be diverted."

After pouring himself a glass of the wonderful Madeira, Hunter waved Charles, muddy clothes and all, into an overstuffed chair and sat himself down on a straight-backed chair with a cushion that matched the rest of the upholstery. "Slow down, old chap. Please. You're panicking and I don't know why. Don't you think I should know why?"

Charles sat, slumped over, his glass dangling between his knees. An ormolu clock ticked on the mantel of a pink-and-white-tiled fireplace. The scent of greenhouse-forced roses wafted from a large vase in the middle of a brass table that appeared to be Turkish.

"Charles?" Hunter prompted gently.

"She's out for blood, I tell you. She said, 'You can't prosecute a body for talking about what she thinks.' I assured her that was generally true, but not always. That made her more quietly angry. She didn't become abusive or loud. Just got up and paced around the room. Then she said, 'They'd better find a way to reverse things, or they'll wish they had.' Told me there were plans already, and she's *just the messenger.* She wanted to make sure I agreed that there was nothing we could do to her for bringing us information. It didn't take a great brain to determine she was talking about the Villiers conviction."

Hunter considered. This case had been bizarre from the outset. Yes, because of the King's gratitude at the outcome, Hunter would be knighted, but that began to resemble an honor that might one day be looked on as thirty pieces of silver.

"Go on," he said.

"She wants the Villiers conviction appealed—and overturned."

"Impossible," Hunter said.

"She wants us to present new evidence. This is evidence she says will be kept in safety until the appeal, then delivered, probably in court."

"And I'm to have no time to prepare?" Hunter scoffed. "If I intended to do what she wants, which I don't."

Charles sweated. His brow shone and he passed a large handkerchief over it. "If you don't, we're finished. That's what she said. Are we prepared to risk hoping that she's mad and will forget all about us by tomorrow?''

''You're not,'' Hunter said shortly. ''You are beside yourself.''

Jumping to his feet, Charles loomed over him. ''She says that if we haven't made some move toward doing what she asks within a week, we'll no longer have the chance to retain at least some respectability by asking for an opportunity to present this evidence of hers and throw ourselves on the mercy of the courts.''

''Charming,'' Hunter said and went to pour himself more Madeira. ''Bloody blackmail by someone we don't know and have no idea whether or not to believe. If we buckle now, she'll be back again and again, mark my words. She asked for money, didn't she?''

Charles went to huddle on a window seat and throw open a casement. He took great gulps of air. Hunter had never seen him like this. ''Not exactly. But we're to apologize to the courts.''

''I'm still not clear what will happen to us if we don't. I presented a solid case for DeBeaufort. The court found for us. What does this woman think she can do about that?''

''Bring you to your knees. Her words. She says she can prove beyond a doubt that Greatrix Villiers was nowhere near Hampstead Heath that morning.''

"Where was he, then?"

"In bed with her friend and sleeping in the same room with her."

Hunter closed his eyes. "How bloody original. Why didn't she come forward during the trial? Why did DeBeaufort set Villiers up—according to the woman?"

"She won't reveal that until we're in a court of appeals."

"Pull yourself together and get home," Hunter told Charles. "So much agitation can't be a good thing. Forget all about this for tonight. Tomorrow I'll find a way to see the woman myself, and I won't be soft with her. A suitable lecture about the penalties for perjury and I don't think we'll hear more from whoever she is."

He held out a hand for Charles's glass and the man handed it over. Charles stood and attempted to close his coat but his fingers wouldn't work properly. "I know when I'm up against a real threat. We're both up against one now. Regardless of the personal cost to you, you're going to have to do the right thing for the firm. As head of Chambers, Parker Bowl will insist on it."

"Sir Parker won't know. Not unless you tell him."

"I'd rather not do that. Make sure I don't have to."

So much for friendship. "You're threatening me. I don't like that."

"I'm protecting the firm, myself and you, Hunter. I'm protecting you from yourself."

"You don't think I'm capable of sorting things out?"

"Possibly. Possibly not, with all you've got at stake."

Hunter wiped all expression from his features and waited.

"The knighthood. Everyone knows the only reason you're getting it is because you're the king's legal puppet."

Cold fury stiffened every muscle Hunter possessed. "You might want to take that back."

"I can't, because it's true. If you go against the king—that is, if you cast doubt on the DeBeaufort case—your knighthood is likely to be withdrawn. That's what's holding you back from doing the right thing."

Hunter set down the glasses, walked to the door and flung it open. "Go home," he said, afraid to let himself go to the smallest degree.

"You're not listening to me. I think there's a lot you don't know and you'd better find out."

"I've listened, and you make me sick. Get out now, before I beat you to a pulp."

"You and I have been friends a long time,"

Charles said. "I don't intend to allow this to come between us. Your happiness is important to me and I hope to God I can help you remain happy."

In a flurry of flapping coat and disheveled clothing, Charles Greevy-Sims stomped past Hunter and into the hallway, passing Jean-Marc as he went. He didn't as much as glance at the owner of the house before letting himself out into the storm.

"Dare I ask what that was all about?" the Count asked.

Hunter reined in his temper and said, "Trouble in Chambers. It'll blow over. I need to leave now. I hope you'll forgive me."

To his discomfort, Sibyl slipped from the dining room and closed the doors behind her. She stood there, her hands laced together, watching the scene.

Jean-Marc glanced behind him, then put an arm around Hunter's shoulders and guided him a greater distance from her. "I have something I should say. I hope you will forgive me if I appear to overstep the mark. But in the absence of a male relative, Sibyl has only me to turn to."

Could this day become any more fraught with challenge? "You are kind to take care of her."

"One can only take so much care of the headstrong ones."

"Sibyl has been gentle and malleable for as long as I've known her."

"Until now, hmm? Now she has approached you with a proposal that leaves you bewildered and exceedingly unhappy, I think. You think a great deal of her, don't you?"

Couldn't he please be allowed time to think about some of these things? Hunter wondered.

"Hunter?"

"You are right on all counts. I'd argue, but there would be no point, since you obviously know."

"Think of me as Sibyl's father."

Hunter wanted to go somewhere dark, cool and quiet.

"I have taken that position because from what I know of the man, I believe he would want me to do so."

"Very gallant of you."

"Very selfish. My wife is the center of my life. I seek to please her, and by caring for her sister, I please her a great deal. Now, can we talk briefly, man to man, without raising suspicion?" He indicated Sibyl behind him.

"I will do my best," Hunter said, glancing at her and finding that his heart made him want to go to her.

"I'm sure you will. Why not marry her?" Jean-Marc smiled but was aware of his audacity, and disquieted by it. "You do love her, don't you?"

This was fantastic. His world, Hunter decided,

had become some sort of play in many disjointed and outrageous acts. "I care a great deal for Sibyl, my lord."

This garnered him a great thump on the back. "I knew it! I knew it! Then our problems are solved, aren't they? You will marry Sibyl, and she will have this baby she wants more than anything else in the world." Jean-Marc knew his mistake at once. "I mean the baby she wants more than anything in the world, except you."

"I think you meant what you said first. And that corroborates Sibyl's declarations. Hardly a match made in heaven, would you say? Hardly a match guaranteed to bring me happiness and a helpmate in my private and professional lives?"

Jean-Marc rocked from heel to toe and back again. He frowned while his mind raced, searching for a way to recover from a frightful faux pas. "A private and professional helpmate is what every man hopes and dreams for. Sibyl will be that for you, Hunter. I know she will. She will keep your home beautiful, and entertain flawlessly. She will make you proud."

"But she won't love me. I shall be a convenience to her."

"By no means!" Jean-Marc laughed heartily, no longer caring that Sibyl must overhear at least some of what they said. "I see how the girl looks at you.

She studies you, touches you—I admit I happened to look under the table to find Halibut and I saw her touching you."

"Rather like a man touching a woman he finds sexually arousing, wouldn't you say?"

"Nothing wrong with a highly sexed woman."

"Or a woman on the hunt for a sire, a man to sire her offspring. Forgive me, please, my lord, but I really must go. Latimer will see the ladies home."

This was a moment that could ruin everything if he didn't act, Jean-Marc decided. "Of course. But before you go, would you step into my study, please?"

"I don't want to be rude, but I find I am exhausted. Could this wait until another time?"

Jean-Marc considered. "I suppose the final arrangements could wait. But I want you to go away knowing how I intend to support you. I know you've done almost everything yourself, that you've had little family support. That should change. I want to make a donation to a good cause, to one of the most gratifying examples of the best British law has to offer. You, Hunter."

"A donation?" Hunter screwed up his eyes and attempted to still his muddled mind. "To me?"

"Absolutely. Perhaps I should refer to it as a plump addition to Sibyl's dowry. And you cannot imagine the joy it will give Meg and me to do this, and to know we have had a part in bringing about Sibyl's happiness. And yours.''

Hunter's head grew cold inside. So cold it felt ice clear. He started for the door, unconcerned with not having his coat. ''You mean, my lord, that I cannot imagine the joy it will bring you to buy Sibyl's happiness, by buying me!'' His voice rang out and it would be surprising if everyone in the house hadn't heard him.

''Hunter, no. Don't listen to any of this.'' Sibyl started running toward him. ''Jean-Marc is trying to do what he considers right. He is misguided.''

''You are all misguided,'' he said. ''Good night.''

7

On the interesting side of thirty, Phyllis Smart filled any room she entered. This wasn't because she was particularly big, although she wasn't particularly small, either, but Phyllis was an impressive presence. She set the mood, so to speak.

This afternoon, about a week after the disastrous dinner party, the only part of Phyllis that did not droop—oppressively—was the boned stomacher in her bodice that was responsible for uplifting her remarkable bosom, which in turn required that the lady keep her chin up.

"Cora's late," Jenny MacBride remarked, sounding even more Scottish than usual, and definitely nervous. Jenny's clothes were much darned and her strained financial state obvious. "She's never late, is she, Phyllis?"

Phyllis turned small, intelligent brown eyes on red-haired Jenny and sighed.

Seated on the very edge of one of Sibyl's needlepoint chairs, Jenny anxiously surveyed the other two women. It had been Phyllis who'd brought Jenny with her to Sibyl's without asking if Sibyl minded. She didn't. Sibyl found Jenny's brilliant green eyes amazing, especially since she'd learned that the girl was every bit as lively as her open face and rapid movements suggested. An apprentice, Jenny worked for one of the finest milliners in London, but her background was vague. Sibyl wondered how the girl, who could not be older than twenty-two or three, thought she could care for a child—given her position.

"Cora's never late, is she, Sibyl?" Jenny said. Freckles stood out sharply from her pale skin. "Och, well, no doubt she'll be along soon enough. This is such a pretty room, Sibyl. Blue is just the color for ye, and—"

"How many times do you intend to repeat that blue is Sibyl's perfect color?" Phyllis wore a fetching walking dress and matching pelisse of gros de naples, vandyked at the hem of the dress, and the edges of the pelisse, in a deep shade of ashes of roses. The lady tended to become impatient with compliments. At least, she became impatient with compliments offered to anyone other than herself.

Jenny drew herself up and her eyes sparkled. "We're about learnin' t'speak our minds and t'feel free enough to take responsibility for our actions. I choose to admire Sibyl and her fine taste—as I admire yours, Phyllis—and I want to thank Sibyl again for being a generous hostess to those of us who've no' enough room t'entertain more than a wee tabby cat."

"Like your sweetest Maximillian," Sibyl said, smiling and feeling lighter of heart than she had since the horrible evening of the dinner party.

Phyllis sniffed. "The cat is a pathetically scrawny mongrel with an unsuitable name. But—" she raised a gloved hand and half closed her eyes "—if the creature is a comfort to a lonely woman who is unlikely ever to have a more worthy companion, then who am I to argue?"

Sibyl caught Jenny's eye and a sympathetic look passed between them. They both regretted that bitter Phyllis had not found the happiness she'd expected in bringing up a son of her own flesh—and that of a pugilist passing through the village where she'd lived prior to her "trip" to the Continent. Both Sibyl and Jenny regarded little Herbert Constantine Smart—adopted children must, of course, take their mothers' surnames—as a loveable boy who had unfortunately inherited his male parent's love of fisticuffs. At the age of two, Herbert entered any room with his fists at the ready and his small face, with its rather scrunched features, set to snarl if the opportunity arose. But he was invariably more than happy to be cuddled, and fed with Barstow's delicious cookies. Phyllis, on the other hand, was of the school of belief that it was not healthy for boys to be coddled and cuddled. They were to be toughened up and encouraged to develop their natural, bestial natures.

So much for little Herbert Constantine, who was not present this afternoon. Currently, Phyllis, whose need for the group puzzled Sibyl, was determined that her son should have a brother or sister.

"Down to business," Phyllis announced. "After Sibyl's distressing announcement, we have no time to lose. If Cora arrives, she must just catch up as best she can."

Just then a tap at the door sent Jenny running to open it. "Cora's such a voice o' reason," she said. "She'll no' let us overreact."

"Where's that book your elevated relative lent you?" Phyllis asked. "I should like a good look at that."

Even the idea of Phyllis poring over the pictures disturbed Sibyl.

"Oh," Jenny said when she'd opened the door. "Ye're no' Cora."

"May I come in and explain myself, do you suppose?" the woman at the door said. "Your dear, dear butler was kind enough to tell me I might come right on up."

"Er, yes, yes, of course," Sibyl said, jumping to her feet. "Do come in and tell us your business."

"I'll do that. My business is, after all, with all of you."

Phyllis sighed yet again at the intrusion and crossed her arms. This feat required that she grip opposing elbows to maintain a hold across her bosom.

"Thank you, thank you," the woman said, advancing into the room. Phyllis might be short, and Jenny petite, but this person resembled a bird in brightly colored clothing. "Very good of you, very good. I am an old friend of your old friend, Cora Mumm. She came to see me and in the course of our exchange, suggested that I might enjoy your little group, so she invited me for today. I'm very honored, I assure you, very honored."

"And you are...?" Phyllis asked with haughteur.

"Oh, I'm..." She frowned. "Ahem. Did I tell you Cora's been called away? She has family up north. Some illness, yes, illness. Cora's got to nurse a relative up north. Through some illness, but I expect I mentioned that already. She told me to tell you she's sorry she had to go so suddenly, but that's just the way it was, sudden. Cora discussed the purpose of your meetings and I was interested at once. You see, I have spent my entire adult life fighting against male oppression." She raised a fist and her lace-edged sleeve fell back to reveal a wrist so thin one might expect the grip of a strong man to break it. ''My entire adult life, I tell you. Spent fighting male oppression. We women must unite to quell weak minds in strong bodies and their conviction that size alone makes them superior to those of us with strong minds and puny bodies.''

Sibyl was stricken silent and noted that Jenny was equally speechless. The tiny newcomer wore a cape of startling red wool, lined with deep-green satin, over a matching green satin dress bordered at the bottom with stiff satin scrolls. Her luxurious muff was of breathtaking ermine, and her red Arcadian bonnet was trimmed with ermine beneath a wide, satin-lined brim. She was a brilliant bird in the midst of some pleasingly feathered but drab fowl. Sibyl almost excused herself to change from her simple flowered muslin into something more dramatic, but since Jenny wore her faded green chintz, that would be unfair.

The woman smiled all around and scuffled in her reticule until she found and withdrew a small box. With evident experience, she pinched snuff from the inside of this box. The ladies gasped and shook their heads when she offered snuff to each of them.

With a small, suspicious smile on her generous mouth, Phyllis silently observed their fluttering, shimmering guest.

"Ooh, tea and biscuits," said the lady in red. "How lovely. Cora said there are always delightful refreshments. She knows I have an embarrassingly huge appetite."

"You didn't tell us your name," Phyllis said, rather loudly, Sibyl thought.

"I didn't?" Fine black brows shot up. Her very dark eyes became distant. "There was something about that, but I don't remember. Not exactly. No, not at all, in fact."

"You don't remember your name?" Phyllis asked.

"Of course I do." The woman laughed, uncomfortably, Sibyl decided. "I'm Ivy Willow, originally of York but more recently of London. I came here to—well, I came to change my life. I'm tired of a solitary existence. I don't want a husband." She shuddered delicately. "But I do want a child. And I also want to learn more about our species—the many things that are hidden from us despite our obvious desire to know them."

"Oh, well," Jenny said. She smoothed back the curls that sprang from her attempt to restrain her hair smoothly from a center part. "That explains why Cora sent ye to us. And it's more than welcome, ye are. When we began our meetings, it was agreed that should we find another body who needed us, and who could add to what we know, or help us in our learnin', she'd be welcome t'join us. So, for myself, I welcome ye."

"So do I," Sibyl said, heartily. "Please sit down and I'll pour you some tea."

"How do we know she is who she says she is?" Phyllis said, still watching Ivy with suspicion. "When does Cora expect to return?"

Ivy looked sad. She set her cup aside and delved inside her bodice to adjust what Sibyl could only assume was her chemise. The woman wiggled around, as if making herself more comfortable. Extraordinary behavior, but Sibyl liked her. "She let me know her relative isn't expected to live, but he is expected to linger. Terrible thing. Terrible thing. She told me she'll write as soon as she's able. But really, ladies, if you are not comfortable with me, I'll just go and there will be no hard feelings. In fact, I understand your hesitation completely. I am by way of being new and uncharted waters for you. It takes courage to explore yet more new experiences and you're already considering a large undertaking. No, no, I mustn't impose." She got up.

Instantly Sibyl went to her and urged her to be seated again. She poured a cup of tea and handed it to her, then offered a plate of biscuits and cakes. "We insist that you become one of our number. We can already tell you will fit in. And we have pledged to seek out and cross uncharted seas in search of answers, and of equality in those matters of the greatest importance to us.''

''Can you tell us what those might be?'' Phyllis asked, refusing tea.

Ivy set her cup aside, then loaded her saucer with biscuits and precariously balanced sticky buns before answering. ''I believe I can. We must be included in matters relating to the politics of our country. Reform, too. All major decisions that have bearing on our lives. And since we are agreed that we are unlikely to have men become permanent parts of our lives, or even to want them to do so, but some of us desire children, we will set forth to make certain this is accomplished. I understand Phyllis is mother to a young son. I congratulate you. Sibyl is taking definite steps to find a man to father a child for her. Jenny is in a more difficult position in that she is Catholic. Difficult indeed, I imagine.'' She pushed the greater part of a pink-iced bun into her mouth, chewed seriously, and sucked in tea rather noisily.

''It seems Cora told you a great deal about us,'' Phyllis said.

Ivy gulped tea, ate three biscuits, gulped more tea, and turned her attention to Phyllis. ''She did. Oh, yes, she did. Cora told me you were all very observant women and would expect to know that she had confided in me so that you would feel comfortable confiding in me, too. And I do have special areas of usefulness to offer.''

''See, Phyllis,'' Jenny said, her freckled face rosy with delight. ''Ivy's going to be able to help us.''

Phyllis's pointed face became pinched and her pale skin took on a luminous cast against her black hair. ''We've done very well ourselves, to date.''

''But we are generous people who are always happy to find a new friend,'' Sibyl said quickly. ''And, speaking for myself, I am in grave need of additional help. I am certainly not doing well with my present attempts to become fulfilled.''

''Hunter Lloyd,'' Ivy Willow said, matter-of-fact. ''Bit of a stuffed shirt. Set in his ways.''

''Not a bit of it,'' Sibyl protested. ''He is a wonderful man. I shocked him, that's all. And certain other things happened that were most unfortunate.''

''You're in love with him. Just need to get into his trousers, hmm?''

Sibyl couldn't remember how to close her mouth, not while her mind jumped about so erratically.

''Natural. It's all part of the female drive to become impregnated. She suffers these emotions, longings, sensations that draw her to the male and turn her into his willing sex slave. Not a thing to worry about as long as it gets the job done, which it usually does, because the male *lives* to satisfy his raging lust.''

Glancing at Jenny, who had plopped down on the chaise and was raptly attending Ivy's declarations, Sibyl determined that no one in the room was about to swoon.

"Do go on," Phyllis said. She, too had moved forward in her chair and no longer looked bored.

"The trick is to push the male past any hope of saving himself. Some don't fight at all. They merely whip out their tireless tools of destiny, flap them around in the long-suffering woman's body until they expel whatever it is they expel, and withdraw in time for a long, satisfied nap. Bit like a tortoise in winter. They're the ones who get up, get dressed, and fly out—usually without a word—to ride, fight or brag at their clubs. Be warned that these men do enjoy discussing their conquests."

"Their conquests?" Jenny's voice broke on a squeak. "How could it be their conquest when it was the woman who peaked their pinnacles? Och, what I wouldna' give t'get a good look at what all the fuss is about—not that I haven't a good idea. After all, I've been about the beasties back home and I've a wee inkling it's not so verra different wi' men. We call those parts pinnacles because we've read that the silly fatbrains consider their manhood the pinnacle upon which the human race rests—" she paused to cross herself "—and upon which women should beg t'sacrifice themselves in worship. Sounds sacrilegious t'me. But then, I'm only a simple Scots lass. Could ye enlarge on the tireless tools o' destiny, d'ye think?"

"Just reporting what I've heard said." Ivy refilled her saucer with food and poured more tea. "And you're not simple at all. Very wise. You're all very wise. Let's move on to the ones who fight desire. And it sounds as if Sibyl has found herself just such a one." She stretched out her short legs, hauled her skirts to her knees and slapped her lips over the latest cake.

"He was a mistake," Sibyl said, "I'm moving on to someone else at once." Even the thought twisted her stomach and made her want to cry.

Ivy took time going through her replenished stock of food. Then she got up and went to stand over—or as over as a very short person could—Sibyl. "Absolutely not. One's first instinct is almost invariably the best. Now, before I came I took the liberty of finding out a little about this Hunter Lloyd. That's why I was late—for which I apologize.

"Mr. Lloyd, soon to be Sir Hunter Lloyd, will make a most excellent father for your child—even for your children, should you choose to proceed on more than one occasion. He is a good man. Ambitious, industrious, honest and virile. Oh, very, very virile. Apparently he's a most talented lover. But you may be in a better position to discuss that matter by now."

Sibyl felt all eyes upon her and didn't at all care for the sensation. "Perhaps we should look at the book Princess Desirée—my brother-in-law's half sister—perhaps we should look at her book. It came into my hands since our last meeting."

"All in good time," Ivy said. "It would be helpful to all of us if you shared the details of your encounters with Mr. Lloyd, soon to be Sir Hunter Lloyd."

"You already said that," Phyllis pointed out.

Ivy smiled. Her face was smooth and unlined. Placing her age was next to impossible. "So I did. Perhaps I'm overly impressed by these things. I can see you are uncomfortable with all this, Sibyl, so I shall help you and make the task simple. Did Mr. Lloyd touch you?"

Sibyl shivered inside her clothes. In a tiny voice she said, "Yes."

"Aha!" Ivy clapped her hands and encouraged Phyllis and Jenny to join her. "Excellent. They are exceedingly susceptible to the feel of a woman. They have almost no willpower at such times. Where did he touch you?"

Jenny blinked rapidly and examined the flowers on her dress.

"Where?" Phyllis asked.

"In rather a lot of places." There, they wanted to know and now they did. "I do think we should study the book."

"Pah," Phyllis said. "Plenty of time for that. Did you touch him?"

"Oh, no," Sibyl moaned and covered her face. "I don't want to think about it. Yes, I did touch him. I was frightful."

"You were marvelous," Ivy said, her voice grown deep. "Where did you touch him?"

"Where he touched me. Although we're differently made, of course."

"Were you both naked?" This was Phyllis.

"Not entirely."

Ivy snickered. "Just mostly."

"To the waist." Sibyl's breasts tingled. She was lost to unbidden desire. Never again would she be able to consider herself an innocent.

"This is absolutely perfect. How about below the waist? Any contact there?" Ivy Willow surprised Sibyl by settling herself more comfortably in her chair and hauling her skirts all the way above her knees in a most unladylike manner. "Did he get inside your drawers?"

Sibyl averted her face. "Yes. And I...I felt him where they put the black squares like the ones they put over certain places in that book, just to see if he was shaped the way I rather thought he might be.''

''And was he?'' Jenny sounded breathless.

''Oh, yes.''

''Was it verra awful?'' Jenny whispered.

''It was...unbelievable. Wonderful. I could feel the power pumping through the pinnacle of life. Oh, I must find out exactly how these things are accomplished. I do believe I should enjoy the process. I think what they say about women not liking their husbands to touch them is poppycock.''

''Y'know,'' Jenny said, still whispering. ''I think so, too. I have for a long time.''

Sibyl turned to Phyllis. ''You've experienced the whole thing, dear friend, yet you haven't shared that part with us and I can't understand why not. Can't you tell us exactly what things look like on a man, and what happens when whatever happens? Please, Phyllis, I've been brave, now it's your turn to be brave, too.''

Phyllis stood up. She seemed more quiet than usual and less certain of herself. ''I didn't actually see the, er, pinnacle,'' she said.

''But ye *did* something,'' Jenny said.

The dejected picture Phyllis made saddened Sibyl, who said, ''You don't have to say another word, my dear. We have always agreed that we will be considerate of each other in all ways.''

"No, no," Phyllis said. "I'm strong and I can explain. Only there's not a lot to say about feeling wind on one's—derriere—and nothing much else. He was sweating and he grunted, and he picked me up off the ground because, well, because he said since he was very big it made it easier."

"What was so big about him?" Ivy Willow frowned intently.

"I really don't know. Nothing I noticed. And it happened so quickly, and I was so afraid of being caught. It was between the third and fourth rounds of that nasty fight. He was knocked out in the fourth round, carried away to a cart by his friends, and off he went. I never saw him again and don't want to. Not that I'd know him. But I have dear little Herbert Constantine and he's what counts."

"Absolutely," Jenny sang out, smiling with tears in her eyes. "Now it's time for Sibyl t'do it. Then it'll be me, I suppose, unless Cora's back by then. And ye, Ivy Willow? Are ye wantin' t'start a wee one?"

Ivy wrinkled her nose, but just as quickly smoothed her expression. "Naturally. Why do you think I'm here? But I'm the last to join, so I must wait my turn. Sibyl first."

"It's going to be harder than even I imagined."

"Stuff and nonsense," Ivy said. "Brave, resourceful Phyllis managed to seduce a traveling pugilist. Hunter Lloyd lives in the same house with you."

"He doesn't live *with* me and he has no intention of ever being alone with me again."

Phyllis rallied. "I seduced a pugilist. You shall seduce a barrister. What's the difference?"

"Sibyl is going to find that out for us," Ivy said. "But first she's got to get all of his clothes off."

"Oh," Jenny exclaimed.

"Don't be a ninny," Phyllis told her. "And all that nakedness certainly isn't a necessity."

Ivy ignored both of them. "A man with all his clothes off and a woman with just enough clothes on to make him want the rest of them off is the perfect recipe for seduction. That inflames him beyond his control. Did he give you any indication that violence might stimulate him—or a little something different?"

All Sibyl could do was gasp.

"Worth a try," Ivy announced. "Sneak up on him while he's sleeping."

"I couldn't possibly."

"You will. And stroke him till he's awake. I'll lend you something I acquired once. Then, when he's trying to decide why his dream didn't go away when he woke up, try something I'm going to explain to you. You'll like it. So will he. This is what I want you to do."

8

This house, Hunter thought, felt empty. On every floor, except Adam's attic, people were in residence and going about their daily lives, but he hadn't seen more than glimpses of any of them for about three weeks—not since dinner at the Etrangers.

Here was a household apparently determined to avoid anything so odious as a "Good morning." Not that he wanted to see a soul here if he could help it, or anywhere else if the truth were known.

And it was snowing. All very well at Christmas, one supposed, but by the time February was in residence, a man who loved the outdoors couldn't welcome the inconvenience.

Above the buildings he saw from the study window, the sky had brightened to an opal film drawn over the sunrise. And a blue glaze hovering just above the land, like thin ice on shallow water, was beautiful, he supposed.

A tap at the door brought the new man Hunter had insisted be hired. Masters had come highly recommended by Meg, whose households, including a shooting lodge in Scotland, and a somewhat crumbling old castle they were slowly restoring, employed an army of help. This man was a cousin to one of the staff in Eton. Hunter said, "Good morning," and smiled to himself. The servant said, "Good morning, sir. And a cold one it is," while he banked both of Hunter's fireplaces.

Shortly another new servant, this one a young girl, delivered Hunter the coffee to which he'd become addicted, a boiled egg, toast and pureed apples. She didn't seemed disposed to speak or raise her eyes, so Hunter said "Thank you," the instant before she closed the door behind her.

The snow was a fact and it had its own allure. He took his breakfast tray to his desk, set it down there, and sat himself beside the tray, where he had an excellent view outside.

The shutters had been closed at Number 17. A minimum staff would be in residence, but the family had returned, with almost suspicious haste, to Eton. He felt uncomfortable lest he had played some part in that, but refused to make enquiries.

At least Adam Chillworth was due to return to Number 7 any day now, and Hunter could look forward to some sensible analysis of recent events. How unfortunate that Latimer More had cast Hunter as a villain out to misuse Sibyl and was, therefore, avoiding him.

Damn, but he wanted to ride. He had several hours before he must be in Chambers—where he would rather not go at all at the moment—and could hardly bear the restless energy that sought an outlet.

With the precision of long practice, he sliced the top from his boiled egg and plunged a corner of toast into the yolk. These were the small joys of eating alone. Who cared if one displayed deplorable manners?

He already wore his boots. Force of habit had allowed him to put them on, and his riding clothes, before he'd opened the curtains. Good enough. The snow was too deep to risk his horse, but not too deep to walk in. A long, brisk walk through deep snow should get rid of a good deal of frustration.

Leaping from the desk, he caught up his coat and hat, and a heavy black scarf, pulled on one glove and carried the second, as well as a cane in the same hand. In the other he gathered together the remaining slices of toast before leaving his apartments. He'd never learned to "pick up his feet," as Nanny had pleaded for him to do. To this day he scuffed his heels, but in deference to those who might still be sleeping, he did his best to move silently.

He reached the top of the stairs. There was no sound from Aunt Hester's rooms. He started down, but stopped when he heard a door open and close below. Sibyl's door. Had it been Latimer's, the sound would be more distant.

Hunter took a chance and leaned over the banister to look down. Indeed it was Sibyl. Dressed in a brown cape that appeared exceedingly bulky—possibly because she had put on substantial clothing beneath—and with the hood drawn up, she had tied a scarf about her neck. She fled rapidly downward on light feet. He could see that she also wore boots and that her hands were gloved.

What possible reason could a female have for venturing forth—alone—on so inclement a morning?

The front door closed behind her and Hunter proceeded much too rapidly to have a care about the noise he made.

When he stood on the front steps he couldn't, at first, see her. Only exceedingly good fortune led him to turn to the right sharply and see a suggestion of something brown slipping into an alley between two buildings.

Hunter dropped his cane by the door, thinking it might become a nuisance after all, and took off after her. Fortunately, he was surefooted and not given to slipping.

The alley she'd taken led to the mews behind the

houses. Her route puzzled him, but perhaps he was about to find out something new about Sibyl.

Count Etranger had tried to buy Hunter for Sibyl. The idea had lost some of its bite and he did regret that she had been a witness to what must have been a frightful experience for her. Also, he couldn't entirely blame Etranger, who, if nothing else, took his family responsibilities seriously. But that didn't alter the fact that a man didn't like to be regarded unprincipled enough to consider a bribe—under any circumstances.

Sibyl trotted some distance down the mews, hopping from rut to rut made by recently departed carriages, and went to a stable door where the upper half stood open and an admirable black of fine proportions stood with his arrogant head pushed out into the falling snow.

Sibyl went to the animal as if to an old friend and stroked his neck, then scratched between his ears while he tossed his head and bared his teeth. Not a gentle creature, and Hunter didn't like Sibyl around those teeth.

Hunter hid behind a hedge softly mounded with white.

"Would I forget you on a day like this?" Sibyl said, her voice muffled by the blanket on the earth. "I know how you are neglected when your master is away. But you are to be kind and not pounce. You hurt my fingers last time.''

Had no one told the silly woman to offer only her palm to a horse she didn't know well, Hunter wondered?

From beneath her cloak she produced a large bag into which she delved.

Before she could remove her hand, her ungrateful friend pushed his muzzle into her chest and knocked her on her bottom with her skirts around her knees and the toes of her boots pointing outward. Her hood fell off, but she tugged it back over her hair.

Hunter smothered a laugh, but wasn't tempted to go to her aid. She wouldn't appreciate knowing her inelegant fall had been observed.

''Why, you bad boy. I've a good mind to leave and take your delicacies with me.'' She scrambled around until she could find enough purchase to get to her feet, then assessed her position cautiously. Extracting a large lump of bread from the bag, she stood to one side, at some distance, and offered the treat—with fingers and thumb.

Hunter held his breath, but the black was on his best behavior and seemed to wiggle his lips with the effort to take the bread gently. He chomped, his great teeth moving in a circular, grinding manner while he tossed his head.

''Was that good?'' Sibyl asked, reaching out her

hand again, this time obviously intending to stroke the bounder's nose. The horse tolerated her ministrations and even managed to make his eyes liquid and soft as he looked at her.

Hunter had no idea Sibyl was interested in horseflesh. Usually he was long away to ride by now and had never seen her leave the house early.

Some greens were offered from the bag, held out like a bunch of flowers.

"Ooh," Sibyl said, and Hunter realized she was keeping her voice down. "That hurt, Nightrider. I think you may have made me bleed." She worked off a glove. "It's time we became much better at this. Just for that, you won't get your whole share. I'm moving on to Libby. She needs it more, anyway." The glove was replaced, so apparently there was no broken skin.

Hunter could watch no longer. He broke cover and said, "Hold up, Sibyl, please," while he walked rapidly to her side. He looked into the bag. Every spare piece of food must have been rescued from the dustbin. "You have to be fair to horses, learn what they can and can't manage according to their natures. This big fellow is always hungry and you offered up your fingers."

He felt her staring at him, but gave all of his attention to the job at hand.

"Thank you," she said.

Hunter selected several scraps, uncurled her fingers and placed the food on her palm. "Always offer the flat of your hand, at least until you know the animal well enough to understand his foibles. Hold it up."

She did as he told her and Nightrider duly ate like a gentleman. "Good boy!" Sibyl said. "Wonderful. You are a wonderful horse."

"And what about me?" Hunter said, drawn in by a pleasant moment of companionship.

"You're wonderful, too," she said. "But I've always told you so."

Instantly he was treated to a view of the top of her hood, and she sped on, passing several stables until she reached the end of the mews. Here she opened the half door and peered inside. "Libby?" she called softly. "Libby, are you up?"

Movement across the hay-strewn floor inside produced the sweet face of a small chestnut. "Nice girl," Hunter said. "I didn't know you were fond of horses, Sibyl."

"Meg and I had an old mare when we were little. She lived to be very old. We couldn't ride her because she had the rheumatism, but we made sure she was happy and Daddy never protested what it cost to keep her."

The chestnut contentedly demolished the rest of

what Sibyl had brought and she carefully folded the bag and put it in a pocket inside her cape.

She looked at him but did not smile.

"The snow cramps a man's style—if he wants to ride, that is—but it's bracing. It's not that I wouldn't ride, but I try to avoid risking an animal when I don't have to."

Sibyl huddled inside her cloak and nodded. Snowflakes found her eyelashes, and the wisps of hair that escaped her hood, and settled quickly on her head and shoulders when she stood still awhile.

"You should go back home to the fire," he told her.

"So should you."

"I need to...an outlet for energy becomes necessary."

"I understand you," Sibyl said. "Particularly when one is troubled."

"As you say. Well, I must be on my way."

"Where are you going, Hunter?"

He brushed snow from her shoulders. "To walk. No particular destination."

"I see. Enjoy it."

Hunter nodded and said, "Thank you. Be careful how you go back. The ground is slippery beneath the snow."

"When I do go, I'll be careful."

She bowed her head and darted away, slipping

through another alley and out of sight. Women were contrary. She obviously hadn't gone in the direction of Number 7.

"Damn it." He followed again and this time caught up when she was walking out of the Mayfair Square on a small street called Bear Walk.

"Oh, Hunter, you are not to think you must watch over me. It's getting quite light and this is not the time of day when ruffians are abroad."

"This is my usual route," he lied. "Hardly makes sense for us to walk it separately. Put your arm through mine and we'll draw on each other's warmth."

Sibyl could not have described her feelings when she did as Hunter asked and put her hand beneath his arm. He had followed her. Now what did that mean in a man who had been so angry with her only days earlier?

He pulled her hand until he could wrap it on top of his forearm and cover it with his hand.

"You don't always come this way," she told him. "It isn't like you to lie."

"Not unless I'm beside myself and unable to decide how to deal with a situation. You, my lady, have presented me with the biggest personal dilemma of my life. I know you too well to turn away and declare that your problems are nothing to do with me. But I should lie if I said I am not both angry and confused."

"Yes." What else could she say? And he wasn't ready to turn from her entirely. If he had been, he wouldn't be with her now, walking companionably and undoubtedly oblivious to the way she trembled in every part of her. To be touched by him, held close at his side, was a dream come true. She would never banish their intimacy from her mind, but this was the next best thing. She would settle for being near to him when he could spare a little time—but first she must try just once more to gain his help in having a child. And she felt it deep in her heart that as he came to understand how much this meant to her, he would give his assistance.

He bowed over her to shield her from some of the snow. When she glanced into his face, he looked intently back at her. His eyelashes were wet and spiky. "Just a moment," he said, stopping and taking off his gloves. Gently but capably, he tucked away pieces of her hair that had worked free and tugged her hood a little farther over her face. Then he tied the scarf more firmly around her neck. His eyes narrowed and he said, "What am I to do about you, Sibyl? It would be convenient to brush off the predicament you've brought my way. I can't make myself do that." This time he wrapped an arm around her shoulders and held her so close it was difficult to walk. She managed. And she trembled with apprehension and with excitement.

"Your behavior confuses me," Hunter said, and a hard edge had entered his voice again. "Why are you so determined to take a very difficult course? Why not search for a husband first?"

"My reasons have been carefully thought out. Why are you angry?"

"It isn't every day that a man is offered money—"

"Yes, yes, of course," she said rapidly, not wanted to hear all the words again. "But have pity on Jean-Marc. Meg is so angry with him she insisted they must leave at once before he could cause more trouble. Naturally he marches around issuing orders and frowning magnificently, but when he and Meg are at odds, then he is bereft. He spends a good deal of time in the nursery with Serena, whom he insists is the only family member who loves him for himself. Then there is Princess Desirée, who is also furious with him, of course, because she has been forced to leave London without... She wasn't ready to return to Eton yet. It is too quiet for her there."

"And Adam Chillworth is not there," Hunter said, beyond diplomacy. "That way lies disaster unless one or the other of them marries soon."

"I know." They crossed to a small churchyard

surrounding a tiny stone church. "Saint Paul's. I like to come here sometimes. But it will be colder inside than out this morning."

Hunter carried on to the porch and heavy, studded oak door. He turned a handle with difficulty and pushed the creaking wood inward. "I'll just take a quick look," he said.

A quick look turned into a hushed stroll to the center aisle of a starkly simple building with stone arches above rows of worn benches. The altar bore a lovingly embroidered cloth and a thick glass jar of evergreen branches. The scent of pine sap brought the outside to the indoors. One stained-glass window behind the altar glowed with the subdued light from beyond.

Sibyl watched Hunter, how he removed his hat and stood with head bowed for a few moments. Suddenly he turned to stare at her and she could not look back at him.

"Enough of this nonsense," he said, his voice harsh. "We should be beyond treating each other like strangers. Silence and anger never solved anything. Words spoken in selfishness or pride will not bring understanding. You and I have unfinished business. Under other circumstances we could go elsewhere, but will you return with me to Number 7? Will you keep and open mind and heart while we resolve our disagreements?"

"I should like that." As if she could see him as he was this morning, or on any morning, or afternoon, or evening—know his nature—and refuse him anything.

They set off for home and Sibyl's thoughts returned again and again to her gatherings with the ladies. She very much liked the rather flamboyant Ivy Willow, but was deeply troubled by her outlandish, even indecent suggestions for "encouraging" Hunter to cooperate. In the end, both Phyllis and Jenny were won to Ivy's side and the three of them had heaped suggestions on Sibyl, or rather Ivy had heaped the suggestions and the other two had urged Sibyl to implement them.

She adjusted her hood and peered up at him through the falling snow. *Creep up on him while he slept? Employ a degree of—roughness—something different? Roughness—she could not even consider the word* violence—*excited men, particularly when they were aroused, and women, too.* They didn't know her, that much was clear. She had learned a great deal about behaving in a manner that should show her interest in a man. And she was nowhere near as shy as she used to be, at least on the surface. But be rough? That far, she could not go—could she?

Hunter looked down at her. They were back in Bear Walk and drifts left only a narrow path down the middle. They were forced to walk close together again, and once more Hunter put an arm around her shoulders. She knew what she saw in his face—bemusement.

"I don't know if I hope to see inside you and find answers," he said, standing suddenly still. "You do not appear changed, yet you are. Sibyl, my life is already very complicated, and to worry about you makes it almost unbearable."

"You don't have to worry about me." Hah, so spoke the old Sibyl. She loved it that he admitted to worrying about her. "I shall find my way. Believe that."

"Exactly, I do believe it and that's what worries me so intensely."

"I will not do anything you need to be anxious about," she told him.

Hunter rubbed a snowy glove over his face. "May God give me patience. I can almost forgive Etranger his audacity, poor fellow."

"Yes." Sybil turned her mouth down and sighed.

"You are impossible," he told her. He turned her toward him and held her shoulders. Without warning he kissed her forehead. He kept his mouth there, then lifted his chin and rested it atop her head. His arms were around her and tightened. "I had no brother or sister. My parents were not a happy couple and died young, perhaps of their unhappiness. I always wished I had a family. If you would allow me, I would be a brother to you."

Her brother? Sibyl filled her fingers with the sides of his coat and squeezed her eyes tightly shut.

"I would protect you and advise you. There are those who think I should move to more sumptuous surroundings, but I don't know about that. Perhaps I should. If I do, would you consider coming there to live under my protection? With a companion, of course. From there you could be properly launched."

"Jean-Marc has made the same suggestion," she pointed out. "I am not interested in all that."

"He is too busy with his own family, including his half sister. I have friends and among those friends there is bound to be a man you *would* like to marry. Anyway, I go too fast and overwhelm you. Let's get back and get warm and begin again."

Sybil made sure he didn't see the tears that squeezed from the corners of her eyes.

Spivey here.

Hunter offers to be Sibyl's brother? The young rattle must have lost his mind—or he's trying to find a way to keep her near because he doesn't think she has any interest in him as a man.

In Ivy Willow I have a mutinous ambassador. Don't ask me how this occurred. I have no idea, although there was a certain spiritedness there on the second occasion when I paid her a visit. And I misjudged her as an ideal subject. When I first saw her she seemed perfect, a drooping drudge with little or no interest in life. I gave her a purpose to leave her home and she deteriorated from that moment. Why, she has done nothing but become more assertive! I work hard to control her. Each time she produces snuff I'm afraid I shall be ill. Never could abide the stuff.

Disaster!

I made certain she forgot the name Ivy Willow and took on Fern Elm. I was once particularly fond of a girl named Fern. But she defied me—or forgot. I rather think the latter. And do you see her clothing? I arranged for her to buy what she needed and she confounded me. It's inevitable she will draw attention. I've considered getting rid of her—I mean, returning her, of course—but it's too late to find a replacement. Hunter must not learn her name. I would rather he didn't see her at all. But, on the other hand, I must be prepared in case yet another of my plans goes awry.

Now, back to the most serious matter in hand. Sibyl and Hunter. He is so obviously besotted with her that I almost ache for him, or would ache, if I could ache. And she is besotted with him, too. I refuse to remember an ache for her because to be so desperate to produce a wrinkled up, constantly hungry, always inconvenient offspring so badly as to risk one's current comfortable life is mad! But I do have to get her out of my house, and I am wedded—nice word, that—to seeing her leave with Hunter.

I had been quite uncertain about the, ahem, notions put forward by Miss Ivy Willow, but such things have been known to work. The surprise element. Preferable when the man is all but asleep and already, well, wishing he weren't sleeping alone. Unfortunately I have no idea if Hunter is likely to respond to what Miss Ivy refers to as "roughness, or something different," but it does have something to recommend it. I seem to recall—not in my own case, of course—that a little struggle, a romp, one might say, with some effort on the part of the woman to master the man—led to a few notable experiences. I wouldn't dream of chronicling them, of course. I leave that sort of stuff to base scribblers with no sense of decorum, and I know at least one.

Could work.

What was Saint Augustine supposed to have prayed in his youth? "Give me chastity and self-control—but not yet." That is the message I must whisper in Hunter's ear until he thinks he invented it.

On the other hand, can we really imagine Sibyl

Smiles leaping upon Hunter in the dark and attempting to subdue him by force and seduce him?

Laughable.

Saint Augustine must be around somewhere. Perhaps he can suggest suitable advice for Sibyl. Or a way to make Ivy Willow keep her hands out of her bodice and her skirts in their proper place.

9

The very last thing Hunter had expected to receive on a day such as this was a summons from Sir Parker Bowl, ancient Head of Chambers. Sir Parker arrived for meetings of the partners—he came for little else—in a wicker bath chair pushed by an officious nurse. At each of these meetings he threatened to retire, then took the mumbles that met his announcement as pleas for him to remain.

Upon Hunter's return to Number 7 with Sibyl, Coot had been waiting with a note requesting Hunter's presence to deal, Sir Parker's shaky hand announced, with a matter of gravest import. Immediately.

With enough regret to disturb him deeply, Hunter took his leave of Sibyl but made her promise that they'd meet as soon as they possibly could.

He had his carriage brought around for the journey to the Inns of Court off Fleet Street. As soon as he was safe inside and trundling through Town, he thought how much more enjoyable it would be to have Sibyl at his side. She would be mostly quiet, unless he pointed something out, when she would show interest, and smile at him—and make him feel as no other woman could make him feel.

Yes, well, the old Sibyl would have been quiet until spoken to. Perhaps the new Sibyl would chatter and laugh, and point things out to *him*.

And would he mind?

An academic question. The city was pristine, every surface coated pure and chill. As his coachman knew he preferred, they went by way of Piccadilly, past Saint James Palace to the Mall, then onward to the Strand and, eventually, to Fleet Street. Today as on every day at this time, scribblers and printers for *The Diary* and *The Chronicle,* and the grand old paper, *The Courant,* dragged to and from their places of business. A ragged lot, their drooping shoulders and the tatty condition of their clothes showed how badly they were paid. No doubt the poor beggars were especially cold today.

Hunter left his carriage and made his way on foot along Middle Temple Lane. A right turn onto Crown Office Row and he was at the Inner Temple and the Pegasus symbol on the entrance gate. The area was silent except for a squabbling cluster of crows fighting over some invisible prize on the buried lawns.

He had been extraordinarily fortunate to be called

to the Bar among young men of considerably higher stations, an opportunity he'd feared would never come his way. And he certainly never expected to be invited to join Sir Parker Bowl's firm at its chambers in King's Bench Walk. But he was grateful for his opportunities, and his studious nature—uncommon among most aspiring lawyers—served him well. He was as likely as Lord Fishwell, second in longevity in the firm, to succeed Bowl, with Charles as a distant third. When certain other pleasures presented themselves, Lord Fishwell did not choose to apply himself to the business of the law, something else Hunter allowed himself to hope would be on his side.

Inside the redbrick building he felt a certain proprietary pleasure steal over him. He hadn't wanted to be here today, but once he smelled the familiar scents of dust and furniture polish—and old books, old papers, and old whiskey—he felt he was where he belonged, where he was most qualified to be.

Some lawyers lived at the Inns—usually in fine quarters on the actual premises where their chambers were situated. Fishwell was among these, but not Sir Parker, or Charles Greevy-Sims. Sir Parker and his much younger third wife had a fine house near Saint James Park. Charles shared a house in Curzon Street and was more than a little famous for both working and playing hard.

Hunter went into the room where two clerks could usually be found, but it was empty. He checked his own quarters and saw no evidence that they had been entered since he was last there.

The air of silent waiting disturbed him.

Charles wasn't in his office and neither was Fishwell. Hunter was hovering outside Sir Parker's sanctum when the old man's quavering voice hailed him. "Your place, if you don't mind, Lloyd. The fire catches so much better in there. Besides, your whiskey is better than mine."

And Sir Parker was a notorious pinchpenny who preferred to save his own coal, *and* his own whiskey. Hunter liked the old man and felt he owed him a great deal. He greeted him cheerfully, and included the fearsome-faced nurse who didn't as much as show her teeth, then led the way to his office, where he quickly and efficiently started a fire.

"Put me over there," Sir Parker said. Hunter had never heard the old man use his nurse's name and so didn't know it.

The nurse positioned him in front of the fire and began tucking a blanket around his legs. Sir Parker waved her away. "Stop fussing, woman. I'm not completely in my dotage yet." His voice grew a little more gentle and he patted her shoulder. "Run along with you and make yourself some tea in the clerks' office."

She did as she was told, a solid person considerably past an age when she should be told to "run along."

By the time they were alone, Hunter had poured whiskey for Sir Parker and water for himself. He wasn't fond of drinking early in the day. "Drink this," he told the man. "It'll warm you. Now, what's up?"

Sir Parker drank, then turned his bright, slightly watery gaze on Hunter. "You don't know yet?"

"You haven't told me, Sir Parker. But I gather it's important."

They drank for a moment before Sir Parker said, "Whole damnable world is going to the dogs. Nothing's the way it used to be. Not much of a legacy to our children."

Hunter thought to point out that he didn't have any children and immediately saw Sibyl's face, framed in a brown hood, looking up at him through falling snow. "As you say," he told the old man. "But you sent for me."

"Because I was warned it could be dangerous if I didn't, dammit. Think I want to venture forth on a day like this? Damnably cold and inconvenient, I can tell you. Wait till you have to be pushed around in a bath chair by some old battle-ax."

"Very trying for you," Hunter said.

Sir Parker aimed his bright eyes in Hunter's direction again and said, "How would you know?"

Hunter inclined his head and waited.

"Girl, or so my butler tells me, showed up with a message she recited. Went something like, 'Go to King's Bench Walk and wait to be told what to do.' That was it. So we wait, I suppose. Damn this new set of rabble that think they can order their betters around. Yes, also said you had to be here. Something to do with the DeBeaufort case, no doubt. You never should have taken that on."

"You mean I should have sent word to the king to the effect that I wouldn't represent his friend?"

"I would have."

"You did, but the circumstances are different for you, and you told His Majesty that I was the man for the job anyway."

"Did I?" Bowl looked up from beneath shaggy white brows. "Well, what if I did? It was true."

Shouting voices sounded in the corridor outside the office, and the clatter of shoes. Perhaps it was only one shouting voice, a woman's. Hunter couldn't hear what she yelled. He strode to open the door and collided with Sir Parker Bowl's nurse.

When they'd finished grappling in order to stop the woman from falling, she said, "Look at that.

There was a woman here. Thanks to you, she's away. I would have stopped her easily."

"Quite," Hunter said, more than a little amused. She had learned Sir Parker's defense by offense tactics well. "Did you talk to her—the woman?"

"I talked to her, you can be sure of that. But did she answer me? Not a word. And she came in through the window in Charles Greevy-Sims's rooms, if you can believe such behavior. Didn't expect me to show up in the doorway, I can tell you. Screamed, she did, and ran for it. What I could see of her was all wrapped up. But she wasn't any child."

"Nurse!" Sir Parker cried. "Would you stop dramatizing yourself and get in here at once."

Hunter gave the woman credit for self-control. She lowered her eyes, dutifully went to her employer, and gave him a heavy sheet of paper folded in half and looking somewhat grubby.

"Both of our names on it," Sir Parker remarked, unfolding the sheet. "Hmm, anonymous sort of thing. Written in red, of all things—printed like a small child. You'd better look at it."

Hunter took the paper and went closer to a window because the light in the room was poor.

"Greatrix Villiers didn't to it. Find out who that DeBeaufort was with on the Heath and you'll know why he accused Villiers of robbing and trying to kill him. It's your job to stop it before sentencing. You got to tell the court there's been a mistake and there's got to be an appeal and a big effort to get the truth about DeBeaufort. If you don't do it quick, we'll have to keep your friend to make up for Greatrix...." Hunter let his hand fall to his side. What friend? Who did they have? He caught up his hat and gloves.

"Where do you think you're going?" Sir Parker Bowl said.

"Home. I've got to be sure everyone there is safe." He must reassure himself that Sibyl was all right at once.

"I had no idea Charles lived in Mayfair Square these days." The man looked deeply puzzled. "When did he leave Curzon Street?"

"He didn't," Hunter said, bewildered, and looked at the note again.

"Can't say I'm too taken with him," it continued. "But your Charles Greevy-Sims is quiet enough right now, if you know what I mean."

"Charles?" Hunter said. "Charles has been kidnapped?"

"If we can believe what they say. I'd say you've got your hands full. Where d'you intend to start?"

"Where do *I* intend to start? I can't do this alone."

"'Course you can. I certainly can't help you.

Need to be in the comfort of my own home. My wife would insist on it. And you can't talk about this anywhere. If word gets out that there's question about a ruling for us, we'll suffer damage we may never recover from. No, you do this alone, my boy. Where will you start?"

Hunter brought his fists down on the edge of his desk. "How the hell should I know?"

"You're considered a man of vision and insight. Your powers of deduction are touted throughout the Inns. Had it been otherwise, the king wouldn't have agreed to retain you. I ask again, where will you start?"

Hunter felt as if a net was closing about him and he was helpless to stop it. "Poor Charles," he said, regaining some of his composure. "I'll go to his place first, I suppose. And I'll pray I find him there and this is all a hoax to force my hand."

"Good plan," Bowl said. "Let's go, Nurse."

"I should appreciate conferring with you and Fishwell," Hunter said. "Only appropriate."

"Keeping your own council is what's appropriate," Bowl said. "Fishwell's gone on a tour, anyway."

"A tour," Hunter said, beginning to pace. "He didn't mention a tour. When does he leave?"

"Oh," Sir Parker sounded vague, "already gone. Left this morning, I think."

"This morning? When I saw him yesterday he was talking about his current case. It comes up in less than a week."

"Got a continuance," Sir Parker Bowl said, suffering to have himself securely wrapped before going outside. "I'm not up to it. So, the good name of these chambers rests in your capable hands. I'll look forward to hearing you've got everything sorted out." He held out a hand for the note, reread it, then tossed it into the fire. "I've dealt with people like these on more than an occasion or two. So have you. Work swiftly and silently. Raise no suspicion and leave no trace of your investigations. Mollify them when necessary. Jolly them along. Then close in for the kill and expose the bounders as soon as you're ready. More glory and honor on your head, I should think."

"Yes, Sir Parker," Hunter said. It paid to know when to give up the argument.

"Good fellow," Bowl said, "and good luck!"

10

Something was terribly wrong with Hunter.

Many hours after he'd left her so abruptly, he'd returned home. Sibyl had seen him from the window when he got out of his carriage and he'd appeared…disheveled. There was no other way to describe him. And even at a considerable distance she'd been able to see his frown.

He hadn't walked rapidly upstairs with his heels scuffing, as he usually did, he'd run. She put her ear to the door and thought he probably took at least two and sometimes three steps at a time. Then, when he closed his door, the noise was loud enough to shake the entire house. Also not like Hunter, who was considerate of others.

After a period of clearing, when a frosty sun shone on a sparkling white world, snow had begun to fall again. She checked the time. Despite failing light, it was only four o'clock.

She would compose herself and be ready for Hunter to contact her. He'd promised they would have a discussion as soon as he got home—or words to that effect. Eventually he would come to her—to reopen his discussion of the morning.

Ivy Willow had called on Sibyl earlier in the afternoon. Alone. Despite the woman's forcefulness and odd mannerisms, Sibyl rather liked her. She said nice things about people, even Phyllis, who could be hard to like. But Ivy was forceful. And she had outlandish notions that disturbed Sibyl. They were quite—no very—exciting, but also disturbing. And Sibyl was absolutely certain she could never follow Ivy's instructions.

On the piano stood a box. Inside lay a coil of rope made from intertwined strands of red and black. There was a tassel at each end. The box and its contents were a gift from Ivy, who said it was very old and had been used by some notable ladies of pleasure. Sibyl hadn't asked for details of the ladies, but Ivy had insisted on telling her about the rope.

Extraordinary.

Interesting, too, actually. One might almost like to see what effect it might have, on…ooh, someone else, because then one could watch, but also on oneself because then one would know how it felt.

What would Hunter think of such things?

Sibyl huddled her arms around herself and shuddered, an entirely pleasant shudder. How had the daughter of the Vicar of Puckly Hinton, a girl considered pure in heart, come to such a pass?

Pah! She marched into her bedchamber and surveyed her clothes. She had come to such a pass after being much too good for much too long. She could still be good and enjoy men—a man—at the same time. And as Ivy had pointed out, whatever it took to obtain what she needed was completely permissible. After all, she would not harm anyone.

In the big mahogany wardrobe she'd once shared with Meg, there were several items she'd had made recently because she liked them, even if she would be the only one to see them. But why should that be? They were perfectly decent, if a little risqué.

Black wasn't a color a person of her current station usually wore, but she would wear it anyway because it made her feel...deliciously wobbly and perhaps even wicked in the best way.

The clock showed after five o'clock already. Still no sign of Hunter.

Sibyl stripped and washed in cold water from a ewer on her marble commode with its built-in basin. She shivered, but became increasingly aware of her own body.

Now *that* was sinful.

The gown was made after a design she'd seen in Ackerman's. A very exotic creation of India muslin that flowed from beneath a high, tight bodice to the ground, where black satin rosettes surrounded the hem. Ackerman's had intended the gown for evening dress. Sibyl had decided she would consider it an at-home dress for occasions when she expected to be alone. On the other hand, she thought Hunter might consider it sophisticated and that would be an improvement over his considering her naive.

A diaphanous shawl, more a voluminous stole edged with strands of jet beads, was to be worn over the shoulders, which were bare. She had black lace stockings—the occasional scarlet rose decorated black garters and black satin slippers. When she wore them all and had brushed her hair softly upward, allowing a good many natural ringlets to fall about her face and neck, her heart thumped harder. Why should it, just because she'd entered into a little charade and dressed up?

Because she wanted Hunter to come, that's why. She wanted him to look at her as she'd seen some men look at some women—as if they were irresistible.

Sibyl had acquired some pots of paint. Actually, Meg had given them to her. A little shiny pink paint on her lips made them appear wet and soft, and color applied to her cheeks warmed her skin. She breathed in before the mirror inside the wardrobe door, watched her daringly exposed breasts rise, and quickly patted a little more of the pale rouge into her décolletage. When she breathed in really deeply, she could also see the tops of her nipples.

She looked away. One of the things the ladies had discussed was the topic of how gentlemen are aroused by certain incomprehensible means. Sibyl looked into the mirror again. First cold, with gooseflesh springing out on her body, then almost unbearably hot, she eased a nipple free of the gown. Sensation, stinging but pleasing sensation, sprang from the place where her thumb rested on her own flesh. She looked in the mirror at her flushed face, then at her partially exposed breast, which was also flushed. Slowly, Sibyl slipped her hand all the way into her bodice and revealed her entire breast. And she remembered how Hunter had passed his flattened palm back and forth across her nipples. Holding her tongue between her teeth, she tugged the bodice down until she could watch the way both nipples grew hard, and how her breasts seemed to stiffen when she passed one of her own palms lightly across them.

She reached for the pot of rouge, wetted it with a finger, and carefully applied it until the pale pink centers of her aroused flesh were red.

Sibyl held herself, displayed herself for her own inspection and dropped her head backward. Powerful throbbing began in her body, and a weakness. She throbbed in her most private places and the greater the sensation, the harder it was for her to stand. With her lips she murmured, "Stop," but with her body she committed to experience these sensations for as long as she could.

She throbbed more insistently as if the pace, the pulse increased, and saw the rise and fall of her breasts. They appeared swollen, the faint blue veins more noticeable. She pressed the heel of her hand between her legs, trying to quell...no, she wasn't trying to quell what she felt. She wanted to feel it more and more and more.

Unable to look away now, she gradually raised her skirts, lifted them inch by inch up her legs, revealing the black lace stockings, the deliberately naughty garters, then her slender white limbs above them. At last she unveiled the reddish blond curls between her legs and when she parted herself a little, she saw moisture.

Her hearted thudded so hard now she thought she might faint. She was a wanton creature beyond redemption.

Tentatively she slid a finger along slick flesh, and jumped almost violently at the spear of heat that racked her. She repeated what she had done, and repeated it, and her legs parted. Bracing her feet apart, she locked her knees and watched the woman in the mirror who couldn't be Sibyl Smiles.

Her stomach showed, flat, and her hipbones

prominent. Her breasts remained bared and straining. The sight of her rouged nipples excited her and she paused to pinch each one and cry out low.

The need wouldn't die, the need for something more that waited between the red-blond curls that glinted in the light of the single candle burning in the room.

Guiltily now, she touched herself in that special spot and gritted her teeth with the pleasure of what she felt. A flick of her fingers and she had to lean against the wardrobe's second door. Sibyl set up a rhythmic stroking. The more she stroked, the harder she had to stroke. Her breath became shorter and she held her tongue between her teeth, where she could watch how the pointed end moved of its own volition.

A moment more and she'd be unable to stand, yet she stimulated herself harder and harder until she ached with the effort and hung on the edge of some precipice, someplace she had never been before and where she must surely fall into an abyss of only sensation, and hunger for more sensation.

Her eyes had closed. She opened them and made herself focus, look at herself, her body, from tumbling hair to lace-clad ankles, and back up.

That's when she saw Hunter standing in the doorway behind her.

11

The woman in the mirror all but brought Hunter to his knees.

At the same time, he wished he hadn't walked in on her. No, that was a lie. To erase this moment from his mind was unthinkable. But he didn't want her to stare at him, her eyes huge and stricken. He didn't want her to slap her skirts down and draw her shawl across her breasts, not remembering that although black, the shawl was transparent and only served to make her more incredibly desirable—and sexual.

Too soon she started to make quiet choking sounds. She turned toward the wardrobe and filled her arms with clothes that hung there, buried her face and sank slowly downward until she crouched on the floor.

So much for being a man of the world and supposedly capable of handling any situation. He found he could scarcely breathe, and that his own eyes stung, but while he searched for a way to comfort her and erase her embarrassment and guilt, he knew he would never forget the picture she'd made as he arrived here. "Sibyl?" he said, but without hope that she'd respond—or hear him.

He had never wanted, or needed, a woman as much as he did Sibyl. And he wanted her now. The devil take the consequences. The desperate figure on the floor was deeply, instinctively sensual. Hunter had seen a glimpse of what must be a shattering self-discovery for her. Sibyl had discovered herself, and she was everything convention said she should not be. Now she ought to be taught otherwise. Why not by him?

Hunter could only guess what she felt about the revelation, especially followed by discovering that he had watched her.

He went to her and bent to touch her back.

Sibyl shrugged him off and mumbled, "Please go away," into the clothes.

"I was worried about you. There was light under your door and I knocked twice, but you didn't respond. So I came in to see if you were all right. I thought I had to. There's nothing to be ashamed of, Sibyl."

"Go away."

"No. I'm not leaving you like this. Let me help you. Let me explain some simple things to you." Simple things that were often not explained even to men, but ought to be. He caught her by the arms. "Up you come."

She shook her head and tried to slap his hands away. A bee would have been more effective.

"Sibyl, enough. This is not the end of the world. So you have discovered you are a woman with the capacity to be a great lover, that is—"

"Loathsome," she said in a broken whisper, and struggled with her clothing. Covering herself, no doubt. She said, "Stop it. Don't talk about it. I am mortified, can't you see that?"

"Any fool could see it," Hunter said with little regret for being sharp with her. "I want you on your feet and walking, my dear. Now." Ignoring her flailing fists, he hauled her to her feet and marched her before him to the chaise in her sitting room.

The moment he sat her down, she bent double and folded her arms around her knees.

Hunter considered taking one of her straight-backed chairs, but scooted a comfortable old arm-chair forward instead. He positioned it on the opposite side of the fire from the chaise, sat down and waited.

Hellfire, he hadn't thought to change his clothes since returning from the abortive visit to Charles's place in Curzon Street. He'd been in his study, sunk in despair, when a longing to see Sibyl had brought him dashing down here. He must resemble a wild man.

But he wanted to be with her and she wouldn't care how he looked.

Hunter cared how Sibyl looked. A great deal. Despite her tears, and the fact that her hair had completely escaped to fall about her shoulders, she made the most charming picture. Perhaps the more charming because she was softly vulnerable and completely undone by her own human appetites.

Sibyl gave a big sniff and sat up. She wiped at her face with the backs of her hands until Hunter got up and gave her his handkerchief. With this she dabbed her eyes, then scrubbed vigorously at her cheeks and lips. A little pink showed on the white linen and she glared at the stain. She folded the handkerchief and placed it on her lap while she tried, and failed, to tame her thick hair.

He smiled, inclining his head to watch her face until she looked back at him. "You are wonderful," he said. "Confused, but wonderful."

"I am *not* confused. I know exactly what I am and I don't like it. But I am responsible for myself."

Her next swallow was audible and she couldn't blink rapidly enough to hide that she was close to tears again.

"You are responsible for yourself, yes," Hunter

told her, trying to appear relaxed. "But friends are also responsible for each other. You're my friend."

"I—I—" Her lips remained parted and she was obviously gripped by something close to horror. "Please go away, Hunter. I am so ashamed, I shall never recover, or forget."

The shawl didn't stay in place. The neck of her clinging black dress was cut so low, and had so recently been disturbed, that her rouged nipples were more than a suggestion. He averted his eyes, not so much for the sake of her modesty as his own. There were times when a man could not be expected to be more than that—a man.

"When I left you, I went to my chambers," he told her.

"I know."

"This has been a difficult day." *In many ways.* "After my meeting there, I paid a visit to a certain address where I hoped to find information that would put my mind at rest. That proved impossible."

Sibyl's expression changed subtly. "You are worried. I see that now."

He nodded, but still didn't allow himself to look at her body. "Anger helps nothing. I have been enraged. I should have come to you the minute I returned home as I'd promised I would. Forgive me for keeping you waiting."

"You didn't promise. You said we should meet again as soon as we could, that's all." Tears did break free then, and coursed down her cheeks. "You mean that if you'd been talking to me, I should not have been tempted by the devil, don't you?"

Hunter paused, at a loss for words, then he laughed, slapped his thighs and laughed.

Sibyl used his handkerchief once more, but watched him through brimming eyes.

"Forgive me," he said when he could speak again. "Tempted by the devil? That is what you said? Yes, yes, of course it is. How often do you pleasure yourself?"

She jumped to her feet and hiccupped. "I have never done such a thing before and I never shall again." Hiccups jerked her throat and chest. "You can't be blamed for thinking me practiced in such things, but I'm absolutely not. I'm not even sure how I managed to discover...I'm not sure how it happened. One thing led to another, I suppose. Oh, I can't talk about it." This time she threw herself on the chaise and pressed her face into a cushion.

Hunter felt a complete bounder, but at least he'd accomplished his aim. Unless he was much mistaken, Sibyl began to see that despite her humiliation, there was an element of humor here.

"I trust you," he said. What, he wondered, could

have possessed him to make that announcement? But he did trust her. "That's what got me out of my chair upstairs and brought me to you. I'm alone with a great dilemma, so I wanted your company."

"If you trust me and I'm your friend—and you want my company—how can you be alone with anything?"

Because there are things I must not tell anyone. "I can't argue with your logic," he told her.

She sat up and smoothed her skirts carefully, set the cushion down and plumped it a little. But she showed him only her profile and kept her eyes lowered. "I regret the nuisance I've made of myself. If you'll let me, I should like to help you. Will you?"

"Well—" to turn her down curtly wouldn't be at all the thing "—well, yes, I'd like that." What he would really like would be to have her waiting for him in his bed when he returned from another, and dreaded trip into the snowy night. He was a scoundrel and a cad and very possibly a lecher to boot. "You would help me if you would be prepared to talk with me when I come back again later. I have no choice but to return to Curzon Street and speak with someone there, but you and I have unfinished business. It would ease things for me if we dealt with that."

"Who do you have to speak to in Curzon Street

at night? It's cold and unkind out there. Why can't your business wait until morning?"

Hunter wasn't accustomed to having his plans questioned. He considered that, and supposed men with wives must be forever answering for their actions. "It can't wait. And I must leave at once. Will you be available later?"

"How much later?"

Dash it all. "I'm not sure. I'll knock and if you don't respond, I'll know you are asleep."

She turned her face toward him slightly. "I won't sleep until I know you are safe."

"But—" This miss had to know how beguiling she was with firelight on her pale hair, on the curls that spread across her shoulders, and fell to the rise of her breasts. "My business involves the law. I can't discuss it with you, neither can I restrict myself with promises that I'll return at a certain time."

"I shall come with you."

Hunter stared at her.

"You go by coach, yes?" The blues she'd used in the room became her, turned her eyes dark blue, and drew attention to her white skin. "Hunter?"

"I go alone. That is the last word I shall say on the matter." He got up, bumped a brass-topped table and barely caught the porcelain figure of a Chinese fisherman before it would have fallen to the floor.

"Latimer gave me that," Sibyl said. "Thank you for saving it."

Hunter examined the figurine and felt unaccountably annoyed. "You like it?" he asked. For himself, he preferred finer workmanship. "But you'd do well not to encourage familiarity in that quarter." Now there was a mean and inappropriate comment, Hunter thought.

"Latimer is a good friend," Sibyl said, with a strange glance at Hunter. "I really like my fisherman very much. I like things that depict people going about their business. I'll get a heavy cloak."

"You will do no such thing, unless you plan to sleep in it, Sibyl."

"I may do that. In the coach. But I can't stay here and worry about you."

Why had he shared any part of his affairs with her? "There is nothing to worry about." In fact there was a great deal, but the worry was his. "I'll be back before you know it. Now, I'll bid you goodnight for a little while."

"Have you already sent for your carriage?"

"Sibyl, you aren't listening to me. I appreciate your concern. In fact you give me a feeling I don't recall having before and I like it. But you are delaying me." He went to the door. "I hope you'll be waiting for me when I get back."

* * *

For an hour Sibyl read a novel of love and adventure. Rather, she read a page, and reread the page, then repeated the process with the next page, and the next, until she grew irritated and set the book down. This was a time when she'd like to play the piano, for it soothed her, but the hour was too late.

The hot chocolate she'd made over the fire had grown thick at the bottom of the pot, but what she had drunk had warmed and soothed her.

The night was even colder. She knew that by the way snow faintly rapped the windows. When she looked outside, she shivered. Every railing, every shrub and tree and rooftop wore a rounded mantle. Gardens in the middle of the square were barely discernable from the surrounding street.

Sibyl fought back weariness. Her days and nights had become trials and she was rarely at peace. If only Meg hadn't found it necessary to rush away back to Eton. If only naughty Desirée were nearby to distract one.

Nothing moved outside. Or inside that she could hear. Everyone had gone to the warmth of their beds.

There would be no question of Sibyl falling asleep. That would be impossible until Hunter returned. She would go to her own bed and rest on top of the quilt.

On her way to the bedchamber, she picked up the box Ivy had left and put it on the bed beside her. The rope inside was soft. She draped it around her shoulders and smoothed the silken fibers. Running her fingers through the tassels calmed her at first, then sent little thrills through her belly.

Ladies of pleasure had used the rope, the tassels.

This time when Hunter got no response to his knock at Sibyl's door, he continued up the stairs to his own rooms. He supposed he was glad she'd fallen asleep.

No, he wasn't.

Somehow he was changed. She had changed him. This damnable disaster with the DeBeaufort-Villiers case had changed him. In all probability his life would never be the same. The emotion he felt welling up inside him, spreading through his veins, heating his skin, was familiar but stronger than he'd ever felt before. *Rage.* In all his life he had made his own way. As an adult he had chosen to live in this house out of a sense of responsibility for his aunt, who was the closest relative he'd had. And she'd been good to him when he was managing to grow up and make something of himself despite the impressive neglect of his parents. But he owed no real allegiance to anyone. He owed little to anyone at all, except perhaps to Sir Parker, who had picked him out to champion.

Closed inside his study, he didn't light any lamps. The fire was all but out. He didn't care enough to do anything about it, didn't even give a damn that a servant should have banked the coals. What pumped through his body was best kept in the dark and cold. He was not fit company for anyone.

Dear God, he was grateful Sibyl had not waited up for him. He would have become a danger to them both.

He stared toward the sky, where a weak moon made sparkling diamond lies of the frozen spicules the snow had become. His own face still prickled from their assault. Sweeping off his hat, he offered a mocking bow to that sky before he spun the hat aside. His cloak he swept off and let fall, together with his gloves. The cane remained in his hand when he went to the bedchamber.

Apparently Charles Greevy-Sims wasn't at the house in Curzon Street. The woman who also lived there, Mrs. Constance Smith, had refused to speak with him at first. He'd explained that he'd been there twice already during the afternoon. He'd given her his card and tried not to notice that she couldn't read. Charles was one of his colleagues, he'd told her, and he was concerned for him. Was he at home? Mrs. Smith had shaken her head. Short in stature, she had eyes that appeared sunk into deep hollows. From her beautiful but gaunt face, he guessed her to be no more than in her late twenties. Her name didn't fit her appearance. He would have taken her for a Frenchwoman. And when she inclined her head just so, her figure was revealed by the touch of light on dark shadow. Her voluptuous body was breathtaking. Only with difficulty did he manage to concentrate on his reason for being there. Could he take a look at Charles's rooms? Hunter had asked. Another shake of the head had been his answer. That had been when he'd discovered that this was Villiers's sister, the woman Charles had referred to offhandedly and with no hint of her relationship to the jailed man.

For so long that he'd grown deeply chilled, Hunter had stood on the threshold of the house in Curzon Street and pleaded with Mrs. Constance Smith through a bare crack in the door. She told him Charles had befriended her and given her a home in exchange for her becoming his housekeeper. He was, she said, a real gentleman. Was she worried about his absence? Hunter wanted to know. The shadows beneath her eyes and cheekbones had grown darker, but she'd shaken her head yet again and told him, "Mr. Greevy-Sims likes his freedom. He don't tell me when he's going away." And that had been the best Hunter could do. He was, however, more determined than ever to find Charles Greevy-Sims.

He would have to find a way into the house without Mrs. Smith's approval. That would mean waiting for a chance to break in like a common thief. He had been brought so low. Fame had come to him by chance, followed by royal honor, and for these he was to become what he hated most: a man defending what he'd achieved by means that made a mockery of his principles.

Charles had begged him to take the threats seriously, to present whatever evidence came forward for the defense and stand ready to throw himself on the mercy of the courts. But Charles was jealous and Hunter knew it, so he'd dismissed the other man's demands.

And now Charles appeared to be missing, almost certainly a victim of ruthless people who, unless Hunter could arrange a miracle, would kill him regardless of what happened. After this, Charles would be too dangerous to them alive because of what—and who—he would know.

The night was neither dark, nor cold enough to match Hunter's mood.

A baby's breath, soft as a snowdrop's caress against her neck. Small, nuzzling face bumping there. Sweet-scented magical creature, tiny hands clutching. Helpless, innocent one who would grow sure in her mother's loving care. Hair a satin cap, gentle mouth reaching. Elfin fingertips tickling. Born from the love of two lives entwined.

How warm and tender, how perfectly right.

Sibyl's heavy eyes opened slowly. She stared at the glimmer of the white ceiling. No infant snuggled in her arms, and she was cold. Sadness crept inside her head and heart. Earlier she had disgraced herself in front of Hunter and all because she had set out on an impossible quest, and explored things no single woman should explore. Her hard-won brazenness had brought her very low. Perhaps she must content herself with the children of her dreams.

She must have dozed for a moment.

Sitting up, she swung her slipper-clad feet over the side of the bed. A great help she would have been if Hunter had returned home too quickly and needed her. What would he think about trusting her then?

A trusting friendship. He had spoken of that and it should be enough for any woman. It should certainly be enough for her.

In the sitting room, she was barely in time to light a fresh candle before the last one alight went out. There was no point in adding more coal to the fire now.

Through the open curtains, she looked down on the street, a gleaming white expanse unmarred by wheel or hoof. She glanced at the houses surrounding the square and saw little or no light. The chill air had driven everyone to their beds.

Number 7 was also quiet. Unusual, since Lady Hester enjoyed being pampered in the evening and the scurry of Mrs. Barstow's footsteps could invariably be heard.

Sibyl looked at her father's angel-encrusted gilt clock that had been a gift from his grateful parishioners. Breath fled her body. She hadn't dozed, she'd slept—for hours. It was almost midnight. Where could Hunter be? She should have made such a fuss that he allowed her to go with him just to silence her. The least she could have done was keep watch from the carriage, and go for help if necessary.

Perhaps he was home and safely asleep in his bed.

Going to find out was unthinkable. She must wait until morning to discover his fate.

And if she did try to wait until then, she would surely die from fear for him.

This was one of those times she'd planned for, a time when she must put the old, shrinking Sibyl firmly behind and march courageously forth to do what was right. The right thing was to make certain the dear friend who trusted her was safe.

Every carefully soft footfall sounded loud in her ears and the air became alive with creaking and snapping. The stairs were the worst part. Once they were climbed, she set off for Hunter's rooms on tiptoe. She reached his study swiftly, but hovered there, not knowing what she should do. No light showed beneath the door, and no sound of movement came from inside.

This was just as she'd feared. He hadn't returned.

Or he could have returned, discovered she'd fallen asleep, and gone to his own bed.

The risk must be taken. Sibyl turned the handle and, when the door opened, slipped inside and whispered, "Hunter, are you here?"

No fire remained, and no light burned. How fortunate the snow cast a pale glow through the window. Sibyl's eyes adjusted quickly and she saw the room clearly enough to make out a heap on the carpet. Closing the door with more of a slam than she'd intended, she hurried forward and went to her knees.

Hunter's cloak. Surely it was the one he'd worn to go out? She looked around and saw his hat, also on the floor and on its side. As if he'd thrown it down, and the cloak.

Sibyl got to her feet again and faced the bedchamber. The door wasn't completely closed. If she went nearer, perhaps she'd be able to make certain he was in his bed.

Slowly, quietly, she approached until she could peer through the narrow opening and see the bed.

Empty.

Blood rushed to her head and pounded. He hadn't come home. She pushed the door open wider and went into the room, went to the bed. Why should it be unmade? He wasn't likely to tolerate laziness in the servants.

Unless he had been here and left again. Without thinking, she slipped her right hand beneath the tumbled quilt and sheets to see if there was warmth left in the mattress. "Oh, Hunter," she whispered, and knelt to rest her head on her hand. "Where are you?"

The bedchamber door slammed. "You shouldn't have come here tonight."

She had no time to react to Hunter's voice before he threw her, facedown, on the bed.

12

Spivey here.

I have no time to argue. Pay close attention to my instructions. Do as you are told at once. Come this way. Make sure your boots are stout, your hats and gloves of the warmest stuff. Now, out into the snow with you. Play. Build a snowman. Run along and run about. Forget everything you've just seen. I'll let you know when it's time to return for cold milk and warm cookies.

Oh, that Hunter. How could I have misjudged him so?

13

Sibyl struggled for air.

Hunter held her by the back of the head, pushed her face into the mattress. She grew still. Fighting him was pointless.

"Yes, you'd do well to be quiet," he said. This was not the Hunter she knew. Once before she'd seen him in this room and noted that he seemed changed, but on that occasion he had been gentle compared to the man who stood over her now.

"Don't move," he told her, releasing the pressure on her head.

Sibyl drew a grateful breath and listened. Hunter paced. Then he lighted a single candle that guttered so low its only purpose seemed to make the room more eerie.

"Do you want me to think you a fool?" he said. "Is that why you're here?"

"You are not yourself." Cora had spoken about the dangers of letting a man see you were afraid.

"How dare you call me a fool. I came to make sure you were safe, nothing more."

"Really? Dressed in a gown intended for seduction—in private? Am I to think that in the hours since we were last together, you've had no time to change?"

"I didn't change because I was afraid I'd miss you when you returned. So I lay down to rest while still dressed, but I fell asleep." She started to get up, but he pushed her down again. "You should be ashamed, Hunter. I would never have thought you capable of violence toward a woman."

"Yet you missed me anyway." He gave a short laugh. "You would not make a credible witness, my dear. But you're afraid of me. Your voice betrays you. And that, my dear Sibyl, is an intelligent reaction. But I have not been violent and you would be wise not to make such a suggestion again."

She rolled to the opposite side of the bed and jumped to the floor. Hunter made to come around to her but she held up a hand. "Don't come near me. I warn you, if you touch me again, I shall scream and the household will come to my aid."

"And find you in my bedroom, dressed in that? How will you explain your presence here? I suppose you could say I captured you and carried you to my rooms. But with not a word from you until you arrived in my bedchamber? How would you explain why you didn't scream for the household every inch of the way up here?"

Sibyl studied her hands. Anyone who forgot that this man's business was to solve puzzles in his mind was indeed foolhardy.

"Not so much to say?" Hunter said. What he felt now for this woman burned him from the inside. "Well, I have more to say. You came here for something, and you shall have it. I am a desperate man tonight and desperate men resort to any means to bank the fire that burns within them—even if only for a little while. You are here to entertain me. I should be rude to deny you your wish."

In the years he had known her, she had walked in her more flamboyant sister's shadow. A shy woman. But what did they say about such people? *Still waters run deep?* He no longer doubted that Sibyl was much deeper, much more complicated than he could ever have imagined. And knowing it only sharpened his desire for her.

She had asked him to help her have a child. The Sibyl Smiles he'd thought he knew could never have asked such a thing. No, all this time she had hidden the woman she really was, but he didn't despise her for it. Circumstances dictated actions. Now she was alone, answerable to no one, and he believed what she truly longed for was sex. A raw, even a crude word, but more descriptive than any other for this particular purpose. He was a sexually frustrated man who had found little pleasure in the services of courtesans—or prostitutes. He needed a woman who wanted him. Perhaps Sibyl could be that woman. He would find out, but without allowing himself to be trapped into an arrangement he could not accept.

Sibyl looked at Hunter again. He stood there, staring at her, searching her as if for something he might see inside her.

Hunter frightened her. Never had she expected to see him as a predator.

All the gatherings and discussions, the poring over texts about situations such as this, had not prepared her for a moment when she might face Hunter as he was tonight.

From his appearance, his tousled hair, he'd been lying on his rumpled bed. He wore his riding breeches—unfastened at the waist—and boots, but no shirt, and the skin over his powerful shoulders and chest glistened—so did the dark hair on his chest. He had not shaved in many hours and the shadow on his cheeks and jaw gave him the appearance of a handsome ruffian.

"Have you seen enough of me for now?" he asked. "Of course you haven't. If I'm to believe your outlandish explanation for this behavior, there are other parts of me that are much more important to you. Fear not, I shall oblige."

"You are being awful," Sibyl said, making fists in the folds of the unsuitable black gown. "Rude and suggestive. Stop this at once."

"*Suggestive?* How would an innocent woman learn such a term?"

"I am an educated woman. I read and I talk. And you mean that you consider me an ignorant woman. I am not."

"And you also learn, do you?" Gripping a bedpost, he worked off a boot. "I believe you've learned very well, and discovered that there are possibilities that excite you. In turn, that idea excites me. I do believe you've considered me a cool, controlled man. You have been wrong." The other boot hit the floor and his hands went to the waist of his breeches.

"Stop at once," Sibyl demanded. "What can you be thinking of?"

"I think you know very well." He undid his breeches and slipped them down. They were tailored to fit as closely as his skin and he had to take thumb and fingers to push the buff fabric over his considerable thighs, and then his calves.

He stood before her naked. Sibyl tightened her lips to stop them from trembling, and stood as tall as she could to show him she was not intimidated.

Oh, but she was very intimidated.

She would never again have the slightest doubt about what was under those black squares. From his gleaming eyes, to his firmly planted feet, he exuded manliness. And the sight of his jutting manhood stole her breath and weakened her, caused her to tighten and hurt deliciously in unmentionable places.

"Come to me, Sibyl," Hunter said in a low, husky whisper, watching for the slightest hint of her real feelings. "Now it's your turn and this time you won't need to do a thing to help yourself."

She flushed, but didn't protest. She would also make no attempt to do as he asked.

Hunter came around the bed until he stood in front of her. He narrowed his eyes and smiled at her. Not a reassuring smile.

Sibyl didn't know where to look.

She shouldn't want to put her arms around him and hold on, but she did. And she also wanted to take off her clothes and feel him against her. She was lost.

"You must share the title of the book that gave you this idea," Hunter said, gathering up both ends of the silken rope Sibyl had forgotten was around her neck into one of his hands and pulling very slowly, pulling her toward him, inch by inch. "*Fe-*

tishes for Beginners, perhaps? Or were you learning about masochism?"

"A gentleman wouldn't make such a suggestion."

"Perhaps a gentleman wouldn't." The idea of her reading a book on sex and wanting him while she did so drove him mad. "You didn't answer my question."

She angled her face and said, "I've read about all those things." Lying didn't please her but he would not be allowed to treat her like a child.

He laughed again, and without warning blew out the candle. "I like to please a lady if I can. Nice of you to bring something to help."

"Hunter—"

"Please don't speak." He used the rope to hold her still while he stripped away the stole and fumbled with the fastenings at the back of the dress. He pressed his face to her neck and kissed her there, and between the kisses, he drew her skin into his mouth. "I want you," he said, as if through clenched teeth. "I've got to have you." His fierce intensity clutched at her, frightened, but thrilled her. She heard her dress tearing, but couldn't have spoken if she'd wanted to. Her chest felt constricted. Dread fueled by desire was a potent enemy.

Hunter gave up any pretense of being careful. He pulled the dress open and tugged it from her shoulders and down her arms. Sibyl struggled to free her hands and attempted to cover her breasts.

He rewarded her with another hard laugh.

He took off her drawers, but not before he reached inside and rubbed a hand back and forth between her legs. She was hot and wet—ready for him. He ached with the force of his own arousal. When she stood before him in her stockings and slippers, he pulled her closer to the window and the sight of her, of her pink nipples and round breasts, awoke instincts he'd thought didn't belong to "gentlemen." She was new, untouched, and his for the taking.

Sibyl panted. Hunter took her arms behind her back and held them there with one hand while he studied her body, and he used a tassel at one end of the rope to make butterfly passes over her breasts. When he used the maddening tassel to barely tease the tips of her nipples, he dipped his head and played his tongue over her mouth. Her lips opened to his persuasive probing and he licked the roof of her mouth. Her breasts throbbed and the throbbing shot to her labia, and between their folds to a burning place hidden there. Each move he made was calculated, provocative, lightly played out, but she felt how he restrained himself. He was as wild as a horse reined in before a hunt.

Too much, Hunter thought. Holding back was

costing him too much. With sudden force and speed, he whipped the rope from around her neck. At one end he made a loop for her left wrist and tightened it deftly before leading her back to the bed. Her attempts to tear free were useless. He bound her loosely to the headboard, lifted her onto the mattress—facedown once more—and leaped astride her hips.

Sibyl panicked and struggled, but he spanned her waist and softly stroked her until she was still.

Hunter started at her waist, and kissed a line to the nape of her neck. She couldn't stop herself from shuddering, or from responding to the feel of his mouth on her skin.

He took her unbound arm and rested it at her side, carefully bent it at the elbow and set it, palm up on the back of her thighs. He changed position and Sibyl held her breath.

"Hunter—"

"Don't speak. This is the time for silence. Just feel, Sibyl."

Then she knew his intention. Into her hand he pressed the part of him that still held so much mystery. He pressed it there and folded her fingers around him. Sibyl held him and felt how smooth he was, and how tight and swollen and hot. Hunter covered her hand and forced her to tighten it. He tightened it and released it, again and again, and when she felt him pulse within her fingers, her mind grew fevered.

He removed his hand, but she continued to squeeze, until the unexpected caress of silken threads against the side of a breast shocked her into stillness.

Too often of late, deep anger had overtaken Hunter. He must control that anger, especially now. Perhaps he was grooming Sibyl to be his and his alone. If that was so, he could not make the mistake of mishandling her, tonight, or on any other night. But the line was fine: to use her innate sexuality, but slowly, very slowly, while building her confidence in him.

She had come to him with her own plan. She intended to use methods she had learned to make him all but lose his mind and do what she wanted.

He removed her hand from him, rolled her a little onto one side, and tucked her hand and arm comfortably beneath her. Comfortably, but where she would be unable to interfere with whatever he decided to do.

If only he knew exactly how she had envisioned this encounter. "I suppose you've discussed violence, haven't you? The excitement of inflicting pain? That's what the rope was supposed to be about?"

"Don't talk about it," she whispered.

Just do it? Violence didn't appeal to Hunter and he doubted it would appeal to Sibyl if she understood its many implications.

The rope was long. He blew into her exposed armpit, the part of her breast pressed outward by the mattress. He sucked, and nipped at that vulnerable flesh. She gave a thin scream and he smiled. He smiled and used the end of her silken rope. He tickled her back and her bottom until she squirmed and cried out. He would never have expected her derriere to be plump. The fact that it was made his sex even harder. Parting her slightly, he traced another line down and then forward between her legs. Sibyl tossed and thrashed. He was surprised she didn't speak.

She stung unbearably and moved her hips, willing the marvelous sensation to come again, the one she'd already tasted, at least a little, but at her own hand. Could this be what Cora and Phyllis had discussed? The sexual climax? Orgasm? Of course it was, and she wanted it to happen again, doubted she could go on if it didn't.

Hunter replaced the end of the rope with the long, heavy, hardened part of him that excited—and terrified—her so, and stroked between the cheeks of her bottom.

Certainly this was wrong. She was wrong. But at least she would not die without knowing a good deal about the pleasure that was possible between a man and a woman.

Sibyl, Hunter was almost sure, was all but tasting each new sensation he offered her. He felt her passion, her lust. Sibyl Smiles, spinster piano teacher, lusted for him. In fact, she lusted for sex and the thrill of experience.

When he parted her thighs, she resisted him, but was no match for his strength. With his knees, he held her legs apart. She was open to him, helpless to deny him whatever he chose to take. This time he indulged himself in the feel of her. With carefully delicate fingertips, he swept forward, past slick skin to her pubic hair.

Then she cried out. And cried out again, a strangled, shocked sound while she writhed, raising her bottom from the bed.

How easy it would be to slide into her. He was so ready.

Sibyl couldn't be ready, not yet. For a while he played, settling fleeting touches in spots guaranteed to inflame her. But even he hadn't been prepared for her upward bucking, the way she tried to trap his fingers when he tweaked the small tag of flesh already engorged and beating against the skin on his finger.

Her body begged for pleasure.

Hunter gave that pleasure, but his mind was made

up. This was inappropriate enough, it would not go too far. Leaning over her arched body, one hand beneath her and holding a breast, he slid a thumb just inside her and rhythmically tapped the membrane there until she rocked back and forth.

"It happens as the books seemed to say, doesn't it?" Sibyl gasped. "The long, hardened part, the shaft, goes inside the woman and then there is a child. The sperm? Is it in the fluid you make there?"

Hunter closed his eyes, attempted to close his mind, too, and gave her an orgasm that should stop her from thinking. She bucked, and breathed in short sobs, and fell, limp, upon the bed.

Still on his hands and knees, Hunter let his head fall forward and waited for his pulse to slow down.

Without warning, she flipped over to stare up at him, and to reach for and grasp him. "This is what I want. You could do it now, couldn't you?"

To be certain, he could thrust himself inside her. He could quite easily use the appropriate protection and enter, and take what he needed more than she did now. But he wouldn't.

Shocking him again, Sibyl pinched his hip. At once she put her hand over her mouth.

"What was that for?" he asked.

"Sorry," she mumbled, but poked him with a pointed finger.

"I'm damned." He released her bound wrist, tugged her off the bed and held her so that her feet were inches from the ground and pumping. "The book says pain induces erotic pleasure, doesn't it?"

"No. I mean, I didn't read about it in a book."

"Really?" He liked having her breasts only inches from his face. "Where did you learn about such things, then?"

Sibyl could not discuss her friends with Hunter. That wouldn't be fair. "I don't remember. I just heard it, I think."

"And erotic pleasure always leads to—the whole thing."

"Yes." Her squeaky voice made her feel silly.

"Very well. You must inflict pain upon me, correct? Because then I'll give you what you want."

"You find me naive and you have good reason. I should leave now and let you get some rest."

His barking laughter humiliated her. "Get some rest? After all you've done here tonight, I'm going to sleep?"

"Put me down," she demanded. "What do you mean, all *I've* done? You've done a lot, too."

"We must experiment," he told her. "Stand right here and take hold of this."

When he stepped away from her, Sibyl felt very cold. Regardless of the huge mistake she was probably making, she did know she wanted the memories she was making, even the embarrassing ones.

"Here." He produced a cane—the silver-topped one he usually carried. "Grab it like this, yes, as if it were a sword without a hilt. Very good. Pokes and pinches won't achieve your ends, my dear. Now, I'm going to turn my back and you're going to beat me."

"*Hunter.* Hunter, that's a terrible thing to suggest. I know you're joking, but it isn't funny."

"Hit me, I tell you. Here." He touched his rear. "I should think one good swat should do it."

After a long silence, the smooth side of his ebony cane settled ever so gently against his buttocks. Hunter swallowed his laughter, took hold of the end of the cane and turned toward Sibyl. "Not into violence after all, hmm? Try again. You can do it. Make it sing like this." He turned the cane in his hand and slashed it through the air overhead, making the singing noise he'd mentioned and bringing tears to Sibyl's eyes.

"You've enjoyed debasing me," she told him. "You may not have physically hurt me, but you have managed to let me know the contempt in which you hold me."

Then he closed her fingers around the cane again. "One more time, Sibyl, just to show me you aren't the teasing flower I think you are."

"Teasing flower? Because the thought of hitting another person with a stick sickens me?"

He laughed aloud. "I knew you wouldn't be able to do it—ouch!"

Sibyl landed a sturdy thwack on Hunter's buttock and looked at the cane. For an instant she couldn't recall why she held it at all.

"Ouch," Hunter repeated. "I believe I have underestimated you all along. I must be sure to watch my rear at all times."

"You are obviously a bored man filling some time by playing with a woman's emotions."

"Your annoyance is showing," he said, gradually pulling the cane to bring her close. "I assure you that it would be impossible for me to be contemptuous of you. You are wonderful. Nevertheless, there are ways things are done, my pet. It is never up to a woman of your sort to seduce a man—regardless of the reason she fabricates."

Sibyl's heart seemed to stop. "Fabricates? What do you think I've fabricated?"

"You are certainly a passionate creature. Being with you is pleasure all on its own. Do you think it's time to believe in your own allure and stop all this nonsense—as enjoyable as it is?"

Their toes touched and he took her face in his hands. He kissed her deeply, not caring that another erection rose against her belly.

The flats of her hands, pushing against his chest, spoiled his warm pleasure.

She pressed until he took his mouth from hers.

"What are you suggesting to me, Hunter?" she asked, sounding calm but too quiet.

"We know each other too well to play these games," he said. "You play the coquette well. I have never met a woman, not even a courtesan, who struck a pose with more sangfroid. No, you have practiced well, you are cool, sensual composure personified. But, Sibyl, I want you as my friend and I think you want me as yours. Let's not risk spoiling the possibilities that friendship offers."

Sibyl dodged away from him and gathered up her clothes, or what was left of them. She began dressing very rapidly.

"You agree, don't you?" Hunter asked.

"I don't know what you're asking me to agree to. I don't understand you."

He tried to help with her gown but she darted away from him.

"Very well, Sibyl. You insist upon being confrontational but you'll get over it. When you do, I hope you'll be ready to admit, at least to yourself, that what you want most isn't a child, it's a lover, a man who will match your rapacious sexual appetites—the perfect husband."

14

Remaining in her rooms any longer—alone—would surely break the very small amount of determination Sibyl had left. She'd remained there since fleeing Hunter the previous night and as this night grew older, her spirits threatened to become defeated.

Hunter didn't understand, or rather didn't believe what she'd told him. All her fault, of course. Rather than try to stand up to him at all, she shouldn't have denied how afraid she was. And when she'd become aroused, then tried to persuade him to mate with her...well, how could she blame him for his conclusions then?

There could be no denying that his touch, the sense of his mastery, his solid assurance thrilled her. Still, she was afraid of his temper when she frustrated him. Never before had she seen evidence of any violence in Hunter. She had now, and the new discovery caused her to doubt her supposed excellent judgment of people.

The saddest thing she would carry with her from the moments before their parting was his obvious disdain of her. She would never recover from his statement that she was trying to trap a husband who was an exciting lover. He had made her feel sordid.

And to say she didn't really want a child? That had been the most despicable cut of all. Perhaps his heartlessness would help her forget him, make it easier to pass him with a civil nod and feel nothing.

Oh, but she would always feel a great deal for him—she couldn't help it.

When she'd reached the door in his study, his parting shot had been to ask to see a copy of the conclusions she came to about the men she intended to approach.

Sibyl had rushed back to 7B and not only had she shed the black gown, but she had rolled it as small as possible and wrapped it in paper to throw away when she went to see the horses in the morning. But she was pleased with her own reaction afterward. She could have crept instantly into her bed and clasped her misery so tightly that she'd have difficulty getting up again—ever. Instead she'd put on a violet-colored gown made of the softest wool, and brushed her hair into a smooth coil atop her head. Absolutely appropriate for a spinster.

And her mind was made up. She would continue her attempts to have a baby, but she must also throw herself into her work and find more students. If she could only find peace and a positive attitude, she'd come to learn that there was joy in teaching children to play the pianoforte, and she'd remember that she should do what she did best, and put as much money as possible aside to give her child a good life.

The plan must be put into practice at once. The rouge was long gone from all parts of her person—but she had applied a little light pink color to her lips.

Yes, she had done well, but now, in the middle of another night, a wild darkness seemed to press Number 7 from all sides. Sibyl found a blue woollen shawl and draped it around her shoulders, as much to find some comfort as to make her warmer. A wind sighed erratically through trees in the park. Sibyl would like to go outside and run in that wind, run, kick her feet through the snow and forget.

Latimer was always up terribly late, but at this hour even he was bound to be less than happy at the arrival of an unexpected visitor. Everyone else would be asleep—Hunter included she rather imagined, not that she'd seen him at all today.

Her sturdiest pair of boots, and the swan's-down-lined black velvet cloak Meg and Jean-Marc had given her at Christmastide would keep her very warm. And she'd take her matching swan's-down muff. The hood of the cloak would shield her head from the wind and any blowing snow.

Careful to make almost no sound, Sibyl left her rooms and went to the staircase with its magnificent proportions. On each floor the satiny oak bifurcated, forming two short and matching flights designed for ease of access to the apartments there. The ground floor had Latimer's flat on one side of the vestibule and rooms that were almost always kept closed on the other. On the first floor, Sibyl's rooms were to the left while the other small staircase led to a library at one end of what had, in better days, been a small ballroom. On the third side was a room of quite beautiful proportions where furniture from the rented apartments was stored.

Above all this were Lady Hester herself, Mrs. Barstow, who occupied a comfortable bed-sitting room and Hunter. And Adam Chillworth presided over all in his attic, where few were privileged to enter. The small household staff lived in a wing at the back of the house, although Hunter's coachman lived over stables in the same mews where Nightrider and Libby were kept.

This, Sibyl thought, was a very fine home and she loved living there.

Tomorrow the ladies' club would meet here at Number 7B. She must explain the turn her dilemma had taken—in delicate terms, of course—and ask for their help.

Sibyl paused, held the banister, and looked down into the vestibule. She had no right to blame Hunter for anything he said. She had thrust a shocking quandary at him and he had done his best. His very best. By turns he had tried to embarrass her enough to change her ideas, or to comfort her. She hugged herself beneath the cloak. When she could settle on a suitable opportunity and means, an apology was required.

Footsteps on the stone flags in the vestibule startled Sibyl into standing still. Carrying a loaded tray, Latimer went into his rooms.

So he was up. He was certainly fully dressed, if a little tousled.

She carried on down to the vestibule. It would be best to make her exit from the house at once to make sure she wasn't seen leaving. But there was Latimer, a solid, generous sort if ever there was one. She could see if he would…

Too much thinking had landed her in trouble on more than one occasion. Sibyl took off the cloak and muff, but kept on her shawl. The cloak and muff she deposited on a chair by the front door before returning to tap, ever so lightly, on Latimer's door. It was opened at once by Latimer, who stared at her, evidently bewildered by her visit.

"I'm sorry, Latimer," Sibyl said, rushing to get everything said. "This is unheard of, for a single woman to invite herself to a man's rooms, his castle, at such an hour. But you have always been so kind to me—I think you have understood something of my unhappiness. I was hoping you might let me sit by your fire and take comfort from the closeness of a friend going about his business. That's all I ask, please. I cannot bear to stay alone up there just yet, tonight, I mean. Of course, I shall soon feel more calm and will be able to return to my own home."

Latimer closed the door, and went silently to the fireplace where he heaped on more coals. "I want you to sit here," he said, and sounded anxious. "On this chaise. I'll move it."

And move the obviously old French chaise with its once gold upholstery turned a faded, threadbare brown, he did. Latimer made several moves, arranging and rearranging. He placed one of three gilt chairs with green upholstered backs and seats as if completing a pleasant setting for conversation near the fire. He caught Sibyl by the hand and led her nearer the fire. Once he was satisfied that she must be comfortable, he sat at the end of the chaise and took off her boots.

"Does your shawl keep the drafts away?" he asked.

Sibyl nodded and said, "Oh, yes."

"Nevertheless, I shall still get a blanket to put over you."

"No!" Sibyl had never felt less like laughing but she managed to do so anyway. "I am not tired or cold, merely lonely."

Latimer looked directly at her. He had the type of dark-brown eyes that appeared black, and curly black eyelashes to compliment them. His scrutiny made her uncomfortable. It had often been suggested that one became complacent toward those who were nearest—geographically. Evidently she had seen Latimer so many times that she hadn't thought to look at him, really look at him. His dark, unruly hair gave him an almost raffish appearance. Like Hunter, he kept his face unfashionably clear of whiskers. But tonight dark, almost bluish, stubble covered his cheeks and jaw. He had a wide mouth and although he was quiet, tended to smile readily. That smile could lighten the heart and world of the onlooker and none should miss an opportunity to see it. He was a man whose face stayed in the mind—if that mind weren't too involved with itself.

Latimer More was a very well-favored man. Before this evening she couldn't recall seeing him other than completely and well dressed, even to his neckcloth. On this occasion it was definitely the man who made the clothes look wonderful, not the other way around.

Of course, it would certainly be interesting to see him without any clothes at all.

Sibyl fell back on the chaise and covered her eyes with the back of a hand. She was a changed woman. Despite the exemplary life she'd led until a few weeks ago, she had welcomed the loss of her moral fibre. But she must not and would not speculate about Latimer undressed. Why, she had become lustful, a blight on womankind, and a man like Latimer would undoubtedly be furious, and rightly so, at the very idea that she had been thinking how he would look without clothes—this very minute. How disrespectful she had been to him.

She sighed, and stared at him, and sighed a longer sigh. Her vision blurred. Latimer's skin was supple—all over. His stomach was wonderfully tight and muscular. Sitting forward at the bottom of the chaise, his flexed shoulders showed solid muscle, and his spine was clearly defined. Hair on his chest shone, as it did on his abdomen, and although he wasn't aroused, his penis was partially erect as if ready to be...ready, at a moment's notice. A good body, although not as appealing to her as Hunter's because... *Oh, heaven help her.* The poor, violated man was dressed yet she had somehow come by an imagination so vivid that he might as well be naked!

He got up and Sibyl breathed a little easier. He paced a very worn but obviously rare Sevres carpet. Black-and-beige scrolls pleased the eye, as did the hint of pink roses. The room was a jumble. Books, scholarly publications, small mountains of correspondence—their envelopes slit open and the contents turned sideways to make them visible. Latimer must be several years behind in his letter writing. Sibyl concentrated on his correspondence. Anything, she must think of anything that could control her errant thoughts.

"All attended to," he said suddenly, surprising Sibyl. He smiled and the imp was back. "I saw you looking at my piles of paper. You seemed worried. Don't be—I attend to them all but never get around to filing anything."

Sibyl made a sympathetic noise and barely stopped herself from offering to devise a simple filing system for him. Her own troubles were overwhelming at the moment. She must not take on new and taxing projects. "You have so many beautiful things. They all look so old."

"They are," he said. "Have you been here since the bookcases were built?" He indicated the cases that covered the walls, the only gaps being created by the door, and the wide windows.

"No," Sibyl told him. "They're splendid. I've seen a lot of books in one place on many occasions.

Meg and I grew up surrounded by books. But I've never seen anything like this. You'll never need to replace wallpaper because you can't see the walls."

Latimer's chuckle sounded gleeful. "I didn't plan them with that in mind, but you do have a point. As Hunter mentioned to me recently, my rooms deserve a complete overhaul. I'm going to do it. Why not? It's true that I have no one to share what I intend to create, but that shouldn't matter. I live here and I like beautiful surroundings. Will you help me make some decisions, perhaps, Sibyl? You have such wonderful taste."

The compliment stole Sibyl's newly developed sharp and witty tongue, but she nodded and smiled at him.

Oh, fie, she should not put herself in the way of opportunities to analyze his body again. Anyway, she knew Latimer well enough not to be fooled into complacency by his smile and his request to carry out a friendly assignment with him. As she expected, all too soon the cheerful demeanor fled, to be replaced by sadness, perhaps, or sadness that didn't quite hide ill humor.

When she had to either speak or explode, Sibyl said, "What is it, Latimer? Are you angry with me? Really, I had no right to intrude. I'll run along and stop behaving like a spoiled woman who can't bear to be alone."

His hands on her feet stopped her from scrambling off the chaise and making a getaway.

Latimer was more than aware that he must tread lightly here. If he didn't, she could be easily frightened away. "I am also lonely," he told her. "I chose a solitary lifestyle a long time ago now. That was when I was younger and even more foolish. You are a generous woman, Sibyl, and I'm sure you would do what you could to ease my way. It would ease my way now if you would allow me to comfort you. I'd like to get hot chocolate, for both of us, but you must promise not to run away."

He watched her make a move to reach out to him, but she drew back her arms and said, "I love chocolate, it calms me. Thank you, Latimer. I'd be a silly to leave before you pour me a little cup of magic, wouldn't I? No, I promise you I won't be running away." Damn, but her arms would have considerably more comforting power than the chocolate. He got up and went to pour the sweet brew into two cups. Dash it all—he couldn't risk checking the cupboard in his bedroom where he kept a tin of biscuits. The tin might well be empty but he didn't want to leave Sibyl alone while he went to forage in the kitchens.

"Tell me about how you have been managing," she said, catching him off guard. "You must miss Finch now that she is Viscountess Kilrood, but she has asked you many times to live with her and her family and make the seasonal rounds of their properties.''

Latimer opened his mouth to swear, but breathed in as slowly as he could manage instead. ''Should make my business so much easier to conduct,'' he said finally. She had no idea how ridiculous her suggestion was.

''It would mean you'd come to London frequently. And, of course, keep your warehouse—even these rooms. You'd have to find someone very trustworthy to take care of the warehouse in your absence, of course. And think of it, my friend, all around this great land there are people only too willing to part with some exotic items—good antique furniture. You could be with your sister and her husband, and their children, and pursue your business at the same time. And you wouldn't be lonely anymore.''

He didn't have it in him to be too cruel, not with Sibyl, but such a bright young woman deserved to have her less-than-noble traits pointed out. ''I'm fully aware of the trend—mostly among women—to pretend there are no differences between the male and female. From what I'm told, it is long overdue for men to assume the same tasks, the same position as women in any domestic situation. It might be a fine thing for this to be so, but it's not. A man doesn't usually attach himself to his sister's household and trail around behind her family as if he were one of their dogs. Any man—unless he is an invalid—who would do so is bound to become the object of contempt. And deservedly so. On the other hand, it is perfectly acceptable for a female to become part of her sister's household. That is a simple and accepted fact."

"As a nursemaid to the children, perhaps?" Sibyl said and her face was suddenly white. "Or as a chaperon for a daughter when she grows old enough? Or I could simply sit in a chair near the fire to which I have no right, and work on my needlepoint. A man with his own considerable means and living with a relative would simply be a bachelor member of the family with his own affairs to attend to. A spinster relation in the same situation would be made aware of her situation and—although certainly kindly in my case—told what was expected of her."

Perhaps the time had come for him to be less gentle. "You are an accomplished pianist, Sibyl. Think how useful you would be to the Etrangers. You could be called upon to entertain their guests."

The flare in her so blue eyes satisfied Latimer. In her understated way, she was lovely, but she occasionally assumed the demeanor of a sulking cat.

"You still teach here," Latimer pointed out,

"and you could have as many students as you chose to take. That young Teddy Chatham has certainly grown up a good deal. He's not nearly so surly, or given to pulling strange faces when he thinks he's not observed."

"Teddy has matured and gained confidence. He is going to be a fine pianist himself," Sibyl said, surprised by her own urge to protect Lady Chatham's child, who had suffered so at the hands of an overambitious mother who ignored him unless he could do something worth bragging about.

Sibyl stopped thinking about the Chathams. There had been a subtle change in the atmosphere. She glanced at Latimer, who stood a few feet away with a small cup and saucer in each hand.

She swung her feet to the floor. "Latimer, what is it? You don't look at all yourself. Are you in a rage? I must tell you that I am not good at coping with rages."

"Get back on that chaise, Sibyl." Hurriedly, she did as he told her to do. A china cup and saucer sprinkled with forget-me-knots was pressed into her hands. "If it will comfort you, I'll sit at the end of this chaise, but perhaps you are uncomfortable with such familiarity."

Sibyl indicated the bottom of the chaise and he sat there with his chocolate in hand. He might well have forgotten the cup. Not a single sip did he take.

The onus to help her was his, Latimer decided. She had come to him in her hour of need.

"Please do share your troubles with me," Sibyl implored him. "I cannot bear to see you so unhappy."

Then he must strive to put a good face on things because what troubled him, Sibyl could do nothing to help. "There is absolutely nothing amiss with me. It was not I who came to your door, remember. You came here because you are deeply saddened, and I'm glad you did. Now, drink more chocolate and decide what you need to tell me."

She didn't need to tell him anything. "I told you I was having a bad night and wanted company. There isn't anything else on my mind."

Latimer twisted to place his cup and saucer on a table. He said, "I should have thanked you for your concern, so I do thank you, and I apologize for my sharpness. No, Sibyl, enough pretense, if you please. What happened to you tonight?"

The manner in which she bowed her head and turned her face away from him struck real fear into Latimer. The last time he'd seen her, she'd been visiting Hunter and the fact that they were close, possibly quite close, could not have been more obvious. He couldn't take it upon himself to ask about Sibyl's relationship with Hunter.

"Sibyl," he said. "You must miss Meg terribly.

You've finally realized your life will never be quite the same. You regret that the family returned to Eton so abruptly. You also miss Princess Desirée and her Halibut—the two of them keep you entertained and while the entire family is in residence at Number 17, you feel happy and secure."

She was right in her conclusions about men, Sibyl thought. They did, naturally, have traits unique to each of them, but they all suffered from an overdeveloped conviction that they knew all answers to all dilemmas. She studied him covertly. He'd pushed his jacket back on one side and rested a fist there. In his usual unconscious manner, he leaned forward, and looked straight ahead. Sibyl could almost convince herself that she heard what he was thinking. She certainly saw the movement of muscle on his thigh, his slim waist, and...

The only way to remain secure in his friendship was through truth—and a *disciplined* mind. "That's not it, you know, Latimer. Well, I suppose there could be some small elements of truth there, but what happened between Jean-Marc and Meg is everything I wanted for my sister. For that I shall always be grateful."

"Of course," Latimer said. His thoughtful pose didn't waver. "That's not it, then, just as you say. Are you short of money perhaps, and too embarrassed to go to Meg and Jean-Marc for help? If money is the problem, then put it out of your mind. You have had quite enough of that unpleasantness in the past. I will work something out with my banker to provide you with a regular allowance."

Sibyl wanted to hug him and tell him he was the best of men, but her natural reticence had returned—at least for the moment. To make any such gesture out of the question.

"Sibyl. Is all this a question of finances?"

"Thank you, Latimer. You have touched me deeply. But I am not short of money. In fact I am quite well fixed from the final settlement of my father's affairs, praise the Lord. And I do intend to increase the number of students I take—and perhaps charge more for the lessons."

"I'm glad to hear it. But you are just as miserable. You hate living here. Is that it?"

"I love living here. This has become home."

"Then we must move farther afield for our answer," said the indomitable Latimer More. "You like it here, but you miss Puckly Hinton."

"I don't," Sibyl insisted. "My father is no longer there and my mother died many years before that. And the village is so changed. Any brief visit I've made there has filled me with such sadness. I belong here. I have made a life here—even if you do pity me for it."

Latimer rose to pace some more. Sibyl had to

crane her neck to see his face. Finally he said, "I do not pity you, Sibyl. But I do grow angry with your evasiveness. No, no, please don't interrupt me. In case you thought to mention that you have adopted a quite forward manner, and that you wear some delightfully alluring clothes on occasion, don't. I have been aware of the changes in you from the moment you began practicing that jaunty and really quite pleasing prance of yours. The sharpness of your tongue annoys me and those stiff-backed females who come to visit you behind closed doors—and rather often—appall me, with the possible exception of the red-haired girl, who seems embarrassed by her companions. But I think you are becoming changed by those people and not for the better."

"Latimer."

"Kindly don't snap. You might want to warn them to lower their noses enough to see where they're going. A fall down the stairs in this house could hurt a great deal. Enough of that. You have collected those females as confidantes because you are embittered by your lot. Am I right?"

If she lied, he'd know. Sibyl had always been certain Latimer could see into her mind. "You are right, at least in general."

"And specifically. What are the specific reasons?"

"I came to you because you are always so understanding. You have tried to guide me on occasion, but without being a boor about it. But you must also be changed because this evening you have become a most arrogant and lordly fellow."

He stared at her for so long, the corners of his mouth twitching, that she expected him to lose his battle with laughter and proceed to insult her with it.

"I would not have had you go anywhere this evening but here, to me. You've avoided my questions about the specific reasons for your unhappiness, but no matter. If I may be so bold, I should be among several who would miss you a great deal if you were to leave us."

This man was unshakable in his loyalty toward her. That's why she'd come here. And he was right, he couldn't help her if he didn't know what was wrong. "I am undone," she murmured.

In a manner that reminded her of watching ice slide from a Scottish mountainside, she felt herself become less certain, letting go and fading away.

"I am completely undone," she told Latimer. "You may not wish to know me once I've explained."

He swallowed and cleared throat. "Whatever has happened, I shall stand beside you."

Sibyl took up a corner of her shawl and used it

to hide the tears streaming from her eyes. "You are much too good to me," she said in muffled tones through the shawl. "Last night I made a terrible mistake and I am mortified by it. I've spent the day hiding in my room because I'm so ashamed."

Latimer pulled one of his gilt chairs close to her and sat down. He eased her hands from beneath the shawl and held them firmly.

When Sibyl could speak again she heard how tears clogged her words. "I'm determined to have a child, an infant of my own body. I have spent considerable time educating myself on the workings of both men's and women's bodies when they set out to accomplish this mystery.

"Please don't think badly of Hunter. He is so logical he can't imagine that a woman might prefer to look for a good man to become her child's father, rather than to concentrate only on the flighty, foolish ritual attached to gaining a husband. For a while, just long enough for me to make a complete fool of myself with him, he seemed willing to help me. But then he made up his mind—and who can blame him—that I was not sincere. He twisted the truth and told me I was far too interested in...I can't say it."

"Sex?"

"Quite so. He spurned me and doesn't want to see me again—not even in passing, I rather think.

He believes I am no better than I ought to be, and perhaps a great deal worse. I should never have gone to him in the first place.''

He must hold himself back from what he really wanted to do, Latimer thought. He wanted to confront Hunter and punch the bounder, but violence would solve nothing. ''You should have come to me for advice first. Surely you know the differences in our spirits, Hunter's and mine? He is a good man, principled and sincere. But he is also the most ambitious fellow I've ever met. No matter, I should not make negative comments about a friend. I am also a good man, or I like to think so, and I am careful of others. I am engrossed in my business, but not so engrossed that I forget my nearest and dearest—both family and friends.''

Sibyl listened closely and became less certain of herself by the moment. He sounded...possessive...of *her*. She liked Latimer, but didn't love him. Not that love had ever been an important component in the plan. For that reason alone she should never have gone to Hunter. The all-too-familiar knot formed in her throat. She loved him so, but if there had ever been the remotest chance for them, it was ruined now.

''Tell me what you would like me to do,'' Latimer said. ''Anything, Sibyl, anything at all.''

Good heavens, could he mean he would be pre-

pared to... No, he would be as horrified at the idea of fathering a child that was not to be his as Hunter had been. But perhaps not.

"You amaze me," she told him. "Your kindness is almost too much to bear. What have I ever done for you that would cause you to make such an offer?"

"You've been yourself," he said. "May I ask you to more fully explain what you need from me? If indeed you'd like my help in this matter."

This was awful, Sibyl thought, another debacle in the making. But if she told Latimer she wasn't interested in his help, he would be so wounded. Anyway, Latimer would be a most marvelous father for any woman's child and she would be a fool to pass up such an opportunity—if it did present.

"It's all right, Sibyl," Latimer said. "I should not have spoken out of turn. Why should you want to share such personal issues with me? Forget I made such an arrogant suggestion."

"It wasn't arrogant. It was generous, so generous I can hardly think straight. You see, I would support my child on my own. The father would only have to be a father through...well, you know. I have arrangements for making sure there will be no suspicion attached to any man because of my actions. I intend to go to Europe and return with a child, a foundling I have championed. That will be my story. But obviously I can't do this with absolutely no help.''

Latimer said ''ah'' with an expression that suggested he'd had a revelation. ''Now I see what this is all about. I made rather a ridiculous assumption, but that's all cleared up now. Sibyl, you cannot go to the Continent alone.''

''No, but one of my friends will go with me.''

Latimer considered how this should be dealt with. Finally he said, ''I think I understand what you've been too shy to admit. It *is* money that's the worry. You need funds to help you make the journey, then buy the child from its wretched parents. You are so brave.''

Oh, dear!

''I must say I'm surprised Hunter wasn't more than willing to help you. I suppose we should remember that he's having some difficult times professionally.''

''I do, Latimer. He is of great concern to me. He keeps going to a house in Curzon Street to look for someone because he needs to ask the person questions, I think. He is so angry each time he returns. He hasn't found him there yet. Do you think he could be afraid for this other person's safety?''

Latimer had grown so tense, his back ached. ''Yes, I do think so,'' he said. ''Is Hunter out now?''

Sibyl couldn't look at Latimer, but she said, "I assume he's in his rooms. Probably asleep as we all should be."

"You're right about that. And since this seems a perfect opportunity to mention another issue, perhaps you should curtail your morning pilgrimages to the mews, at least until the snow is gone and there are more people about at that time of day."

"You spy on me!" The outrage in her voice was funny. "I go to feed two neglected horses, that's all."

Latimer made a decision not to laugh. "Spying, as you put it, is another symptom of a narrow life, I'm afraid. We know the footsteps of each person in this house and we tend to wonder where they're going. Rather like Miss Sibyl Smiles of 7B and the way she watches Mr. Hunter Lloyd's comings and goings."

"As you say." She became haughty. "I'll leave you now."

"Very well, but will you promise to come again? I should really like that."

"Thank you. Of course I will."

"If you get the appropriate information to me in the morning, I'll arrange to have money transferred to your account for the, er, little venture you have in mind."

Sibyl got up and wrapped her shawl firmly about

her. "Unfortunately, you have not quite understood me. That is because the subject is embarrassing and I hurry to finish what I need to say.

"You weren't listening when I said I wanted a child of my own body. I have no intention of buying and adopting a baby."

Latimer touched her face fleetingly, and regretted even that small lapse in propriety. "I heard, but I thought I had misunderstood. After all, why would you insist you want a child, but not a husband? Surely that is not a good thing for a child. And how very dangerous to go overseas and..." The enormity of what she suggested finally registered. Until this instant he'd preferred not to look too closely at what she seemed to propose. "You intend to take some stranger, some foreigner into your bed to accomplish your needs, then to await the birth of your baby and return home pretending... Hell's teeth, Sibyl. What will Meg say? What would your father have said?"

"Meg already knows and is worried. I'm sorry about that." She rubbed her eyes. "I ask Papa's understanding every day."

"Surely the count forbids this."

"He is *not* my father or my guardian." She tossed her head and the new, spirited Sibyl was very evident. "I know this all seems a dangerous undertaking, but it's not as daring as you think. I had thought to look for a willing mate, someone from a traveling circus, or in a great house where I could go into service and expect some gentleman to take advantage of me. I ruled out an interlude at a brothel almost at once.''

Latimer couldn't speak.

''But now I have put aside all thoughts of mating with a stranger—I am well-informed, by the way, and becoming more so. I am no longer a green girl, I can assure you.''

''I see that,'' Latimer said, and he didn't recall ever feeling as desperate and helpless as he did now. ''This is an exceedingly delicate matter. You will need careful guidance.''

''Most certainly. Oh, I do agree with you. And I have just made up my mind about something. This is not a new idea, although I thought I had to set it aside. My child's father cannot be a stranger after all, but someone I know and respect. The man must be comfortable with becoming my lover, a dear and admired lover, until I am increasing. Then I would leave for the Continent. Some months later, when I returned, this man would see the child, but since I will have been absent a long time, he'll have moved on in his life and will have no more than kindly feelings toward the baby. Not a soul would know he was the father.''

''I see.'' What Latimer saw was the impossibility of seeing one's own child and being expected to behave as if that child were a stranger.

"Do you agree with me that I'm right in wanting a man I respect to be my baby's father?"

"I think it most wise." Surely she couldn't be heading where he thought she was heading, Latimer thought.

Sibyl went to open the door. "Good night, then, Latimer. I know it's too much to expect an immediate answer, but it would be useful to have your decision by sometime tomorrow. There are decisions to be made about such things as logistics. We would manage well enough, I'm sure. If not at Number 7, then elsewhere."

"So," Latimer said. "You are actually saying that you'd like to... You would like me to agree to make you with child, but without the protection of marriage. You are telling me you wish to be my mistress, but only till the baby is conceived."

"Your own life may be too full for you to consider involving yourself in this," Sibyl said. "I should, of course, understand. But if that is so—and you have said you will help me and never turn from me—then perhaps you can guide me toward someone else. Bear in mind that no joining of hearts is at stake and I shall do my best to complete the job as soon as possible."

Latimer swung her to face him, rested his hands on her shoulders, and looked into her eyes. "Will you promise me something? Will you promise to keep me informed every step of the way?"

"Yes," she murmured solemnly. "I promise."

"Then I will get back to you tomorrow with my thoughts. And, Sibyl, I am exceedingly flattered that you are considering me for this challenge."

She nodded and gave him one of her disarming smiles, then closed the door as she left.

Latimer took the place on the chaise where Sibyl had sat. She had come to him. Offered herself to him with absolutely no ongoing responsibilities. They would become lovers—he gritted his teeth at the thought of this marvelous thing. And when she was with child, she would never again come to his bed, never place any demands on him, and make sure that if they were all still in this house, Latimer and his child would be strangers.

He stretched out and let his legs trail from the end of the couch. Firelight shooting and subsiding across the ceiling gave a pleasant impression. No doubt something nasty and wet still fell from the sky, but in here he heard and felt nothing. Except the loud voice in his head:

You're a sexual man, very sexual. Your current misery of spirit arises from being tired of casual affairs, and longing for a wife—and children. So why would you put your own desires aside and agree to sleep with Sibyl Smiles just to give her what she wants?

Because although you don't love her now, you're sure you could come to love her. And you think you can change her mind about not wanting or needing a man except to sire a child.

She is naive. You have never set out to educate a naive women, but the prospect isn't without appeal. And, after all, in certain quarters there are those who are more than willing to fight, physically, to share a bed with you, with "The Most Daring Lover in England." Some time has passed since you frequented the houses or the hells, but you haven't forgotten what you're so good at.

Poor little Sibyl, without as much as guessing the implications, had approached the two least likely candidates to help her carry out her mission in a quiet—and boring—manner. The only man whose secret reputation equals your own is Hunter Lloyd. Of Hunter it is said that he can climax more frequently than any other man, and that it takes a strong woman to keep up with him through a single night. Fortunately, Hunter has managed to maintain great discretion about a reputation that would only shock his own circles.

Hunter would eat Sibyl alive. While, with certain modifications to avoid hurting her, Latimer believed he could make certain he was a drug to which Sibyl became addicted. He believed they'd be a fine, well-matched couple.

15

Sibyl stood in the vestibule, cold following heat across her skin, and attempted to convince herself she could not possibly have made the suggestions she knew she had made to Latimer.

What had possessed her?

The familiar comfort she felt with him?

Desperation?

The sudden onset of madness?

No, no, no, please, no. Not satisfied with causing a terrible situation with Hunter, she'd now set a second disaster in motion.

Now she had invited Latimer to be the father of her child and she'd also given him more than a vague idea of how Hunter had treated her.

Latimer would never brush her visit to him aside. He would take what she'd told him seriously and try to help her. And, because she had been indiscreet in mentioning her visit to Hunter, there could very well be bad blood between two men who had been such good friends.

Outside his work, Latimer seemed to live a cloistered life. Hunter, on the other hand, was so much more a man of the world and, since he was her friend, he would pretend their encounters had never taken place and in time would probably believe they hadn't—as long as Latimer didn't confront him.

Sibyl sat on the bottom step of the staircase. Her experiences with Hunter would be forever vivid to her. And even if he never mentioned their outrageous meetings, whenever she looked at him she'd assume he was recalling her behavior.

She would recall her behavior, too—and his. She had another piece of the mystery about men now, or about some men. Contrary to the claims of the text she had read on the subject, copulation was not as transporting and memorable to men as it was to women. In fact men had a need to copulate because their bodies demanded it. Little had been mentioned about the male brain playing much part in these events. However, in another book there had been a suggestion that a clever wife could captivate and bind her husband to her through creative play and teasing. Sibyl wasn't certain exactly what was meant by the two latter suggestions. After all, surely a wife would not be expected to produce silk ropes—or even the odd cane—whenever she and her husband entered the marriage bed.

She had a fleeting recollection of her very real

image of Latimer. Latimer, naked. She would not dwell on that disturbing incident and she was sure such a thing would never happen again.

But what if it did? What if she started seeing all sorts of people as if they wore no clothes? She shuddered.

She was in a pickle. All the academic study of human sexuality would not erase the stupidity she'd been guilty of such a short time ago. Never mind, she was no longer naive. Why, she had added a most important piece of knowledge to her mounting body of information. All the black squares in the world wouldn't stop her from knowing exactly what was supposedly hidden. And grateful for the insight she was, too. Hunter's penis had become much bigger by the time they had been together on the bed for some minutes. So she knew that part of a man changed when aroused.

She made two fists and placed them end to end. When she held them up and studied them from all aspects, she was amazed. Not long enough to be an adequate study, but still impressive. Gradually, she uncurled her fists in an attempt to approximate the circumference. In fact, because one of her arms had been restrained, she had to improvise in this instance. Later, she would use a measure to gauge how long and large these jealously guarded secrets became. Possibly eight inches, or even ten inches, and as big around as a brass doorknob, although blessedly warmer—hotter actually—than a door handle, and decorated with distended veins. The tip had truly stunned her. A single dimple, like that in a ripe peach, scored the very tip, and the color reminded her of purple hyacinths—or a plum.

And the entire contraption swayed when he walked. Oh, dear. How very odd that must be and how inconvenient it might become in some circumstances.

Her own fixation on these things tightened her tummy. She was going out into the cold, beautiful night to clear her head, to completely forget all the complications in her life.

Sibyl got up and paused. A sensation—no, more a feeling that she was not alone unnerved her. She peered in all directions. There was nothing untoward to be seen and nothing, other than the old house's creaks, to hear. Yet the feeling was there and it climbed her spine slowly.

From outside came the wailing of cross cats. Sibyl imagined them with spikes of fur sticking out all over their bodies as they performed that miraculous feat of walking on their extended claws, their tails pointing at the sky, rows of sharp, white teeth shining in the darkness.

Perhaps she should go to bed after all.

That's what the old Sibyl would have done, slink

away and hide again. The old, shy Sibyl, not the evolved Sibyl. If only she could receive the gift of the kind of confidence she had worked to find—discover that it was a natural part of her, that is.

The slightest sound reached her, a man quietly clearing his throat. She looked upward to see Hunter with his arms crossed on the banister while he watched her.

Two stories of the house might separate them, but she saw his amusement clearly. He thought her ridiculous. Oh, no. Had he seen her gauging the proportions of his penis with her fists? Or at least guessed that's what she might be doing? *Oh, Sibyl, be sensible. How could he possibly guess that?*

Hunter gave her a smart salute.

Sibyl found the wit to drop a graceful enough curtsey. And she had thought he might already be asleep. He was probably planning another expedition to Curzon Street. He was desperately worried about some matter there.

Hunter pushed himself upright and moved out of sight.

"Piffle to you," Sibyl muttered. "Why did I have to fall in love with that man?" She had quite enough problems of her own without adding the burdens of the man she adored.

She retrieved her cloak and tossed it around her. A black velvet band on the muff allowed her to hang it around her neck. She pulled up her hood before checking inside the cloak, where she'd made openings in the lining in order to pop away the scraps destined for Nightrider and Libby. Once satisfied that she hadn't forgotten anything, she let herself out into a night so cold it stole her breath and she had to stand still until the shock of it passed. A wind had picked up, the kind of wind that ebbed and flowed, fading away only to launch a fresh assault when it was ready.

Darkness still seemed absolute, although the gleaming snow cast an eerie light. Fine flakes fell again. In the distance, narrow ribbons of inky smoke breached bands of deep purple above rooftops. The acrid smell of that smoke was in the air Sibyl breathed.

She went slowly down the steps, holding the railings as she did so. The square felt so odd. Silent, as if waiting for something. Ominous. Breaking the silence, occasional small avalanches of snow slipped from a rooftop, or a tree branch, ice-encrusted snow that landed with brittle skitterings.

She set off, remembering the pact that she'd made with herself to run and kick up snow with her very good boots. A larger chunk of snow let go from a roof and whooshed down in front of her. A strong rush of wind caught at the freshly fallen load and whipped it into eddies, some of them tall enough to become skeins of icy needles over Sibyl's face. The fine snowfall grew heavier and she smiled as she ran on to the alley.

The feeling came again. A watched feeling. She turned about, but saw nothing unusual. Despite the wind, the scene was static. The occasional shadow stretched from a doorway or tree, nothing more. And more snow slid from high places to join the fresh fall. This was a deserted night.

If Nightrider's lazy groom was true to form, that arrogant animal would have had no fresh food today and might not even have water. She knew where to find a pump, but she was suddenly anxious just to greet the horse.

In the alley, she sped along with her hood pulled as low as possible. And a conviction that there was danger nearby grew with each step. She kept moving but looked over her shoulder. There were no doorways or trees in the alley, just impenetrable gloom—and the possibility that a villain in dark clothing could be crouched there, following Sibyl at a distance.

Why?

She was absolutely nobody.

Hunter had seen her in the vestibule. He'd dropped out of sight, but that didn't have to mean he'd gone to his rooms and stayed there.

Of course it was Hunter. He was playing his big

brother role again. The brotherly suggestions still rankled, but she didn't mind the thought of him keeping an eye on her now. No doubt she would pay for her venture with a tongue-lashing. And perhaps she'd deserve a lecture.

Smiling, she walked confidently to Nightrider's stall. He'd heard her coming and pushed out his big head. For once he wasn't tossing that head or making ferocious noises. Rather he sagged, and when Sibyl got close to him, he nuzzled the side of her head.

Several wrinkled apples disappeared in quick succession, followed by some rather soft carrots. A raised water trough to the right of the horse had a coat of ice over whatever water remained. Some help would be very useful now. She turned around and said, "Stop creeping around, Hunter, and help me here."

Hunter didn't step forward and such behavior infuriated Sibyl. She gave Nightrider some pieces of bread and found another apple. Near the stable wall she saw a snow-covered rock and lifted it with both hands. By leaning inside the building she could smash the ice in the trough repeatedly until slushy ice mixed with what was left of the water.

"Very well, young fellow. I shall have to make some enquiries about you. I can't believe your owner would condone such neglect." She scratched between his ears, and smoothed his soft muzzle. "Time for you to get some sleep now."

She pushed him gently back and started to close him in.

Sibyl didn't get any farther.

Someone yanked her hood down over her face. She screamed and kicked, but her assailant was a much larger person. He had little difficulty pulling the big hood completely over her head and using something to tie it in place around her neck. It made the perfect, and suffocating blindfold. "Who are you?" Sibyl called out. Panic clawed at her. If she became hysterical she'd be unable to do anything to help herself. "Why are you doing this?"

Her answer came in the form of a blow to the side of her face, quickly followed by a second that caught her eye. She shook so badly, the creature had to hold her up. He hauled her from the cobbles and slung her over his shoulder. Then she heard a snort from Nightrider and the sound of the lower part of the stable door being opened.

From the smell, and the rustle of the ruffian's boots in straw, she knew she'd been taken inside Nightrider's home. The next sound was of another door being opened. This could only lead into the tack room. Sibyl had seen it standing open on several occasions when she'd visited the horse. She smelled oil and wax and listened to the man who had captured her mutter oath after oath under his breath.

He was going to kill her in here. There were so many things one could use as weapons of murder.

"Please let me go," she said. Sometimes you just had to give up and beg. "I only come here to feed two horses who are neglected. Nothing more. If you'd like me to count to a hundred while you get away, you have my word I'll keep the bargain. I won't make a sound."

The creature laughed, and with no attempt at gentleness, he deposited her on the stone floor and administered a kick to her middle that caused awful pain and made breathing impossible. He must have moved around her because the next kick was equally hard but aimed at her bottom this time and followed by several more to the back.

"What have I done to you?" Sibyl asked finally, not caring that she cried openly.

"Nothing," the man said, surprising Sibyl. "Except you're a close friend of Hunter Lloyd. You're useful. We may even let you live if you do exactly as you're told. Hunter's got to do something for us. All he has to do is what we say and everyone will be happy again. But he's being difficult now, isn't he? Fortunately for us, we found out he's got one or two people he really cares about. We're sure you are one of them—though why you'd be soft on a man like him is a puzzle, given his reputation with women. Since you're important to him, we're going to let you help him. This is what we want you to do. When he gets here—and we'll make sure he does—tell him you were told the only reason you're still alive is to give him a message for us. He's going to be beside himself when he sees you. That'll help."

Sibyl tasted blood in her mouth. Her lips were swelling. She'd heard the suggestions this man made about Hunter. They were, she was certain, meant to make her angry at Hunter so she wouldn't balk at doing what this person asked. "What am I supposed to tell him? If it's something that could put someone else in danger, he won't do it."

The slow, steady thud of boots circled her. "He'll do it," the man said and trod on her bound wrists. She cried out and prayed he wouldn't do anything to harm her hands.

"That one hurts, doesn't it?" he said. "When Lloyd shows up, you've got something simple to tell him. All you've got to say is that there's no point in looking for Greevy-Sims until Lloyd's ready to do what he's been asked to do. Can you remember that?"

"Y-yes."

"Good. Then you tell him that if he doesn't do as he's told, we'll bide our time till you're on your own again. We'll take you on a little trip and you won't be bringing back more messages. You won't be seen again."

Hunter cursed himself for waiting too long to locate Sibyl. Unable to stay away any longer, he'd left his rooms intending to pay her a visit, only to discover she'd obviously sought comfort with Latimer. Why should that matter? It did, that's all, and being such a mature man of the world, he'd waited until he was sure she'd seen him watching her in the vestibule, then taken himself, and his temper, to bed. *Damn.*

How in the name of hell was he to know the annoying little madam had left Number 7 at such an hour, and in such weather conditions? If he hadn't decided to get up again, go to her, and try to mend some of the things he'd said, he'd still assume she was at home. But he had—and she wasn't. Her rooms were empty and gaining entrance to Latimer's digs on the pretense of remembering a book the man wanted to borrow convinced him she wasn't there, either.

The very brief visit to Latimer established another unpleasant truth. Hunter had already decided he didn't like Latimer hanging around Sibyl, giving her gifts, being too familiar. Their latest encounter suggested the dislike went both ways. Latimer had warned him off Sibyl. There was, Latimer had said, no other way than bluntly to put "If you do anything to make that wonderful woman unhappy, you'll have me to deal with." So that's what he was doing, being blunt. To which Hunter replied, "Stay away from Sibyl, More. If I see you hounding her again—pressing cheap figurines on her because you know she's led a quiet life and wouldn't know a good piece of art from a deplorable one—just to curry favor with her—well, if I catch you at it, you'll rue the day."

Hunter had left the room and breathed a sigh of relief when Latimer didn't follow. On a whim he opened the front door, gritted his teeth against the cold, and noted footprints on the front steps, and going downward.

The footsteps were still clear and not large enough for a man, but since little snow was falling, the footprints would take a long time to fill in anyway. He grabbed the serviceable cloak and hat he kept in a cupboard near the front door, and was grateful to find a pair of gloves, too. He took off in pursuit of the footsteps. When they made a sharp left turn at the alley leading to the mews, his relief was marred only by his annoyance. She was an idiot. A headstrong idiot. Going to feed horses? How could she go on such an expedition, at such a time, alone, and not be exceedingly silly?

He speeded up his progress until he emerged into the mews proper. The footsteps were there all right, but so was a second set, these made by much larger feet. They were probably present as far back as the flagway outside Number 7, but he hadn't noticed them.

Hunter proceeded cautiously, staying close to the garden walls belonging to the Mayfair Square houses. The walls faced the stables, some of which had living quarters on top and were used by married servants.

Sibyl had trotted ahead not knowing she was being followed, but then, in front of Nightrider's stable was a sight that made Hunter break out in a sweat. The snow was churned for an area of several feet. There had been a scuffle. He'd call it a fight, but even if Sibyl was capable of fighting, evidence suggested her assailant was much larger.

Hunter walked on a little way, then crossed to the stables and doubled back to approach from the direction where he would not immediately be seen by someone leaving the stable.

He reached the corner of the building and realized both the upper and lower parts of the door stood slightly open. Not a sound came from inside.

Damn, this was his fault. Why had he been so harsh with her when she'd come to him? Only a man with no feelings at all could fail to understand what it must have cost her to come to him at all. And what did that make him?

Because his ego was wounded by finding out she wasn't interested in marrying him. The new experience had made him as petulant as a girl making her first season, a diamond-of-the-first-water who had discovered the man she'd set her sights on didn't want her.

There was no choice but to go in, and quickly. Hunter produced the small pistol he carried and pushed open the door. The only light he had to work with was a reflection off snow.

He made out the shape of the big black. The creature stood, unmoving, near the right wall. Hunter approached him confidently. Horses had always been part of his life. "Cold, old chap? Wouldn't be surprised given the chill. We'll have to do something about you." Not even a blanket had been thrown over him.

Hunter saw something else. Behind the horse was a door that the animal had effectively blocked off, against which he all but leaned, in fact. Hunter didn't waste more time before going to the horse and rubbing him down with gloved hands. He stroked the creature's head and murmured to him, all the time turning him gradually away from the door. The instant there was a small space cleared, Hunter lifted a rusted latch and threw the door open—and the horse tried to crowd into the second room with the man.

"Okay, old fellow, okay," Hunter said softly. "Stay right there."

He made out a jumble of shapes. Shelves heaped with things, tack trailing from hooks on the walls, boxes stacked around piles of what appeared to be logs. "Nothing in here," he told the horse. "Except a blanket for you, perhaps."

A blanket was heaped on the floor in a corner.

Hunter approached and the thing moved; it moved, then let out a long sigh and a moan. His heart beat painfully hard. He strode the rest of the way and said, "Sibyl? Is it you?"

Another moan came, this one louder.

On a shelf Hunter saw the obvious shape of a lantern. He'd rather not use flame in here but he had no choice. He took the lantern and used one of the matches he always carried to light the wick. He almost cheered when the thing worked. He'd fully expected to discover there was no oil.

"Oh, my God," he muttered and without pausing another second, went to work cutting the pieces of rope that bound Sibyl. Only Sibyl came to this place to visit this horse. Only Sibyl would do it in the wee hours of the morning if the fancy took her. And Sibyl owned a beautiful, swan's-down-lined, black velvet cloak with a hood.

Nightrider whinnied softly and pawed at the straw in his stable. "It's all right," Hunter said, speaking to both Sibyl and the horse. Fury and fear made him clumsy and freeing her took too long. At last the rope that secured the hood of her cloak over her head fell away, but rather than look at him, Sibyl turned her face to the filthy floor. Next he released the bond that held her wrists together, then the one at her ankles. Another long rope had been wrapped around and around her body as if there were some likelihood that this small woman could do something about the way she'd been tied up. "Let's get you up and back home. You've had a horrible ordeal." He dreaded discovering just how horrible. "We'll get you warm and make sure you eat. You can tell me what happened as we go."

The only movements Sibyl made were some sort of attempt to curl into as small a ball as possible beneath the cloak.

"Sibyl?" He began to roll her over but she immediately rolled back. *My God.* "Let me help you."

"You can't," she said. "That's what the people who did this want you to do. They want you to care so much about what happens to me that they can use me to threaten you."

Hunter didn't have to ask who "they" were. Now Sibyl had been dragged into the Villiers-DeBeaufort case.

"I don't care what they've told you. I decide what I do and what I allow the people I care for to do for me. You will not remain on this cold, hard floor another second." With that he abandoned delicacy and forced her to sit up. She cried out and balanced all her weight on one hip. "What has been done to you? Don't hold back. How have they hurt you?"

"They haven't. I'm shaken, that's all. A good sleep will put me to rights."

Hunter went to his haunches and pulled off the hood—and his blood ran cold. "Oh, Sibyl. And this is a warning to me? Isn't that what you've already admitted?" He raised her chin and instantly wanted to start punching people.

"Yes," she said through cracked and swollen lips. Hair stuck to a wound at her temple and blood caked the side of her head.

He looked closely at the injuries. "How many men were there?"

"One." Her left eye was swollen shut. "A big man with heavy boots. A rough person with a gruff voice."

"He's going to wish he was already dead," Hunter said. "These will all heal and disappear within days. He will not be so fortunate with his injuries."

"No. Violence is wrong. I've seen enough violence to know how evil it is."

Hunter didn't argue with her. He knew what had to be done. "You must be so cold. You aren't hurt anywhere else, are you?"

"Oh, no."

A very hasty reply, Hunter thought. "Good. We'll get you home. Here, put your muff back on." He held it toward her but she didn't take it.

Gently he undid the cloak and reached for a hand. She pulled it back and whimpered. Hunter set the muff down and eased her arms forward. Both wrists were swollen and bruised. On one there was a wound about two inches long. "What did he do here? This wasn't just the rope."

"He stamped on my wrists," she said. "God makes people like him suffer, so he will."

"Oh, yes, he will. But I can't bear it that you must suffer like this now. He liked kicking, didn't he?"

Sibyl shook her head slowly but said, "Yes."

"He kicked you in other places?"

She got to her feet, but stumbled as if her legs might collapse. "I'm going to be fine. You've already said so."

"Do you have other injuries, please, Sibyl?"

"Nothing serious."

She stood against the shelves, her back hunched over.

Hunter removed her cloak and confirmed his suspicions. There was blood on the back of her neck and a small patch seeping through near her waist. When he ran a hand very carefully down the length of her spine, she cried out, then settled into steady sobbing.

He wrapped her not only in her own cloak but in his as well. The muff he used to keep her hands warm, and to support her wrists.

"Here we go," he said, managing to sound calm while his mind darted through the steps he would have to take first thing in the morning. He swung Sibyl into his arms and managed to ensure she was well covered. She'd closed her eyes and he was certain she'd done so to pretend, catlike, that if she couldn't see him, he couldn't see her. He kissed the end of her nose, and the cheek that had been spared by the fiend whose days were numbered, and set off, making his way past Nightrider and securing the stall as best he could behind him.

"Please don't worry about Nightrider. He's strong and I shall look into his care myself. We'll enter the house through the back fence and the kitchen gardens. The snow will be more of a challenge going that way, but there will be less likelihood of our being seen. Is that all right with you?" He was going to try to learn to be a modern man.

"Thank you, yes. All I need is my bed. After I clean myself up. I'll plead sickness for a few days until I'm not so frightening to look at as I must be."

"You aren't frightening. But neither will you be cleaning your own wounds. Fear not, the entire household will rally. You will never be left alone. And you will sleep in my bed until you are completely recovered. Aunt Hester and Barstow will make fine guards. But even then, when you are healed, I will know where you are at all times until the guilty are punished."

Hunter entered the gardens at the back of Number 7 and waded through the untouched snow.

"Oh," Sibyl said at last. "You've muddled me so. Of course I cannot remain in your bed. Even if you didn't think I was a liar and a manipulator, I would never consider inconveniencing you so. You are so good to put aside your true feelings just to look after me, but it won't be necessary."

"My mind is made up," Hunter told her. "You came to me with a request I didn't like and we parted on bad terms. What has occurred is dreadful and I take full responsibility for it, but we shall make the best possible use of the circumstances. Proximity, close proximity is the best means for making decisions about one's feelings about another's notions. Perhaps you will change my mind and show me that everything you said came straight from your heart. Perhaps I will decide that I should make a sacrifice and help you with your project—if you persuade me.''

Sibyl's breath made sharp puffs of white vapor in the darkness. ''Well,'' she said. ''I'm grateful for your help, Hunter, but I am an honest woman and I'm forced to tell you that I have never, ever, encountered such unconsciously pigheaded arrogance as you have just shown.''

Hunter smiled to himself. Now there was some spirit again. He found he liked the spirited Sibyl Smiles better than the docile one.

''Don't overset yourself,'' he told her. ''Although hysteria would be understandable after such an experience. I am sorry for what you've been through. But please don't argue with me further, because I will have my way. For the foreseeable future you will live under my protection....''

16

Spivey here.

When I was other than I am now—in a tangible condition, shall we say—I was known as a calm man, coolheaded, not given to muddled feelings.

Well, my feelings aren't muddled now. It's just that the unbelievably extraordinary developments of the past few days have left me convinced that my responsibilities have never been more serious, or more desperate. But I have had one or two feelings that don't fit in with my character at all. Whimsical feelings? Regretful feelings? Very puzzling. They concern me because I am forced to wonder if I am being tested in some way and if so, why? And how am I to respond? What if I beg for an audience with one of the Elevated Ones, bare my soul, explain what is happening here at Number Seven, and explain these odd sensations I've experienced in other areas, then throw myself upon his mercy and beg for sympathy and guidance? And what if he doesn't have the slightest idea what I'm talking about?

It was that comment about Reverend Smiles and what he might think about Sibyl's behavior that did it for me. Even the humans are wondering about reactions in higher places. So far I'm squeaking by. I give the fellow a few mild remarks about how well his children are doing. I mention the infant, Serena, and watch Smiles turn pink and soft and ruffle the feathers on his wings. Those wings, by the way, are becoming quite frighteningly large. The man has a good deal of power now and I should not wish to become a reason for him to practice meting out mighty punishment.

If Hunter has a child with Sibyl Smiles—out of wedlock—I am doomed. And not only Up There.

She will want to remain at 7B—with the infant—and Hunter will not want to leave the house, either. Hester has a sharp eye, behind all that pretense of being fluffy. She will figure everything out and become possessive. After all, this will be a child of her own blood. Instantly the house will become akin to an asylum. Hester will press for a marriage and set about creating a home for the dear little family—right here.

I was so hopeful that Hester's friend would send her chick to stay here and that the she would manage to beguile Hunter into her claws, but the mother had found a more eligible suitor for the girl and won't allow her to visit Hester at all.

Hester is tucked away and planning already. She doesn't know about the baby, of course, but she has sniffed something in the wind—between Sibyl and Hunter and she wants Sibyl to stay here. It's absolutely certain that although Hester would be glad to see Hunter go, she fears they may marry and move on. If that were the case she would encourage long visits. The result is that Hester has already invited "suitable" candidates to do rough renderings of the house. But I heard her whispering to Barstow about asking Adam Chilworth if he'd like to help—since he's an artist. The fool woman doesn't even know how different a dauber like Chillworth is from a highly trained architect.

Hell's bells, how dare she?

I must take deep breaths—I mean, I must think calming thoughts.

This is no good. Even if it were true that I'm a trifle tetchy—which I'm not—I am honest to the core and I've been bending the truth, not quite admitting the reality of it all. The truth is that there is considerable gossiping Up There, if you know what I mean, and Reverend Smiles has been asking pointed questions about Sibyl.

I have refrained from mentioning the situation with Latimer More to you because I refuse to believe that silly girl would turn to him if she can't get Hunter to comply. But he is another complica-

tion and certain meddlers have taken note of him. I know about his reputation with the ladies. For that matter, I know about Hunter's. But both men show definite signs of deep interest in Sibyl.

This is terrible. What if the angel courts become involved? I could be called before a tribunal and the whole business of my life—my afterlife mission—brought out. Whatever happens, I must deal with it and come out looking like a saint. I must do everything in my power to stop Sibyl from pursuing single parenthood. If she insists on sexual interludes, fine, let her make love while sliding down the banisters. No one in the courts is going to take much notice of such trifling matters—because they're too busy elsewhere. But a new soul? Now that's a different matter. Each new soul must be registered. A person can't hide one of those, so there will be no new soul born to Sibyl Smiles, spinster.

Dear readers, you know me well enough to recognize my distress. I would never share such private matters otherwise. But if you should feel inclined to reveal anything I've told you to others, well, don't do it. I'm not threatening you, but I am always on the hunt for the mindless, just in case I need a host body to perform some service for me, and you could very well be exactly what I'm looking for one day.

Ahem, forgive me. I tend to get carried away when I'm distressed.

I must employ every possible means to bring about my own ends. Adam Chillworth, or so I'm told, may be here before long. He will be at Sibyl's—Hunter's, that is—bedside in a trice. Without tight control, the presence of all three men could bring about a shocking situation.

Hester—and wretched Barstow—must discover the overwhelming depth of their feelings for Sibyl and watch over her. They'll pay frequent visits.

Old Coot could easily become soppy—arriving with chicken soup and so on. The thing is that Sibyl must not be alone with any of the eligible men.

Ivy Willow has improved greatly and becomes quite useful, but her leaning toward rebellious behavior confounds me. I could make her life miserable, or I could reward her for helping me manipulate Sibyl's plan. Ivy could confuse Sibyl with vague references to the need for a husband—for the child, if not for herself. The beauty of a family...

My God.

No, there's something I'm missing here. I—Sir Septimus Spivey—could not have made such an horrendous mistake.

Where has my mind been?

This is disaster, my dear friends. Think, please think—help me discover a solution.

You see, it won't really matter which course Sibyl takes, will it? I am doomed to fail anyway.

As I've already mentioned, if Hunter and Sibyl have a child, but don't marry, Hunter will remain in his rooms and Sibyl will remain in hers. Nothing will get them out because they'll want to see each other and Hunter will want to see his child.

They could well continue as lovers.

And the child will grow. The more it grows, the more it will explore—and damage. There will be no peace to be found anywhere, not even in my beautiful newel post.

And if Hunter and Sibyl marry, this house will be changed, ruined, and then there could be more children.

But there is more and this is where I really don't understand why I didn't think more clearly.

If Chillworth or More can be removed from this house, and I have great hopes for my plans in those areas, isn't it perfectly possible that Hester will find more lame ducks to take their places? This isn't a certainty because it could be decided that Hunter's family needs the space, but Hunter is also too generous, and that Sibyl would give away her last shilling.

There may be nothing for it. If these sickening developments take place, I shall probably apply for angel school. I understand this takes years and may really muddle up one's true nature. I'd have to start by being nice to everyone, helpful, sharing, offering my support whenever someone needed it—actually go out of my way to be charming.

This is unfair. I am besieged on all sides. Here comes that maudlin meddler, Sir Thomas More. Now, I may believe in standing up for what I believe in, but to die rather than give a man a divorce?

"The man was King Henry VIII," Thomas More says to me. He has that irritating ability to know what one is thinking. "I have reason to believe you might need my help, er, Spivey? Is it Spivey?"

Insulting cur. "Sir Septimus Spivey. I need no help, thank you."

"Forgive me for not knowing your name. I have a great number of protégés and it does become difficult. I am in charge of angel school, you know."

This is unbearable. He is so holier-than-thou. Look at him. His face is so cadaverous his skin seems stretched over the bone.

"I always was exceedingly thin, but I must tell you that cadaverous is not a favorite word of mine."

Of all the outlandish comments to make. Can you imagine that I would be so foolish, my friends? I must work hard to avoid saying, or even thinking things that might be embarrassing.

"Wonderful. I can't tell you how delighted I am

to hear that you are determined to improve. Come, we will start your instruction at once."

This is how absolute desperation feels. "I say, Sir Thomas, perhaps you'd better make a dash for it. Isn't that King Henry VIII coming this way?"

"By the odor, I'd say you're right."

"It doesn't smell good, that's true." Rather like exceedingly old blue cheese, in fact.

"I have no reason to fear that man now," says Sir Thomas. In my opinion, he shows more satisfaction about that than might be expected of one so angelic. "He is condemned to remain just as he is forever."

The king shambles and limps, with the entourage of his wives, in various conditions, trailing about him, even though he repeatedly waves them away.

"He doesn't appear well, Sir Thomas."

"Frightful what selfishness and greed and debauchery will do to a man. That one enjoys absolutely nothing. He rots as he drags himself around. Should certainly give someone second thoughts about meddling with others' lives just to get one's own way. "I say, is it true that you know a relative of mine?"

Not if I can help it. "No, Sir Thomas, I doubt it."

"What makes you loath to know one of my descendants?" The man's laugh sounds like marbles rolling inside a jar. "It's been a long time since I

observed Latimer, but he seemed a sterling chap—if somewhat wild in areas unknown to the people he shares that house with. In Mayfair Square, I think. Good grief, now I remember it all. Latimer lives in the house you built. Think of that. How fortuitous that I should remember. I must pay a visit sometime, just to check the boy out. Remind me in class, there's a good fellow."

Thank goodness he's drifting off again. I won't scream, I won't. I will return to the work at hand with increased fervor.

And I will never attend angel school.

17

"I will leave when I decide to leave and at no other time."

Sibyl listened to Hunter's mounting fury through the drumbeat of a headache.

"We'll just have to see about that," Barstow said. "Her Ladyship will be here shortly. Never mind that it's barely dawn and she should sleep for hours yet. Lady Hester insists on getting the necessary things for cleaning Miss Smiles's wounds herself. She's in the kitchen making supplies. When she comes, we'll see who will or won't stay in this room."

Sibyl kept her eyes closed, not a great feat since one was already swollen shut. Perhaps if she pretended to sleep, they'd be quiet.

"This room, Barstow, belongs to me," Hunter said. "As you well know."

"If her Ladyship was to tell you to leave, you'd go. You shouldn't be here anyways. It's unseemly. Miss Smiles needs to be out of those clothes and into something soft on her skin. She'll have to be washed, too."

"I shall remain here," Hunter said, much too loudly. "When my aunt arrives, I shall explain the reasons for my presence and she will understand. A man must be here to guard Sibyl at all times."

Sibyl hoped the bruises on her face would hide her blushes, and that they did think she was asleep.

Conversation had ceased. She listened to the clomp of Hunter's boots and the rustle of Barstow's gray dress.

The door to the study opened and closed. Light footsteps rushed into the bedroom. "Oh, what has happened to her?" Lady Hester's round tones were unmistakable, even when she was as shocked as she clearly was. "Oh, Hunter, why didn't you tell me how bad it is? The poor child. The doctor must be summoned at once." Whatever she had brought with her smelled strongly of vinegar.

Sibyl opened her one functioning eye and said, "No. No doctor. Everyone is making too much fuss. If I sleep and keep a little quiet for a day or two, I—"

"You will what?" Lady Hester asked, snapping out the last word. She came closer and bent to look at Sibyl. "You have been attacked," she said. "Hunter, kindly leave at once. Send for Dr. Enditt."

Hunter wished, more than he remembered wishing for anything, that he could be alone with Sibyl and take care of her. All this female chattering and wailing was unbearable. He and Sibyl needed only each other.

He felt his breathing stop, and his heart appeared to follow suit. What *did* he feel for her? What were these repeated sensations that clenched his gut yet expanded his heart? There was euphoria in the mix when he thought of her—with him. He wasn't sure he wanted to analyze his feelings for Sibyl. She had made hers for him quite clear: she was fond of him, admired his mind and his honor, and thought he would make an excellent father for the child who had become the center of all her hopes. She had not mentioned having any affection for him, not the kind of affection that led to intimacy.

Aunt Hester's hand, settling on his forearm, made him jump. She was a tall woman, and statuesque. Lady Hester Bingham was accustomed to commanding attention, and to being obeyed. "I'm sure you are as appalled by Sibyl's appearance as I am," she said. "But pull yourself together, boy, and do as you're told."

Sibyl barely stopped herself from telling Lady Hester she had no right to speak to Hunter like that. He was too good and successful a man to put up with such treatment.

Hunter looked into his aunt's very blue eyes.

"There are things you don't know, Aunt. Things you won't know. I am asking you—and Mrs. Barstow, of course—to help me keep Sibyl safe."

"He was always like that," Barstow said. "Full of secrets and things he couldn't tell you because they'd get someone in trouble. Twaddle. That's what I say. There's more here than meets the eye, all right, but if you ask me it's not so complicated—if you know what I mean, my lady."

Aunt Hester glared at Barstow. "If you're suggesting what I think you're suggesting, then I think you'd better think harder before you speak the next time. If, as seems to be the case, you're suggesting some sort of romantic attachment between by nephew and Sibyl, well then, how do you connect that to the dear girl's condition? Surely you aren't suggesting that Hunter—"

"Oh, no, my lady," Barstow said. "I would never suggest such a thing. Mr. Hunter is a gentleman in every way. I wasn't really thinking, I suppose. I was just putting together his concern for her and him thinking he ought to stay in the bedroom with her, with wanting a private tryst. I'd forgotten how she's hurt for a moment. Forgive me, Mr. Hunter. And I'll take the very best of care of Miss Sibyl. Not a soul will get past me, I can tell you. I'll have her in my sights every moment of the time."

"Very generous of you, Barstow," Hunter said.

I shall go completely mad, Sibyl thought. She shivered, as she had since she'd been on the floor in the tack room. Her teeth chattered.

"There," Lady Hester said, "we have it all decided. Barstow and I shall take care of Sibyl's wounds, and...why should we not call the doctor?"

"Because I was hurt in unusual circumstances," Sibyl said, desperate to have this over with and go to sleep. "Dangerous circumstances. We have to be very careful to keep the events of this morning quiet. No one should know. A doctor might think he should talk to someone—or even mention what he saw here in passing. That can't happen at the moment. Lady Hester, please believe me, if word were to get out, a person might die. And although I am certainly sore and in need of rest, I believe I shall be fully recovered very soon."

She was marvelous, Hunter decided. Beaten, wounded, yet completely competent to assess a situation accurately and put forth her case with the appropriate passion and conviction.

Sibyl observed how her ladyship breathed deeply, raising her considerable bosom. She wore a voluminous and beribboned white nightgown with a heavy green velvet robe on top. Green ribbons decorated her white nightcap, from which long, blond ringlets trailed. She was really a beguiling person.

"Very well," she said at last. "Hot water will be here soon and we shall wash you. Meanwhile, I have my tested recipes to deal with your injuries."

"Wash me?" Sibyl said, horrified at the thought. "No, I can't let you do such a thing."

"Barstow and I are surprisingly strong, aren't we, Barstow?"

"I'm not considered a reed in the wind," Hunter said. He waved a hand to stop their arguments. "This is an emergency. Wrap her in a sheet and I'll turn her for you. And keep my back to you all while you attend to her, of course."

"You, Hunter Lloyd, will put more coal on the fire. Then you will go into the study and make sure we are not interrupted. I begin to think there's more truth to Barstow's notion than I gave her credit for. You're behaving like a moonstruck whelp. Tell me, how did you happen to be there when Sibyl was attacked?"

"He wasn't," Sibyl said quickly. "He found me and if he hadn't I might not be here now. Hunter is brave and good, and very, very kind, and I can't allow you to treat him badly. He is my good friend. He has never let me down." *Almost never.*

Hunter observed Aunt Hester's disapproving expression and smothered a groan, but he also basked in the words Sibyl had spoken. She didn't sound like a woman who didn't care about him.

"Where did this happen to Sibyl?"

"In one of the stables in the mews," Hunter said. "She was shut inside the tack room, in the dark."

"Hunter," Sibyl said. She turned her head, attempting to see him better. "Nightrider. We didn't get a blanket on him."

He went to her and carefully brushed back her hair. "I will see about the horse later in the day." Looking up at his aunt, he added, "Sibyl visits a horse that's ill-treated. His name is Nightrider." Better to answer the questions before they were asked.

"So you went to visit a horse in the early hours of the morning?" Lady Hester said.

Hunter took lint, dipped it in the bowl of water laced with vinegar, and went to work on Sibyl's facial cuts and scrapes.

"And you, Hunter, what were you doing there? Do you visit abused horses, too?"

A wound on the side of Sibyl's head was shaped like an arc. Hunter separated the hair and cleaned away dried blood. "He kicked your head," he said, fuming at the idea that a man would take his boot to a woman's head.

"As you said," Sibyl told him, "he was fond of kicking. It hurts so." Those were her first words of complaint.

"I know. I take pleasure in the thought of finding the man who did this."

"Hunter, I asked you—"

"You asked what I was doing at the stable, Aunt. I followed Sibyl. There, the truth and exactly what you wanted to hear. I couldn't sleep, I discovered she wasn't in the house and was fortunate enough to open the front door before she'd gone from sight."

"Well, then, we were fortunate," Aunt Hester said.

Barstow had puffed up her cheeks, but now she let the air out. Her face was pink, the only color on her gray person. "Well, I don't like to point out troublesome things, but how would you know if Miss Sibyl was at home or not? You said you *discovered* she wasn't here. At that time the only place you'd expect her to be was in her rooms—in her *bed.*"

When Barstow paused for breath, Sibyl said, "If he wanted to find me, Hunter would knock on my door, just as I would knock on his. And if I didn't answer, he'd pop his head inside and call to me. So if you're trying to suggest Hunter must have gone into my rooms looking for me, you're right." She turned her face into the pillow to stop herself from crying out as Hunter wrapped cold cloths around her wrists.

"Enough from you, Barstow," Lady Hester said. "You have always looked for the worst in people. Hunter, we'll take over now, please. I must see her back. Latimer has a spare bed. You know he'd be more than glad for you to—"

"No." He'd be damned if he'd be ordered about, not that he'd approach Latimer for anything. "Did you make sticking plaster, Aunt?"

With pursed lips, Lady Hester uncovered a bowl and lifted a strip of linen from inside. On this she spread a thick, syrupy concoction Sibyl knew to be diachylon and rosin. While Hunter held the edges of a wound carefully together, his aunt applied the plaster crosswise. They continued until each cut was closed.

"Now, out with you, Hunter," Lady Hester said. "At once. I must deal with Sibyl's back. If you don't want to awaken Latimer, sleep in Sibyl's rooms."

"Absolutely not. Do you have what's needed for the bruising?"

Lady Hester's eyes flashed. "You might leave a woman's work to a woman. Elder flowers, vinegar, bread crumbs. In no time her bruises will resolve. Now, Adam Chillworth isn't back yet. You could sleep—"

"Out of the question. I shall rest on the couch in my study. I'm going there now. When you have finished tending Sibyl, you are both to go to bed. She will be safe enough with me close by."

"Depends on what you mean by safe," Barstow muttered.

Hunter let her insolent comment pass and went into his study, to a shabby but comfortable red brocade couch he knew he should replace.

At the sound of the bedroom door closing, he looked over his shoulder. Aunt Hester stood there. She was pale and rubbed her palms together repeatedly.

"Aunt? Oh, you're tired out, of course you are, and I've been thoughtless. Forgive me, but I feel responsible for Sibyl. I want to feel responsible for her." The instant he closed his mouth he knew his mistake, but there was no taking the comment back.

Aunt Hester walked slowly to stand before him. "She's the most special girl I've ever had the good fortune to know. I well understand how you could fall for her."

He met her gaze steadily.

"Are you in love with her?"

"Things will go faster in there if you help Barstow," Hunter said. He stretched out on the couch and stacked his hands beneath his head.

"Are you?"

Hunter closed his eyes. Even if he were absolutely certain of the answer, his aunt wouldn't be the first person he told.

"I see," she said. "Your silence tells me what I want to know—eloquently."

18

Constance Smith felt sick. An excited sickness when fear and arousal churned low inside her. She'd heard him come in, heard the curses and the sound of fists and boots connecting with anything in his path.

He would be wild, and demanding—and appreciative in that certain way of his.

Constance had managed to get ready for him, but it hadn't been easy. Whenever she knew he was coming to her, the most important thing she could do was set the scene and do what she knew he liked best—to make sure he was intrigued, that he confronted the unexpected and that he came close to meeting his sexual match. Close was the best it would ever be, but the fact that she never let him get what he wanted too easily provoked his need to dominate. She hoped she hadn't gone too far today, but she must find out what was planned to gain the release of Greatrix Villiers.

He was coming. The battle of wits and endurance was coming.

"Constance," he called. "Constance? Where the bloody hell are you?"

She sat at a round table in the elaborate second floor boudoir that had belonged to some former mistress of the house. The draperies were drawn, closing out the gray light of the winter's afternoon. A fire provided the only light in the room. Constance wore a hooded, lavishly full tunic made of red gauze with satin stripes. The hood was up and pulled forward, but her dark hair was free of its chignon and trailing over her breasts.

The table was of ebony with a mother-of-pearl inlay depicting the five-pointed star. Constance had designed the scene with care. She had spread a deck of gypsy tarot cards and lit nuggets of incense in a small stone mortar. A valuable piece of lapis and another of sodalite, both known for their clairvoyant qualities, occupied the very center of the table.

Simian, a huge and eerily silent man that George, Lord Fishwell, had returned with from the American south had been her guide in all this and the fact that he hated George—who treated him like the slave he'd been for a wealthy plantation family near New Orleans—had made him very enthusiastic.

"Constance," George bellowed this time. "If

you're hiding from me then you are being too clever for your own good. I want you. I want you now."

Constance spread her hands on the table and bowed her head. Simian hovered near the fireplace and a disguised door leading to a space in the walls, where the former lady who used this room might well have hidden a male friend when necessary. "Go in there now, Simian," Constance said. "And remember. Tonight you leave and never come back."

"Yes, Miss Constance. Thank you. But you be careful."

"I will. Don't forget you are not to return—ever. Or answer questions about what you've seen here."

"Yes, miss. But I'm mightily afraid for you with this monster man."

"Thank you. Please go or he'll find you here."

Simian did as he was told.

George had crashed his way around on the lower floor and was now mounting the stairs. By the slightly stumbling sound he made, she thought he might be drunk. Not an unusual condition for him.

The incense sent thin, bluish streams into the air.

"Constance? Damn you, where are you?"

He would find her without her having to utter a word. George would never admit it, but searching for her heightened his desire and allowed him to exhibit his forceful temper.

She stared at the lapis. Its deep-blue mystery calmed her. But it didn't soothe away the tingles that covered her skin, wave after wave.

The boudoir door slammed open so hard it hit the wall.

Constance closed her eyes and spread her hands on the table, felt the inlaid star with her fingertips.

"What the hell—" George cut off his words abruptly and there was a sudden silence. Silence but for the click of the door shutting and the steady thud of his boots as he approached her. His shadow fell over the table, but he had placed himself on the opposite side to observe what she was doing.

Constance smiled a little. How like George to assess a situation before making his first move.

"Is this witchcraft?" he asked at last. "Voodoo? Black Magic?"

She pulled the sodalite toward her and studied its pitted blue surface. "You are angry with Charles," she said. "You have had difficulty persuading him to leave London entirely." George was always angry with Charles, and ever since Charles had agreed to hide in the attic and pretend to have been kidnapped, the two men had been squabbling because Charles wanted the matter over and done with, but George would not risk moving too quickly.

"So now you are clairvoyant," George said, his deep, rumbling voice starting to rise to its usual booming pitch. "You knew I was coming. That means you should be ready for me."

George didn't always understand the more subtle points of seduction. Constance looked at his face and said, "I am ready for you, George. But I have been interested in the man you are. The real man, not the one you show the world. Wouldn't you enjoy my knowing what you want, what you will enjoy, almost before you know it yourself?"

He swung his cloak off slowly and put it on a chair with his hat and gloves. His cane he leaned into a corner. He never took his dark eyes from her. A man of fifty, he was big enough to be overwhelming to many. He had a large face, the forehead wide and the nose flat. Beneath a swarthy complexion, his skin was pockmarked. A fleshy mouth promised passion and George had never disappointed Constance with that mouth. His black hair was brushed straight back and it curled along the bottom. He had a luxuriant mustache. Lord Fishwell prided himself on his strength and what he considered the magnificent condition of his body.

"You think you can know what I want before I know myself, hmm? I think perhaps you have overstretched yourself, my dear. That could lead to abysmal failure on your part but no matter, I should simply have to take things into my own hands."

Constance summoned all of her very considerable

courage. "Kindly take a chair and be seated, my lord. Across the table from me."

"I don't want to bloody well—"

"My lord."

He stood there with his hands on his hips and his massive legs in light-fitting buff trousers, braced apart. He glowered, but then he grabbed a chair, swung it around and mounted it as if it were a horse.

Constance moved the crystals aside and offered him her hands, palms-up. He hesitated, then settled great, beefy hands on top of hers. He was a very hairy man and his hands were no exception. "You have a moment or two," he said. "No more."

She slid her palms backward beneath his until she could lace their fingers together. Then she closed her eyes and raised her face toward the ceiling.

"You've got something gold on under that thing, I can see it."

"Hush," Constance told him.

"Charles said Hunter keeps coming here and you've got him fooled into thinking you're little better than a skivvy. He says you speak like a street urchin when it pleases you and you've got Hunter convinced you're some poor, misused creature."

"His pity for me may become useful." She was misused, had been forced to become submissive to Charles Greevy-Sims and Lord Fishwell in order to try to secure Greatrix's release. She wanted him freed because until he was, she was captive to two men she hated, but Fishwell and Greevy-Sims's plans ran on different lines. They wanted only to stop Hunter Lloyd from receiving a knighthood and from becoming Head of Chambers. It was fortunate that she was very much a woman of the world or this situation would be impossible to endure.

"Oh, stop this nonsense," George Fishwell said. "I'll decide what you're to do. Stand on this wretched table and strip. Slowly."

Constance kept her eyes closed but offered him a serene smile. With her forefingers she made small circles on his palms. He jerked. Her smile deepened.

"You have been so deprived, George. Forced to leave a passionless wife in the country and make your way alone—without a hostess even, a woman to run your house—in a world where such things are expected. You have too many decisions to make, too much responsibility. Let go, dear one, and allow Constance to give you what you want. Trust in me. Just a moment." She removed one hand and passed it over the lapis, then she pressed the hand over her left breast. Once more she allowed her head to hang back. She stroked, found the nipple and stimulated it until it stood out, a large, firm bud, pressing into the gauze.

"God, what tits you've got," Fishwell said. "Let me do that for you."

"Stop," she said. "Stop behaving as you're expected to behave. You want more than you have ever had, George. That's what you want today, and that's what you shall have. I see that in you—the lapis clears my mind and allows me to see into your deepest longings."

She took her other hand away and rested it on the rough sodalite. Fishwell had grown quiet, from the inside out. That much she really could divine. Both of his hands remained on the table.

"Such need," she told him. "Take off your boots and your trousers."

He guffawed. "I'm the one who gets the show, my love."

"But it's habit. It's not what you always want. You want something different. Take them off. I promise you'll be glad you did."

"Oh, bloody well, why not?" Grinning, he swung a leg over the chair and set about working off his boots. Then he stood up and stripped off his trousers. Constance kept her fingers moving slowly over the sodalite. Praise be that she found him exciting. He was probably the most masculine man she had met and he was the first who had fulfilled her.

Constance got up slowly and circled the table, keeping a light touch on the rim. When she drew close to George, she stopped and inclined her head to study his legs. "Take off your coat."

He did so. And his grin disappeared. His hands hovered over his waistcoat.

Constance nodded. He was enjoying himself. If he wasn't, he would never follow her orders. But his jaw was rigid and his nostrils flared. She looked at him, and he looked at her.

"Undo your shirt," she said. "Slowly."

His big chest rose and fell more rapidly while he pulled off his neckcloth and unbuttoned his shirt. Once more his hands returned to his hips and he braced his feet apart.

Constance went to him. She stroked his shoulders beneath his shirt, pinched his nipples hard enough to make him breathe in sharply, and held his bulging forearms while she stared down at his manhood. She'd heard talk about men who were endowed like horses. But she hadn't seen such a man until George, Lord Fishwell. She sank to her knees, but didn't touch him. While she watched, he grew full and firm, rose to immense proportions that thrilled her. With difficulty, she looked up at him, ran her hands over his belly and up his chest, combed the graying black hair there. He watched her face while his own was grown so stark he unnerved her. The brief confidence she had gained threatened to break. There were signs in his eyes that he could turn on her at any moment and she knew what that was likely to mean. He would mount and enter her, and use her until she cried for mercy.

There was one way to stop that quickly—if not for good. She hefted his erection with both hands and squeezed. His legs unlocked the smallest amount. Constance took him into her mouth as deeply as she could. His cry was low but clearly audible. She used her teeth on him—gently but firmly—and raked back and forth along his shaft. With each stroke, his hips followed her mouth and he began to pant.

Knowing she took her immediate safety in her hands, she withdrew her mouth and scrambled to her feet, keeping her head bowed. "The shirt," she told him, crossing her arms and holding her breasts. She backed away until she pressed into the edge of the table and turned to remove the crystals and the cards. These she placed carefully on the floor.

George took off his shirt and tossed it to the elaborate oriental daybed. "Don't take long," he said in a tone that left no doubt about his frame of mind.

Panting, Constance moved her eyes over him, scrutinizing every inch.

She tossed back her hood, revealing the thick, black hair that reached her waist. She pushed it behind her shoulders and, with her attention always on George, began undoing the tapes that closed the tunic. Not hurrying, making little attempt to show him how she was dressed beneath the tunic, she untied the narrow ribbons, one by one.

George's expression changed. He stared at her neck and Constance knew what he saw. Gold braid around her neck, crossed, and disappeared again.

Constance undid another tape, and another, and the tunic began to fall open.

"My God," George said, "You are a sorceress. Let me touch you."

She shook her head. Her skin she had oiled with a fragrant potion that left her shining. The gold braid crossed at her collarbones, wrapped above her breasts and beneath her arms to surround her body, crossed over behind her and returned beneath her large breasts, crossed again between them and passed over her shoulders.

George took a step toward her but she held out a hand, urging him to stay back.

The fire was bright enough to send the reflection of its darting flames over everything in the room. Constance knew what it must do to her glistening, braided skin.

She finished undoing the tunic and let it fall about her feet.

The braid traveled on to make a circlet around her small waist, then wound downward, around her thighs, her calves, her ankles, and there it was knotted.

The man who watched and made half lunges at her, groaned at the sight of her. His shaft stood out, unmoving and so big around that most women would wonder if they could take it inside them. Constance already knew the answer to that question.

Always supple, Constance dropped to her back on the table and spread her arms. All it took to start the top of the table rotating was a push on the floor with one pointed toe. Slowly, it turned, then a little faster until it spun and she took her toe from the ground. Tossing her hands over her head, she writhed, turning, stretching, drawing up her knees and letting them fall open, turning onto her stomach so that he could see her finely made derriere.

Finally she allowed her arms and legs to trail, lax—her knees parted, and the table slowed down. "You have often been lonely, George," she said. "You have wanted desperately to fill that loneliness but you have been used."

"Yes," he whispered in the flickering darkness. "They always thought wealth took the place of any need for affection. They were wrong. Power is the better weapon."

Ah, yes, your power, George. That is why I am here. I love every moment of our charades, but I doubt you would be the man with me today if I didn't need to free Greatrix.

Before she could guess his intention, George took hold of the lips between her legs and spread them apart. He bowed over her and the delving of his tongue, the rhythmic massage, the closing of his teeth on engorged and throbbing flesh, brought her hips bucking from the table. No more than a few seconds and a climax ripped through her, forced sweat from her pores, heated her to burning. She grabbed for his rod but he pushed her away. Bracing her thighs apart, he pushed partway into her and pinned her shoulders to the wood while he sucked her breasts.

"I want you," Constance said.

"Do you think I don't know that? You were right when you said you knew my heart and I didn't want the rutting to be always the same. You bewitch me with your courtesan's imagination, bewitch me and show me a new way. Holding back, that's it, isn't it? By holding back you can drive me more wild. But you are a lusty baggage with a need for sex to rival many men's." He drove all the way inside her and the shock sent her hands flailing about, searching for something to hold on to. Just as quickly, he withdrew. "We are matched."

She would not let him tease her now. Quicker than he was this time, she captured his shaft and pushed it inside her. When he would have pulled back, she grasped his ballocks and squeezed, milked him until he shuddered and moved in her, moved back and forth with his thighs pressed to the rim of the table between her thighs. He caught her beneath the knees and hooked them over his shoulders, and drove into her so far she was shoved, inch by inch across the mahogany and mother-of-pearl.

Any self-control left him. She felt brute strength curl within him while he constricted his buttocks and thighs and pounded into her.

Grunting, without gaining release, he withdrew, then caught her up and threw her over his shoulder to stride to the door. Constance gave a thought to Simian and thanked the heavens he was not a man to make an unfortunate entrance.

George leaped downstairs, taking several at a time. "You shimmer, you witch, but then, you know that. You set your scene and I liked it. I will only want more and more of you. What a pity I am a married man. If I could, I would marry you and parade you around on my arm. I can't, but I can come to you more often. And I will."

Constance said nothing. She had heard variations of the same lies from him before. And, as tempting as it might be to find a way to spend time with him in the future, she would get what she wanted and move on.

He took her to the huge old pantry where utensils hung around the walls and huge pots for boiling and bottling sat, cold, upon the stove. Jars of fruit lined shelves, and cones of sugar stood ready to be used by the woman who came in to do the cooking. Simian cleaned and did all other household tasks. This was a house kept very private.

George slapped Constance's bottom hard enough to make her squeal, and he slapped her again, and again. She rose up and pummeled his shoulder. Her hair, hanging in front of her face, hampered her. She angled an arm upward to pull the hair back and laughter rumbled in George's throat as he caught her breast in his mouth and held her while he rubbed his face against her and drew on her nipple repeatedly, not stopping even when she beat on his head and pulled his ears.

At last he swung her around and smiled down at her. "All your fault. You made sure I wouldn't be able to get enough of you."

Constance wiggled and said, "Put me down." He liked to bring her here for some of his favorite games, games that sometimes frightened her.

George gritted his teeth. "You think you can move against me like that and cool me off. Up you go." And he put her on a scrubbed wooden counter beneath a bank of shelves. "So soft and slippery." He stroked his stubbly cheek over her body and his mustache tickled everything it touched, especially the insides of her legs.

"Now," he said, baring his teeth, "Let's see what we can get up to here."

Constance moved fast. She swung her legs past him and leaped to the stone floor. She shot away, skirting the big table in the middle of the room, making for the door.

George got there first. His laughter went on and on. He raised his right hand and tossed a heap of sugar grains at her, covering her skin where it stuck to the lotion.

"Don't," Constance yelled, dashing away from him. He followed her, chased her around and around the table. She felt more sugar rain on her, this time on her back, and she squealed.

He got a hold on her and spun her to face him, but Constance dropped down and through his legs, giving him a squeeze as she went. She grew freshly excited and laughed, too.

They dodged and darted, jumped over piles of unused jars on the floor, and scrambled under the table—until the time when George was waiting for her when she'd passed through and come out on the other side.

In a trice she was stretched on the counter again. "Ouch," she said. "The sugar scratches." He ignored her complaint and kissed her, kissed her hard and deep, and immediately moved down to kiss her between the legs, licking off sugar on the way.

She batted at him, overwhelmed by his energy. From a sink filled with ice and water, he lifted a bowl of whipped, red-wine syllabub and settled it on her stomach.

"George, it's freezing," she cried. "Take it off."

"Oh, I will," he said, and with that he scooped the creamy, pinkish mixture from the bowl and spread it over her while she squirmed. "Tell me again why I should force Hunter Lloyd to put off the sentencing of Greatrix."

She twisted, tried without success to squirm away. George lifted another heap of the syllabub and continued to coat her with it.

"Constance, have you forgotten why I should do this for you?"

"No!" she said, attempting to scoop the chilly sweet stuff from her body. "He's innocent, but who would believe me against the likes of this Hunter Lloyd?"

"Be grateful it wasn't I who took the case," George said.

"I am," she murmured, although she already knew the man, Lloyd, had been handpicked by the Head of Chambers. "You're torturing me, George. And it's going to be such a mess." If George had been given the case she doubted they would be here, although Greatrix would still be in jail.

"You look good in pink. Be grateful. I'm finding out what suits you. That woman is a wonderful cook. See what I've found here. Do you like currant jelly? I do." He opened a small jar, took a glob on a forefinger and coated one of Constance's nipples. He repeated the process the other side.

"How shall I explain such a disaster as this pantry?"

"You have no need to explain," George announced. "I'm thirsty. Anything worth drinking in here?"

"Cherry brandy. Please let me down."

"Absolutely not. And I hate cherry brandy. Where is it?"

She pointed to a cupboard and George removed not one, but two bottles. He opened one and upended the bottle, pouring the fruit brandy straight down his throat. Then, before she could protest, he poured the drink into Constance's mouth and she choked and rocked her head from side to side.

Her coughing all but stopped her breathing. This mad game playing was a diversion she hadn't anticipated tonight and nothing was really happening as she'd hoped. The two of them, Greevy-Sims and Lord Fishwell, had their own ends in mind. The least of their concerns was Greatrix. True, freeing him and ruining Hunter Lloyd's name was the quickest way to get what they wanted. But how could she be sure they wouldn't decide to kill both Greatrix and herself to ensure their silence afterward?

Before she could think further, George leaped upon the counter and straddled her thighs. Smiling down at her, he said, "You look good enough to eat, my dear." And he buried his face in her lap, and laughed as if this were a jolly feast. His tongue probed where he knew he could be sure of a reaction. Constance rocked her hips. George, Lord Fishwell, sat up again and looked at the shelf beside him. His grin did nothing to reassure Constance. "Look what we have here," he said, opening a jar. From it he removed a pickled cucumber. He reached around to dunk it repeatedly in iced water.

"I'm very cold, George. Let's go to bed."

"Without supper? Never."

"I want to talk to you about your progress with getting Lloyd to approach the judge."

"There is progress," he said and rubbed the cucumber over her clitoris. "And you? Are you feeling some progress?"

Constance couldn't speak. The sensation he caused was indescribable.

He took the cucumber away. "Charles is growing impatient, you know. He says the agreement was that you would go to him regularly and keep him company."

"I live in fear that he will decide to come down from the attic," Constance said.

"You don't have to fear that. He won't. I thought the same thing for a while, so he is locked in. And fuming. He must not be fed unless Simian is with you to make sure he doesn't try to escape."

"I see." Constance liked Greevy-Sims as a man, except for his greed and jealousy. He was polite to her and tried to reassure her that Greatrix would be all right.

"You go to him tomorrow and have Simian guard the door until you're ready to leave."

"Very well." She must not argue.

"Yes, very well. Very, very well."

Again he rubbed his obscene weapon over her erogenous flesh. Sensation mounted rapidly. Faster and faster he went, bringing her to the edge of release, only to push the thing inside her where the little knobs on the vegetable's skin stimulated her until she was weak with longing.

That was when George tossed the cucumber aside. He sucked the currant jelly from her nipples and made satiated noises, then opened his mouth wide and filled it with the wine syllabub. Holding his weight on his arms, he slipped inside her and his eyes closed. "I can never let you go," he murmured. "I hate that bastard Greevy-Sims. Give him as little as you can."

Constance's hips were moving, meeting each of George's thrusts. "Say you won't do anything more with him than you have to," he said.

"I won't." And she would tell the other one the same thing if necessary. "Of course, I won't. Do you think Lloyd will go to the judge tomorrow?"

"Leave that to me, Constance. When your brother is free it will be time to send him on his way, you know. I will never let you leave me."

She must be...careful. Another stroke or two and she would explode. But she must not let George guess she had no intention of remaining with him. No, the moment she could, she would leave.

Without warning, George spread himself on top of her. He was heavy, too heavy, but the strength of the man was an irresistible lure to Constance.

He slithered against her and she giggled. Reaching between them, she found enough syllabub to rub in his hair.

George chuckled, hooked another cucumber from the jar, and thrust it between her lips. "It's good," he said. "Try it."

She took a bite and chewed. "Very good."

"Eat some more." He held the vegetable between his teeth, while she chewed off a piece, and when she'd swallowed he had her keep it in her mouth while he had his own bite. They ate from either end until there was no more. George pressed his face into her neck and the movements within her started again.

This time he didn't stop until he had her sobbing beneath him. She heard him cry out as he spilled his seed.

Fighting for breath, George rested his face beside hers. "We'll take a bath. Together. Simian can heat the water and fill the tub. You do know I mean it when I say I want you, don't you?"

She held still.

"Constance?"

"I know what you mean."

He rubbed his fingers back and forth along the sides of her breasts. "I'm going to buy you a house and you shall have anything you want. Anything. Jewels, gowns. I'll take you away somewhere and we'll be completely alone."

"That sounds wonderful." She was scared. He frightened her. What would she be able to do if he decided he really wanted to carry all this out?

"In theory you will be my mistress, Constance, but we will think of ourselves as husband and wife."

"I will have to—" She'd almost fallen back on suggesting that Greatrix told her what she must do.

They would kill him if they thought he could interfere with their plans. Any of their plans.

"What?" George said. He kissed her neck, then gradually slid down over her until he could lick more of the syllabub from her breasts.

"I was wondering how I am to deal with Charles Greevy-Sims. If he decides he also has a continuing right to me."

"If I have any trouble controlling him, then he must be dealt with in the same way as Hunter Lloyd."

Constance knew what he meant because she knew what George and Charles planned for Hunter Lloyd.

George discovered his hands could span Constance's waist and the discovery pleased him.

"Tiny waist," he said. "Just as easy to have two men kill themselves as one. Both will have every reason to do so."

19

"Get out of my rooms, More," Hunter said. "You haven't been invited and I'm not inviting you now."

"Mannerless popinjay," Latimer responded, unaccountably satisfied with Hunter's reaction to seeing him. A man who sensed no threat wouldn't be so annoyed at the sight of another man. "If you insist on keeping Sibyl up here for days, then you must expect visitors. She has a lot of friends and they have a right to see her if she's ill. If you don't like that, then you'd better let her come to me. I'll make sure anyone who comes will be made welcome—including you."

Hunter, constantly worried about Sibyl and longing to see her all the time, was exhausted from nights spent on his lumpy couch, being frequently refused entrance to his own bedroom by Barstow and lectured by his aunt. He didn't have the energy to spar with Latimer. "Over my dead body, she'd come to you," he said. "Kindly leave my rooms.

Leave the flowers, if you like. And whatever else that is you've got there. I'll make sure she gets them."

The adage about how much more one might catch with honey made Latimer decide to try a different approach. He put his bunch of pink cyclamen on the mantel, set down his elegantly wrapped box, and returned slowly to confront Hunter. He flipped the tails of his jacket aside and sat down. "We've been friends a long time," he said. "Don't you think we can work out what's going on without becoming enemies now?"

Hunter didn't want to feel kindly toward Latimer, but, dammit, he liked the man and now he was making it hard to be aloof. "I've valued your friendship," he said. "These are difficult times."

"Sibyl said she was worried about you. I don't know what you told her, but she's got wind of Curzon Street and some trouble in Chambers. She thinks you're in danger, and I think she's right."

Hunter leaned back in the couch and crossed his arms. "No point in arguing. You know about the Villiers-DeBeaufort case. It's become really ugly. A lot of threats thrown around and some serious events, I can tell you. I've got some heavy responsibilities to discharge. But I'm not a man to shirk responsibilities."

"It's obvious you're afraid for Sibyl," Latimer

said. "Could it be you think she's been drawn into the events surrounding the case? She can keep her own counsel, you know. Might be a good idea to tell her what's going on and try to put her mind at rest. She worries about all of us—including you."

Hunter looked at him sharply, but would not be baited. "I'm concerned for Sibyl. She was attacked early on the morning after she visited you, and beaten. Bound to be concerned."

Skin tightened all over Latimer's body. "Beaten how? Where?"

"At those damnable stables where she goes to feed the horses. Beaten up. No other way to put it. Black eye, wounds on her head, bruises on her face, cuts on her back. Whoever the bastard is likes to use his boots on helpless women. Sent a message back with Sibyl—for me—about the case. So we know there's a connection."

Latimer leaped up. "I'm going to find him and kill him," he said. "You didn't see him at all, you say?"

"I didn't. Big, according to Sibyl, and cruel as they come."

Latimer took up his flowers and package and marched to the bedroom door. He knocked solidly and opened the door. Hunter heard him whisper, "Just heard the real seriousness of all this, Mrs. Barstow. Is it all right it I just watch her sleep for a moment and leave the flowers and a little gift? She's so quiet and kind. What kind of monster would do such a thing?"

"The world's full of monsters," Barstow said. "A gentleman like you would find that especially difficult to understand. Go ahead and watch her. I think the sense that people care about her helps. But don't take long. We mustn't overdo."

Hunter pushed to his feet. "Of all the damned nerve. He marches in and gets told he can stay, and what a gentleman he is. I'm polite enough to ask if I can go in and get turned away if the mood strikes that woman. And what about her feeling *my* concern for her? Wouldn't that help? Blasted audacity."

Within minutes, Latimer came out again. He was pale and sweat stood out on his forehead. "How could a man do that to so gentle a creature? Hunter, what can I do to help? I know you prefer to work alone, but an extra pair of hands could be useful in something like this."

Yes, they could, Hunter thought. "I do need help. I'm going back to Greevy-Sims's place in Curzon Street tomorrow evening. The housekeeper—did I tell you she's Villiers's sister?—she never answers the door by day. I have no legal reason to break in so I must keep trying to get the woman to relent when she does appear at night. This evening I'm staying here because I want to see Sibyl looking better and I think the moment for that is close. If there's no sign of anything amiss with Charles's things tomorrow and no clue to what might have happened to him, then I'm going to talk very seriously to the housekeeper—and insist on searching the whole house. She wouldn't like that, I'm sure."

"And I could help out?"

"Don't see why not."

The study door opened again, without a knock, and Adam Chillworth extended his handsome head into the room. "Aye, well there you are, then. Hello. It's good to see all of you. Look what I found?" To Hunter's amazement, Adam swung Halibut, Princess Desirée's very fat gray tabby cat, into the room. Large yellow-green eyes surveyed the surroundings and the animal seemed to smile. He was happy at 17, or 7 Mayfair Square because he got spoiled in both places.

"Where was he?" Latimer said.

"Your windowsill. Sitting out there in the snow as if it were as normal as his battered fish on Sunday. I would have run him straight back to Number 17 but I didn't see any sign of life over there."

"Put that thing down," Hunter said, referring to Halibut. "First tell us how you are. How did you fare? Did you meet some fabulous woman with a fortune? Are you here to stay, or only passing through to pick up your things and go on to grander climes?''

''I fared well. Saw wondrous things. Met a lot of fabulous women whom I didn't mind leavin' since I'm so shy.''

The other two men guffawed at this.

Adam, ever the dour north countryman, pretended a puzzled air and said, ''I'm here to stay and glad t'be back. There's no place like London, and no place in London I'd rather live than Number 7 Mayfair Square. There. Now you've learned all.''

Latimer grew serious. ''Sibyl's in serious trouble.'' He indicated the closed door to the bedchamber. ''Some ruffian beat her badly several days ago while she was feeding a horse in the mews. She's in there.'' Latimer hooked his thumb in the direction of Hunter's bedroom. ''Barstow's keeping watch at the moment.''

''By hell, someone's to answer for this.'' Adam paled beneath his tan. ''She's in danger still, you say? Because of her health? Or because of something else?''

''She'll do well enough,'' Hunter said. ''She's got some lumps but they're healing.''

''Because of Hunter's celebrated case,'' Latimer said, ''She's at risk of another attack. Not that it's Hunter's fault.''

''Thanks,'' Hunter said. He hadn't taken his eyes

from big, glowing, far-too-handsome Adam Chillworth. Now there was stud material if Hunter had ever seen it. Oh yes, indeed, there couldn't be much doubt that the stuff of fine children ran strong in the appropriate places in Adam's body.

Adam would not be allowed to be alone with Sibyl.

Neither would Latimer. And the main thing there was that nothing intimate should even start. A little of Latimer's celebrated sensual imagination, and his antics might well appeal to Hunter's darling, highly sexual Sibyl.

"She's asleep," Latimer said. "She looks lovely even with the bruises. A beautiful creature. I must admit that although I always thought of her as pretty, I'd never noticed that she's a late bloomer. She's burst forth into a complete charmer. There's a sensuality about her. Her body is still small because she's small of stature, but it's full and ripe, now. You take a look for yourself, Adam."

Hunter seethed. He'd like to take Latimer by the throat, but if he showed any reaction at all he'd give his feelings away and he wasn't ready, might never be ready.

"She's changed," Latimer said, apparently blissfully unaware of Hunter's mounting rage. "She's more outgoing, more—more worldly, but in the best possible way."

"I've also thought she was beautifully made and ready to mature into a very desirable woman," Adam said. "I'd like to paint her nude. I'd want to capture that blossoming into full womanhood. Excuse me." He went to the door of the bedroom, knocked and walked in. "Hello, Mrs. Barstow, it's Adam. Just got back and heard about Sibyl. Terrible thing. Lucky there's you to watch over her. I've brought you a little something from France, by the way. You shall have it as soon as I unpack my bags. Halibut was outside so I gathered him up and brought him in. Sibyl loves him. Animals are supposed to be good for someone who is sick. All right if I put him on her bed to keep her company?"

Latimer and Adam spoke about Sibyl as if she were a marriage-hunting female at a ball. And Adam wanted to paint her nude. The gall of the man.

"Oh, Mr. Adam." Barstow twittered. "We have missed you. You look so big and handsome. Enough to sweep all the girls off their feet."

Adam chuckled. "You'll be turning my head, Mrs. B. What do you think about the cat?"

"Good idea. Very good idea. Put him beside her carefully. I've got her on her side to keep the pressure off her back."

Hunter mimicked Barstow's simpering, caught Latimer's amused eyes and looked away.

"That's the way," Barstow said. "A kiss from a strong, caring man can be a powerful healer, or so they say. I wouldn't know."

"Damn it all," Hunter muttered. "Taking advantage of a sleeping woman."

Latimer frowned deeply and said, "Don't think much of that myself. Shouldn't think it a good idea to let the man be alone with Sibyl, should you?"

"Absolutely not. No, that's absolutely not on."

The bedroom door closed and Hunter looked at Latimer. "Now why would that be necessary?"

"It isn't," Latimer said. "But Barstow's in there. Take comfort in that. Why would you have Sibyl here rather than in her own place?"

The question made Hunter uncomfortable but he was well set with his excuses now and he had Sibyl where he wanted her and where he intended her to stay. "I was the one who discovered her and what had happened to her—and why. I must take responsibility for taking care of her—in particular of guarding her against any possible new attack. I can't be running up and down the stairs to check on her, or sleeping in her sitting room to guard her. The other rooms on Sibyl's floor need a thorough cleaning and rearranging, and they would all be too distant if someone crept into her apartments."

"Admirable," Latimer said, but he looked sour. "I should point out that there are two bedrooms in my flat. Finch's is still in perfect condition. I could work at home and keep watch over her for you. I don't have to leave the house as you do."

And wouldn't that be convenient? Hunter almost asked Latimer what had transpired between himself and Sibyl when she had been with him in his room for so long. That would be a foolish move.

"This is *my* affair," he told Latimer. "*My* fault. No one else's. Sibyl will not be moved from these apartments and no one new is to be introduced into this house. The staff will do what's necessary and my aunt is more than anxious to help."

Latimer bristled. "You aren't her husband, you know, old boy. But you're remarkably possessive for a man who treated her so badly when she visited you a few nights ago." Color shot across Latimer's cheekbones.

Hunter shot from his seat. "What the hell do you mean by that?"

"Keep your voice down," Latimer told him. "It was the following night when she came to me. She was desperately lonely and couldn't sleep, and then she saw me crossing the vestibule to go to my rooms and found the courage to knock on my door. She made up all sorts of nonsense about just needing to be with a friend for a little while, but gradually it all came out, you cad."

Hunter made fists, but shoved them in his pockets

out of harm's way. "We had a small disagreement. Nothing more." Why had he let her leave as he had? He'd been a thoughtless bastard, and this was the result.

"I'd hardly call it small to turn aside the overtures of a shy girl."

"A shy girl with a ripe body who has matured into a worldly woman of the best kind? Your words, not mine." Hunter closed in on Latimer. "You want her for yourself, don't you? Come on man, have the courage to confess your true feelings."

"I want her for myself," Latimer said calmly. "Frankly, I don't think I'd ever looked at her in the light in which I saw her during that visit. And the request she made—I don't think she intended to make it to me, but she did—she had made it to you and you turned her down. You made her feel lewd and no better than she should be. You are an old-fashioned man. I am not."

"You mean she asked you to do something directly? She spelled it out?"

Latimer raised his already arched brows. "I am to think about it and give her my answer. I'm ready to do so. And it's all your fault, Lloyd, for treating her so shabbily. She turned to the only true friend she has in this house and I can't tell you how glad I am."

"Because you love her?" Hunter detested himself for the mistakes he'd made.

Latimer paused a little too long. "I care for her a great deal."

"And you care for her ripe body more," Hunter said, knowing he was pushing the mark and not caring. "Thank you for comforting Sibyl when she needed it. Consider your task done."

The door to the bedchamber opened and both men jumped when Adam emerged, smiling. *Smiling,* mind you. Hunter chafed his palms rapidly together. "How does she seem to you?"

"Well, there's a chap out there who'll get his just reward. I'll hunt the devil down and give him some of his own medicine."

"*I* will be the one hunting him down," Hunter said.

Adam smiled his charming smile that didn't appear too often. "And I'll be helping you. But she's coming along. She woke a little and smiled at me. And any man would enjoy being that cat. Took him right into her bed, she did."

"Have a care," Hunter said.

"My." Adam chuckled. "When did you become possessive over Sibyl? Can't say I ever noticed it before I left."

"I'm not possessive. She was hurt because of me and I must protect her—from dangerous villains, and from any who would take sexual advantage of her.''

Adam sputtered. ''Sexual advantage?''

''Hunter's a bit put out about a lot of things,'' Latimer said. ''You'll have to forgive him. He's not himself.''

Sibyl heard raised and angry voices from the next room but they quickly dropped to a quiet rumble.

She smiled at Barstow, who had been so kind, and the housekeeper smiled back. ''I'm afraid tempers are running high this afternoon,'' she said. ''You know how men are. They can't make a point without shouting and posturing. But I'd say all three of those strapping—and elegant—males are taken with you.''

''Oh, fiddlededee,'' Sibyl said, her face suddenly too warm, ''Why would men like that look at me?''

Barstow gave a secret smile and went back to her crocheting. ''Some things are obvious if we use our eyes and our heads. That cat shouldn't be inside the bed.''

''He comforts me,'' Sibyl said, ''although I'm worried about him. I suppose he got himself into trouble at Riverside Place and Jean-Marc has dispatched him back to London with a coachman to be taken care of by the staff at Number 17. They will not care about him, so I shall keep him here. After all, he is a member of the family and I must ensure his safety for Desirée.''

''The Princess Desirée,'' Barstow said dreamily. She had always been overwhelmed by people of rank, particularly people of royal rank.

''Yes, and don't you agree with me that nothing should be said to my dear Meggie about what has happened to me? I really wanted to ask your advice and help in this matter. If she were to find out, she would rush back here, terribly upset. And there is dear baby Serena. It would be bad for Meggie's milk and the baby does so thrive on being nursed by her mother.''

''You have my support,'' Barstow said, sitting up straight in her chair. ''That Meg is a sensible woman. She's gone against what's expected of women of her rank because she wants to do what's best for her child. An admirable woman, that. You've got my promise of help. We just won't say anything.''

''Thank you, Barstow.'' Sibyl's eyes grew heavy. She still ached considerably and the villain's boots had left such painful welts around her eye.

She sank low under the covers and pulled a satisfied Halibut into the curve of her body.

And realization, a string of realizations, hit her so hard she almost sat up. Instead, she pulled the sheet halfway over her face and concentrated furiously.

Hunter and Latimer were two very different men but with one common trait. They were both a bit shy. Hunter was especially shy—when it came to women. She had shocked him and he was posturing as a man of the world who was completely unaccustomed to being so boldly approached by a female. She felt completely awake and amazed she hadn't thought of this before. From her reading she knew that men suffered from sexual frustration and vented this in different ways. Hunter rode his horse like a fiend in all winds and weathers. Latimer worked especially hard. Adam—she smiled at his sweetness and soft kiss—well frankly, Adam was rather obviously masculine and sexual and he chose to lock himself away with his painting. Most of which no one ever saw. And who knew what he did when he went out—which he did quite frequently? She blushed beneath the sheet. There were places for men with fierce appetites and no outlet to go.

But back to her dear Hunter. He even moved excessively rapidly. Yes, yes, Hunter needed to sleep with a woman, regularly, and he needed intrigue and vigor in that part of his life. Out of concern for her—possibly because he didn't believe the reason she'd given for wanting him—he'd drawn back exactly when he should have, well, *gone on.* And she knew the truth. He was definitely frustrated and a little afraid of her.

Never mind. Soon she would be well, although perhaps she wouldn't let everyone know how well she was, not at once, and she would simply find her time to pounce on him. Oh, that was a dreadful way to explain what she had in mind. She would, after returning to her rooms, go to him and explain how exhausted and frightened she was. She'd also explain she felt she needed his protection. She fully expected that he would tuck her away in his bed again. Her job was to tuck him away with her.

Very carefully, Sibyl turned over. Promptly, Halibut slithered his considerable body over her waist to settle against her tummy again.

Two more revelations had presented themselves and they were both concerning.

Her child's father could only be a man she loved as well as admired. Now that was unfortunate. The love of a child was almost definitely tied up with love between the child's parents. If Hunter absolutely refused to comply with her wishes, but Latimer offered to deal with the difficulty like a man and sacrifice himself—what then? She liked Latimer, in a way she loved him, but only like a brother.

She shouldn't even think of Adam. He was virile and strong. She had felt his strength, carefully harnessed, when he had kissed her a little earlier. He might help her, or his strong sense of right and wrong might put her request on the "wrong" side and leave true trouble in its wake. It didn't help that her new curse—the one that caused her to see handsome men nude even though they were fully clothed—had come back in Adam's presence. She had deliberately checked the condition out on Old Coot, and on a number of other men of mature age and there had been nothing, no change at all. It never happened at all with women. She had relaxed about the whole thing, but then Adam arrived.

Oh, dear. Oh, how fortunate she was not attracted to him. He had stood by the bed with the hard muscles in his belly contracted in ridges. His chest was extremely broad and the hair there was as curly and dark as the hair on his head. His shoulders could easily belong to a field hand who actively used them all day. So strongly made were his thighs that one or two parts of them didn't entirely come together.

She remembered a little of the old nursery rhyme: "The better to grasp your body tight while I pleasure, then enter you." Well, maybe that was Little Red Riding Hood and the grandmother and somewhat different words. But there was something of the wolf in Adam and it excited Sibyl. His penis all but defied description...but not quite. To accommodate it somewhat more tidily inside his trousers, and, no doubt, to attempt to make its proportions less obvious, he pressed it back between his thighs. Unfortunately, when he became a little aroused it began to slide forward, and when he became considerably aroused, it released itself entirely and thrust out. Only his clothes held it somewhat in check. That part of him was long and full and hard, with the circumference of a quite considerable wine bottle. The end made a small bead of fluid, promising its readiness to perform.

Sibyl pushed deeper beneath the bedcovers. Adam's most private flesh was pale against the thick thatch of black hair at its base and the hair on his chest was curly and black, but looked soft. He was beautifully made and it was more than fortunate that she knew the one and only man for her was Hunter, who was also fabulously made.

But this was dreadful. *She* was dreadful. She was a dreadful woman and must go to church to discuss her sins.

"Are you sleeping, Miss Sibyl?" Barstow whispered.

Sibyl held very still and didn't reply.

A creak and a rustle let her know Barstow had got out of her chair. She tiptoed to the door, rustling with every step, and opened it. "Just going to get a cup of tea," she told whoever was outside. "No one in this room, mind. Miss Smiles is sleeping. She needs her rest."

The door closed again and Sibyl was left alone.

Another revelation emerged. There was no longer anything artificial about her manner, the way she moved her head, looked at someone, walked. She had changed. How did that make her feel? Well, people changed, that was all, and there was no reason why she should be less likely to change than any other. She had become more mature, more sure of herself, more sure of what she wanted. And she had become interested in men. Not just interested in their appearance and the way they spoke or danced or any of those other unimportant things. She was interested in men as men, most particularly in their entire selves, the way they looked, and moved—with women—when they made love.

To the church with her the moment she was well enough to face the derision she was bound to meet.

Could it be that some of Hunter's odd behavior toward her, his almost violent behavior, then his clear desire to be with her, and, yet again, his rude rejection was the result of his deep concern about something professional? After what happened a few days ago, there was no doubt that a great deal was amiss. She'd been the vehicle used to deliver a threat to him.

The door handle turned slowly and carefully. Someone was opening the door and trying not to make a sound. Sibyl held her breath.

Someone crept into the room. A man. She heard his boots creak. It wasn't possible that Hunter, Latimer and Adam had all left and this was a stranger—was it?

The door closed again.

Sibyl had been able to eat little since the assault and her stomach burned. She was tight all over—she hurt all over, even more than before.

She kept very still and pulled Halibut close. The cat complained a little, but then held still. Dearest of cats.

"Sibyl? Are you really asleep, my darling?"

My darling? She opened her good eye and looked into Hunter's face. He knelt beside the bed and ducked his head until his concerned face was on a level with hers.

"You aren't asleep," he said, stroking her cheek with the backs of his fingers. "How do you feel now?"

She smiled and knew swelling made it a lopsided smile. "Forgive me for looking so awful," she said. "I feel better, really I do."

"Already you are much improved. You are a brave woman. A beautiful, brave woman."

If she weren't already lying down, she'd faint. "Thank you."

"If fate smiles, perhaps we shall work something out together."

"Work something out?" Oh, no, it was happening again. Fortunately she could only see his upper body, and a fine body it was. She loved the way his muscles distended when he held them stiff as he did now, and the veins that rose over his arms and over his shoulders. And the perfect pattern of hair on his chest.

Oh, really, she must find something else to do other than look at the hair on various parts of men's bodies—when she wasn't looking at other things, that was.

He offered her a hand and she pulled one of hers from the bed. He took it to his lips and his eyes closed while he kissed it gently, repeatedly, in every spot imaginable. "Perhaps we can work something out for the future," he said at last. "Perhaps there is some future for us if we can be patient."

Her heart beat uncomfortably. "Perhaps. What made you think of this now?"

"The terrible weight of responsibility on my shoulders. Do you remember exactly what that wretch said about Charles? That there would be no need for me to look for him unless I did as they'd asked me to do. You know what that means?"

"That you are to take steps to have the sentencing delayed pending the production of new evidence."

"Correct." He stared at her until she lowered her

gaze. "Yet my superior has advised against it—at least until there is definite evidence that we should act." Then she felt his lips on her neck. He kissed her there, and trailed his tongue over the skin until she shivered and her nipples became stiff with longing, and other parts of her ached and grew moist. "You are the most sensuous creature I have ever met, Sibyl. And I had no idea. How could that be?"

"We have been polite neighbors. The topic never arose."

He laughed lightly. "Perhaps that's it. I have something to ask you."

She held her breath again. What would be her reply, her answer?

"May I ask you, Sibyl?"

She nodded.

"Thank you. I beg you not to mention what your attacker said about Charles Greevy-Sims."

A wretched blush shot over her face and she felt weak with disappointment and embarrassment. "I promise I won't."

"Bless you. I have no doubt he would carry out his threat and kill him. Tomorrow I intend to go to that house in Curzon Street and demand access. Then I shall search it from top to bottom. If I am confronted by an enemy, I shall tell him I have spoken to the courts but that it is my job to continue looking for my friend."

"And I shall come with you."

Hunter stared at her, his lips parted. "Don't be foolish. You are injured and need rest."

"I don't intend to run a race, merely to accompany you. And we will make sure there is someone nearby in case we don't return in reasonable time. Latimer will do that."

"Latimer is already coming."

"Good," Sibyl said. "Then he'll drive the coach and wait for us. I suggest that I go in with you because I will not be a threat and the woman in the house is more likely to speak to me. Don't you agree?"

He touched her mouth and looked at her. His tough expression softened. "I agree, yes. And I think you are remarkable. You are a clever manipulator but you are also...clever. I must warn you to remain close to me, though. It could well be that someone with a connection to that house is responsible for beating you."

"I know that," she said quietly. "We will be vigilant. But we move tomorrow? And you'll speak with Latimer this evening while my ladies meet here with me? They sent a letter to Lady Hester, asking to see me, and she agreed."

Hunter's expression gave away that he'd had no idea about any meeting. But then, why should he? He'd never been told about it.

"Will you, Hunter?"

"For you, Miss Smiles, I would do almost anything. Yes, I will talk to Latimer."

"And you will not try to sneak away without me tomorrow?"

He paused with his lips parted, then pursed them and blew air out slowly.

"Hunter?"

"Er, no, no, I absolutely shall not attempt to sneak away without you. Sibyl, I will not leave the house without you when next I go to Curzon Street. Do you trust me in this?"

She looked back at him and the power of her feelings for him brought her close to tears. "I trust you absolutely."

Once more he kissed her neck. Then he stood. "Barstow will return and I'd better be in the study."

"Yes," she said, afraid her voice would break. "You must go quickly."

Still he stood, looking down at her, his eyes filled with some emotion she couldn't decipher.

"Go," she said, "Now."

He nodded and walked to open the door. Once it was open, he stood there, staring at her.

"Hunter," Sibyl said. "I must say something to you, but then you absolutely must leave or Barstow will tattle and make a great deal more out of this meeting than she should."

"Say it, Sibyl."

"I love you. I think I have loved you from the first time we met. That love has only grown stronger. I know there are things that cannot be between us, so I do not long for them. But I do still pray that you will help me achieve what I so want to achieve."

"Sibyl, my dear. This is so difficult. Do you think—"

"I think I hear Barstow coming. Go now. I shall always love you, Hunter."

20

Later that evening when Hunter returned to his study, his aunt waited for him wearing the kind of smile that unnerved her nephew. "Good evening, Aunt," he said. "I had to go out and do a little business but I'm back now. Once Barstow is ready to retire, she should do so. I'm more than comfortable on the couch."

"Oh, Hunter, dear boy," Aunt Hester said, hurrying to him and wrapping her hands over his. There was something vaguely pitying in her voice, a hint of his not being quite mature enough to handle anything even slightly taxing. "You are taking all of this far too much to heart. Accidents happen. Sibyl would be the first to agree with me. She is so much improved already. And we all think it would be for the best if you slept in her rooms tonight. Run along and get a good night's sleep."

"Absolutely not," Hunter said. "We've had this discussion and I've told you my place is near Sibyl. She went through a terrible experience because of me and I have vowed to look after her. I left this evening because Adam promised he would be at home and Barstow agreed to send for him if necessary."

"Yes, yes, yes," Aunt Hester said. "But everything is all right and there's no need for you to lose sleep now. I just took dear Sibyl the gift of a small book of poetry. Actually some of Lord Byron's pieces. They are a little flamboyant for me, but the young are so much more open-minded. Barstow is going to read to her later when she's ready to sleep. For now she is not to be disturbed."

Hunter looked around. If Aunt Hester intended to make things difficult for him, then he could only show her that he would not be treated like a child. "There is the little library. There's a couch in there. Not as comfortable as that in my study, but it will do. I shall stay there."

"Hunter—"

"Aunt. The subject is closed. Except that I'd like to know why you are so determined to keep me away from Sibyl."

Aunt Hester arched her neck and leaned her head from side to side as if easing some stiffness. "I don't know what you mean."

"Yes, you do. You don't want Sibyl and me together, especially alone, even though you know I can be trusted." Might he be forgiven for lying.

"Hunter, it's time you looked for a wife."

Closing his mouth took several seconds. "Oh, really."

"Yes, really. You need a wife and I hope you will bring her here—to visit. She would certainly be welcome. It's time I spent money on this house."

Spivey here. My bones ache and my spirit shivers at the very thought of what Hester may have in mind. But it is not my place to interrupt. Not now. We'll speak again later....

"We both know Sibyl is only your friend," Aunt Hester continued, "but sometimes proximity confuses rational thought and one becomes muddled. You might give her notions you wouldn't want her to have. Sibyl is of simple beginnings, certainly not a suitable partner for you. Even if you were thinking of such a thing, which I know you aren't. But have a care, nephew. You could hurt a girl and neither of us should like that. In time Sibyl may meet someone suitable—although I doubt it. Not that it matters because she will always have a home here. And think of it—while you are being so very protective of Sibyl, you are missing opportunities to make a brilliant match."

Hunter stared hard at her. In other words, Auntie dear wanted to keep Sibyl for herself and she'd like

Hunter to leave with a woman likely to advance his stature. "I'm going to read," he said abruptly. "So I'll wish you good-night."

Once closed inside the library, he stripped off the sheets that had covered the slippery leather couch, shook them out, and hoped he didn't sneeze to death when he tried to sleep beneath them.

Damn it, but he would have expected his aunt to be more supportive, more interested in his getting whatever would make him most happy.

Spivey here again. Just had to drop in and give you a more detailed progress report. Terrible pity about Sibyl. Disgrace, that man beating her like that. I fear there will be more nastiness before we are done here. Although I assure you I shall do my best to avert any repeat of the last debacle. Too bad that very nasty cat, Halibut, is in residence. Now that one can be a terrible nuisance.

Ivy Willow has come along very well and she has promised to reveal our newly agreed-upon excuse for her calling Hunter away to his chambers only if that becomes necessary. She also promises to behave herself and do what she can to further my cause, my cause to empty this house of interlopers. I do believe I grow better at dealing with my human helpers. After all, on the occasions when I need a visible emissary to intercede for me, I must be cer-

tain that emissary hears only my thoughts and speaks only my words.

I'm bemused about which course to take with Hester. Hunter's right. The woman wants to keep Sibyl at her beck and call. In fact it's certain she doesn't wish the girl to marry at all. I rather think Hester really did hope Hunter would fall for her friend's girl, marry her, and set up a home elsewhere. She most certainly wants him to leave Mayfair Square. Mercy me, I am not opposed to the idea of Hunter leaving this house, not at all, but I cannot bear to think of Sibyl producing an infant by one of her willing sires, and then staying here with the child.

Hester is continuing with her potential plans to remodel the house, you know. I heard her ask to speak to Adam a little earlier and I'm sure the subject will arise then.

Mark my words. If Sibyl were to have a child by Hunter, this entire house would become a shrine to the family. Give me strength.

Good heavens. Here comes Reverend Smiles—here—in this very house. I thought he wasn't allowed to visit as yet. "What ho, Reverend. Out of your precinct, aren't you?"

"I learned my daughter, Sibyl, was hurt by some madman. I was given leave to make sure for myself that she is well enough."

"Oh, Reverend, I must appear distraught to you."

How I hate this play-acting. Wringing my hands and shaking my head doesn't come easily.

"A dreadful thing, Reverend. I had hoped she would be completely well before you needed hear anything about it. She is certainly recovering. And the good folk of the household are keeping careful watch over her."

Look at that, my friends. The way in which the Reverend's nose is in the air as he glides up the stairs. Even the most humble of these people become haughty once their wings are bigger than they are. I shall wait here to show respect, and wave him out as he goes.

"Spivey!"

He's back already? He only just went up there. And he looks most displeased.

"At your service as always, my dear Reverend."

"There is a gaggle of females in the room with her, so I shall not stay. But you're right. She looks quite glowing. Listen to me well, Spivey. You are being watched. It's possible that there may be higher things in store for you if you perform well. If you don't perform well...I regret to say it, but if you don't look after Sibyl and make sure she comes to no more harm, there is a place for a washroom attendant at the school for retraining those with a

penchant for making themselves vomit—not that there's much success with the retraining.

"Do you get my meaning, Spivey?"

"I do indeed, Reverend."

Adam crept down the stairs from the attic. Barstow hadn't come for him, but he heard odd sounds. Scrapings and carefully soft footsteps. By damn, if anyone was sneaking up on Sibyl, God help them.

A light shone under Lady Hester's door but it was firmly closed. If he had to guess, he'd say Barstow was still with Sibyl. He put his ear to a panel in the study door to Hunter's suite and heard the distant sound of light voices. Barstow and Sibyl, he imagined. He'd given considerable thought to painting Sibyl nude and was convinced it would be a most beautiful testimony to emerging womanhood, even though Sibyl was cmcrging a littlc latc. From hcr appearance she could very well be no more than nineteen or twenty.

He stood still and listened. There it was again, that swishing sound, a creak. He didn't like it that he lived on the floor above. Might take him too long to get down here if he was needed. Given Hunter's foul mood, he dare not wait in the man's study where he could be comfortable. No, it would have to be the broom closet behind the staircase. He let himself in and was ridiculously excited to find a shooting stick. He opened the small seat, balanced on its single leg and leaned against the wall. But he must not sleep or he'd overbalance and the result would be disastrous. He almost wished the villain would make his move. They'd be bound to catch the slimy fellow and he'd be no more threat. Plus, Hunter's mind would be at ease and perhaps they could all return to some sort of order.

Inside the cupboard that smelled of beeswax and Fuller's Earth, he settled himself as comfortably as possible and held very still. The soft swishing sound continued to come, but less frequently.

Hunter tried repeatedly to arrange the dusty sheets over him. With the extremely slippery surface of the couch, the task became almost impossible. The fact that he must pause every few seconds and listen to unexpected creakings, apparently on this floor, was of considerable concern. He looked through the keyhole, but the landing was dark and he saw nothing. He took heart in the certainty that if anyone tried to get to Sibyl, Barstow would scream bloody murder and the noise would be heard for miles around. He visualized Barstow trying to read the sensuous, overwrought lines of Byron aloud to Sibyl and the thought made him smile. "Bide your time, Hunter, and you'll get what you want." Sibyl's declaration of her love for him had all but undone him. She had looked at him, her pale and bruised face filled with that very love and with uncertainty, and almost definitely with the conviction that he would deny her.

He had neither denied, nor given her his love in return.

Please let him have the courage to do what he must do, what he wanted to do.

"Now, you're sure you wish to remain with us, Barstow?" Sibyl asked, although, kind as she was, she rather wished Barstow would return to her rooms now that the ladies of her club had arrived.

After seeing Sibyl's plasters and the bruises that were now more green than purple, each woman had held her hands and dropped kisses on her brow. Jenny sat beside her on the bed and her eyes were still filled with angry tears.

"If it's agreeable with all of you," Barstow said, "I should love to remain. After all, this is a meeting for unmarried females who have not had particular luck with members of the opposite sex. I do fit those criteria."

"Bravo," Ivy Willow said, resplendent in her favorite purple. "You certainly do fit those criteria, but don't you think we should make sure Gertrude is comfortable with certain other elements of our discussions, ladies?"

"Absolutely," Phyllis Smart said. She was in dark yellow today and appeared much more cheerful than usual. "You see, Gertrude, we are dedicated to open conversation about the male, including those parts of him that they would keep secret from us."

Barstow's hands flew to her mouth, but she recovered quickly and appeared pleased with the idea. "About time," she said. "You have no idea how long I have wondered about such things."

"We try t'be circumspect," said sweet Jenny. "But we've all one thing in common."

"Barstow," Sibyl said in a great hurry. "Do you think you will be able to keep your counsel from Lady Hester? At least for the moment?"

"Certainly," Barstow said.

"Then we are agreed." Ivy gave the rest of her group her sharp look. "We will start you off by showing you the most interesting book that has come to our attention. And we will be able to tell you exactly what is hidden there."

Desirée's precious volume was produced and opened on Barstow's lap. Sibyl whispered in Ivy's ear, "There are things I must discuss and Barstow cannot be present." Ivy's serious response was, "Leave that to me."

"Well," Barstow said, but rather than falling back in her chair, she bent over the pictures. "Well,

I never. Imagine that real men allowed themselves to be painted for such a volume.''

''Ye have no idea,'' Jenny said. ''We've the truth of it all now.

''We've been able to verify what's underneath those black squares. Not frightening at all, Gertrude. Verra interesting and rather exciting, in fact.''

''Really?'' Barstow's gray eyes were growing larger by the moment. ''Oh, I should like to see that with my own eyes, shouldn't you?''

Sibyl smiled, but she studied Barstow. And a very sturdy, upstanding woman she was. Somewhat plain, but with fine eyes and a good, comely body. Perhaps there was some sensible man somewhere who would do very well for her. After all, as Ivy said, this was their purpose.

''Oh, Gertrude,'' Ivy said, the picture of a brilliant creature not quite of this world, ''If I could go and make some tea, I would, but I doubt I'd do well in that kitchen of yours.''

''I'll be glad to go,'' Barstow said. ''I'll turn the book upside down not to lose my place. The rest of you must promise not to take your eyes off Sibyl.''

''Och, we will'na,'' Jenny said. ''Poor, wee thing. We'll watch her every minute and that's a promise.''

They waited until the door closed and a few

minutes passed before they all started whispering at once.

Latimer watched through the crack in his door as Barstow, an unfamiliar bloom on her cheeks, descended the main staircase and made for the kitchen. Perhaps what he'd heard had been her moving about upstairs. He stepped out into the vestibule, stood at the foot of the stairs and closed his eyes to concentrate.

There it was again. A scraping sound, as if something slid along the wall, only to be quickly caught. He went up the stairs on tiptoe and into the sitting room at 7B, where he breathed deeply of the lovely clean scent of Sibyl. Why, oh, why had he hesitated in accepting her proposition? No matter, that would be put right in short order.

In the darkness, he stood with the door open the smallest fraction and his ears straining for any sound. There is was again, the odd sound of something slipping suddenly sideways along a wall, only to be stopped quickly, and he could have sworn he heard a muffled oath. Then there was, from time to time, a thump as if someone or something fell on the floor, following by a great shaking of fabric and then silence again.

What the devil was happening here?

* * *

"So, you actually spoke to him again and—and—oh, Sibyl, you actually asked Hunter if he would be the father of your child?"

"I did," Sibyl said. There would be no dishonesty with her friends. "And he refused again. Or he certainly didn't say he would.... There were some fascinating interludes, but he stopped short of actually, well, doing it."

"Oh, Sibyl, you poor thing. So close and yet so far away."

"You'll never know how close," Sibyl said.

"What does that mean?" Phyllis asked. "Did you take off all your clothes this time? Did he take off his?"

There was a communal holding of breath before Sibyl said, "Yes, on both counts."

All that breath expelled like a gale. "Did you, well—" Jenny's green eyes were round. "Was it all it the dark—as I expect it was—or did you *see* anything?"

"I saw everything," Sibyl said, not without a certain pride.

"Oh, my." Phyllis's hand went to her breast. "I have a child, but I saw nothing, I tell you, nothing. And was left with a most unpleasant impression."

"That will be changed," Sibyl announced. "Not a woman in this room will go without finding joy with a man. I'm convinced this can be achieved."

Jenny's response was a serious and rather small, "Oh."

"I must hurry or Barstow will be back. In time she may earn full entrance to our club. Unlike some, I do not believe that people become too old to find love, but she isn't ready, particularly in such difficult times. Now, I need your help. I know I promised I wouldn't fall in love with any man, but the truth is that I love Hunter."

"I think that's lovely," Jenny said.

Phyllis's response was, "A useless disaster. You must get over it."

Ivy sighed and said, "He is rather lovely. But you said he will not agree."

"He will not."

"Then we need another."

"Latimer More may help me."

"I'm not sure I know who he is," Jenny said.

"Big quiet fellow at 7A," Ivy said. "Good-looking and I always think these quiet types can be veritable storms between the sheets. Pursue him, Sibyl."

"How would you know?" Phyllis asked, her eyes narrowed.

Ivy blushed. She found her abominable box of snuff and partook deeply. "I've embarrassed myself," she said. "I don't suppose I do know. I let my imagination go too far."

''Regardless,'' Sibyl said. ''I want Hunter.''

Ivy put the back of a hand to her brow and tottered backward to sit in Barstow's chair. She popped up to remove the book Barstow had been studying, and plopped down again. ''This is always the danger. That some silly girlish nonsense will interfere with common sense.''

''She canna help it if she's in love with Hunter,'' Jenny said. ''Perhaps we should be helping her work out how to succeed with him. After all, they've been naked together.'' She shivered again. ''What does he look like, if ye don't mind me askin'?''

''Never mind that,'' Phyllis said. ''The sooner we dispense with foolish dreams about a man who isn't interested in anything but getting inside your drawers, the better. But you are here in his bedchamber, Sibyl. Would a man with absolutely no interest in you have you in his bed?''

''He feels guilty that he wasn't there to protect me.'' She explained the details.

''It's all horrible,'' Jenny said, ''but I think he loves ye, too.'' She avoided Phyllis's sharp gaze.

''I told him I loved him,'' she said quietly. ''He didn't answer me.''

''You silly, silly girl,'' Phyllis said. ''Now he knows he has you exactly where he wants you and can use you as he pleases. Oh, fie, you have ruined everything."

"Why?" Jenny asked. "What can be so wrong with honesty? If all he can give you is the child you want, Sibyl, then you still have a very good thing—a wee baby by a man you adore. And if he cannot say he loves you, too, then he is an honest man. And that is a fine thing. What did you say he looked like—without clothes?"

"He's more long and lean than Latimer or Adam. Adam is, of course, exceedingly tall with such broad shoulders one would think he had done manual labor all his life rather than been a painter. Hunter has broad shoulders and I like the way his muscles are delineated. His chest is broad, his waist narrow and the hair on his chest smooth and black. Around his—well, his shaft, it is more coarse, but from what I've seen of Latimer and Adam, that tends to be the case."

At first the utter silence in the room made Sibyl insecure, but then she realized she was telling her sisters in the quest the very things they so desperately wanted to discover.

"Um, Latimer and Adam?" Jenny said, but she shook her head and said, "Go on."

"Hunter's legs are perfect. Long and so well-shaped. And his buttocks are marvelous. Solid. I should think the riding had a great deal to do with that. When his manly part was fully distended it was so firm that it scarcely moved. It could obviously be embarrassing to have it bob around when a man is working. Adam is extraordinary in that respect. He has to tuck himself back between his legs to keep things a little neater. But once he becomes aroused, it pops out. Quite extraordinary.

"Now Latimer is a spectacular specimen. His stomach draws in, accentuating the fullness of muscle in his thighs. Not a pinch of fat on him anywhere. Not on any one of them. Incredible men among men, I can tell you. But Hunter will always be the man I love."

"The body ye love?" Jenny said quietly.

Sibyl pursed her lips and said, "Well, yes. But that is secondary to the man himself. He is a gem. Intelligent, honorable, so wise and kindhearted, but sensible. Perfect."

Phyllis fanned herself and said, "Let me get my breath. You have quite overcome me, Sibyl."

Ivy cleared her throat. Her face was as brightly painted as usual. "I wouldn't wish to be judgmental, but I am surprised that you found opportunities to be naked with all three men."

Sibyl blinked rapidly, then said, "Oh, no. Only with Hunter." She sighed and closed her eyes. "Oh, my goodness, no wonder you are all shocked. I'll explain. But first, thanks to your silken ropes, Ivy, that evening will live with me forever. But as to the other things. I don't even know how to tell you this. But I have developed this gift—if that's what you want to call it. I can see through men's clothes. Young and virile men. It doesn't happen with older gentlemen or with women. Now, what do you think of that? Have you ever heard of such a thing before?"

Silence fell as if a bride had just entered a chapel.

"It is all absolutely clear, I tell you. I had not known that some men pop their private parts away to the left, and others to the right. They do, you know, except for Adam."

"We heard," Phyllis said. She looked dreamy. "I should like to see that myself. But Sibyl. Seeing through men's clothes? Are you sure?"

"Sure enough to wish the curse would leave me at once. When any one of those men turn around to walk away, you have no idea what it does to me."

"I could take a good guess," Ivy said.

"I actually have to stop myself from reaching out to take hold of their buttocks."

Jenny dropped on her back across the bottom of the bed and started to giggle. "It's wonderful. Wonderfully dreadful, but I'll happily look after the curse for you while you take a little break if you like."

* * *

Latimer went swiftly and silently up a flight of stairs. There was no doubt that the noise and general sensation of unrest came from the next floor after that. Before he could set off upward again, the red-haired girl, one of Sibyl's friends, came tripping downward. She held her yellow chintz dress well above neat ankles and playfully hopped down from stair to stair. He stood aside and at first she didn't see him in the failing light.

Her auburn hair had been braided from the crown, a very thick braid that doubled up on itself, and she'd tucked some small yellow flowers in one side of it. He got the impression she hadn't much money. Possibly a hole in her white cotton hose helped that idea. He partly turned away as if going downward, then looked at her as she drew level and said, "You startled me, miss. I didn't see you coming. Latimer More, at your service."

"How d'ye do, Sir. Jenny McBride, I am. From just outside Edinburgh. D'ye know Edinburgh? A very beautiful city it is—and I say it even though I was born and bred there."

"I have been there and it is beautiful. But not as beautiful as some of its women." Good grief, he was becoming a man of true charm. Charm had not always necessarily played a part in that for which he was famous. "Have you just come from Sibyl?"

"Aye. And she's full enough o'life to gladden me heart. I'm away down t'see if I can help Barstow wi' the tea and biscuits."

"That accounts for all the noises up there," Latimer said, rather disappointed at the thought that this encounter could not last long.

"Not a bit o' it. We've been like church mice. Sibyl's t'be quiet." She raised her shoulders. "Not that there isn't plenty that's better whispered about."

"You haven't been creeping from room to room, or sliding things along walls?"

"Absolutely not." She looked into his face. Her own eyes were that lovely Scottish green that offset the auburn hair so beautifully. And her white skin was sprinkled with freckles over her nose and cheeks. There was silence, but not exactly awkward silence, more preoccupied if anything. Jenny held her head to one side and looked at him—really *at* him. She left no part of him unexamined and, to his amazement, lingered longest on his private parts.

Latimer was disposed to laugh, but managed to control himself. She was curious about him and evidently her curiosity extended to his male attributes. He would have to blame the devil's doing for his behavior, but he braced his legs apart, pushed back his jacket to place his fists on his hips and made no attempt to disguise the fact that fair Jenny's interest had aroused him.

She stared and stared, lips parted. Latimer grew more stimulated, and Jenny's eyes grew more round. She cleared her throat, said, "Well, I'd best be about my business," and went to pass him.

Latimer set the lightest of touches on her forearm and said, "Jenny McBride, do you like living in London?"

Her pink cheeks were a delight. "I do indeed, sir."

"And how do you make your way here?"

"Och, I'm nothing, really. I work in a milliner's shop sewing, sir. It doesna pay well, but the materials are so fine, they make me happy, and I've enough to get by. And one day, if I'm verra lucky, I'll be a real milliner myself."

Latimer turned the tables and treated Jenny to the type of scrutiny she'd used on him. By the time he looked at her face again, she was scarlet, but her chin was held high. He didn't care that her dress was threadbare or that he'd noted holes in her stockings and in her slippers. He said, "You sound as if you're in heaven when you speak of the fine things you work with. The women whose hats you work on are very fortunate." He also didn't say that despite a shapely body, it was too thin and she appeared in need of a few good meals. "Perhaps one day you'll have your own millinery shop."

She shook her head emphatically. "Oh, no, not

me. It's not that I canna design the hats, but I'd never have the... Well, I don't think that's in my future, sir. Thank you for talking to me. You're kind. And nice. I must be getting along."

"Yes," he said, watching her go.

The instant before she passed behind the staircase where the door to the kitchens was located, she glanced back at him. Latimer smiled and nodded and carried on upstairs.

An interesting creature, but not for him. He wasn't in the habit of taking advantage of girls who were down on their luck.

At the top of the second flight of stairs, he looked at the door to Hunter's rooms and immediately discarded that as a route to take. Out of the question also, were Lady Hester's rooms and Barstow's sitting room. Very little was left. His best course was to find a place to hide and wait.

There was a small library that hadn't, as far as he knew, been used for years. In there he could make himself as comfortable as possible and wait to see if he heard stealthy movement anywhere. It didn't help that apparently Sibyl was holding a meeting. She must be recovering well.

He slipped into the library, pulled a draped chair near the door and sat. He covered himself with the sheet, ready to listen and wait.

* * *

Adam placed his eye to the keyhole in time to see the library door close. Now that was damnably queer. That room was never used. Of course, it could be that the villain who attacked Sibyl earlier was skulking about in there waiting for a chance to injure her again. While he watched and tried to decide the best way to deal with this, Lady Hester's door opened and that lady, all afloat in pink muslin, trotted across to Hunter's rooms, let herself in, and closed the door.

Now that was either an even bigger nuisance, or it would help keep the enemy at bay, since he was unlikely to want to involve more people in his sinister plot.

There was nothing for it. He would have to confront the scoundrel in his lair.

Cramped from spending so much time in small quarters, Adam let himself out. He hadn't completely wasted his time in the cupboard. Expecting no real danger, he'd come from the attic unarmed. But in the broom closet he'd found a heavy clothes brush with a solid back and hard, brand-new bristles. A strong man could do some damage with that. As long as he wasn't facing firearms or knives.

Armed with the brush and bent double, Adam skirted the landing, swinging this way and that, watching for any sign of approaching interference.

He encountered none. Soon he noiselessly turned the handle on the library door and stepped inside. The heavy curtains were drawn and all he could make out were draped forms around the room.

A draped chair stood near the door and Adam sat on it, prepared to be ready for action.

"Get the hell off me," a voice roared, Latimer More's voice. "What in God's name do you think you're doing?"

Adam jumped up. So did Latimer. In the almost darkness they faced off and Latimer landed a solid blow to Adam's jaw. "If you want a fellow's knee to sit on, pick another, my fine fellow." He went to hit Adam again and his arm connected with the solid back of the clothes brush. Adam positioned himself as for a fencing match and went at Latimer, swinging the brush bristles from side to side.

"Damn your eyes, Chillworth," Latimer said. "You've injured my arm. Put that weapon down now."

Rather than put the brush down, Adam swung it in circles through the air, landing the stiff bristles on any unprotected part of Latimer he encountered. "You were waiting here for an opportunity to spend time alone with Sibyl. Admit it. You have eyes for her and you'll take advantage of whatever opportunity you have to get to her."

"And you?" Latimer said loudly. "What of you?

What are you doing creeping around down here when you're supposed to be in the attic? You were the one who talked about painting her nude, not me."

"And you were the one who pointed out how ripe she's become, how lush, how lovely despite her bruises."

Latimer grabbed up a figurine. "She is going to be mine. Put that in your pipe and smoke it. *Mine.* She's going to have my child."

"I beg your pardon?"

Latimer swung the figurine and broke it against a mirror, which also broke and fell down the wall in shards.

"The hell she is." A figure draped in sheets rose from a couch and rushed at them. "Just because she came to you when I said I needed time to think about impregnating her without marriage, and you're so desperate for a good poke that you could hardly wait to agree, now you say she's yours. Well, she isn't. Never. She's mine."

Adam blinked in the darkness. For an instant he forgot to defend himself and allowed the brush to fall to his side, at which point Latimer whacked his arm with what was left of the figurine.

"I say," Adam said, "Isn't it Hunter you should be thrashing? Or rather, isn't it time for a bit o' common sense here and a talk to get things straight?"

"Get things straight?" Latimer said, going into *en garde* position with the base of the figurine. "She asked him to father her child. He turned her down. She came to me. I didn't turn her down. How much straighter can it get than that?"

"Sibyl loves me and I love her," Hunter said. "That's how straight it can get."

"Hush, all of you." A short figure limped into the room and the door was closed again, shutting out any light. "If you have any feeling for me at all, be good enough not to toss around my problems."

"Sibyl dear," Latimer said. "I'm ready to give you my answer and it's yes."

"Thank you," she said. "But I've decided I ought to wait, at least for now." She lighted a lamp and surveyed the damage. Both Latimer and Adam sported bleeding noses and Latimer had masses of little puncture wounds on the side of his neck caused by the brush bristles.

"Ye could have come t'me," Adam said. "As it is, I think ye'd be better off up in the attic where ye're the farthest from anyone who tries to get in."

"That's what you think," Hunter said, snorting. "And how would she have come to you in Europe?"

"You always were a dreamer, Chillworth," Latimer said.

"Off with the pair of you," Hunter told Latimer and Adam. "And you can bury any notions you may have about getting your paws on Sibyl."

"Because you've got plans for your own paws in that direction, you mean," Latimer said.

"She asked me first." Hunter told him, his teeth bared.

Sibyl took the brush from Adam's unresisting hand and gave Hunter a single, resounding thwack across his buttocks. She looked at the brush with an amazed smile. "I...well, I don't think I ever hit anyone spontaneously before. But you deserve it, Hunter. You have treated me cruelly."

"I said I loved you."

"Yes, *now* you say it. *Now* you say a very personal thing in front of an audience, rather than to me and in private. And you only say it to try to lay your claim to me. You'll have to do a great deal better than that to convince me."

21

"Don't move," Hunter said. "Don't make a sound. I hear someone creeping up the stairs."

"You're imagining things now," Latimer said. "Are your ladies leaving perhaps, Sibyl?"

Sibyl yearned for peace and a place where she didn't have to meet Hunter's searching eyes every time she looked up. "They were on their way out when I came in here," she said. "It seemed best with so much noise and nonsense going on."

Adam held up a long hand and approached the door with exaggerated steps. "Hunter's right. Someone is moving about with great caution."

"It could be my aunt, or Barstow," Hunter said, continuing to look directly at Sibyl. "Or one of the servants."

She swallowed with difficulty. "Mrs. Barstow has gone to bed. Her ladyship retired some time ago and the servants don't come this way unless they have a specific purpose. But I don't hear anything."

Hunter came to her and put an arm around her

shoulders as if he had a right to do so in front of whomever he pleased. Sibyl studied her toes and didn't want to remove herself from his embrace. "Don't worry," he said. "You should be in bed, and so you shall be very soon. Just let us be sure there is no threat here. You can't blame us for being zealous, right, Latimer, Adam?"

Latimer's expression suggested he'd like to cut Hunter's heart out, but Adam said, "Absolutely, old chap. Well, will you listen to that? You could knock me down with a feather but I think someone's on their way to my attic. Bloomin' nerve. Stay put, all of ye."

"I'll come," Hunter said.

Latimer immediately added, "Me, too."

"Ye'll both stay with Sibyl in case it's a ruse t'get the men out of the way," Adam said, and slipped from the room.

Latimer toured the dusty room.

"Sibyl?" Hunter put his mouth near Sibyl's ear. "I do, you know. Very much."

"You do what very much?" she asked quietly, not looking at him.

"You women never will let a fellow off even a little, will you? I love you, dammit. I love you so much it hurts. I want you and I'm going to have you."

"This isn't the time."

"Isn't it? How soon do you want that offspring?"

She felt weak and clung to him.

"Answer me," he murmured, making sure Latimer was engrossed in old volumes. "When do you want your baby? When do you want to start? Tonight?"

Her knees were weak. She shook her head and couldn't keep tears from her eyes. "You don't want one, do you?" she said.

"Yes, dammit, I do. If I have it with you, I want it badly. What say we wait until all is quiet tonight and see what we can do about it?"

"I think I'm going to faint."

Hunter pounded a fist to his brow. "Forgive me. I'm a bounder. Of course you aren't ready for such things. You've just had a terrible shock. Let me know what you want and when."

Sibyl raised her chin and inclined her face. Hunter's green eyes looked down at her through lashes tinged light at the ends by sun. "Tonight," she said. "I don't want to wait."

"There's a condition."

She could not believe they were having this conversation while Latimer strolled about the room. "What?"

"You must promise that you won't ever take the child away without telling me you're going. And I should like to be allowed to know him—or her. Fair enough?''

He wanted his child. If hearts really broke, hers would break now. ''It may not happen tonight.''

''Then we'll have to keep trying, hmm?''

She bowed her head and said, ''Yes. And I promise what you ask.''

''Thank you.'' His fingers dug into her shoulder.

Latimer went to his haunches to open doors beneath a bookshelf. He took out several jade figurines. ''By God. These are worth something,'' he said. ''Odd place to be shut up like this. The room has pretty proportions. You'd think it would be used. And why hide away such beautiful pieces?''

''My aunt was on hard times at one point,'' Hunter said pleasantly. ''That was before she came into her inheritance from my uncle. She closed up as much of the house as possible and cut the staff to almost nothing. I suppose old habits die hard because she certainly has no need to be frugal now.''

''Perhaps she'd rather not have lodgers anymore,'' Sibyl suggested.

Hunter smiled broadly, and her heart all but stopped. ''She lives for her protégés. She thrives on the company. She was never a particularly social woman. In fact, I've seen her go about more since some of her new family—that's what she calls all of you—since some of you have had reasons for her to get out that I never did before. My uncle was a dour, penny-pinching fellow. But she would defend him regardless. She is a faithful woman.''

''I think she's the kindest woman I ever met,'' Sibyl said, still allowing him to hold her at his side. Tonight they would try to start a child growing inside her.

''She has certainly given me the home I never had,'' Latimer said. He had opened the curtains a little to look out at the purplish wintry sky. ''Finch and I never knew much kindness at our own home in Cornwall, but we found it here. More snow coming, I'm afraid.''

''We've had a lot of it this year,'' Hunter said.

Sibyl liked the feeling of his warmth at her side, his heavy arm over her shoulder. ''I like the snow,'' she said. ''Her ladyship has also been my champion.''

''She'd like me in my own home now,'' Hunter said, a trifle too offhand, Sibyl thought.

A scurry of feet, Halibut's clear complaints, and a sound like a subdued struggle sounded from the landing.

Before either Latimer or Hunter could go to check the cause, the door flew wide and Desirée stumbled into the room. Had she not been clinging to Adam's arm, she would have fallen. Adam appeared dazed. Halibut shot to a high spot on one of the bookshelves and glowered down, his eyes slitted and his beautiful fur standing on end. He held a small fish in his mouth, the head trailing from one side, the tail from the other.

"Men," Desirée said. "They are so unreasonable. Every single one of them is unreasonable. Look what this oaf has done to my darling Halibut. Frightened 'im so much 'e must hide."

"With a succulent fish in his mouth and looking fatter than ever," Latimer remarked mildly. "Where did he get the fish?"

"He hid it," Adam said. "It had been on my dinner plate and I didn't recall eating it."

Desirée tossed her head and those curls that had not already come down did so now. She wore no bonnet, no slippers, no mantle or cloak, and her mint-green sarcenet gown and robe looked unsuitably light for so cool an evening.

She pointed at Adam. "I came looking for my darling cat. Jean-Marc said I might return to London with my maid, Fanny, and that Sibyl and Lady Hester would make sure I was all right. He has written to you. I just haven't had time to deliver his communication. Well, I haven't felt too well for a day or two, so I remained at Number 17. Not surprising when your brother has been so horribly mean to you. But there has been a great deal of coming and going here at Number 7, I must say. So, tonight I come to see Sibyl and I cannot find her, so I go in search of her.''

''Why didn't you send for me the moment you arrived in London,'' Sibyl asked, ''rather than watching in secret from across the square? Jean-Marc and Meg will be awaiting word from me of your safe arrival.''

Desirée raised her fine brows and said, ''I wrote for you. I didn't want to put you out and they will never know the difference.''

''You are so bad, Desirée,'' Sibyl said. ''And you searched for me in Adam's attic? What would I be doing there?''

Desirée's very enticing lower lip trembled. ''I could not find you elsewhere.''

''Leave the girl alone,'' Adam said, frowning mightily. ''I've already shocked her out of her wits, sneaking up on her like that.''

''Adam's had Halibut for almost two days. Surely you brought the cat up from Eton with you,'' Sibyl said.

''Of course.''

''But you didn't miss him when he disappeared?''

''I told you I wasn't feeling well. And I saw him come over here and Adam take him in, so I knew he would be safe.''

Sibyl, already exhausted, didn't say the obvious,

that the princess had used the cat as an excuse to get to Adam, she hoped alone, but with so much going on at Number 7, she'd been unable to time her visit well.

"Where are your slippers?" Sibyl asked.

Desirée started to cry. "They're upstairs in the attic. I was so tired from all the waiting and trying to decide when I should come that when I found Adam wasn't at home—or I thought he wasn't—I decided to take a little rest. How was I to know you were all here? I saw all those strange women leave and I thought you had gone, too."

Sibyl thought she was hearing a great big fib but even if she had the energy she would not embarrass the girl in front of the object of her desire. "It's all right, dear one," she said. "You do need to rest. I shall tuck you up in my bed."

Hunter squeezed her shoulder and one look into his face left her in no doubt that he intended nothing to change about their night's plans. Sibyl said, "Now, why did Jean-Marc allow you to come back to Town alone?"

Desirée, her gray eyes huge and doleful, said, "He is tired of me. He said so. He said I complain all the time that I am bored so I might as well come to London if I want to be here so badly. Then I will soon find out that I can be just as bored here when there is nothing going on." She smiled a little. "But

I am allowed to shop all I please, so I shall have a new wardrobe and he said you are to have one, too. He also said you are to let him know if I am bad.'' She wrinkled her nose and cast frequent longing glances at Adam.

''I was quite getting to enjoy that wild beast o' yours,'' he said. ''I suppose I'll have to give him up, now. Who's in charge of you at Number 17, apart from the maid?''

Desirée wrapped her hands around one of his forearms and gazed raptly into his face. ''Please keep Halibut here with you. He likes it here.''

And, Sibyl thought, Desirée would have such a perfect excuse for spending time with Adam. ''Fanny's a tartar,'' she said, catching her bottom lip between her teeth. ''Between Fanny and me—and Lady Hester—we'll make sure Desirée gets up to no nonsense.''

Princess Desirée tapped a foot. ''One would think I might be nine rather than almost nineteen,'' she said. ''Jean-Marc said this would be a good time for my portrait to be finished. If it will fit in with your schedule, Adam. I'm afraid we will need another gown since, well—'' She glanced down at her more mature figure. ''I just will and I know that will mean more work for you.''

His study of her could only be described as speculative. Sibyl saw Hunter and Latimer catch each other's eyes. The girl was obviously suffering from a bad case of puppy love where Adam was concerned, and Adam knew it, as did the other men.

"You think it a wonderful idea, don't you, Sibyl?" the princess asked.

"It will probably have to go somewhat slowly," Sibyl said. "We are all quite busy at the moment." What with worrying about people's lives or being beaten in the dark, she thought.

"Sibyl!" Sibyl saw the moment when Desirée noticed that her friend was bruised and cut. "Oh, my dear, Sibyl, you are injured. What has happened?"

"I can't talk about it anymore tonight," she said, and meant what she said. "I was assaulted some days ago. Hunter found me before I was in even worse condition. I'm getting better. That's it. Please ask no more."

"But you didn't let Meg and Jean-Marc know," Desirée said and a sly light crept into her face.

"Why worry them?" And bring Jean-Marc charging up to Town to create the kind of row that might bring about disaster.

"So you don't want them to know?"

"No, Desirée, I don't."

"I understand. In fact, I'm sure we understand each other very well."

Sibyl pursed her lips and shook her head.

"You are quite the handful, Your Highness," Hunter said. "Too bad you will soon learn that Jean-Marc is correct. London is exceedingly boring at this time of year." He gave Sibyl a sideways look. "Or it can be."

"Where is Fanny?" Sibyl asked, most annoyed with Desirée's manipulation.

"Asleep in her bed, I should think," Desirée said with no sign of remorse. "She is a terrible sleepy-head and will not awake before morning, when we can send word that I am with you, Sibyl."

"Very well," Sibyl said, too emotionally drained to argue. "We'll send one of the staff first thing in the morning. Now. Off to bed with you. Come along."

The moment they were inside 7B with the door closed, Desirée threw her arms around Sibyl and kissed her on both cheeks, careful not to hurt her where she was bruised. "Whenever I am away from you, I miss you," she said. "You are more a mother and a sister to me than any relative of my own."

"You don't have any sisters," Sibyl pointed out, but hugged her back. She loved this headstrong girl. "And I'm sure your mama is lovely."

"She scarcely knows I am alive."

She stood back and held both of Sibyl's hands. "What are you going to do about it?"

Sibyl frowned. "About what?"

''Don't be coy with me. You and Hunter are in love with each other.''

In the mood to be hospitable, Hunter invited the other two men back to his rooms, where he served them some of his best hock. He knew Sibyl would wait for him to come for her and he'd better give plenty of time for her to get the princess settled.

''Change in the wind, is there?'' Adam said suddenly. ''With you, Hunter. Seem a bit more pleased with life than ye did a short while ago. Did I miss something?''

''Not unless you count relief,'' he said, pleased with the speed of his response.

''Speaking for myself,'' Latimer said. ''I'm no more comfortable with the idea of Sibyl being unprotected now than I was an hour or so ago. I can't understand why you are, Hunter.''

''I'm not,'' Hunter said, feeling the pleasant warmth from the hock spread through him. ''But Masters—that's the new man—is on the door. I went to speak with him and he said, correctly, that he couldn't imagine we'd object to the princess coming in. He's a brawny fellow and he'd make enough fuss to rouse us. If anyone braves the snow in the back gardens they'll walk into a booby trap I erected with Old Coot's help earlier. Thoroughly enjoyed himself. But if it goes off, we'll have the neighborhood on our necks for disturbing the peace.''

''Fair enough,'' Latimer said. He held up his glass and smiled at the warm liquor swirling inside. ''Something tells me you and I are about at the end of our, um, days of merry debauchery, hmm, Hunter?''

The surprise in Adam's expression made Hunter uncomfortable. ''Come now, Latimer, we haven't exactly cut a swathe through London with our antics.''

''Haven't we?'' Latimer poured more hock and refilled Hunter's glass. Adam declined. ''Well, here's to you, my friend, the man who can—''

''Latimer.''

''Dammit. Be proud. Here's to the man who can climax more frequently than any on record.''

''The devil, you say,'' Adam murmured.

Hunter waved his glass. ''Tomfoolery. All in the past.''

''Like a few months ago,'' Latimer. ''And here's to me—'' he drank deeply ''—the most daring lover in all England.''

''Good God.''

Latimer bowed and made a leg for Adam's benefit. ''And not in the past at all. Except I begin to think I'd better give some thought to finding a winsome female with a taste for the unusual, and see about getting married. Doesn't mean I can't teach her the ecstasy of love on horseback, or whatever else appeals at the moment."

Hunter gave up. There was no stopping Latimer when the wine was in, and both the wit and the reserved man—out.

"Look," Latimer said. "All that whispering in the library didn't completely escape me, you know. You intend to get between Sibyl's legs tonight, don't you, Hunter?"

"Shut up, man," Hunter said. "And don't ever speak of Sibyl like that again."

"Not if ye don't want my fist in your mouth," Adam said. "There's women, and women. Sibyl isn't the kind of woman you treat like a whore, even with words."

Latimer waved his arms. "Sorry, sorry. Look, all I was going to suggest was that we take a little turn down to Willie's Alley—just for old time's sake. Say goodbye to one or two old friends. Nothing more. No mischief—or not much. I'm not going to try to get you to Madame Sophie's or anywhere like that. What do you say?"

"No," Hunter said.

Adam shook his head repeatedly and set aside the dregs of his hock. Halibut, who had not followed his mistress, landed with a thud, rather like a small feather mattress, on the carpet, where he set to work delicately cleaning every one of the hapless fish's bones.

"What could it hurt?" Latimer cajoled. "Come on, man, just for my sake. I'm going to cut all that off after tonight and find myself a nice girl."

"You still want Sibyl," Hunter pointed out.

"Not really," Latimer said. "She's so lovely, and she was needy. And so was I. It would never have worked. There'll be someone for me. Come on. A drink at Willie's for old time's sake?"

Hunter looked at Adam, who shook his head again. Hunter couldn't decide what to do.

"Just one drink," Latimer said.

"Oh, what harm can just one do?" Hunter said, and to Adam he added, "Watch the women. We won't be long and that's a promise."

"I'll watch them," Adam said, but the downward turn of his mouth showed his displeasure.

As they left the house, Latimer said, "What's wrong with Chillworth? Some sort of religious fanatic, is he?"

"He's a good man," Hunter said, wishing he'd stuck with his original refusal to go with Latimer.

Willie's Alley was some distance through heaped snow and ice and when they arrived, the windows were frosted and the sign outside too frozen to swing. They pushed inside to be met by the customary blast of beer-laden air, smoke, body odor and heat—and raucous laughter laced with bawdy female shrieks.

Taking off his hat and working on removing his gloves, Hunter tucked his cane under his arm and followed Latimer to a table near the bar. Delighted shouts greeted them. Not for the first time he wondered how the folks at 7 Mayfair Square would react to the easy camaraderie between Hunter Lloyd, Latimer More and the motley bunch at Willie's Alley.

Seated at their favorite table near the vast fireplace hung with glittering brass, in only moments they each had a female on a knee, and were pressing large tankards of beer to their lips. The innkeeper, one Silvester, slapped a bottle of evil, oily, colorless liquor and two small glasses down in front of them. He gave a huge wink and said, ''Missed wot we got to offer 'ere, 'ave yer? Thought fer a bit we'd seen the last of yer. Too good ter give up fer good, though, right?''

The brunette on Hunter's knee leaned against him and indicated she wanted a small glass of the strong liquor. He handed one to her and she tipped it down.

The woman had a hand in his crotch and he thanked fortune alcohol had slowed him down, but not enough, evidently. He began to harden and the woman smiled. A pretty creature.

Latimer's armful had already mounted his lap, but Hunter saw weariness in the other man's eyes.

The brunette loosened her blouse until it hung open, revealing her considerable breasts. Then she sat on the edge of the table, pulled up her skirts and spread her legs. Hunter knew he didn't belong there, not anymore, not ever again.

"C'mon, dearie," the girl said. "You'll get me in trouble if 'e thinks I don't know me stuff."

Hunter leaned toward her and spread her skirts over his belly and thighs. "He'll never find out from me. You can make enough noise for both of us, so do it."

On cue, she panted and her naked breasts heaved. She used her heels on the sawdust-strewn floor and jounced, shrieking and throwing her head back.

Hunter looked beyond her and into the sneering face of Constance Smith. Constance was leaving a private room near the door in the wake of a large, shadowy man swathed in a many-caped cloak—a familiar figure but Hunter wasn't certain why. His eyes went from the man's huge shoulders to his feet, feet clad in heavy bespoke boots.

Then the man was gone, and a second later, with a final, knowing glance, Constance followed.

22

With Desirée finally asleep in Sibyl's room, Sibyl sat on the edge of what had been Meggie's bed. Desirée had taken a long time to fall asleep. Sibyl loved having her company. Thoughts of loneliness didn't come often, but with Desirée there, chattering, asking what Sibyl thought about this dress design or that, or this dance or that, it seemed almost as if Meggie were back. At least, it was like having a younger version of Meggie back.

Desirée was no fool. Not once did she directly mention Adam Chillworth, but Sibyl knew the girl's mind rarely strayed from thoughts of him.

And now the princess had finally fallen asleep in Sibyl's own bed because it was well aired and Sibyl sat, listening so hard for any sound of Hunter and Latimer returning, that the very air seemed to hum.

Tonight.

They had made an agreement to attempt to make her with child tonight. Just like that. And afterward they must behave as if there were nothing different between them.

Sibyl would not waver from her determination to help Hunter with this dreadful case. She would like to know more about it. She touched the side of her face. Not surprisingly, she was still very swollen. And her back and bottom were sore and she did not know how long it would be before she could play the piano again. Her left wrist bore welts filled with blood.

Surely Hunter would not come for her and he knew she would not go to him.

Sibyl heard a carriage in the street. The horses clattered to a stop, blowing, their harnesses creaking and clanking. She sat very still. Her hair was combed straight back and wound in a single braid that reached well below the middle of her back. Her nightrail and robe were of simple white lawn but beautifully embroidered in pale pink—made by Meg, of course, who had once earned her living as a seamstress and who could create magic with a needle.

The front door opened and there was laughter in the hall. It sounded like Latimer's voice, and the man, Masters, who guarded the door.

How could anyone laugh on such a serious night?

Hunter's scuffing heels came up the stairs, paused

before her door, then carried on upward until there was silence again.

Still Sibyl sat, her hands folded in her lap, her eyes lowered. He might not come for her, but he might, and there was nothing else she knew to do in order to be more ready.

Her spine ached from tension.

Hunter had told her he loved her and she had told him she loved him, too. What better start could there be for a baby?

She would not think of more, except that Hunter wanted to play some part in his child's life.

If there was a child.

Please, God, let there be a child.

The very air breathed now. And pressed in on Sibyl.

A tap at the door to the flat was so light she scarcely heard it, and when she did, the furious hammering of her heart made it difficult to pull her wits together and go to answer.

Hunter, in shirtsleeves and trousers, but having removed his jacket, waistcoat and boots, looked at her briefly. He spoke not a word before pulling her onto the landing and closing the door quietly behind them. He led her upstairs to his rooms and locked them inside. "Just in case Barstow or Aunt Hester decide to check on me." He laughed softly. "I want you to sit with me awhile. There are things to be said."

"I'm afraid, Hunter."

"Of course you are. That's why we must talk."

"Before I could almost make it a daring game. It all seemed so simple, and earlier, when... Well, not simple. I was terrified, really, but although I was so easily hurt by whatever you said to me, I did half expect you to laugh at me. Not believe me and think I was joking and that would be that. But then I knew more and more strongly what I wanted and I couldn't stop pursuing it. You see, I am changed in some ways, I am grown stronger and more sure."

"What you wanted?" Hunter said. He stood with her in the middle of his study and lightly touched the injured side of her face. "And what did you want exactly?"

She swallowed and covered his hand against her face. "A child of my own," she whispered.

"And you came to me for help—with your odd, incomplete ideas of how such things were accomplished. Why? Why me? Because I'm the man you know best and I seem brotherly enough to approach. I offered to protect you as if I were your brother."

"I don't want the protection of a brother."

"No," Hunter said. "I rather thought not. Which leaves us with the question as to why you chose to come to me. I suppose it must have been because I am familiar, hmm, rather like a comfortable old chair that's been around a long time."

Unaccountably, Sibyl felt angry with him. "You are baiting me, Hunter. You want me to repeat what I've already told you. You confuse me. But I have come to understand that the thought of having a child with someone I don't respect is dreadful."

"So any child of ours will be doubly blessed because we respect each other. Yes?"

"Yes," she said.

He slipped the robe from her shoulders and let it fall to the carpet before the fire. The curtains were open and the never-ending snow hit the windowpanes in big blots that spread and slid. A beautiful night. Pristine without, warm and magical within.

"You don't think it might be a good idea if this possible child of ours had parents who were more than good friends who respect each other?"

She felt disappointed. He no longer sounded excited about the future. "I don't think it would be fair to you to back you into a corner. You are to be knighted."

"If I am not thrown in jail first," he muttered.

She angled her head to frown at him.

"Forgive me," he said. "The hock still talks a little. I can become a little maudlin." He didn't mention the beer and schnapps at Willie's Alley, or the look of disgust he'd got from Constance Smith as she left.

"You will not be thrown in jail," she told him. "Tomorrow you, Latimer and I shall work together to search the house in Curzon Street for signs of your friend, Charles. We will find him somewhere. Mark my words."

Hunter wished he felt as certain. "We digress. Perhaps our child's parents should consider being married?"

"Because I approached you? Propositioned you? Oh, no, I think there would always be that between us. At the moment there is no child. If fate smiles and I become pregnant, perhaps I should consider a good man of my own class to—"

"*Never.*" Hunter lowered his voice. "Never make such a suggestion again. This class thing remains out of hand in England. And it has nothing to do with us, or with any child we might have. Class didn't stop your Meggie from marrying a European count."

"Meggie is different. She has...well, she is different."

"Different, yes. Better, no. One day I will tell you all I think about you, but tonight there are other things to do." He used a knuckle to raise her chin, and he kissed her, a long, light kiss that made it impossible for Sibyl to keep her eyes open, or to stand on her own feet. She slipped her arms around Hunter and leaned against him. ‘‘Ah, yes,’’ he murmured. ‘‘Other things. You have a great deal to learn about the simplicity—and the complexity—of genuine affection. They are one and the same.’’

Threading his fingers into the bound hair on either side of her head, he held her carefully, aware of the blows she'd suffered. To look into her face was bliss, to look into her face and know that when she looked back at him he was seeing only truth in the sweet longing her eyes held.

Sibyl warmed inside, and grew pliant, and ready for whatever was to come. There would be no silken ropes or canes, this she knew, even though she didn't know exactly what to expect this time. She did know she must try not to dwell on his references to affection rather than love.

Releasing her, Hunter took off his shirt. His trousers followed quickly. Naked, as she already knew, he was even more imposing than when he was perfectly dressed. Unclothed he became all male, all flesh and blood and longing and arousal. However many times she was to be allowed to look on him like this, she would never grow tired of the sight of him.

His smile, the smile that made him appear younger and more mischievous, turned up the corners of his mouth and he kissed her again while he smiled, his teeth meeting her lips before he nipped the moist membrane just inside, then the end of her tongue. He curled his own tongue into the roof of her mouth and pulled her upper lip into his mouth.

Sibyl tried to copy each move he made, but she would need practice—practice she started at once.

Wherever she held him his skin was smooth. Sweat had broken out between his shoulder blades. The ends of his hair, where it curled, was soon damp. He was holding back, she felt it and she felt what it cost him to keep himself rigid and to make sure there were those inches between their bodies.

A little bolder, she flattened her palms and fingers to his chest where the hair was rough, then at his sides, where the skin was smooth and damp, and, gradually, slid her sensitive hands downward to his narrow hips and around to his buttocks. He seemed to hold his breath when she reached to cradle him in one hand while she surrounded his shaft with the other.

His hands on her shoulders were leaden. He trembled.

They kissed as if to devour each other.

Hunter found the ribbon at the neck of her gown, pulled it wide and gave the garment what little help it needed to join the robe.

"You see," he said. "So simple, yet so complex. I want to love you now, Sibyl, with my body. And we will hope there may be a child. Probably there won't be, but this should be the reason for our lovemaking, the gentleness of it, the fervor. Do you understand at all?"

"Yes," she told him. He would love her with his body and the reason for this lovemaking was to produce a child.

Hunter settled Sibyl on the bed of their clothes before the fire in his study. Shadows danced on the walls and the snow continued to fly at the windows.

He kissed her lips again and again, and kissed her body. Every touch, every suckling of her breasts, was like nothing she had ever dreamed of. He drew life from her and seemed to hold it within him. And where his mouth went, his hands followed with fleeting touch.

At last he said, "I don't want to wait any longer."

Sibyl shook her head.

His fingers locked with hers and held her arms above her head. He put his lips by her ear and said, "Are you in pain anywhere?"

"No," she lied. What did it matter if there were bruises that would ache for some time?

"There may be some discomfort when I enter you completely for the first time. It will not last and any soreness afterward will soon pass. You are already partly prepared."

''I'm not afraid of anything you will do, Hunter.''

He slid downward, pushing himself between her thighs, and in one smooth lunge drove the length of his rod inside her. Sibyl felt only intense excitement, a burning ache she wished would never stop. She closed herself around him as tightly as possible.

''Oh, Sibyl. My Sibyl,'' he panted and began to move. ''If this is too much, let me know. We have all the time we need to allow you to adjust to me.''

''Don't stop,'' she said, breathing hard. ''Don't ever stop. Yes—yes—yes. Please, don't stop.''

He released her hands and placed his thumb where his manhood made its repeated entry into her body. The sensation stole her heartbeat, her thought.

Hunter smiled through clenched teeth. This was the woman meant for him. All this time she had been so close and he hadn't really known. He'd wondered, but never dared to give in to that wondering. From beneath his thumb, waves of her climax rippled and she arched, shocked, her weight resting on her heels and shoulders while her head turned from side to side.

He had waited as long as he could. His seed poured into her and his own release racked him. Every inch of her glistened in the firelight. Her hair remained in its thick braid and she reminded him of a medieval princess, her gown and robe and his clothes like rushes beneath them.

It was over.

Hunter went to his side on the floor and pulled her into his arms.

At first he didn't understand what she said, but when she repeated the word, he said it after her: "Perhaps."

23

"Mr. Hunter? Mr. Hunter. Wake up now. At once."

Sibyl rolled over in Hunter's arms, opened her eyes the merest fraction and peered at his sleeping face.

Ouch! Her pains of the previous day were nothing more than remembered twinges compared with this morning's deep aches. But her memory was exceedingly good and every discomfort was a testimony to a glorious night.

A great hammering set up on the outer study door. "Mr. Hunter, sir. Oh, sir."

Hunter's green eyes opened, looked at Sibyl, and gained complete consciousness at once. He sat up in bed and listened to the furious banging and thumping and the cacophony of raised voices. Sibyl thought they both heard a carriage and horses, and the shouting in the street at the same time.

"Good God," Hunter said at last. "The city must be on fire." With that he leaped from bed, pulled on a robe, covered Sibyl with a mountain of bedclothes and peered at her underneath, causing her to giggle. "I'm sorry. The moment I can return to you, I will. First I will check outside."

She heard his rapid progress to the window, then another silence, then an amazed oath. His feet returned to the side of the bed and he raised the covers again. "A rich-looking coach—very rich and plain as if it were deliberately devoid of any distinguishing markings," he said, and dropped the bedcovers again.

He left the bedroom and she soon heard the calmer rumble of his voice interjected into the excited rushes of words from others. Then, "No!" came clearly from Hunter.

More argument followed until Lady Hester's distinctive, much slower tones could be heard saying, "You have what you need. And you have no choice. This is when I wish I had insisted you have a valet. I wonder if that man Masters can help."

A shakier, quieter voice spoke and Hunter said, very firmly, "Exactly. Coot will do anything necessary. The rest of you, go away."

Another blossoming babble followed while Sibyl cowered beneath the covers. She did not even dare try to go into the study to retrieve her nightclothes. But even in such extreme circumstances, she smiled at the thought of the night, and of Hunter, and of herself with Hunter.

"And be laughed at for the rest of my life?" Hunter said loudly. "Absolutely not. And have the man think I sit around in satin drawers waiting for his call? What's he doing at Carlton House anyway? I thought he was in Brighton with his dreadful mistress—or at Windsor—with his dreadful mistress. Satin drawers?"

"Hunter." Lady Hester's voice was ominous.

"Satin breeches, then. The answer is still, no, and now, with due respect, kindly vacate my rooms so I may do what the man says and get there with haste, dammit."

"It's the opening of parliament he's here for," Coot said, and coughed.

Hunter grumbled but said, "Of course it is. I knew that."

Sibyl scrunched up as small as she could and burrowed to the bottom of the bed.

The voices had faded away, all but that of Old Coot and Hunter, and they continued a quiet conversation in the study.

The bedroom door opened and Sibyl covered her ears.

A hand, definitely Hunter's hand, extended beneath the covers with a fistful of something. He said, ''All's well, sweet. Coot and I are very old friends.''

''I hope you're feeling much improved this morning, Miss Sibyl,'' Coot said.

Sibyl covered her ears again and didn't manage to shut out a sound.

''We'll return in a few minutes,'' Hunter said.

The instant she knew the coast was clear, Sibyl struggled into her crushed night rail, then gave thanks for her considerably more presentable robe and for the fact that her hair, although awry, had remained caught in the braid. Within moments she had herself straightened and lying in Hunter's bed with the covers pulled up to her chin.

Not more than another minute passed before Hunter put his head into the room and said, ''I have an urgent summons. Should you mind if I removed some clothing from the wardrobe?'' Old Coot was behind him and coughed too significantly. Hunter gave Sibyl a purely wicked grin.

''Of course not,'' she said. ''I shall cover my head at once so you may dress.''

''No, I can—''

''Good idea,'' Coot said. ''Time is now of the essence. Then, once Mr. Hunter is dispatched, I shall bring you chocolate and make sure Barstow checks your discomfort.''

Sibyl didn't dare look at Hunter.

She slithered beneath the covers once more.

"Now, you're sure, sir?" Old Coot said. "A point's a point, but—"

"Absolutely sure and this isn't a point. Nothing to do with a point. Common sense purely. I'm a barrister and as such, I shall arrive looking like one."

"That'll mean powdering a wig and getting the robes pressed, Mr. Hunter. Might take rather long."

Both Coot and Hunter laughed together, the one a rusty old laugh, the other young and robust.

For some time the talk was of nothing more momentous than boots. Then Coot became agitated. "I do think it should be a white neckcloth, Mr. Hunter."

"It will be black."

"Definitely white."

This went on for sometime before Hunter said, "Dash it all, white then. But only because of your extreme age and my fear that you will die of apoplexy if this continues."

Sibyl smiled beneath her sheets. This love was a thorny thing. With each small mannerism, each new revelation of strength, even the strength to give in, the thorns took deeper hold.

"Slick it back," Hunter said.

"Hmph."

"Don't argue with me on this, Coot," Hunter

said. "You have now had your point for the morning."

Sibyl popped from beneath the covers and settled herself on the pillows. She looked at Hunter, who looked back while pulling on his black waistcoat and checking his fob watch.

"You are magnificent," she said. "If it is the hair he wants slicked straight back, then he is right, Coot. Otherwise he looks entirely too young and handsome to be allowed out at all."

Hunter scowled a warning at her, which she ignored, feeling far too sunny to be made unhappy today.

Coot brought a chair and Hunter sat, suffering to allow Coot freedom with the silver-backed hairbrushes.

Then it was finished.

Coot tossed a beautiful black cape with a satin-lined collar around Hunter's shoulders, and handed him his hat, gloves, and a silver-topped cane.

"I'm going to see the king," Hunter said, spreading his arms. "How do I look?"

Coot made a face and said, "Passable."

Sibyl followed suit and said, "Passable."

24

Hustled in. That was the only way Hunter could describe his entrance into Carlton House, the extraordinary monument King George IV had renovated for himself—and intended to discard in favor of what would become Buckingham Palace.

The atmosphere within the excessive lavishness of silk, satin, gold and marble was hushed. Flunkies moved with stately precision about their business. Obviously no suggestion of anything but absolute order would be tolerated.

A gentleman in satin breeches and a dark-blue jacket with a great deal of gold braid bowed to Hunter and whispered for him to follow.

They went, between a phalanx of more bows from more liveried servants, along fabulous corridors lined with too much splendor for Hunter to do more than note vaguely. He wished Latimer could be present—alone—to enjoy peering at, and muttering over it all.

At last they arrived at a door where a gaggle of

serious men huddled outside. These were not liveried but had an air of great importance. They turned to study Hunter with grave suspicion.

His companion said, "Kindly wait," opened the door and slipped inside. He returned quickly and said, "Follow me, Mr. Lloyd."

When Hunter entered the room beyond he knew he would look back on this occasion and wonder if he had imagined it all.

Half-reclined on a vast chinoiserie daybed that groaned beneath his every move was an excessively obese, red-faced man in a plum-colored velvet dressing gown. Matching slippers seemed tiny on feet overhung by puffy folds of white flesh. White lace dripped from his wrists and frothed at his throat, but this was the rich decoration on his nightshirt. He wore a wig, slightly askew and badly combed, and someone had added an inadvisable swathe of rouge to each cheek and to his protruding lips. He frowned at Hunter.

"The barrister," a fat woman to his right said. A satin-clad creature so covered with gems that little skin showed, even where her huge bosom was amply revealed, she looked upon the king with adoration—and he returned that devoted gaze. "Remember Neville, dear one? The fellow Elizabeth—my daughter, Elizabeth—the fellow she was rather taken with. Well, actually I thought—you know."

Her lower lip trembled. "I had no idea I had made such a dreadful mistake in not preparing quite adequately, or that he might mistake her for a... Think of her reputation if it had ever got out about Hampstead Heath. Well, this is the man who successfully defended that naughty Neville. Thank goodness. All my silly fault. Of course, if that Villiers person hadn't been there, we might have had a wedding by now. That could have been a blessing. Daughters can be such a trial."

"There, there, dearest little soft, white dove," the king said, reaching into a drawer beside the daybed to produce a green velvet box. "No tears, now. You only did what you thought was best. But in future you must confer with the one who has your every safety and concern at heart, hmm? We shall find Elizabeth a fine husband."

"Yes, I know," she said, very softly.

Lady Conygham, as Hunter knew the king's mistress to be, opened the box with fat, white, jewel-encrusted fingers, swept out a necklace of perfect white diamonds the size of peas and started to weep aloud, throwing herself at her protector's knee while he fumbled to fasten them around her neck.

Patting them straight among the multitude she already wore, she asked, "How do they look, my iron warrior in velvet?"

"Magnificent," he whispered.

Hunter wondered how one picked them out from the rest of the array. Now he certainly understood what was meant about the lady having a perfect balcony on which to display such objects. King and expensive ladybird kissed noisily.

Hunter assumed a deep bow and remained there now.

"Got to stand up," the king said. Then, abruptly he added, "Can't do this sitting down. Sword?"

To Hunter's absolute amazement, another liveried man appeared from an almost concealed corner, with a sheathed gold sword balanced on a pillow.

The king tried to get his feet over the side of the daybed but made little progress. Hunter, all but overtaken by a desire to run, knew better than to touch the man at all.

"May I assist, Sire?" asked the man who had accompanied Hunter.

Lady Conygham nodded to the man, and with the aid of the other, who juggled the sword and pillow beneath his arm, the ailing monarch was balanced, swaying, on his feet.

He pointed to the floor before him, and hands on Hunter's shoulders, made sure he understood he was to kneel before his king.

He heard the sword unsheathed and could probably have done nothing at all had the decision been made to slice off his head. Instead, words were uttered. He was dubbed this and that and told to rise, at which point, King George IV bestowed a smile that could only be described as utterly charming.

"Greatest pleasure, Sir—" he muttered, and looked to one of his attendants, who whispered in his ear. The king said, "Sir Hunter. Not usual, but there's a portion in Cornwall for you. And a purse. A relative of yours did some service to a relative of mine before, y'know. Architect, he was, or so I'm told. Not sure what it was he did. Give Sir Hunter the necessary, Soams."

He was handed several scrolls and an exceedingly heavy silk purse.

"Place in Cornwall's remote but nice, or so I'm told. Never been there. But there's nowhere like England, no matter where in England."

Hunter wasn't sure how one thanked a king for giving one a knighthood, a piece of land and money, so he said, "Most gratified," or some such thing. "I am your most devoted subject."

The king gave another of his almost childlike smiles. "And now the matter of DeBeaufort is forgotten. Correct? Other fellow is where he belongs. He'll be punished appropriately. And the rest will be forgotten?"

Something within Hunter grew very cold. He looked into eyes that were still sharp and had turned cunning. There was more than a little wrong here.

He was being paid to be silent. With absolute conviction, he came to the conclusion that Greatrix Villiers had somehow been wronged.

"He's not answering," Lady Conygham said.

The king's gaze became fixed. "Overwhelmed, I wouldn't doubt. Come along, fellow, we do understand each other?"

Hunter began formulating how he might explain that he thought there should be a stay of sentencing while all evidence was reevaluated when a hard rap came at the door and a fierce-looking, self-assured young buck strode in. He wore dark-green velvet and exuded privilege.

The appearance of Neville DeBeaufort shocked Hunter deeply. The man did no more than flash his former barrister a superior, assessing stare before going first to Lady Conygham. He executed a respectful bow, observed with evident pleasure by the king. DeBeaufort said to Lady Conygham, "Getting this audience has taken weeks or I would have come much earlier. I hope I am forgiven, most beautiful lady. My apologies have been delivered and I'm assured all will be put behind us. Had I had any inkling, things would have been very different."

Lady Conygham patted his cheek. "I'm sure everything happened for the best." She smiled and dimpled and tucked at the dark shining curls surrounding her face. "How are the wounds that dreadful man inflicted on you? Recovered are you? Such a terrible experience."

Satisfied, yes, Hunter decided, she appeared exceedingly satisfied. Was this all as simple as it appeared to be? Lady Conygham had already made mention of her daughter, Elizabeth, who, it was to be assumed, had been the "wronged" woman with DeBeaufort on Hampstead Heath. Hunter would dearly like to know the details that had caused such strife. Not that he dare ask under these circumstances—but ask he would as soon as he could get at DeBeaufort without his royal bodyguard.

"I am feeling quite fit," DeBeaufort said. "My arm will take a little time to recover completely." He demonstrated what was apparently some loss of movement in his left shoulder. "But one must be grateful for one's life."

"Indeed," La Conygham simpered.

A compelling fellow in his green, DeBeaufort went to the king, who smiled at him and suffered his ministrations as he helped seat him again and lifted his feet onto the daybed before murmuring a lengthy message to him.

"The devil you say?" the king said, glowering at Hunter, who had become too numb to be nervous. "Well, it's too late now. It's done. Can't take it all back, can I? Not at all the done thing. Probably looks good, anyway."

"You can be off with you, *Sir* Hunter. Make sure you're a credit to me. You might want to know that Greatrix Villiers was found dead this morning. Fight, apparently. Got himself stabbed. Obviously the weight of his guilt was too much for him."

25

Spivey here.

Surely you've heard the saying: Everything comes to he who waits, or is that "him" who waits? I don't care. I am beside myself with glee. The light has shone upon me. I have already gone to that dear man, Thomas More, and put in my application for his school. He is delighted, I can tell you.

You see, I shall soon not be needed here anymore. Oh, I shall return from time to time to nestle in my newel post and watch—well, watch almost nothing happen.

The joy.

The perfection of it.

Hester is not by nature a social woman. She has lived a little, vicariously, through her—oh, let's call them protégés. I am feeling particularly generous today. But left to her own devices she is a quiet soul and will become so again after all these interlopers have left.

What, you ask, of Adam and Latimer? Simple.

Adam has, I discover, developed quite the reputation for himself as a painter of note. Unusual during life. But he is most talented with portraiture and is expected to go far. Clearly, he cannot go far in the attic of Number 7 Mayfair Square. So, before we know it, he will have a large studio in an even more salubrious area of London and his subjects will pour to see him. Hah, perhaps he will even make time for that persnickety Princess Desirée who is far too advanced for her years. Mr. Chillworth must be at least ten years her senior. Not such an unusual state of affairs, but he will soon have other, more interesting women to occupy him.

And Latimer? London's most imaginative lover, hmm? I do believe I sense a certain ennui about our great lover, a need to settle down. If this business between Hunter and Sibyl had not straightened out so nicely, I think Latimer might have slipped in there—so to speak. Now he has seen the possibilities and he will look elsewhere. See if he doesn't. Also, with no other young people in the house, he'll grow bored.

No, not a thing shall dampen my spirits—my mood. My lovely house is to be returned to its former glory and Hunter will be in a position to make sure that happens. There will be an appropriate staff and even I admit it may be time for some, well, brightening up here and there. Not a lot, mind, but a little.

Did you hear that popinjay George IV talking about "some ancestor" of Hunter's who was knighted for service to the Crown but that he didn't really know the reason? Buffoon. I was that ancestor and I refuse to shout about my accomplishments.

Oh, bliss.

Hunter with a knighthood. I always knew that brilliant boy had it in him to carry on in my footsteps. Now he will marry Sibyl—have to. Can't very well have an innocent girl he's compromised in his aunt's own house on the loose, very probably increasin', can he? He'll marry her and tuck her away down in this remote place in Cornwall that the King's given him. It's bound to have some sort of shabby little hovel on it. Sibyl can oversee the building of something a bit suitable. Meanwhile, Sir Hunter will trot dutifully back and forth, no doubt find himself a nice little bit of muslin to occupy himself in town and set her up somewhere comfortable—where he can also be comfortable. And that will be that.

I admit, I do rather wonder how much our friend, the king, gave Hunter. Perhaps I shall have to make the effort to find out. Should be simple enough.

Oh, peace at last. And blessings on every one of them, and every one of you—with the exception of you know who. No doubt scribbling away out there looking for more trouble to make.

I must run along and make sure Reverend Smiles is aware of the wonderful news, then present myself to Sir Thomas. He's bound to want to use my extensive knowledge of the nature of mankind as a resource for his classes.

26

"What do you think?" Desirée said, afloat in chiffon that was sometimes lavender, sometimes rose, depending on which way she turned. "Do you think it would look good in my portrait?"

A week had passed since the amazing night Sibyl had spent with Hunter. She sat in his big, worn leather chair near the window in his study and stole every opportunity to watch for his return. At least Desirée had never commented on Sibyl's disappearance from 7B during that momentous night. Or the fact that although Sibyl was almost completely recovered, she continued to spend time in Hunter's rooms, especially when he was out. She liked to be among his things and if he objected, he hadn't told her so.

"The gown is beautiful," she said. "But I thought Adam had already begun painting you in that wonderful costume that was made for the Eastern Ball Jean-Marc had for you that time. To change everything will take so much more time."

"Pah," Desirée said. "I was *so* much younger then. And *so* much thinner." She quite baldly ran her hands over her breasts, which were, undoubtedly, considerably filled out.

"I liked you in it," Sibyl said honestly. "It was sensual, and so are you. With all those artful, winding panels that appeared to be skin rather than material. It's such a match. You and the dress. Very clever. It could easily be altered."

Desirée pushed her mouth out. "There is that."

The ladies of Sibyl's group had gathered for a late-morning chat and Mrs. Barstow had provided delicious sandwiches, small pies and fruit—in addition to tea. She appeared concerned about Sibyl, hovering over her and pressing more food on her whenever possible until Sibyl wondered what Coot might have suggested to Barstow on the day Hunter was knighted. An ottoman had been placed beneath her feet and Barstow would not be appeased unless Sibyl remained covered by a quilt. Masters appeared from time to time to build up the fire.

"I wonder if Adam is at home," Desirée said. "We could ask him what he thinks."

"Perhaps he has other things to interest him than your portrait," Phyllis Smart said, quite kindly. "We do, too, really, Your Highness. We have a feeling that there is a great deal Sibyl could tell us if she had a mind to and we're all anxious to hear more about how she sees through gentlemen's clothes."

Desirée laughed aloud. "You don't really believe that, do you? Sibyl may have been a quiet one, but she always had a naughty sense of humor. She's pulling our legs."

Jenny McBride caught Sibyl's eye and there was a wicked smile if ever Sibyl saw one. "I expect you're right, Your Highness," she said. "She just wanted you to think she could see Adam Chillworth nude when you never have."

Desirée snatched up poor, complaining Halibut and stroked him fiercely. "You were just teasing, weren't you, Sibyl?"

"No. I wish I were. It's been most embarrassing."

"I shall test you," Desirée said. "That servant. Masters. He can't be more than in his twenties and he's nice-looking."

"You shouldn't be studying the servants like that," Sibyl pointed out.

"Does he have broad shoulders?" Desirée said, not to be deterred.

"I don't have to see him nude to know that he does."

"And his legs? Are they fine?"

"Shame," Jenny McBride said and immediately

covered her mouth, but Desirée didn't seem to notice any disrespect.

"Masters is a nicely built man," Sibyl said. "Here's a carriage. A beautiful carriage. Yes, it's stopping here. Hunter's home." She was helpless to stop the thrill in her voice, the color rising in her cheeks, or the instant glisten of joyful tears in her eyes.

"Guess who's in love?" Ivy Willow said. "And very good taste you have, too, Sibyl. How lucky he obviously loves you, too."

"If you marry him, you won't stop helping us learn, will you?" Desirée said, her eyes filled with worry. "Not the way Meg did?"

"At this moment there is nothing to get excited about and nothing to worry about," Sibyl said.

Without warning, Lady Hester sailed into the room. Occasionally she wore a subdued color but today she was in the signature mauve that had replaced her mourning black more than a year since. She glanced around at the gathering, her disapproval evident until her gaze came to rest on Desirée and she managed a smile.

"Your Highness," she said stiffly. "Ladies." And she went to the window to look past Sibyl. She was in time to see the top of Hunter's head as he entered the house.

She crossed her arms and waited, one slipper tapping. Sibyl's guests looked at each other, clearly uncomfortable.

Hunter's footsteps sounded on the stairs. He called something back to Coot and sounded somber. Lady Hester stared from one woman to the other until they made motions to leave.

"Ah, a party," Hunter said, entering, but his smile was thin. "I don't think you've ever formally introduced me to your friends, Sibyl."

"Phyllis Smart," Phyllis said promptly and with a remarkably nice smile. She dropped an abbreviated curtsey.

Jenny McBride followed suit and Sibyl saw how Hunter could not help but return Jenny's cheerful grin.

"Ivy Willow," Ivy muttered, lowering her head as she introduced herself. She didn't curtsey. "And before you think you remember hearing the name before—you have. I was the one who asked you to meet me at your chambers, then I never turned up. I was worried about Sibyl, that's all. I was afraid you'd hurt her and I wanted to warn you not to."

Hunter stared at her, then at Sibyl. "Ah, well," Hunter said, "Nothing wrong with wanting to protect a friend."

Once Hunter had met Sibyl's eyes, it became obvious he didn't want to make small talk with anyone else.

Adam wandered in with Latimer. ''Door was open,'' he said, his too serious expression in place. ''We thought we might be missing a celebration.''

''Hardly,'' Lady Hester said, her face without expression.

''It's about time I was off then,'' Jenny said. ''I'm behind on my work and I'm expected at the shop.''

''It's Saturday and getting late,'' Latimer said. ''Seems a shame someone so young has to spend her weekends shut up in a shop.''

''Och, I dinna mind. I'm fortunate t'have such good work and I'm learnin' a lot. I love makin' hats. You've no idea how beautiful some of them are.''

''I'm sure they are.'' He watched her closely. ''I'll take you, if you'll let me. I rarely use my carriage. The horse could use some exercise.''

Jenny's fair skin glowed, but she nodded and let Latimer usher her from the room.

''Tea,'' Adam said, his eyes lightening. ''You have no idea how hard it gets makin' your own tea when you've no talent for the job.''

''I've developed a talent for it,'' Desirée said. ''Sibyl has taught me. Come, Adam, I'll make you a fresh pot of tea in the attic and we can talk about my portrait. These poor souls are getting very bored with the topic, and who can blame them?''

Adam had two choices: go with her, or be rude. He went with Princess Desirée, bowing as she passed before him, but not without definite signs of concern.

"I'll have Fanny join you," Sibyl said, smiling at him. She pretended not to see Desirée's annoyance.

Hunter stood beside Sibyl and stroked her hair. He bent to examine the side of her face, and checked the place behind her ear where the stranger's boot had connected. Then he held out his hands for her to present her wrists. She did so and he said, "Getting better, but you must still be careful."

"Thank you for the lovely lunch," Ivy said, donning her buttercup-yellow pelisse and matching bonnet. "Shall we walk together, Phyllis?"

With her head cocked on one side, Ivy smiled on Hunter and Sibyl. Then she sighed before the two women left. Lady Hester remained.

"I'd offer you tea, Aunt," Hunter said, "but I imagine it's cold by now, isn't it, Sibyl?"

"Oh, yes. Barstow made it a long time ago. She's been so kind to me. I almost think she dreams up kind things to do for me."

"Who wouldn't?" Lady Hester said. She dropped a small lace-covered pomander on Sibyl's lap. It smelled of roses and seed pearls had been sewn into scallops around its edges. She said, "I thought you might enjoy this. Now, Hunter. Share your news."

Lady Hester's rude manner toward Hunter disquieted Sibyl but it wasn't her place to comment. She said, thank you for the pomander, and held it to her nose.

"I've discoverd the land I was given in Cornwall is a delight," Hunter said, without to-do. "The house is Elizabethan and called Minver Place. It's on Minver Bay and the place is well maintained."

Sibyl averted her eyes. He was a knight. A knight with land. He wouldn't want—

His hand settled on her shoulder. "I have no immediate plans to do anything about Cornwall, or to change my life in any way. There is far too much to do here. And my work is here, too, remember." His hand tightened and Sibyl's spirits lifted. She wasn't imagining that he was giving her a message that what they had together wasn't yet over.

"You're going to need a place of your own here in London," Lady Hester said to Hunter. "Something suitable to your station. And a wife of the same type, no doubt. Congratulations, nephew. Your parents would have been very proud."

Sibyl looked at the woman's face and realized that the lady was holding herself very rigid, as if to control anger—or tears.

"My parents," Hunter said, "were never proud of anything I did. But that's in the past. Unless you insist that I must leave at once, I should like to remain at least for the foreseeable future."

Barstow had entered and quietly began placing cups and saucers onto a tray.

"It's long past time I had this house to myself," Lady Hester said.

"To yourself?" Hunter set up a steady massage of Sibyl's shoulder. "Does that mean you will ask Adam and Latimer to leave? And Sibyl?"

"Adam needs a place where clients can come and be comfortable. I understand famous people want to sit for him now. And Latimer is a successful man in his own right. He won't want to remain for long."

Barstow stood up so suddenly she knocked a cup to the floor, shattering it. "It's not my place, my lady, but I've got to say it. You're driving out your own nephew even though you love him. You had a child once and she died—"

"Barstow! Leave at once."

"No, my lady. This house is partly Mr. Hunter's anyway."

"*Sir* Hunter's," Lady Hester said.

Barstow's face glowed with delight and she said, "Sir Hunter. How lovely. This house is half yours. I know you'd never do anything about that because you're too kind. You'd give it to your aunt. But there are things you don't know."

"Don't," Lady Hester said. "I can't bear it. Please don't say any more."

Barstow scrubbed at her face. "Lady Hester had a baby girl who died when she was only weeks old. Some say it was because Lord Bingham was so cruel he wouldn't let her ladyship go to the little one when she was ill and the nurse wasn't capable."

"Stop it!" Lady Hester begged, tears flowing. "It's not true."

Sibyl got to her feet and put her arms around the woman.

"She loves you, Sibyl," Barstow said. "She thinks of you as the child she lost. I've heard her say how she thinks her Catherine would have been like you if she'd been allowed to grow up. And now she's afraid Mr.—Sir Hunter will take you away and she can't bear to lose you. It feels like losing her child all over again."

Sibyl held Lady Hester tightly and let the woman cry. When she looked at Hunter she saw his pity and his helplessness and thought, wryly, that she was seeing the difference between men and women and their ability to comfort the grieving openly.

"No one's going anywhere," he said finally. "Barstow, would you please take my aunt and help her settle and be calm.'' He went to her and awkwardly patted her back. ''I'm only your nephew, Aunt Hester, but I shall never forget your kindness to me. You aren't going to be alone. Just remember that. I will make certain you are never alone.''

Lady Hester straightened. She touched Hunter's face, smiled at Sibyl, and actually tucked an arm through Barstow's when the companion led her from the room and across the hall. Her ladyship's walk had lost its spring.

''Did you know?'' Sibyl asked. ''About the child?''

Hunter shook his head. ''This hasn't been a happy family. We aren't good at—at relationships and caring.''

Sibyl's heart squeezed so tightly, it made it hard to take a breath. Was he telling her he wasn't interested in trying to break that mold?

''How do you feel today?'' he said. ''You should try to stay off your feet.''

He closed the door and when he returned she said, ''Why? I'm not having any difficulty walking.''

Hunter looked at her intently. ''I've heard it said that if one is serious about starting a pregnancy, it's a good idea for the woman to remain as still as possible.''

''Oh, have you? I believe that if I am meant to

be pregnant, now or at anytime, walking, or normal activity of any kind, will not interfere.''

He continued to look severe. ''When did you last bleed?''

Sibyl thought she might faint from embarrassment. ''Two weeks ago. Perhaps a little more.''

''I see.'' He smiled a little. ''Do you think we should keep working hard at this project, then?''

She didn't answer the question. ''Sir Hunter. How does that feel? To be Sir Hunter?''

''Unreal. Sibyl, I've held back talking about this but what does feel real is that I've been used. My own fault. I accepted the evidence presented to me and that poor devil Villiers never had a chance. He was up against the King of England. Guilty before the opening arguments were read. Now I am more determined to put things to rest. We had no luck at Charles's place that night, but I'm going back—after midnight. This time I'll use a different approach. Charles must be found.''

''Hunter,'' Sibyl said, deeply concerned by the flat tone in his voice. He had explained all the details of the case to her. ''If Villiers is innocent, then prove it. Get him freed. Allow the woman, Constance, to tell you what she says she knows, and see what can be done.''

''Right.'' Hunter took a heavy-looking silk bag from his coat pocket and tossed it on his desk. The bag opened and sovereigns poured out. "Do you know what that is?"

"Money," she said, feeling stupid.

"Right, first time. I haven't known what to do with it so I decided to bring it here today. Lots of money. I don't even know how much, but we'll call it thirty pieces of silver. A gift from a grateful monarch to a faithful subject. Blood money. I haven't wanted to tell you, but Greatrix Villiers died days since. He was killed in a knife fight in jail. Perhaps the money should go to Constance Smith since Villiers was her brother."

Latimer couldn't keep his eyes from the faces of his companions. Even in the darkness, with only the help of an occasional gaslight in the street, Sir Hunter Lloyd and Sibyl Smiles were the two most unhappy-looking people he'd seen in a very long time.

"You'll stay with the carriage again," Hunter told him.

"So you've said several times," Latimer reminded him.

Hunter turned to him. "Then I'm saying it again. I've also told Sibyl to remain here. You see how far I get with her."

"Constance will need the care of another woman," Sibyl said. "You know as well as I do that they may not even have bothered to find her and tell her about her brother's death yet. With me I hope she'll be able to show her grief and let me comfort her."

"You aren't up to this," Hunter said. "You should be taking it easy."

The coach ground to a halt, and Latimer ducked to see through the window. "The house is the one two from the end of this terrace? The coach shouldn't be visible from there."

Still breathing hard, Hunter said, "Correct. Sibyl, I don't want you to come."

"Neither do I," Latimer agreed. "Stay with the coach and go for help if necessary."

"I belong with Hunter," she said, not caring what either of them thought of that statement. "Where he goes, I go. Even if he'd rather I didn't. And I've already told you I think I will be badly needed."

"You can't argue with women," Hunter said. "If there's no sign of our return in forty-five minutes, bring help."

He rapped for the coachman, who jumped down and set the steps. Hunter leaped out first and helped Sibyl to the ground. A few quiet words between Hunter and the coachman and Sibyl was hurrying along at Hunter's side.

The house was in darkness.

"She must be asleep," Hunter said.

Sibyl gulped. "And we have to wake her with such terrible news."

"Perhaps she's already been told." He knocked at the door sharply.

Almost at once a flickering light showed somewhere inside the house.

The light didn't come closer and no footsteps sounded.

"She's afraid," Sibyl said and Hunter knocked again.

A window opened overhead and they heard a whispered, "Who is it?"

"Hunter Lloyd and Sibyl Smiles," Sibyl said. "Hunter's told me about you, Constance. We need to talk to you."

"What about?"

Sibyl closed her eyes. "Why not just come down and talk to us?"

"Not unless you tell me what it's about."

"It's about Greatrix Villiers," Hunter said. "We've got some news of him."

"Oh, my God," Constance said. She left the window open and the sound of bare feet quickly descended the stairs. The door was opened and Constance waved them inside. She looked around outside and Hunter was grateful the carriage was out of her sight.

"Tell me, then," Constance said, standing there in the cold hallway, shivering violently, far more violently than could be accounted for by the chill night air.

Hunter pushed the door shut while Sibyl put an arm around the woman's shoulders and led her into the closest room. It was well furnished, obviously without expense being spared, and the remnants of a fire still burned. Hunter immediately added coals and used the bellows to bring it back to life.

Constance's beautiful dark eyes stared. Her black hair stood out in shiny curls. A lovely woman caught in some nightmare that might or might not be partly of her own making. She wore a fine beige robe over her night rail and much expensive lace was in evidence. It was clear to Hunter now that she was nothing like the illiterate housekeeper she'd led him to believe she was.

"Let's sit here," Sibyl said. She didn't need to be told that Constance hadn't been given the kind of bad news Hunter and Sibyl brought. That much was obvious from her reasonably calm demeanor.

Sibyl took Constance to a comfortable needlepoint-covered couch with finely carved ebony arms and legs. Constance sat on the edge of the seat and completely upright. "Very well," she said. "We've dealt with the necessities. What's happened?"

Sibyl didn't wait for Hunter to come from the fire. "Greatrix Villiers is dead."

Both of Constance's hands slapped over her mouth and nose and she screamed.

Sibyl tried to hold the woman but she shook her off and the eerie, keening noise went on. "How?" she choked out at last.

"There was a knife fight. He was killed."

Hunter had turned and Sibyl saw him searching the room for something he could give Constance to drink.

"When?" Constance asked.

"I think it was sometime on last Saturday morning," Hunter said.

"But they didn't let me know," Constance said. "It wouldn't have been a fight. And his death was no accident. He didn't fight. That was part of it. He couldn't have hurt anyone like they said he hurt DeBeaufort. Greatrix was marked to die from the moment he walked on the Heath and saw that DeBeaufort man with the woman."

"You're absolutely sure your brother was innocent?" Hunter said.

"He was innocent of what he was charged with," Constance said. "He shouldn't have been there. He'd probably been with someone himself. But I'll always believe it was what he saw that finished him. What does it matter now? He's dead. He wasn't a good man, but he didn't deserve that—and neither do I."

Sibyl couldn't believe her reaction. "You're shocked," she said. "That's natural."

"I'm only shocked it didn't happen sooner." Constance began to cry silently. Tears slid from open eyes. She wrapped her arms around herself and rocked.

"That's better," Hunter said. "Let it out." He had finally located the decanters in a corner cupboard and poured a small measure of cognac.

"You don't understand," she said, choking on each word. "He wasn't my brother, he was my husband. There are reasons I had to pretend I wasn't married."

"Oh, Constance," Sibyl said. "I'm so sorry. I don't know what to say to you."

"Of course you don't. But I'll tell you what I want to hear. I want to hear how I'll get Birdie back now. How will I find her? Greatrix used her to keep me in line, to make sure I did what he wanted. If I didn't follow his orders, I'd never find out where she was."

Hunter came to Constance and held the glass to her lips until she drank.

"Constance," he said, "Who is Birdie?"

Sibyl couldn't look at him but she knew he was as aware of the answer as she was.

"My kid," Constance said. "She's six."

27

Two riders approached. Cloaks whipped, crops flailed at straining flanks, snow and mud flew in clumps. A frenzied flight toward the shadows where Latimer waited.

The coachman had drawn the carriage—with Latimer inside—partway into a passageway between two buildings. The new arrivals never knew it was there.

Pulled up by their riders, the horses snorted and bellowed, sent plumes of vapor into the dark sky. Streams of foam shone on their sweat-slick hides.

Latimer slipped from the carriage on the side farthest from the newcomers. He crept around until he could catch the coachman's attention. The fellow jumped and grabbed his chest, but managed to be silent. "Stay," Latimer said. "Something feels very bad here, but stay as long as you can. If you have to go, we will understand."

"And leave Mr. Hunter?" The fellow was old, his eyes no more than glints beneath flaps of sagging flesh. "I'll be 'ere all right. God bless 'im. 'E's the best of men."

Latimer nodded and continued on. He hid behind a metal railing where a snow-covered hedge grew, and listened to the muffled voices of the horsemen.

"Stand off, then," one said. "Go back by the Snuff and Bottom. That'll be good enough. I'll finish here quickly enough, and it won't take me more than ten minutes to run that far."

The other man said, "It's back the way we came?"

"Yes. And you'd best be saying your prayers. You heard the king. If even a whiff of this gets about, we'll be dead men and he'll never have heard of us."

Latimer knew the pub the first man spoke of. Blessedly it was in the opposite direction from the coach's hiding place.

"I'm on my way," said the second man. "The horses will be in the yard and I'll be raising a tankard for both of us." He laughed softly while his companion slid to the ground.

Latimer didn't recognize either man's voice. He also hadn't noticed before that the man on the ground carried a bundle over his shoulder—and when his cloak flew open, firearms or knives—or both—shone.

Immediately the horses were wheeled around and on their way with the single rider.

Hunter's forty-five minutes had passed but this was not the time for Latimer to burst into the house.

And he dared not leave to find additional help. This was a dangerous dilemma indeed.

Crouching, the big man, and he was very large, went to the front door and used a key to let himself in. He slunk noiselessly inside, leaving Latimer with one crumb of hope. The door wasn't shut.

He waited a few seconds and hoped it was long enough, before following in the other's footsteps.

In a room to Latimer's right, voices carried on a conversation and, occasionally, a woman—definitely not Sibyl—cried and was hushed.

Straight ahead was a staircase.

More rooms had to be beyond the one he knew was occupied, but he heard the slightest sound, a soft bump, as if something brushed a wall above him, then the bump came again—and once more.

Hunter and Sibyl could be in the room with the crying woman, or they could be upstairs and about to be ambushed.

Latimer chose the stairs.

He climbed three flights and knew he was closing in on the other when he heard him breathing hard. Anxiety tightened Latimer's own chest. He'd reached a junction where doors covered with heavy curtains to keep out drafts flanked a few narrow steps leading to another door at the top.

The big man was entering through that door as Latimer arrived at the bottom of the steps. Latimer managed to pull himself back and out of sight behind one of the dusty curtains.

Thumping followed, the sound of flesh on flesh, but not a spoken word. A crash had to be furniture falling over, perhaps breaking.

Cursing his stupidity for not arming himself, Latimer left the curtain and started up the steps.

A single shot rang out.

And another.

"Constance! For God's sake, woman, where are you? What's happened? Constance, answer me."

"*Fishwell.*" Hunter didn't hesitate an instant before grabbing Sibyl and pushing her behind the couch. He glared down at her. "Do not move from there. Or you," he told Constance, taking her by the arm. "Get down. I don't know what that man's doing here, but I soon will."

"You don't know what you're talking about," Constance said, twisting away from him. "Don't interfere or we'll all be dead, do you understand me?"

Sibyl began to rise, only to be pushed by Hunter, without ceremony, back where she'd been.

"Set up by Fishwell and Greevy-Sims," Hunter said, shaking his head. "And not a single pointer—except Greevy-Sims trying to push me into going to the judge. Stand aside," he told Constance.

"No," she said. "He'll kill us all."

"He's already fired two shots," Hunter pointed out. "Upstairs, from what I could tell."

"That was nothing," Constance told him. "He likes to play act up there sometimes. He sneaks into the house and does things like that. Then he wants me." She looked at the ground. "Fishwell likes his games."

Sibyl had stood up again. "Fishwell may have arranged for your husband to be killed," she said.

"And left you not knowing where your child is," Hunter added.

Constance lifted her hair from her neck and wouldn't look at either of them. "But I need him. I've got to go to him. And if you let me, I'll make sure you get away safely because you've been so nice to me."

"And let that man get—"

"That's really nice of you," Hunter said, interrupting Sibyl. "We have to do the best we can for ourselves now," he told her. "Even if it goes against your principles."

"Constance, come to me now," Fishwell bellowed.

"I have to go," she whispered. "If he comes here, you will both die."

"And if he doesn't," Sibyl said, "He'll get—"

"He may get away," Hunter said in his most civil tones. "Off you go, Constance."

"Yes," Sibyl said, "Off you go, Constance. I hope your poor little child has found a good home. Come, Hunter, we'll climb out of the windows."

He rolled his eyes, and Constance said, "That's not a good idea. There's broken glass set in the windowsills."

She left and soon, from some distant part of the house, came wails of passion that resembled the mating sounds of cows. Sibyl covered her ears while Hunter put his time to better use. He looked into the hall and noted the front door was open. No doubt that was how Fishwell had slipped in and gone upstairs to prepare for his little orgy.

Hunter could take Sibyl and leave.

He could force Sibyl to go alone—no, he couldn't, since he suspected—hoped—Latimer might have sneaked into the house again.

"Fishwell and Greevy-Sims did this together," he said.

Sibyl, frowning unbecomingly, said, "Of course they did."

"I'd like you to go to the carriage.... Where the hell is Latimer?" He thought of the shots. "Go to the carriage at once, Sibyl. Go back to Mayfair Square and see if you can find Adam. Didn't you say Jean-Marc intended to return to London shortly? By tonight, even?''

''And what will be happening while I'm driving around London looking for help?''

I will be attempting to rescue Latimer, capture Fishwell, subdue Constance and find out where Greevy-Sims is hiding. ''Just keeping a watch on things,'' he said. ''It would be nice to have at least Adam for a backup, though.''

''You have me for a backup. Be grateful. Tell me what to do. Oh, dear.'' Another bellow boomed through the house, followed by a scream of ecstasy, and Sibyl put her fingers in her ears. She shouted, ''Be patient, Hunter. Constance said that man always behaves like that. I'm sure Latimer's going to come at any time and there'll be three of us against two of them. More, if he had time to find...well, find another helper.''

''Keep your voice down,'' Hunter said against her ear. ''Three of us and one of us possibly with child, hmm?''

She breathed through her mouth and he saw she'd never given the idea a thought. ''Please don't go alone,'' she said, and her eyes brimmed with tears.

''I must.'' The love he saw in her face, and he knew it was love, made him strong. He seized her shoulders. "I agree there isn't time for you to get help, but right now you're delaying me from trying to make sure Latimer doesn't get killed—if he hasn't been already. For my sake, and possibly for—" he pressed a hand to her belly "—just in case, do not take terrible risks. I will come for you. That I promise." He only wished he could be sure.

When had there been that moment, that sign he'd missed of all that was to come?

Hunter didn't start up the stairs. Instead he stood flattened against the banisters at the bottom with the room where Sibyl waited behind him.

Be it ever so subtle, there had been a warning about all this, but he hadn't seen it. In every case, whether while reading evidence, or perhaps interviewing the principals, some important clue came to light. What had it been in this case? He had not wanted to take the case, but it had been pressed upon him and as junior in the firm, it was his place to do as he was told.

He hadn't been offered the knighthood until after Villiers was found guilty of wounding DeBeaufort and fabricating a story that he'd stopped DeBeaufort in the act of raping an unwilling maid on Hampstead Heath. True, he'd known the king wanted DeBeaufort cleared, but a man could have friends in high places and not be a criminal. He also knew that the king's mistress had some reason for not wanting the truth to come out. The Elizabeth she spoke of was her daughter and he'd lay odds she was the "maid" with DeBeaufort on that fateful morning.

And it had all come down to Fishwell and Greevy-Sims being jealous of Hunter for one reason or another. Despite his insistence to the opposite, Fishwell wanted to be the next Head of Chambers. Greevy-Sims didn't want the knighthood bestowed upon his rival—or for Hunter to look good to Sir Parker Bowl.

Now they were faced with disaster, all of them, with no hope of turning back.

Fishwell's voice rumbled again. "Get your things, Constance. We've got to leave England for a few weeks."

"Leave England?" Constance said, her amazement obvious.

"Do as you're told. I'm not even supposed to be in England, remember? It'll all be simple enough. I was never here through all this and I'll take you somewhere safe."

"But people know I was here," Constance said, her voice shaking.

Fool, Hunter thought. *Don't remind him.*

"Not to worry, my dear. I'll take care of everything. Into your room with you. That's right. You won't need much because I'm going to make sure you have everything your heart desires. Everything new and rich, and exquisite.''

''Oh, Fishwell,'' Constance said, any concern apparently fleeing while avarice rushed in.

The next gunshot shook Hunter to his feet.

He had to go up, and he had to pray that if Latimer was in this house, or somewhere nearby, he had not been on the receiving end of one of Fishwell's shots.

Taking two steps at a time, treading on the balls of his feet to make as little sound as possible, Hunter arrived at the next floor. To his left, a door stood open to a feminine bedchamber overloaded with lace and dried flowers and fripperies. On the floor beside an unmade canopied bed lay Constance Smith, facedown on a pink carpet turning rapidly red with blood.

Fishwell routed through a chest. He held a pillow slip and tossed what appeared to be an odd collection into it. Fancy stockings, lace underthings, a packet of letters tied with ribbon, several beautiful fans and some jewelry boxes.

He was, Hunter realized, getting rid of evidence by removing gifts he must have given Constance.

''Drop the bag and put your hands up where I can see them,'' Hunter said, and when the man made a move toward his belt, added, ''Do it now, or you join your lady friend on the floor.''

Lord Fishwell dropped the pillow slip and raised his hands. "Can I turn around, Lloyd?" he said. "It's better to look an enemy in the eye, don't you think?"

"Turn if you must, but turn slowly."

Soon he was faced with Fishwell's meaty, florid countenance. Hunter had never liked the man. Now he hated him.

"Oh, Constance." Sibyl's voice came from behind Hunter. "I must go to her."

"Don't come a single step into this room," Hunter said, cursing that he should ever have trusted her to remain downstairs. "Constance is dead. There's nothing you can do for her."

"No," Sibyl said. "Oh, no, no."

"Sad," Hunter agreed, although he mourned the woman less than Sibyl seemed to.

"She'd have done anything to be a lady," Fishwell said, sneering. "Laughable."

"It's him," Sibyl murmured. "Why didn't I recognize his voice before? The man who beat me. He shot her, didn't he?"

Once Hunter digested Sibyl's revelation, he didn't have time for a conversation.

"She loved her child," Sibyl said to Fishwell. "Now her husband's dead and who knows where the little one is?"

"Villiers's bastard," Fishwell said. "A nothing

and no relative of hers. No loss, I can assure you. Connie didn't love her but she put up with the child in part because it was one way to manipulate her husband. When he took the girl away he taunted Connie by saying his daughter was worth her weight in gold—the gold Villiers kept sewn inside the brat's clothes. Connie wanted it, that's all. The money. Not the brat."

Heavy footsteps thundered on the attic stairs and Latimer yelled, "It's me, Latimer. I've been trying to help Greevy-Sims. Fishwell shot the poor devil. He's still alive, but he won't let me do anything much for him."

"I'll go up at once," Sibyl said.

"You'll stay here," Latimer and Hunter said in unison.

Hunter said, "Help me tie this bastard up," to Latimer.

"No time." Latimer backed away. "You'll have to manage. This one's got reinforcements at the Snuff and Bottom. Some pub up the road. By my calculations, the fellow's likely to have given up waiting there and be headed back here by now. I'm going to intercept him if I can. Wing this one in the leg with a shot. Or knock him out. Then—"

"Thank you for the advice, Latimer," Hunter said. "You'd better get to the other fellow before he gets to us."

Sometimes, Latimer thought, it was hard being a foot soldier rather than whoever it was who gave out the orders in these situations.

He clattered down the rest of the stairs and through the front door.

Damn. It was cold and growing colder.

Whatever hit the back of his head turned it numb before he slid downward and lost consciousness.

Almost as soon as Latimer left, Sibyl heard him returning. "He's coming back already," she said to Hunter. "Look, why don't I hold the pistol or whatever it is, while you tie Fishwell up? I really do have very steady hands. And I might even try to give him a kick. Just because I ought to, really."

"Steady hands, eh?" Sibyl swung around but didn't recognize the man who had arrived. "I wouldn't be surprised if you've got lots of nice things. Good idea to keep facing away from me, both of you, but you may drop your arms, Lloyd. I have both you and your lady friend covered. And, by the way, even if your friend doesn't freeze to death outside, he may not recover consciousness anyway. I'd have shot him if I could have afforded the noise, but he won't be going anywhere again."

Lord Fishwell said, "What ho, DeBeaufort," with obvious glee. "Jolly good fellow."

"They've both got to be finished," DeBeaufort

said. "You understand that, of course. Greevy-Sims is done for, isn't he?"

Fishwell turned an unpleasant shade of red. "Apparently not quite. But I'll just pop up to the attic and do that."

"We'll all just pop up to the attic then," DeBeaufort said. "Nice for them to be among friends in their final minutes."

DeBeaufort, in green once more, herded them all—including Fishwell—ahead of him and up the stairs until they reached the attic, where another horror scene awaited.

Charles Greevy-Sims, curled in a grotesque ball on his stomach, had a good part of his left shoulder shot away and the arm trailed at a sickening angle. He appeared unconscious.

Fishwell said, "All for king and country. We make a fabulous team, DeBeaufort. I say, you'll put in a good word for me, won't you? With his majesty, that is?"

DeBeaufort felled him with a single blast and went to a rough table. He kept his second weapon trained on Sibyl while he reloaded the other with one hand. He glanced to a corner, where a lumpy, blood-stained bag lay, and narrowed his eyes. "At least the fool did something right. The child's done for." He pushed at Greevy-Sims with the toe of a boot. "I think he's finished, too. Let's get this over with."

"You." He indicated Sibyl. "Over here."

She didn't move.

Hunter broke out in a sweat. He had a second knife in his boot and knew how to use it. Just give him the smallest diversion, but not at Sibyl's cost.

Both of DeBeaufort's pistols leveled at Hunter as he said without looking at Sibyl, "If you care about him, do as you're told, bitch." Before Hunter could say a word, Sibyl walked toward DeBeaufort who told her, "This side of the table. Lift your skirts and lean forward. Shame to waste absolutely everything, what?" He was contriving to loosen his trousers. "And you get the pleasure of watching, Sir Hunter."

Hunter stopped thinking. He heard another gunshot, but his feet had left the ground and the knife was in his hand. He landed on DeBeaufort and brought the knife down at the same time. The curved blade entered the man's throat and blood sprayed Hunter's face.

He raised the knife again, but stopped. DeBeaufort had slumped on his back, his eyes wide-open.

"Greevy-Sims did it," Sibyl said. "He shot him. He must hate these men more than he hates you."

Hunter looked up as Latimer staggered into the

room. "I saw him. He got Fishwell's pistol and shot DeBeaufort." Holding his head, he crumpled to his knees.

"Heavens, what a terrible mess," Sibyl said.

Hunter jerked upright to look at her. She stood by the table, staring around her. Standing on top of the table, clinging to the collar of Sibyl's pelisse, was a very thin child who might have been no more than four, rather than the six Hunter thought her to be, and he was almost certain he was looking at Birdie Villiers. "Where did the little girl come from?"

"So many dead people." Sibyl spread a hand over the back of the child's head and pressed her face to her chest. "That man Greevy-Sims had the child under him. That's why she's alive, I expect. He's dead, too. I suppose he wasn't all bad. But all the blood. All the death."

Latimer and Hunter exchanged long glances. "Time to get out of here," Hunter said. "And find a comfortable place for this little girl. Let's get the coach, Latimer. Once we're in Mayfair Square, we'll notify the authorities, not that anything will be done."

"What's in that bag over there?" Sibyl asked. She moved so quickly they couldn't stop her from opening the burlap bag. Her face was white as she parted the top. Hunter saw her let out a breath.

"Gold," she said, holding up a candelabra. "With a Royal coat of arms. DeBeaufort biting the hand that fed him."

Latimer helped him get a very quiet Sibyl downstairs. Hunter carried Birdie, who had yet to speak.

They were in the carriage and almost back at Mayfair Square when the truth came to Hunter. There had been two moments of revelation, not one, and he'd totally missed them both. The first had been Fishwell. The man had left Willie's Alley ahead of Constance, but there was something much more sickening to live with. The second clue to his own entrapment had come from his champion. Some men were never too old or too ill to be avaricious and power hungry. So it was with Parker Bowl.

But he doubted tonight's disaster had been exactly what Sir Parker Bowl had in mind when he made his deal with a king.

28

"Odd how the entire household decided to make journeys this spring," Sibyl told Hunter. "Everyone's gone away. But you didn't have to take pity on me, you know."

Although a pale sun shone, he saw that she shivered a little. Since the night of horror in Curzon Street she had been almost cool toward him. "It was you who took pity on me. The journey from London to Cornwall would have been a lonely one to take by myself. And we've had Miss Ivy Willow's company to boot. What more could we have asked for? Are you cold? The breeze is quite fierce up here."

Sibyl chuckled at the thought of ebullient Ivy gasping at every new sight along the way. "I'm not cold, thank you, Hunter. Minver Bay." Below them, new, soft green grass covered cliffs that fell to the gray-mauve waters of that bay. "It's a pretty name and such a lovely place. And at first you thought you had been gifted with a useless piece of scrub land in the middle of nowhere."

He smiled. "How could I know otherwise?" They looked at each other and unspoken was the knowledge of the sadness and violence, the bizarre events that had led them to Cornwall and Minver Place, Hunter's small gem of an Elizabethan house and estate which he'd seen for the first time yesterday.

"Everyone's so pleased you're here," Sibyl said, breathing deeply of the fresh salt air off the sea. "Who would expect a household staff in place and waiting like that? And the villagers."

At that Hunter laughed. He longed to take her in his arms, but knew better. He felt as if he were on a precipice with his back to the water far below. Sibyl stood before him to push or pull. For the first time he was convinced his life was completely in another's hands. "All eleven families. One schoolteacher. I'll admit the teacher really did surprise me—and the schoolhouse, tiny as it is." He sobered. "But it's a responsibility I'd never expected to have. They fish. Hah. What do I know of fishing? Not a thing."

"You'll learn. And you won't be here often so they'll carry on as they always have when you're in London, won't they?"

He nodded, driving his hands deep in his pockets.

"I suppose they will. But my life will never be quite the same for knowing they're here."

"Of course it won't. You have such a sense of responsibility. Did you notice the vicar didn't come to greet you?"

Hunter had noticed. "I shall go to him. I understand the church barely accommodates the flock, and we know how large that is."

"He's probably afraid the unmarried lady with you is no better than she ought to be," Sibyl said and felt furious with herself for breaking her personal promise to avoid careless comments. She shrugged. Now it was too late. "And he's right. But forgive me for mentioning such things."

"Thank you for mentioning them." Hunter could have grabbed and kissed her for what he knew was a slip on her part. "It's May, Sibyl. February is long behind us. Couldn't we put any differences behind us, too?"

Sibyl began walking again. "One would have thought the house had never been without its master," she said when Hunter fell in at her shoulder. He placed her on his uphill side and she was warmed by the small gallantry. "Did you sleep well last night?" She looked at her boots. Hunter sleeping was something she tried not to think about.

"Very well, thank you." He lied, but then, he'd spent weeks lying to her with every polite word spoken on their occasional walks together, or when he took her to visit Nightrider and the little mare, Libby, who now both belonged to him. He'd lied with each calm smile when they passed at Number 7.

He had not slept very well, dammit. He rarely slept well anymore. He was a desperate man who wanted the woman he loved.

She said, "Good," and the breeze pulled a long lock of pale hair from beneath the brim of her soft gray bonnet.

"Except for some wretched cat that decided he had the right to sleep on my feet." In truth he'd been grateful even for the company of a feline.

"Is that what they call marram grass?" Sibyl asked, although she didn't care. "It's so long and coarse. See how the wind turns it into waves." She allowed the wind that made a little sea of the grass to push her along.

"I don't know much about what grows here yet," Hunter said. Somehow he must say what he'd set up such elaborate plans to say in this isolated place. "You didn't answer me when I asked if we could forget anything that may have been unhappy between us. I don't pretend to understand what I've done to make you cool toward me, but I would mend it if you would let me."

She looked at him over her shoulder and

smiled—and was his familiar Sibyl again for that moment. "You've done nothing. Consider it forgotten."

Ah, yes, he thought, but you will say whatever you have to say to make this day easier, won't you? "Do you really like Minver Place?"

"I do. Very much."

"Should you enjoy visiting here from time to time?" He did not have the best way with such words.

She tossed her head, and for the first time since that dreadful night, affected a little of the strut she'd so quickly forgotten afterward. "If that is an invitation, then it's a very nice one. Thank you."

No commitments, not even that vague one.

Sibyl turned her head toward the house. It was beyond a wooded rise and not visible from there. Her throat was so tight, it hurt desperately. When she had accepted this invitation she'd thought it the best possible opportunity to do what must be done. How foolish a woman without options could be.

She stood quite still, staring toward the trees. They weren't far distant from the water and fairly sparse at the seaward border.

"What is it?" Hunter asked.

"Nothing." How could she tell him about her struggle without just telling it all? "I think there are deer in your woods, Sir Hunter. This is an idyllic place."

"Don't leave me, Sibyl." He brought his teeth together and fought for breath. His heart beat too hard. "Please, don't go away."

She turned from him and ran a few steps.

"Did you think I wouldn't find out what you were planning?" he asked, going behind her and holding her arms. When she didn't pull away, he closed his eyes.

"Who told you?"

Why lie anymore. "Latimer."

"Latimer?" She shook her head in disbelief. How did he know?

"Ivy told him. She asked for his help. But did you think I wouldn't see the moment you started to change?"

Ivy, her companion and confidante.

"There's no need for more sadness, Sibyl. There's been enough of that."

"You have your own life. You're important and I'm a reminder of something that shouldn't have happened. To myself as well as to you."

"If you go away—to the Continent or wherever—I'll follow. I will not allow you to close me out. I'm begging you. Please have our child here in England. In London, or here in Cornwall. Wherever you choose as long as I can be with you and you can be among family and friends, where you belong.''

''Oh.'' She bowed her head and wrapped her arms around herself.

Hunter caught her against him, slid his hands beneath her elbows and spread them on her stomach. ''There isn't so much to see,'' he said, kissing the back of her neck. ''But there's enough when a man spends as much time looking as I do.''

''That isn't seemly,'' she murmured.

''This—'' he stroked her through the thick pelisse ''—is mine as well as yours. It's seemly for me to look. We've admitted we love each other. I love you and this child so, Sibyl.''

She didn't speak and he turned her around. Her eyelashes were wet and there were tears on her cheeks. She looked determinedly downward.

''Stop punishing me for my mistake, Sibyl.''

''I'm not punishing you for anything.''

''Yes. Oh, yes. Because I didn't have the sense to ask you to be my wife years ago. That was my mistake.''

When she raised her eyes, they stunned him. So blue, so honest, so filled with longing and uncertainty. ''But you didn't mention marriage seriously even when we became lovers. Of course there was no reason you should have, except for the love I declared and the love you implied. When I knew about the baby, I wanted to come to you, but you were so withdrawn. And then I decided your aunt was right. You need a more important wife."

"Dammit." He paced and fumed. "You are the most important woman in my life, and she has been selfish in trying to keep you from me. That's what she's done, you know, tried to keep you for herself. Believe me. You want to. It's the truth. I think I told myself you'd be there waiting for me whenever I was ready to think about having a wife and family. How arrogant can a man get? Or stupid? Let's not discuss, or argue, or talk about who should or shouldn't have done what. Or when."

Could a man who was only trying to do the right thing look or sound as Hunter did? Sibyl no longer knew. "Just do what I want to do, you mean? Stop punishing myself? Be sensible, intelligent, self-serving and greedy enough to find joy in this child I want so much—and become your wife as well? Is that what you mean?"

Hunter framed her face, knocked her bonnet off, and kissed her soundly. "Yes," he said. "Yes, that's exactly what I'm suggesting we do. Why not? It's right and Sibyl..."

She waited, peering at him.

"Sibyl, I don't want to sleep with a cat again. And I hate sleeping alone."

"Yes." Her gloves made the task difficult, but

she did up another button on his coat. "Yes, I understand, and I agree with you. So we will, Hunter. All right? We'll get married."

"Oh, thank God." He wrapped her in a hug that stole his own breath, then eased his grip quickly. "Sorry. I forgot the baby for the slightest moment there. Is it true I produced this infant the first time we made love?"

Sibyl looked past him and saw more than the suggestion of a deer moving through the woods. Gradually shapes, human shapes, emerged and came toward them. In fact, these people were running rather than walking, and showing absolutely no decorum.

"That could well be the case, Hunter," she told him. "A tribute to your manliness, I suppose, hmm? And just because I'm having a baby it doesn't mean I'll break if you hug me. We should continue this topic at another time. We are about to have company."

"Hello, oh, hello, you two," Lady Hester Bingham called, her blue skirts flying. By the hand she held Birdie, who looked quite happy to be dressed like a miniature sugarplum fairy and to have her rather thin hair twisted into tight curls beneath the brim of her velvet bonnet.

"Hello, Aunt," Hunter said, determined to forgive anything today. As the new man he now was, he wouldn't lie to himself again. He'd known this gathering was likely, but he didn't have to be happy at the interruption.

Ivy Willow twirled in her red-and-yellow velvet, laughing and flapping her black eyelashes at a stocky, white-haired gentleman accompanying Meg, Jean-Marc, and little Serena, who wore so many clothes her arms stuck out straight. The other ladies of Sibyl's group trotted behind.

The Etrangers grinned, a bit foolishly, Hunter thought. But Desirée, the breathtaking swan in pale green, studied Sibyl with tearful seriousness, and neither Adam nor Latimer showed either amusement or joy in the moment.

They were worried in case all had not gone well, he realized, and winked at Adam, who only frowned in response. Adam could be obtuse on occasion, or perhaps unworldly would be a better description.

"As they say, the company is all present," Jean-Marc announced. "It happened too unexpectedly for my good friend Kilrood and his Finch to get here in time. But they will join us soon."

"If there's anything to join us for," Latimer said in morose tones. "Is there?"

"Of course there is," Meg said. "Look at them."

"I am looking." Desirée looked very closely. "You have cried, Sibyl. That's not good for—"

''Everything is absolutely wonderful,'' Sibyl said rapidly.

''Wonderful,'' Hunter agreed, eyeing the stranger. ''We seem to be missing a few people. The Minver staff, perhaps? The staff from Number 7? Couldn't you manage to round up the villagers, too?''

''Oh, forgive us,'' the stocky man said. ''No intention of offending, I assure you. I'm sure we can round everyone up in no time.''

Hunter grinned and stuck out a hand, which the other man shook firmly. ''Forgive me,'' Hunter said. He put an arm around Sibyl's waist and she leaned against his chest. ''I was joking. This is...yes, this is my family and they are incredibly good at getting together on very short notice.''

''We are,'' Meg said. ''Hunter and Sibyl, let me introduce you to the Reverend Telskuddy, Vicar of St. Piren's here at Minver. Reverend Telskuddy, Sir Hunter Lloyd and Sibyl Smiles, the engaged couple.''

Epilogue

7 Mayfair Square
London
June, 1822

Friends—English or misbegotten—well-wishers, and traitors:

This newel post is the only thing, earthly or otherwise, that I can rely upon. Regardless of how cruelly I am treated, this fine, beautiful piece of art awaits the return of my exhausted mind and spirit at any hour, day or night. But I have learned, oh dear me, yes, I have learned a great deal.

Hester's keeping the lot, you know. Absolutely. That is to be my reward for trying to do the very best for this fabulous house. They're all staying. Oh, Hunter and Sibyl—and their offspring—will spend time at that pathetic little Minver, but it's as I feared. Hester has decided Sibyl is the perfect wife for Hunter and already has the most inept clods hammering and banging amid all this perfection. Designing suitable apartments for the family, they are. Pah.

Every room is open again. Something I might have welcomed had the reason been that they were needed for my family, but no. Strangers are the cause. A six-year-old orphan of dubious lineage must have her own ridiculously expensive quarters, mind you.

Latimer is still here. Adam is still here. People come and go, tramping through as if this were part of Fortnum and Mason. I should have designed and had shelves installed for jams and jellies.

Forget I mentioned jellies, please. Some things are better forgotten.

And you have not helped. You have stood by with the other one—how she must be laughing, the wretch—and seen signs you failed to warn me about.

Well, I hope you are all satisfied. As I've said, I've learned a great deal and most important is that this being nice business is a dangerous waste of time, and to be avoided at all costs.

No more Sir Nice,

Spivey

Frog Crossing
Watersville
Out West

Dearest Friends:

My father was a reading man who didn't consider "scribbling" a suitable occupation for a woman. He never read anything I wrote, other than letters, and these he sometimes returned with the grammar "corrected." There are times when I think he and that inept manipulator, Spivey, would get along famously. But I'm wrong. My father had a sense of humor.

Oh, and my father told wonderful stories, too.

Spivey takes himself too seriously. Finally I've realized that this is the root of all the trouble he makes. The poor, horrid creature actually thinks he's important.

Thank goodness for the insight. I'm just going to have to loosen him up a bit. But perhaps a little progress has been made already. I am almost certain he shows a ghost of a conscience. This will all be very interesting.

Stick around.

I am, as ever, your devoted scribbler,

Stella Cameron

Secrets, lies, blame and guilt.
Only love and forgiveness can overcome the mistakes of the past.

Witt Matlock has carried around a bitter hatred for Hardy Wingate, the man he holds responsible for the death of his daughter. And now, twelve years later, the man he blames for the tragedy is back in his life—and in that of his niece, Joni.

Widow Hannah Matlock has kept the truth about her daughter Joni's birth hidden for twenty-seven years. Only she knows that her brother-in-law Witt is Joni's father, and not her uncle. But with Hardy coming between Witt and Joni, Hannah knows she must let go of her secret...whatever the consequences.

A JANUARY CHILL

"A magnificent presence in romantic fiction. Rachel Lee is an author to treasure forever."
—*Romantic Times*

On sale April 2001 wherever paperbacks are sold!

Visit us at www.mirabooks.com

MRL802